"It is never the same, is it?"

"Never," Julia said so softly, it was almost a whisper.

Richard had taken another step to stand even closer to her, in order to get her perspective of the scene. Now he stood directly behind her, brushing her shoulder blade. Julia leaned back ever so slightly to rest against his chest; it was so strong, so broad, so . . . right. Richard, in the motion of a dream they both were unwilling to disturb, raised his hand and laid it gently against the front of her shoulder; with the barest increase of pressure it might have been called "clasping her to him."

"Things change so quickly, do they not?" she murmured. "One believes they will always be the same, and then suddenly everything is different."

"What is familiar becomes unfamiliar," he said.

Whatever else they were discussing, it had ceased to be the painting. . . .

Dear Reader,

As the holidays approach (at much too fast a pace for most of us) we, at Harlequin Historicals would like to take the time to wish our readers well.

This month, *Christmas Miracle* by Ruth Langan tells the story of a Southern family displaced by the Civil War. Though their lives would never be the same, Lizzie Spooner was determined to show them all that life was still worth living.

Impetuous Julia Masonet had always chafed under her guardian Richard's watchful eye, until she was faced with losing him. With *Tender Journey,* Sally Cheney has written a delightfully different story of a free spirit and the proper gentleman who has captured her heart.

China Blossom, Margaret Moore's second historical for Harlequin, offers the reader a glimpse of 19th-century England's elite society, and a young woman who dares to defy its strictest rules.

When a handsome drifter saves the life of an Irish-Mexican beauty, their love threatens to destroy them, in Elizabeth Lane's tale of the old West, *Moonfire.*

Also this month, keep an eye out for the HARLEQUIN HISTORICAL CHRISTMAS STORIES 1992 collection, wherever Harlequin Books are sold.

Thanks again for your continued support.

Sincerely,

Tracy Farrell
Senior Editor

Tender Journey
Sally Cheney

Harlequin Books

TORONTO • NEW YORK • LONDON
AMSTERDAM • PARIS • SYDNEY • HAMBURG
STOCKHOLM • ATHENS • TOKYO • MILAN
MADRID • WARSAW • BUDAPEST • AUCKLAND

Harlequin Historicals first edition November 1992

ISBN 0-373-28748-8

TENDER JOURNEY

Books by Sally Cheney

Harlequin Historicals

Game of Hearts #36
Thief in the Night #112
Tender Journey #148

SALLY CHENEY

was a bookstore owner before coming to her first love—writing. She has traveled extensively in the United States, but is happiest with the peaceful rural life in her home state of Idaho. When she is not writing, she is active in community affairs and enjoys cooking and gardening.

Sincere appreciation to my friends, Professor Vaughn Stephenson and Don Royster, Ph.D., who know France; my sister, Melanie Metzger, who knows art; and my father, who knows how fast a horse travels, among countless other helpful bits of information.

Prologue

Thump. Thump. Thump.

The dull, steady throb of the locomotive was relentless, yet somehow soothing in its endless repetition. The iron wheels had always clicked against the rails; the coach had always swayed thus. And so it would continue on and on. Like the ticking of a clock or the passage of years.

Julia Masonet leaned her head wearily against the cushion and considered ironically the passage of years. Years she had hurried through so impatiently. Despairing of her youth and dependence, she had rushed headlong to this moment, ignoring the reality that surrounded her, with her eye only and always on this goal.

Now, at last, all that she had been waiting for was hers.

Any observer in the passageway would have been struck by the stunning picture presented by the beautiful woman in the railroad car. Her raven black hair, red lips and light olive complexion suggested exotic romance, intrigue and *mystère*. Her attitude of languid repose led to the assumption that this was a woman accustomed to having her own way, of imperiously directing the course of her life.

Julia would have been amused by those conclusions. Smiling, she would have dismissed the claim that she was beautiful, and it was only within recent years that anyone would have disputed the point with her.

And she might very possibly have laughed out loud at the implication that she was the Captain of her Fate, the Mistress of her Destiny.

Until now.

She closed her eyes, drawing her long black lashes down to rest against her cheekbones.

Thump. Thump. Thump.

Against the throbbing background she saw her life, in that moment, stretched out behind her like the receding train tracks. It all seemed an indistinct progression of days, with only here and there highlighted moments, brightly illuminated milestones along the way. And just as the iron rails beneath her would inevitably take her to Gretna Green, so the course of her life had brought her to this moment.

Rather than a journey *to* some destination, it had often seemed a flight *from* a pursuing evil. A stalking nemesis. A direful ogre.

There was no question who was the ogre in her life from whom she had so often fled. She remembered vividly the fateful day, that mournful time, those dark and silent chambers where she first set eyes on Richard Edmond. Cousin Richard. The title was almost laughably inappropriate. Almost.

Cousin Richard had been standing behind Uncle Charles's chair, the two of them looking like the formally posed subjects of a pretentious portrait painter, both in black suits, eyes directed emotionlessly ahead, tall hats held in their hands. The solicitor's richly flocked walls formed the stately background.

His most striking feature was a mustache, not bushy or unkempt, but adding age and distinction to, she realized only now, a young man's face. Next she became aware of his clear blue eyes, though of course in the subdued light of the office she could not distinguish their color. But she could see that they were direct and unflinching. A girl of thirteen could not appreciate the dedication those eyes and that firm jaw promised, as much as she would have appreciated a slightly less severe, a slightly more tractable countenance.

His shoulders were broad; he stood above average height. When he spoke, his voice was low and educated. He was young and handsome, responsible, yet ready to befriend the lonely girl. Julia only wished she had seen all that then.

Instead, she only knew she was alone and frightened, determined to care for herself.

That was no doubt a trait she had inherited from her father. That, and her exotic coloring, which made her look almost Mediterranean in descent, and her distinctive bone structure. Her mother, who had left her with so much by way of tangible wealth, was nowhere reflected in the girl. Any other mother might have felt slighted, but Julia's mother would have considered her daughter the luckiest child in the world.

Julia did not feel lucky. At thirteen she felt lanky and awkward, and at thirteen she was right.

Chapter One

Milestone Thirteen

Gérard St. Pierre Masonet had come across the Channel twenty-five years before to see how these *riches Anglais* could contribute to his well-being and the comfort of his life. They, not collectively, but in the person of Colonel George Parson, contributed Miss Sarah Parson, who did all within her power to ensure the well-being of her handsome French husband. And considering that Sarah's father owned a great deal of land around Tunbridge, England, and her mother's father was both titled *and* wealthy, which advantages do not always go together, Sarah Parson Masonet's contribution toward the comfort of Gérard's life were considerable.

She was a pretty little woman, with a soft English complexion that was reminiscent of the little pink primroses she never ceased trying to transplant into the window box of their Parisian apartment.

The primroses from her English home never did well in France. Unfortunately, neither did Sarah.

In the first year of their marriage Sarah bore Gérard a son, a beautiful, delicate baby who did not live long enough to lose the fine translucence of a newborn. The wee fellow grew weaker and weaker, and despite the loving arms that held him, he slipped away a month after he was born.

Masonet, with the ebullient emotion of a Frenchman, was boisterously grief-stricken. Sarah's grief was much quieter but unreleased it seemed to draw in her cheeks and bruise the flesh around her eyes.

Two months after the baby's death, she was with child once more and nine months later presented her husband with a daughter. The baby was named Julia after a spinster aunt of Sarah's, but she was a Masonet from heel to head. She had her father's well-defined bone structure, her father's dark coloring, her father's snapping gray eyes and her father's fiery temper.

Sarah was a gentle, docile creature whose every intention had been to bring comfort to her husband's life for years to come. But the birth of two children only a year apart required a grave toll of her body, and the heartache for the one and the care required by the other drained her. Drained her of more than she or her husband knew.

She continued to oversee the care of the Masonet *appartement,* but she did it more and more from the chaise longue and less and less from a position of cooperative labor.

One day when she was almost five, Julia's father took her hand and said they were going to see her mother. To Julia's surprise he led her toward the front door instead of the bedroom.

"Where is *Maman?*" the child asked.

"She has left us, *ma chère fille,*" Masonet said.

Sarah's goodbye had been long and, like her, gentle, so her daughter laid the lily on her cold hand with only a few tears. Marguerite was still there to care for her, she knew.

Marguerite was an old woman in the little girl's eyes. Much older than *Maman,* not nearly as pretty, never as soft-spoken and larger. By Julia's calculations people got bigger as they got older, and therefore Marguerite was very old indeed. She had been Julia's nurse and nanny since the day the little girl was born. Caring for the child was a job at which she worked to earn money; no love or even tenderness had grown between them, but at least the woman was a reliable constant in the child's life.

And then again, in a pattern that should have become familiar to Julia, her world was turned topsy-turvy.

It was some time after her mother's death that Marguerite stopped nagging her about bathing and picking up after herself and acting like a lady. In fact, she very nearly stopped coming into the nursery at all. Julia did not regret that fact. She reveled in her freedom and regularly pulled out all of her play things at once, whether or not she had any intention of playing with them. And she found she could leave them out for days without the nurse getting cross with her.

Gérard St. Pierre Masonet and his daughter were so exactly alike that they did not always enjoy each other's company. Masonet might have been fonder of the child if she had been more like her mother, like the blond and pretty Sarah Parson who had come home with him from England.

Instead, Julia was dark and wiry. Her face had the high cheekbones of the Masonet's, and her hair, pulled back in the severe *chignon* prescribed for proper little French *jeunes filles,* did nothing to soften the sharp structure of her face. Her limbs were thin and seemed awfully long, especially when she was around fragile glassware.

There was simply nothing soft and cuddly about little Julia Masonet, so unlike her mother, whom Gérard had loved so tenderly.

It was a surprise to the girl when, one day shortly after her seventh birthday, her father called her to join him in his study.

"*Comment vas-tu?*" he asked.

"*Très bien, merci,*" she replied.

"*Tu es jolie aujourd'hui.*"

"*Merci bien, Papa.*"

Like schoolmaster and student going over a French lesson, the two exchanged the prescribed pleasantries.

"Julia," Masonet said, at last coming to the point. "Your mother has been gone two years now and I have decided to remarry."

Julia's dark eyes opened wide, but not nearly so wide as they did when Masonet stood, smiled and extended his hand to someone standing in the doorway. That someone was Marguerite.

"You must call Marguerite *Maman* now, Julia," Masonet told his daughter.

Being a child of seven, Julia had neither the insincerity nor the vocabulary to offer congratulations. Instead, shaking her head, she said, "But Marguerite is so *old!*"

That remark, naturally, did nothing to endear the child to her erstwhile nursemaid.

Papa saw that she had a new dress for the marriage ceremony, so it was not a complete loss. And Julia was not the poor, abused orphan of fairy tales. She and her stepmother were not tenderly affectionate, true, but the second Madame Masonet was unfailingly polite, and Julia was tolerant.

Upon Julia's eighth birthday her father called her into his study again. That is not to suggest that father and daughter had not spoken since his announcement of his intent to remarry, but the formal audience in his study was a rare occurrence that usually portended some sweeping change.

"Julia, if I am not in error, you recently reached your eighth birthday."

"Oui, Papa," the girl said. She had taken her place of formal audience on the rug in front of her father's chair.

"And your reading and figuring—coming along, are they?" he asked.

"Not as well as I would like, Father."

"Ah," Monsieur Masonet said, bringing his hands together in front of his chest, his index fingers forming a steeple upon which he rested his chin. "It is as I thought. And you would like to become more proficient in your studies?"

"Oui, Papa," the girl said, not that she had actually given the matter much thought. A child of eight does not usually contemplate her future estate, least of all the advantages to be gained by an education. But it was the response her father expected and Julia dutifully supplied it.

"Splendide. Anticipating your desires in this matter, *ma fille,* I have been making inquiries of various boarding schools. A Madame Chevous is the mistress of a fine school

located outside of Paris in the country. I was confident you would enjoy the change.''

"Of course.''

Actually, having spent all of her short lifetime in the wonder and excitement of The City of Lights, Julia did not share her father's confidence at all. But when she stood on that rug in front of his chair, her argumentative impulse was quelled.

"Madame Chevous's school enjoys an impeccable reputation. She enrolls only four new girls each year, and she has accepted your name on her list. Her girls receive the finest education in both academic pursuits and social training. More than an *école primaire,* Madame Chevous calls it *école d'arts d'agrément pour les jeunes filles.* A finishing school.''

"It sounds lovely, *mon père,*'' Julia murmured.

"This is what your mother would have wanted for you,'' Masonet said.

"I am sure.''

"If you have no objections, then, Berte will help you pack your things. You need to be ready to leave in a fortnight.''

"Very well, *Papa,*'' Julia said, putting one foot behind the other and executing the little curtsy Marguerite had taught her, while she was still Marguerite and not yet *Maman.* Then dutifully she left to find the maid.

Berte Simone was the behemoth of a serving woman who had replaced the cute, friendly little Michelle shortly after Masonet and Marguerite married. Besides being bulky and generally greasy, Berte was practically inarticulate and evidently on bad terms with the entire world. Marguerite Masonet considered her the perfect maid.

The help she provided now for Julia's packing consisted of throwing clothes and toiletries over her shoulder with a casual aim toward the bed.

Julia gathered her strewn belongings, stuffing them into a trunk. Eventually she and her trunk were loaded into a coach that bore her away to the French countryside. She and her father and her stepmother found distance to be the ideal leaven for their mutual affection.

Julia wrote loving letters home to *Papa* and Marguerite, describing her studies, classmates and funny Madame

Chevous, who walked with a cane and had long black hairs growing out of her chin. That last, Madame Chevous's hairy chin, seemed to particularly fascinate the girl. Almost every letter had some mention of it.

Monsieur and Madame Masonet sent her trinkets and elegant tidbits and occasionally small change.

They were all pleased with her enrollment in the school.

Her best friend at school was Bethany Beatrice Augustina d'Arnez. Over the next five years they grew to adolescence, passing the rigorous initiation year, the *élémentaire* years, and advancing arm in arm to take their places in the top form but one.

Bethany's father owned a men's clothier shop in Paris. Haberdashers in England or the New World could hardly afford to send their daughters to exclusive boarding schools with the proceeds from their businesses, but this was Paris, and Monsieur d'Arnez's customers paid for a good deal more for the d'Arnez family than Bethany's stylish education.

The girl was a pale duplicate of Mademoiselle Masonet: her hair was dark but not black, like Julia's; her skin lacked Julia's exotic hue. She was tall, but not quite as tall; bright, though not quite as bright.

"Beth, are you awake?" The girl's whisper was surprisingly audible in the quiet dormitory.

"Yes."

"I saw him again today."

"I did, too."

The two girls lay in narrow beds near to each other. It was late at night. Lights had been extinguished an hour ago, and any of the younger girls disturbing the quiet so long past bedtime would have had her hair pulled, her toes pinched, or even felt the *thump* of Madame Chevous's cane on her heavily padded derriere—under nightgown, blanket and coverlet. But Julia and Bethany were, by reason of their greater maturity, immune to such ill-usage.

Julia had only last month turned thirteen.

At that age, awake together late at night, they were, not surprisingly, discussing a boy. The delivery boy who brought fresh vegetables and cheese to the school kitchen from the market in the village. The *école* was pleasantly situated on an acre or two of good French farmland, but the parents of these girls were paying for them to learn how to be ladies, not gardeners or milkmaids. The groceries consumed were ordered twice a week from the marketplace and delivered by Philippe.

Philippe was an unremarkable farm lad. He was deliberate in his actions and speech, probably because he was lazy rather than stupid. He was also usually dirty, his hair grown long and clothes almost grown out of. He was nevertheless a source of consuming interest in the school and an almost universal topic of discussion. Considering which, it was curious that none of the girls knew his surname.

"'*Bonjour, mademoiselle,*' he said to me," Julia whispered.

"He *spoke* to you?" Bethany asked, thrilled to think the acknowledged "pillar of stone" had made verbal overtures to her friend.

"I said, 'Yes, it is a good day, Philippe.'"

"You called him Philippe—to his face?" Now Bethany was scandalized, the story enhanced considerably by the relish of unseemliness.

"It is his name," was Julia's unconvincing defense.

"And he said?"

"Oh, something about the onions being in next week. I could hardly hear him at all," she confessed to her friend, dropping her voice so that Bethany strained to make out her words. "My heart was pounding so, I thought he would surely hear it."

Both girls sighed deeply.

Lying in the dormitory bed that night, the windows on either end of the long hall open to admit the cool night air, Julia thought she could see the set destiny of her life in the blackness overhead. Hearing the hum of insects in the meadow under the window and the sleepy coo of one of the turtledoves that nested in the linden tree, she thought the course of her life was as plain and predetermined as any of the lives of those tiny, contented creatures: she would remain at Madame Chevous's for a few more years, perhaps taking her place as one of the instructors when she had completed her studies. All the time, however, she and Philippe would be growing more and more intimate. He would ask her next week if she liked onions, perhaps. She would tell him no. He would agree. They would discuss at a later date how powerless they felt at times in this world managed by others, how they were forced to eat onions against their will. Which discussion would naturally lead to another about a shared ambition they had to decide for themselves, about onions—and everything. Her father would most assuredly not approve of Philippe—which further glamorized the boy's short, stocky figure in Julia's eye—but they would be in love and Philippe would know the curate, and they would marry and continue to live lives of peace and harmony in a charming little cottage in the country.

How beautiful. How serene. How inevitable.

It was the next day that the note came from Paris.

Julia, your father is very ill. Return home at once.
Marguerite Masonet.

"We lay to rest the body of Gérard St. Pierre Masonet, in the sure and certain hope of the resurrection."

Madame Masonet nudged the slender, black-clad, heavily veiled figure at her side. Julia stepped forward, gathered a small handful of the upturned dirt in her gloved hand and sprinkled the grains over the open hole in front of her. She could hear them clatter on the wooden lid, but she did not look into the hole at the casket lying below. Instead, tears sprang to her eyes at the indignity of the raucous bits of loam clattering above her father's face like that, and she stepped back quickly.

When Marguerite Masonet finally sent her note to Julia, the girl's father was breathing his last. He had expressed no particular urgency about saying *au revoir* to his daughter, so it did not occur to Madame Masonet until it was too late that the girl would want to see her father before he died.

A coach was sent for the moment Julia showed Madame Chevous the note. The girl took only a small bag with a few personal toilet articles and kept urging the driver to greater speed. Nevertheless, when the coach finally stopped in front of 417, rue Saint Jacques, her father already lay cold and in state, the funeral arrangements made.

Though they had not been close, this was a much harder death for Julia to accept than her mother's. It was such a surprise, so unexpected. She had not been able to bid him farewell, press his hand, murmur *"Je t'aime, Papa,"* into his ear.

His last letter had said something about hoping to get to the new revue at the theater. When last she wrote, and it had been some time since she remembered to send off a few lines, she told them she was enjoying the summer in the country and would not plan on coming into the city until *saison de Noël.*

Marguerite told her that Gérard was caught in a shower walking home one evening two months before. He contracted a cold, which he did not worry about. The cold seemed to settle in his chest, which he also did not worry about. Finally, his breathing became so labored that they called in a physician, but by then the pneumonia was too far advanced.

"We thought all along he would get better. My dear, you have seen much grief in your short lifetime." Marguerite patted the girl's hand, her eyes filling with tears. "We both have, have we not?" she asked.

"Oui, madame. But it is the way of the world, *n'est-ce pas?"*

Julia did not feel as coolly philosophic as her words and tone of voice seemed to suggest, but she did not want to share her grief with this woman.

Marguerite had usurped the position of her dear and beautiful mother, and the fact that her father had not exclusively enjoyed his second wife's affections became obvious with the ubiquitous presence of a Monsieur Henri du Prés. Monsieur du Prés was already at the house, consoling Madame Masonet, when Julia arrived from the school. Monsieur du Prés accompanied them to the cemetery and for an unconscionable length of time sat silently in the darkened parlor after the funeral, ostensibly sharing their grief but usually dozing in the big stuffed chair that had been her father's favorite. That Madame Masonet and Monsieur du Prés were seen together frequently was a fact casually accepted in the easy morals of French society. It was naturally acknowledged that they were enjoying, as well, certain pleasures outside the sanctity of marriage. Julia, ingenue and cosseted schoolgirl, was not graphically aware of all of the details of her stepmother's *affaire de coeur,* but she suspected that with more consistent and reliable care her father might not have gotten sick in the first place. Where was Madame Masonet when her husband came home wet that evening?

If Marguerite had known what her stepdaughter was thinking, she might have opened the girl's eyes concerning her father. For instance, she might have told her that Gérard was caught in that rainstorm leaving a clandestine meeting with one Thérèse Sanette. Her husband and Mademoiselle Sanette had been keeping company long before she met Monsieur du Prés, and he offered his friendship and company for those long evenings when she would otherwise have been alone. Actually, Marguerite felt rather sorry for the silly Sanette girl, because her husband had been her sole means of support. The woman would just have to find herself another wandering husband, which would not be difficult; the Paris streets teemed with them.

The day after the funeral Monsieur Naft, Masonet's solicitor, sent word to Madame and Mademoiselle Masonet that certain legalities concerning Monsieur Masonet's estate and the monies left in trust for Julia by her mother would have to be discussed. He suggested a meeting in two weeks' time. Julia and Madame Masonet both wondered at the delay, but they sent back word that the fourteenth of September would be perfectly acceptable to them.

So Julia's return to her school was put off at least until then. She knew that her mother had left a trust fund for her that had been supporting her and paying for her education all along. There was no reason to believe that, even with both parents gone, her life would necessarily change now.

She missed her schoolmates, especially Bethany. But the two girls wrote long letters to each other, which is as signal a pleasure for a young girl as talking face-to-face. Even while at Madame Chevous's, Bethany and Julia had regularly exchanged lengthy epistles.

Julia's letters were filled with details of her father's funeral, the changes that had been made in the house since she had last been home and how lonely and empty her life was now. Actually, since her father had never been an obtrusive factor in her life, she would have been hard-pressed to detail exactly how her life had been emptied by his passing. But Bethany never questioned her friend in the depth of her loss.

Bethany's letters to Julia were filled with minute descriptions of Philippe: what he did—he delivered foodstuffs twice a week; what he looked like—he evidently had not changed a hair of his head since Julia left or, very likely, combed one, either; what he said, if he ever said anything, which he usually did not. But just in case he ever let slip with a monosyllable, Bethany's pen was there to catch it and preserve it for her friend.

Every night, after her dutiful prayers, Julia would whisper a little message to her true love, trusting that the Holy Spirit would pass it along.

"Philippe," she would whisper, "I have not forgotten and I will return, *cher ami.*"

The offices of Monsieur Daivde Naft, avocat, were dark and heavy and absolutely silent. Monsieur Naft himself greeted them at the door, speaking softly, as if welcoming Julia, her stepmother—and, of course, Monsieur du Prés— into a house of pagan worship. The image was not inapt, since most of his clients came to discuss their money, the idol that, for some, had replaced Baal and Moloch.

"Madame Masonet, Mademoiselle Masonet..." Monsieur Naft spoke in hushed tones, bending over their hands, then raised his eyebrows questioningly toward du Prés. "Monsieur?" he inquired.

"Henri du Prés, at your service." The gentleman introduced himself and bent politely toward Monsieur Naft, but having less height, more width, fewer hairs upon his head and a good deal more flesh distributed lavishly over his short body, he did not inspire the same nervous respect as the cadaverous lawyer.

Naft nodded to the other man, but returned his attention to Julia with no further comment.

"Mademoiselle Masonet, permit me to introduce Monsieur Edmond and his son, Richard. I understand you have never met each other, though looking over the papers of your mother I gather she meant that you should. Before this unhappy time. You will meet now. Messieurs Edmond, this is Julia Masonet—your ward."

Chapter Two

Julia inhaled her breath sharply, though not audibly. She looked at the two gentlemen in front of her in frank amazement. Not that their appearances were outlandish, but it was startling to discover she was the legal responsibility of someone she had never heard of before.

The persons of Major Charles Edmond and his son, Richard, were actually quite presentable, even distinguished. Particularly that of the elder Monsieur Edmond. His rugged, tanned features and erect bearing suggested campaigns waged while leading brave fighting men in exotic lands. He had a full head of white hair and darker mutton chops that followed the line of his jaw. His eyes were a sun-bleached blue, which further enhanced the image of years spent on foreign desert sands.

Richard Edmond was even taller than his father, and though he was a young man, still attending university in the winter months, he looked to Julia to be nearly as mature as the white-haired gentleman at his side. It was the mustache above his unsmiling lips that made him seem so very *ancien*. His hair was light brown, his features as well-defined as his father's, and though his eyes were darker, still there was a resemblance that verified these two were father and son.

The younger man remained where he stood as his father stepped forward to greet Julia.

"Mademoiselle Masonet. It is a profound pleasure to meet you at last." He took the girl's hand and nodded stiffly.

"Monsieur Edmond, so glad to meet you."

Madame Masonet, unlike her stepdaughter, had been looking not at the two handsome gentlemen but rather at Monsieur Naft this whole time, so she had not been as pleasurably employed. She did not seem as willing to be civil, either.

"Monsieur Naft," she barked. "What is the meaning of this? I am the girl's guardian."

Monsieur Naft shook his head, seating himself behind his desk as he did so.

"Not legally, Madame Masonet. Not in the eyes of the law." He held up a handful of papers that had been lying atop his desk and offered them to the lady. These evidently were the letter of the law and held more sway than Marguerite's thirteen years of caring—more or less—for the child.

"I do not understand," Madame Masonet said. Even if she had been able to read, she still would not have understood the complicated French and Latin legal phrases.

Monsieur Naft extended his hand for the papers and Madame Masonet returned them.

"I will not suggest that it is simple," the lawyer said. Any such suggestion would have insulted the intelligence of the people before him. "Monsieur Charles Edmond is an acquaintance of the Parson family in England and shared certain—" he glanced down at the papers "—military exploits with George Parson. Your grandfather, Mademoiselle Masonet."

"I served under Parson on the Peninsula, miss. Finest soldier I ever knew. Good man." The elder Edmond clipped his words in crisp, military fashion, but even then he was unable to disguise the ring of emotion in his voice.

"Your mother, Sarah Parson Masonet, consulted me a number of years ago," Monsieur Naft said. "When she knew her health was failing, I believe. Her own father had passed away, leaving his daughter, your mother, a sizable estate. Madame Masonet, the first Madame Masonet," he clarified, "came to me to complete the matter of putting that money into a trust for you, *mademoiselle,* and at that time she made certain other arrangements for your well-being, education, care and legal guardianship." Monsieur Naft was a devoted follower of his profession and always used as many impressive-sounding words as possible to express a single idea. "She named at that time Monsieur Charles Edmond as your legal guardian should you be left without parental influence. Not knowing how long her husband would outlive her, or even, perhaps, if her own weakening condition was mortal, she also named Monsieur Edmond's son and heir, Monsieur Richard Edmond, as cooperative guardian of that trust. The trust to which I refer is both yourself, Mademoiselle Masonet, and the considerable personal properties being held for you until you reach the age of legal maturity."

"What about me?" Madame Masonet demanded bluntly. All of this nonsense about Julia was very interesting, she was sure, but what did that handful of papers say about her and her consolation now that Gérard had left her—and Thérèse Sanette—*sans* support?

Monsieur Naft looked at the woman with a cold, blank stare, eyes like the glass eyes of stuffed game, displayed by proud huntsmen in their dens or libraries and finally consigned by wives or weary housekeepers to attics or trash heaps.

"Monsieur Masonet left you twenty thousand francs, *madame,* as we have discussed. You are not mentioned in Madame Sarah Masonet's papers. Monsieur Masonet was quite generous in his bequest."

"Generous!" Marguerite cried. "He might have been remembering his cook. I was married to the man. Surely I may claim more than a bequest? In the eyes of the law, Monsieur Naft, the eyes of the law." Marguerite Masonet had evidently latched on to that phrase in the assumption that it possessed some of the same awesome power as Aladdin's "Open Sesame."

"Monsieur Masonet properly disposed of all of his holdings in his will. He made a number of gifts to friends and relations, yourself included, *madame*. He evidently believed twenty thousand francs would maintain your current way of life, until you chose to alter your situation." Naft looked pointedly at Monsieur du Prés, who colored visibly.

Madame Masonet was rather a vivid color herself, but not from embarrassment. She sputtered furiously, but Monsieur Naft held up his hand impassively.

"Your husband has not left you destitute, *madame*, but he has, quite correctly, I assure you, left the balance of his property to his daughter, his only heir, and issue of his first marriage. These are the terms of your husband's will. The terms of Madame Sarah Parson Masonet's will are of no concern to you, nor are you in a position to contest any of this.

"Now, Mademoiselle Masonet..." Naft returned his attention to the girl, dismissing Marguerite as completely as if he had sprung a trapdoor under her chair and dropped her into a deep pit. "Though Monsieur Edmond and his son are strangers to you, I believe, or rather, Sarah Masonet, your mother, believed they would have your best interest at heart if you ever found yourself in a position of guardianship."

"Indeed we do, Miss Masonet," the major assured her brusquely.

"And knowing that a certain understanding would have to be reached between you, I contacted these gentlemen and asked them to join us today. Which they did, I might say, at considerable personal expense and inconvenience, dropping matters of business and leaving their native soil on such short notice."

Edmond cleared his throat gruffly.

"Nonsense, Naft, old man. Not much doing on the old place right now. I suppose it was not too difficult for my son and me to come across and meet George's little granddaughter." He smiled kindly down at the girl with the black hair and olive skin, so unlike Parson's ruddy mien or little Sarah Jane with her milk-and-strawberries skin.

"Because you are here," Monsieur Naft continued blandly, "you have the occasion to become acquainted. You are welcome to use this office while the three of us step outside. Madame Masonet, Monsieur du Prés, will you join me?"

Monsieur Naft stood and seemed to draw Marguerite and du Prés to their feet like rigid marionettes attached to strings. In a moment the door shut, very softly, behind the three of them, and Julia found herself alone with the two strange men.

The white-haired gentleman took the chair nearest to the girl, the one Madame Masonet had just quitted. The younger man remained standing silently behind his father's chair, saying little but watching the dark child carefully with his razor-sharp blue eyes.

"I know this is rather awkward for you, my dear, and something of a surprise, too, I gather?" The elder Edmond paused and Julia nodded. "Your mother was very like a niece to me. The colonel, your grandfather, insisted we keep in touch, and we've all been like family over the years. Isn't that right, Richard?"

"Like family, sir," the young man agreed.

"Then you knew *Maman* before she and my father married, Monsieur Edmond?" Julia asked.

"Knew her? Why, I took little Sarah on her first buggy ride. She was the flower girl when I married my own sweet bride."

"How fortunate for you, *monsieur.* I never really knew her. I have only a few vague memories of a pretty woman with golden hair." She smiled faintly. "We have been reading the Greek myths at Madame Chevous's and I have come to embody her as one of the Grecian maidens or even—" she smiled again "—one of the goddesses." She stopped and laughed self-consciously. "Silly of me, I suppose," she apologized.

"Nonsense, my girl. Your mother was very like one of those Grecian . . . whatsits . . ."

"Nymphs," his son supplied.

"Yes. Well. She could charm at least one old soldier, or even a young buck, as I was in those days. But see here, miss, all this formality will never do. As I said, we are more or less family here. Certainly in Monsieur Naft's 'eye of the law,' so you had better call me Uncle Charles and this young fellow Cousin Richard. What do you think?" The gentleman paused expectantly and Julia obediently tested the strange names on her tongue.

"Uncle Charles. Cousin Richard."

"That's the ticket! Now, let us find out a little about one another. You know I served in the military with your grandfather, but when I returned to the old home soil I thought the peaceful country life would be too dull for such a heroic soldier of fortune." The elder Edmond stopped and cleared his throat self-consciously. "I and a friend of mine from the Forty-ninth decided we would do a little speculating and try to make our fortunes in, oh, this and that. Oil, land, corn—you could throw a stone and hit something the two of us took a chance upon. Eventually, surprisingly, we actually succeeded. It was South African diamonds that finally made us both indecently wealthy." The gentleman stopped again and Julia was fascinated by the dark red flush that gave his tanned cheeks an almost purple hue.

"But enough of that," he said, summarily dismissing the stroke of fortune that had provided for a lifetime of ease and pleasure. "Suffice it to say that with the means in hand I found that what I wanted most in the world was to enjoy a peaceful country life. So Brewster and I abandoned our active pursuit of riches, though we still maintain a casual partnership and a warm friendship, even after all these years and the different directions our lives have taken us. I married a lovely young lady and set up housekeeping on a modest country estate. Brewster married a pretty girl from the London stage. Poor Elsie died quite young, I am afraid, but they had one daughter and we were blessed with one son." Major Edmond leaned toward the girl and spoke in an undertone, as if imparting a well-guarded secret. "I will confess to you, Miss Masonet, that both the Edmond family and the Brewster family hope that fact is significant." He looked fondly over his shoulder.

The young man who stood behind him cleared his throat uncomfortably. The major smiled and then continued his history. "The Edmonds now inhabit a modest home in the English countryside. Myself, my wife, Jenny, that is, Guenivere, Richard here, when he is not off being educated, and Millie, who orders everyone around as if she were the commander in chief, though she is in our hire and ostensibly at our beck and call. I raise expensive Hereford cattle, which cost me a great deal and which I sell, usually at only a small loss. Fortunately, my early financial success allows me to indulge my cattle hobby with no serious consequences. All of which, I am sure, is of consuming interest to a schoolgirl of, let us say—" he paused and squinted his eyes thoughtfully at Julia "—fifteen."

"Thirteen...Uncle Charles," Julia said, smiling and flattered that she had been mistaken for a fifteen-year-old.

"Thirteen, of course," Major Edmond corrected himself. Julia did not catch the twinkle in his eye that suggested he probably could have guessed her age more accurately. "And you are attending school?"

"*Oui, mon oncle.* At Madame Chevous's in the country." She waved her hand vaguely, implying that France was made up of two segments: Paris and "the country." "I am in the top form but one."

"And your studies?" Edmond asked.

"They are many," Julia said, not grasping clearly the meaning of his question.

"Are you a good student? Are you able to comprehend the lessons?" the major expanded.

"Oh, *oui*, Uncle Charles. I enjoy especially chemistry and mathematics. It no doubt questions my femininity to make such a claim, though."

"Not at all. Young ladies may be as smart as they please, I say. Smarter than me by a long shot. Just like Richard here. Attends the university and puts his own father to shame. I don't mind it. Let him do all the work now that he has the education, I say."

Julia looked up toward the younger man.

"London University?" she asked, impressed by the wisdom and maturity the words suggested.

"*Oui, mademoiselle.* I, like you, am in the top form but one of my school."

"Oh, not like me," Julia said, flustered that her poor schooling would be compared to his.

"Julia..." Major Edmond recalled her attention as much with the serious tone of his voice as with her name. "In our discussions with Monsieur Naft, and from letters from your own dear mother, it is our understanding that you consider us more than the legal trustees of your inheritance until you come of age. You are, quite literally, to think of the Edmonds as your family. We do not want to disrupt your life so much as provide you with a home. You are to come to me, or your Cousin Richard, when anything troubles you, when you are faced with a problem, if, even, you are lonely and find yourself at loose ends for a few days or a few months. Do you think you can accept us as your ready made family?"

"*Certainement,* Uncle Charles."

"You must not be shy around us."

"*Non,* Uncle Charles." Julia earnestly nodded and shook her head to reinforce her responses, but glancing at the figure who stood so straight and stiff behind her new uncle, she was not at all easy in her mind about approaching *that* gentleman as a confidant. Tall and forbidding, Richard Edmond did not really seem to invite the confidences of a thirteen-year-old schoolgirl. After her recent comparison of her mother and the classic Greek figures, Julia mentally clothed the gentleman in the skimpy attire of one of the Greek heroes and the setting seemed to suit him well. He could easily claim as home some lofty pinnacle on Mount Olympus. Though Uncle Charles Edmond had generously suggested she share that home, she was relieved that her heart was already claimed, her home already decided: a little country cottage outside of Paris with Philippe.

There was a muffled knock at the door.

Monsieur Naft opened it and peered around the panel.

"Is everything all right?" he inquired.

"Yes, everything is going quite smoothly, Monsieur Naft. We have gotten to know each other a little. Julia tells me she is going to school."

"A boarding school. *Oui.* That is correct."

"We do not want her education to be discontinued, naturally. But she knows she is welcome at the Edmond manse whenever she can visit. Julia, your Aunt Jenny is anxious to meet you and would have liked to make this trip with us. Too strenuous for her, I was afraid. But do not put off a visit too awfully long, my dear."

"I will, Uncle Charles. Or rather, I will not."

"Then it is your intention that Mademoiselle Masonet return to the Chevous school?" Naft inquired, sitting behind his desk once more and taking up his pen, ready to seal irrevocably Edmond's decision.

"Oh, yes," Major Edmond said, but his son bent over his chair and spoke into that gentleman's ear. Neither Julia nor Naft could hear the words, but they saw young Richard Edmond's brow furrow seriously and various expressions of surprise, question and finally understanding settle on his father's face. Finally, Major Charles Edmond nodded and turned back to Naft.

"Or no," he said.

"Wh-what?" Julia gasped.

"My son brings it to my attention that since her guardians will be in England, as well as her bank accounts and the property her mother left her, it would be logical if the girl were in England, as well. Therefore, we will arrange for Julia to attend a school on our side of the Channel."

"*Très bien,*" Naft said. It did not matter to him in which country the child attended school. His hefty bank fees would continue to be issued from her estate as long as he was alive and wrote her one or two letters a year.

"But my friends . . ." Julia protested.

"Not to worry. You will make plenty of new friends in England," Edmond remarked, casually dismissing the girl and her objection. "Come along, Richard. Unless Monsieur Naft can think of anything else?" The lawyer shook his head, signifying they had completed his agenda. "I believe our business is finished here, then. We will contact you shortly, Julia, as soon as we have seen to your enrollment in a suitable school. Monsieur Naft, Mademoiselle Masonet, *à bientôt.* Convey our regards to Madame Masonet and the gentleman."

The lawyer showed the Edmonds out while Julia sat stunned and brokenhearted in the dark office. Just like that, with no more thought given to it than to the slapping of a bothersome gnat, Charles Edmond, and more specifically that odious son of his, had razed the structure of her universe, of her life and of her destiny. There would be no

idyllic cottage in the French countryside; there would be no
peace and harmony. There would be no Philippe for her.

Alone in the quiet office, young Julia Masonet put her
head down into her hands and wept.

Major Edmond let no grass grow under his feet.

Within the week a letter was delivered to Julia, inform-
ing her that a suitable school had been located for her.

Neither Mrs. Edmond nor I have had a great deal of
experience with schools for young ladies, Richard being our only child, and he having been tutored in our
home until he was ready for secondary school. I was
dismayed by their scarcity of number and appalled by
the shabby state of maintenance and inferior instruc-
tion available in some of them. One would think with
good Queen Victoria on the throne a more concentrated effort toward the education of young women
might have been made in this country. Fortunately, my
son and Miss Brewster were able to locate a school for
you that meets all of our stringent requirements. It is on
the other side of London from Tunbridge, near the little town of Barnet. It is farther away from us than we
would have liked, but Richard assures me it is a top
drawer establishment. Better than anything in this immediate area.

Arrangements have been made for your enrollment
the first of November. That will give you a few days
with us anyway before you have to go on. Shall we say
October, then? Mrs. Edmond thinks a month is not
nearly enough time to have you with us, but I ask her
what pleasure a young girl like yourself can take with
two old relics such as ourselves?

Then, in a different, more feminine hand, a note was jot-
ted across the bottom of the paper.

You must not mind the major, Miss Masonet. Aspen
Grove is admittedly small, but I believe all the more
charming for that. And I am eagerly looking forward

to meeting you. Richard tells us he can take another few days away from his studies and has agreed to come across and fetch you. God be with you until we meet, Guenivere Edmond.

Julia had steeled herself for the pain of this uprooting. She was very fond of Major Edmond, and Mrs. Edmond's note touched her motherless little heart deeply. But she was not at all pleased to hear that the younger Mr. Edmond would be the one to cross the Channel and fetch her—like a sack of turnips.

Her pique was necessarily thrust into the background. The timetable the Edmonds had laid down barely allowed her time to gather her things from Madame Chevous's and complete her packing here in Paris.

Madame Masonet had been cold and distant ever since the meeting with Monsieur Naft. Relationships in the *appartement* at 417, rue Saint Jacques, steadily deteriorated. Marguerite, when she was present, became very short and impatient with the girl. Perhaps it was fortunate, therefore, that Madame Masonet was absent more and more often, until a brief encounter once a day was as much as the two saw of each other. Having failed to find consolation in Masonet's will, Marguerite was evidently faring better with Monsieur du Prés, whose company she was keeping almost exclusively now.

Julia was forced to rely solely on Berte's heavy hand to help collect her things. And then, hiring the coach herself, she returned quickly to the school to pick up her possessions and say her *adieux*.

"Bethany, whatever am I going to do without you?"

"You without me? What of me without you? Oh, this Monsieur Edmond of yours is a *bête!*"

Julia's eyes narrowed. *"Un ogre!"* she breathed furiously.

The girls were not talking about the same Edmond generation, but as long as their anger was interchangeable, they did not stop to define just which of the Edmond gentlemen was a *bête* and which an *ogre*.

"You must come and visit me," Julia urged. "Now promise that you will."

Bethany promised with all of the passion and sincerity of her powerless little soul. "And I will write to you," she also, more practically, promised.

"Oh, yes! Every week! I want to hear about everything and—" Julia hesitated. "Everyone," she finished.

"Do you mean Philippe?"

The two girls had been walking arm in arm around the grounds of the school. It was the first week of October now, but the weather was still mild. Even if the weather had been much cooler, the girls would have been comfortable, huddled as they were with heads bent together and tears occasionally threatening. Now, though, at the mention of the boy's name, Julia stopped and pulled away from the other girl.

"No," she said. "Not Philippe. You must never mention Philippe to me again. It is too painful."

"Certainly not, *chère amie,*" Bethany said, claiming her friend's arm again. "I would not cause you distress for the world." She patted Julia's hand consolingly, but in the back of her mind was a certain guilty relief.

Bethany Beatrice Augustina d'Arnez really was fond of Julia and would have, honestly, rather she stay than go. But Julia did have that olive complexion and black hair that overshadowed her paler friend. Since she had been away, it was Bethany, not Julia, who was hearing reports on the onion harvest and now predictions of a cold winter from the delivery boy. Now it was Bethany who was the envy of other girls in the school, and she was sorry, but if Julia was going to move to England and never wanted to hear of Philippe again, Bethany was certainly not the one to say her nay.

Even before Julia returned for her things, Monsieur Naft had informed Madame Chevous that her student would be leaving the school. She found her trunk and carpetbag packed and waiting, looking deserted and forlorn, outside of the dormitory. A sob caught in Julia's throat when she saw the luggage, abandoned vessels after a storm. She might have climbed back into the coach that brought her and returned immediately. That would have been her wisest course, as a matter of fact. But Julia could not leave this, the most important part of her life so far, without saying good-bye. So she stayed.

And for one last time, Julia spoke with Philippe.

Bethany, ashamed of her hidden felicity over Julia's departure, saw to it herself that her friend and the young man would be alone together. The occasion was his delivery of winter squashes, which were to be kept in the cellar. His load was larger and his stay would be the longest for several months. This was a noble sacrifice on Bethany's part.

"Bonjour," Julia offered shyly.

The young man arrived on the day and at the time Bethany had promised. He had drawn his loaded cart up to the cellar door and was just getting down when the girl came through the back entrance that led to the kitchen.

"Bonjour," he said.

"You have brought the squashes, I see."

"Oui."

Julia watched him take one of the large, heavy vegetables off the cart and carry it down the cellar steps. His muscles bulged provocatively, but...oh, it was just that she remembered him as being a little taller, with less hair in his eyebrows.

"What is that?"

"You looked thirsty. I thought you might like a drink." Julia held out the tin cup. The boy took it and drank, then grimaced sourly.

"De l'eau," he complained.

"Oui," she agreed. "Water."

"I hoped it might be a sip of wine. A fellow needs a little something to keep up his strength, you know." He winked broadly at the girl.

"We...we have no wine," Julia stammered, surprised and offended by his manner and the wink.

"No wine?" the boy scoffed. "A French house with no wine? Ridiculous!"

He pulled another large squash into his embrace and turned toward the cellar.

"I am going away soon," Julia called after him desperately.

"Going away? What a shame."

Julia scurried to the cellar door and met him, eyes wide when he returned.

"Are you sorry, Philippe?" she breathed.

"Sorry about what?"

"Sorry that I am going?"

The boy stopped and studied the girl with an amused expression. Suddenly he grabbed her two bony shoulders and pulled her to him. He planted an awkward, moist kiss on her lips. Then he stepped around her to get another squash from his cart.

Tears had sprung to Julia's dark eyes. In dumb misery she watched Philippe empty the cart and then climb up onto the driver's seat.

"I am going to England," she called up to him frantically.

"*Bon voyage,*" he said, jouncing the reins.

"*Au revoir, mon amour,*" she said softly as the cart pulled away.

With only a week until Monsieur Richard Edmond's scheduled arrival, Julia was finally obliged to leave the dormitory and classrooms that had been more her home than the Masonet rooms in Paris. Everyone received a final hug: all the little girls; Madame Chevous teetering clumsily without the support of her cane; Bethany and Julia dampening each other's cheeks with their tears one last time.

"Write," Julia sobbed.

"I will," Bethany returned.

The ride back into town took less than two hours, but it seemed so much longer than that to the girl, and so much farther away. Her whole life, she knew, was being left behind her. Soon she would bid dear Marguerite goodbye, as well. As her departure drew nearer, the memory of her nursemaid and stepmother softened. Now she allowed her eyes to fill with tears quite as often when she thought of Madame Masonet, as when she thought of Bethany.

At last, the coachman pulled the horses to a stop in front of 417, rue Saint Jacques. When he open the carriage door for the girl, Julia was surprised to find the town house locked up tightly, nor did anyone come to answer her knock. She would not have been surprised if Marguerite was not there, what with Monsieur du Prés and all, but it was strange that Berte had been allowed the night off when she was expected home.

With her own latchkey, however, she unlocked the door and held it open while the driver carried her trunk and boxes inside the front door. She also paid him herself from her small supply of French coins.

"Marguerite! Berte! Is anyone here?" she called as she left the tiny vestibule inside the front door, the space almost completely filled by her trunk. But as she stepped through the archway and turned into the apartment, her words stopped suddenly, her eyes grew large and her mouth dropped open.

The rooms had been stripped bare. Evidently Madame Masonet had decided to make the best of a bad deal and had taken, and most probably sold, every sliver of furniture, stroke of artwork, glimmer of silver and thread of rug or wall hanging.

The wallpaper in the dining room had even been pulled off, exposing the plaster-dabbed, unpainted gray wall behind it.

The rooms were dim, filled with afternoon shadows, and in the echoing stillness Julia could hear a tree branch striking the eaves overhead intermittently as the October breeze picked up.

Chapter Three

Julia wandered from room to room, stunned. She walked through the sitting room, into the dining room, beyond it to the kitchen. She mounted the stairs and stood at the doorway of each bedroom, and then, like a sleepwalker, she retraced the entire circuit.

Downstairs for the third time, she became aware of the moaning sounds she was making. Tears had started falling when she first looked into the room that had been her bedroom since before *Maman* died, and had fallen faster and faster with each trip through the house. Her moans, though, were new and like those of a wounded animal. Unconsciously she backed into the corner of the sitting room, and with her shoulder blades supported by either wall, she slid down to sit on the floor.

Where was everyone? Where was everything? What was she to do?

"Papa, why did you do this?" she sobbed aloud. It was somehow all her father's fault for dying and leaving her at the mercy of that woman. Why would he go? What had she done to make him leave her like this?

She put her head down on her knees and could actually feel the anger course through her body. Anger at her father for dying, dying of something as foolish as pneumonia.

Her fists were clenched and with a shot of pain she felt one of her nails break the flesh of her palm.

The wind moaned through the Paris streets and now the branch rapped against the roof frequently, but without a steady rhythm that might have calmed the girl.

She thought about her stepmother and transferred some of her anger to this more legitimate object. The woman who had cared for her since the day she was born had betrayed her, abandoned her, thrown her onto the trash heap, robbed her and deserted her and might as well have physically assaulted her. A knife through her thin chest would have left no more frightful a wound.

The ruddy light of sunset was filtering into the room from the window that faced west when Julia transferred her anger once more to the author and engineer of all of her terrifying woes: Richard Edmond. *Cousin* Richard.

Her life had been fine. Not happy, not with her mother gone and now her father leaving her, but it had been safe, familiar. She had friends and there were adults who would have cared for her. But Edmond had ripped her from that place and left her forsaken here.

Tears no longer fell from her eyes, but her dress was damp where the moisture had soaked through the material. Now a shudder racked her frame. She was cold and very thirsty. She pushed herself up against the wall again and stumbled first into the kitchen, where she put her face under the spigot and pulled on the pump handle. A flood of water burst through the hole and drenched her face. She gasped and pulled water into her lungs. Falling back, she coughed and sputtered, rubbing the water from her eyes, pushing a streak of rust and dirt from the pump handle across her face.

When she could breathe again she gathered the water in her cupped hands on her next try, sipping at the water as it quickly drained from them. Then, wiping her hands on her skirt, she returned to the entrance hall and the heavy trunk that still sat there, keeping watch at the door.

She opened the box, letting the lid fall sharply against the wall. There was no *Papa* or Marguerite or Berte to scold her. She rummaged down through the folds of material until her fingers recognized the thick fabric of her woolen cloak. Naturally it was at the bottom of the box, and pulling it out, she also pulled out almost all of the other contents.

She had been cold, and after her drenching in the kitchen, she now shivered miserably. She wrapped the cape around her and returned to the sitting room and her corner. The rooms were dark, but the wind outside had evidently died down, since she could no longer hear the pounding of the branch. She sank to the floor and looked out into the room. She still shivered and the floor was like a slab of cold marble. Now there were noises inside the house, amplified in the empty rooms. Her eyes were wide and suspicious and very frightened. It was not safe in her dark corner, but it was safer here than any other place this night.

The night was long. She did not remember ever closing her eyes, but she dozed fitfully and at last woke to see the room growing light again. She was recumbent on the hard floor and rose slowly, stiffly. She returned to the kitchen for another drink and realized, as the cold water hit her stomach, that now her two major discomforts were cold and hunger.

Last night she had been too shocked and frightened to feel hunger, but in the light of day her mind was able to concentrate on other ideas.

She had a few francs left, enough for some bread and cheese, and she knew the way down to the little marketplace Berte had frequented. Stepping around her open trunk and scattered belongings, she opened the door and then carefully locked it behind her. Having so very few possessions left to her in the world, she was very careful of them.

The bakery was two blocks away, and the little grocer who sold cheese was on the next street after that. By the time Julia reached the cheeses, half of her loaf of bread was already gone. She purchased a small chunk of the mellow white cheese, counting the coins that were returned to her, calculating other purchases her dwindling fortune would buy. Two more loaves of bread and one or two of the small kippered fish, perhaps. But not today. Having already been parted from more money than she had expected, she could not bring herself to buy anything more today.

Instead, she turned her troubled thoughts to the problem of finding something to burn, some way to keep warm tonight. She was walking with head bent, worrying over the problem, when her eyes fell on a little scrap of wood, perhaps four inches long, lying against one of the buildings.

She snatched the wood up as if it were encrusted with diamonds, then continued on her way, still slowly, but this time with eyes darting back and forth, prying under every window ledge, back into the shadows of every alleyway. By the time she reached number 417 she was carrying, besides half a loaf of bread and the paper-wrapped cheese, a dozen odd scraps of wood. But she had seen a whole pile of discarded boards and bricks back in the last alley, and after depositing her precious freight in her corner of the empty sitting room, she hurried back down the street to the treasure trove of flammable material.

The pile contained many more broken bricks than boards, and Julia, retrieving what she could, was forced to continue her scavenging.

It was afternoon before she was satisfied that the wood stacked on the apartment floor would last all night. The rooms were already cold and the girl carefully piled her smallest, driest bits of wood around a crumpled news sheet she found discarded on one of her forays. There were, surprisingly, a few lucifer matches left on the fireplace mantel, although there was no wood in the cradle and certainly no coal in the metal bin.

She struck the match and bent over to ignite the paper, unwilling to let any of the warmth escape up the chimney. A glow of keen satisfaction warmed her every bit as much as the embryonic fire. She had food, she had fuel, there was water, and the bare walls, which if they provided her with nothing else, were a protection from the elements. Her skirt, she noticed, had been torn, and even by the feeble light in the sitting room she could tell that her ankles were filthy. But everything considered, she was very pleased with herself.

That night was long, too. Julia was still angry with her father and Marguerite and Cousin Richard, but not wildly furious. She did not feel desperate or terrified or even as physically miserable. But her life, which had been filled with family and friends only yesterday, was today totally bereft of any kindly influence. Alone in the empty apartment, crouched over her little fire, dully munching the bread, which was stale by now, and the cheese, which had grown soft, she might have been some solitary explorer in the gloomy forests of the Dark Continent. Surely the fiercest flesh-eating jungle cat could be no more frightful than the beasts that beset her here.

She was able to sleep more soundly that second night and woke to find the room light and a faint warmth still wafting from the ashes in the grate.

She ate the heel of the bread and most of the cheese from the wrapping, leaving only morsels she would finish tonight with the bread she bought today. And the smoked fish.

Awake and alert, freshened and strengthened by her sparse meal, she decided that her first order of business must be wood. She had gathered every scrap she had been able to find in a two-block radius and realized that today she would have to range farther afield.

Once again she locked the door securely behind her, but she brought with her the canvas bag that had held her schoolbooks. She would not have to return to rue Saint Jacques as often this time. She would go down to the park. There would be fallen twigs and branches under the trees and papers tossed about in the grass. She had her bag filled once before she reached the park and returned to empty it near the fireplace in the sitting room.

She found the park to be the bonanza she had envisioned. There were leafy limbs, sometimes whole branches under the trees, and one log that was as long as Julia was tall and as big around as her waist. That she was forced to leave it where she found it almost made her cry.

There were also geese on the pond and smiling people sitting on the benches or strolling along the walks. One young man was playing with his dog, throwing a stick and then urging the big mongrel after it. Julia started watching the two of them to see where the man would discard the stick. Then she became interested in them. The carefree lad appeared to have nothing better to do than play with his dog in the park, no worry of greater moment on his mind than getting the dog to bring him the broken piece of wood.

When the two of them, master and mutt, left the park, Julia watched their departure wistfully, the stick entirely forgotten.

With her bag filled and bulging, she sat beneath one of the trees to watch the carnival swirling around her. A lady and a gentleman passed on the walkway. The lady had a parasol, and the gentleman a tall top hat and a cane. The lady wore a shawl and had her hand linked through the man's crooked elbow. The man chuckled; the tinkling crystal of the woman's laugh floated across the parkway to Julia. Then the woman turned her head, saw the filthy little urchin under the tree and grimaced, pulling the man the other way, hurrying him from such a distasteful sight.

Julia stuck her tongue out at the departing couple and was inordinately pleased when the woman turned and saw the mocking expression on the little girl's face.

There were other passersby to see, and the birds on the pond, the ripples in the water, the clouds in the sky. Julia was fascinated by it all, as if she had never seen anything like it before, as if she were a stranger to the world around her which, to the world in which she now found herself, she was.

She felt the rumblings in her stomach and had decided to start away to the bakery and the grocer's that sold smoked fish *and* cheese, when she noticed the man on the park bench. She noticed him because, other than the fine lady with the parasol and the tinkling laugh, he was the only person who had noticed her all day.

He was whiskered and slovenly and grimy. Julia was somewhat slovenly and grimy herself, but she had been slovenly and grimy only since the day before. This man had been slovenly and grimy for years, since the day he was born, perhaps. From the dull gloss across his eyes one knew he would be slovenly and grimy until the day he died.

Julia looked away, uncomfortable and strangely alarmed. From the corner of her eye she glanced at him. He was looking out toward the pond, too. She breathed easier until she dared another glance in his direction and found he was looking at her again.

Fighting the panic, but now definitely alarmed, she scrambled to her feet and bent to clutch the drawstrings of her bag, and when she stood she saw that the man was standing, too. Looking toward the water, but standing.

Julia gasped. She threw the heavy bag across her shoulder, which staggered her, then struggled up the steep incline that led to another walkway. By the time she reached level ground again she was out of breath, panting like a winded greyhound. She finally dared look behind her and nearly collapsed with relief when she saw she was not being followed.

She paused to catch her breath, then lifted the bag again, this time gently dropping its weight onto her back.

"I will stop at the bakery on the way home," she mumbled to herself. "There is no need to get the fish this afternoon. I could not eat a bite of it. Not very hungry at all. I shall get along very well on a loaf of bread and a drink of water. That sounds delicious, in fact. Perfectly filling. And if I am very careful, this wood will surely last me two days. It is not so cold out here. I will put my cloak around me and not light a fire until it is quite dark in the *room.*"

Her last word was forced out of her suddenly when she ran directly into a person on the walkway in front of her. Or rather, he ran into her. She looked up with the *"Pardonnez-moi!"* on her lips. He reached forward to grab her arm before she recognized the whiskered face and the bleary eyes.

She stumbled back; he lurched forward. She turned and ran in the other direction, the bag of branches banging against her back and ribs. She thought she felt the weight of his hand against the bag, the pull of dirty fingers grabbing at the bulges, but she never stopped to look, never even slowed down. In a few minutes she was out of the park onto the thoroughfare, but her flight had taken her in the opposite direction from rue Saint Jacques, and she did not dare enter the park again to retrace her steps.

She decided she must circumvent the square, but it was a very long way around it. She was in a part of the city she did not know. Or did not know well. Unfamiliar signposts of *rue* this and *place de* that were on every hand, and Julia felt as if she had never been in this city before.

Eventually, at long last, she came to a street she recognized and knew she was only two crossings away from her street and home and food. But at that crossway she passed another man, this one clean-shaven, face washed, hair combed. He noticed her, too; watched the slipshod, lanky girl hauling the heavy sack behind her. If Julia had stopped to consider the picture she presented she might not have wondered so at the interest she inspired. But she thought only of the man in the park and his filthy hand reaching toward her, and she vowed if she could only make it to number 417 she would never budge from its safe confines again.

She arrived at the blessed portal at last. She did not find her key in the first pocket she explored, and panic almost claimed her again before her fingers closed around it in the flat strap she wore across her bosom, which she and Bethany had euphemistically titled a *brassière*.

She slammed the door behind her, locked it and then pulled the heavy trunk in front of it. She staggered into the sitting room, where she dumped the heavy canvas bag onto the hearth before she collapsed onto the floor herself.

She waited a while before she lit the fire, but not as long as she promised herself she would. She sat very near the flame that night, partly to capture all the warmth and partly so the crackling of the flames in the sappy branches would drown out the rumblings in her stomach.

Her vow never to leave the confines of the apartment again lasted until the next morning when hunger woke her. She would have to get something to eat. She knew Monsieur Bonét, the baker, and decided it would be safe to travel the two blocks to his shop and back again. After all, it had been a safe trip for the previous twelve years.

She bought her bread, two loaves this time, which left her with only two small coins that looked as forsaken in the bottom of her coin purse as she felt. She hurried back to the apartment, closed the door, pulled the trunk in front of it again as an added safeguard and spent the rest of the day inside. She sat by the window looking out at the neighborhood she had called home, in which she had been born and grown up, at least as "up" as she was now. Today she looked through the glass suspiciously, until one of her neighbors would pass by, and she would slink back around the windowsill and only peek out until he was out of sight.

The bread she bought to last until Monsieur Edmond arrived was three-quarters gone by the time the rooms grew dark again and she knew she could sleep. She only started a tiny fire and wrapped her cloak around her for the night until the flames had time to warm the room. She might be forced to buy more bread, but she had already decided to burn her trunk before she ventured out after any more wood.

The next morning, chilled to the bone, she hurried down to Monsieur Bonét's and with her last copper coin purchased a half loaf of day-old bread. Back in the stripped rooms she followed the sunlight from window to window, then still not completely warm, she was forced to start the fire even before the sun went down.

It had been four days, or maybe five, since she arrived in Paris from Madame Chevous's. Julia looked down at her soiled, torn skirt and found that hard to believe. It might have been a millennium.

However long she had been here, though, it was surely past the time when Cousin Richard was scheduled to come for her. Something must have happened, or perhaps the Edmonds had changed their minds about taking her and had written to Madame Masonet, which message Marguerite also took with her.

But Julia simply could not stay here any longer. She would start out tomorrow, taking a few things with her, and return to the school. They would give her a job and something to eat if they could help her no other way. It would take two days, perhaps three, possibly another entire week to find her way through the city and out into the countryside. Perhaps she could sell something: her books, her half-empty bottles of *eau de cologne,* her other school uniform, which was only slightly less worn than the torn, dirty ensemble she was wearing now. Something. For just enough money to buy another loaf of bread or two. And maybe the fish. By now, the little kippered herring she had seen, but decided against that first day, had achieved a fabulous quality, was the tastiest morsel she could possibly imagine. Her mouth watered and her stomach growled every time she thought of it. And as the days had passed and the bread became so unvarying, she found herself thinking of it often.

She placed the last small branch, the leaves dried and crisp by now, onto the fire sometime after nine o'clock, if she had counted the faint *bongs* correctly that she could hear from the clock tower down near the center of the city. She wrapped herself in her heavy school cloak, which by now looked as if it had been dragged through the city behind a dogcart, and promised herself that she would be on her way as soon as the sky was gray in the morning.

A sharp rap at the front door woke her the next morning. When her eyes sprang open she noticed the sun shining through the sitting room window onto the hardwood floor. The sun never came through that window until after nine o'clock.

The rap was repeated. It was so loud and sharp it must have been produced by a cane or an umbrella handle against the door.

"Madame Masonet! Miss Julia! Are you in?"

She recognized the voice. It was her *horrible* Cousin Richard. At last. She threw her cloak off and struggled to her feet, her sharp bones stiff and sore after her long night on the floor.

"I am here!" she called hoarsely. In front of the door, she put her weight against the trunk that she pulled across the entranceway every night.

"Is there some difficulty?" Edmond called on the other side of the door, confused by the sounds of struggle.

"I am coming," she repeated crossly.

"Good heavens!" Edmond gasped when she finally opened the door. "What have you been doing?"

Julia ran her fingers through a few inches of hair before they were stopped by snarls. The action hardly tamed her wild appearance, especially since she was glaring furiously at the young man, who dared to make it sound as if this situation were her fault. In fact, she had firmly decided during the lonely hours of the past week that *all* of her troubles were directly attributable to *him*.

"I have been taking care of myself."

"Taking care of yourself? What do you mean, you have been taking care of yourself? Where is Madame Masonet?"

"Gone."

"Gone? Where? When?"

"I do not know. But she has taken everything."

"What do you mean, 'everything'?" Edmond asked.

Julia gave him a look that expressed, better than words ever could, how abysmally stupid she considered the question and the questioner.

In reply she opened the door wide and motioned the young man across the threshold.

Richard needed only to look through the front hall and the sitting room to understand what the girl meant by "everything."

"How long have you been here, like this?" he asked.

"Since Saturday," the girl said.

"Saturday!" Edmond barked. "You have been alone, in this apartment, like this, since Saturday? Where is your stepmother?"

"As I told you, I do not know."

"Did she leave no word? No message?"

"Nothing."

"Could you not contact Monsieur Naft?"

The girl shrugged her shoulders helplessly.

"I did not know how to get to his office."

"An address? A letter from him?"

Julia shook her head and Edmond had no difficulty deducing that Madame Masonet had also taken away every bit of correspondence from the lawyer's office and every scrap of paper that might have had his address on it. Perhaps she had made a studied effort to keep the girl and her legal representative incommunicado, but more likely her intent had been to leave nothing behind her.

"Did you seek out *un gendarme?* Go to the *poste de police?*"

Now Julia's eyes grew wide in surprise. That possibility had obviously never occurred to her.

"A policeman might have set up an immediate search for your stepmother and the stolen property. He could have directed you to the offices of Monsieur Naft. He even could have contacted us.'' Edmond stopped, the expression on the girl's face stabbing him as surely with a dagger of guilt as she could have with a dagger of metal.

"I did the best I could," she said, tears in her eyes.

Edmond looked chagrined at the girl, a girl who was barely more than a child.

"And you have done very well," he said, his voice no longer strident but edged with shame—though Julia had not recognized that. Now it was soft and soothing, and had in it another note that Julia also could not exactly identify, though she found she liked it very much. It was profound respect.

"I have been lonely," she whispered, a quiver in her voice. "And frightened."

Edmond stepped to the girl and put his arms around her shoulders, holding her trembling body—all knobs and bony limbs and smelling as though she had been in these same clothes for a week—against him very tenderly.

"And hungry, I would wager," he said.

"I would like some salted fish," Julia murmured hesitantly.

Richard Edmond laughed. Julia thought he was laughing at her, but she was too weary and his arms were too comforting for her to stiffen and pull away from. But once again she was wrong. His laugh was one of aching relief.

The young gentleman did all within his power to ease the trauma of the harrowing experience. The child's only remaining belongings were the things strewn around the trunk.

Though he had promised his parents he would return with the girl the next day, Edmond was forced to spend several days in consultation with Monsieur Naft and going from shop to shop, outfitting the young lady. Richard Edmond had a true eye and Julia might have fared much worse with an adviser.

On the evening of his arrival, the young man secured rooms for them in one of the better Paris hotels. He loaned Julia his own brush set, and when he tapped on her door to bid her good-night, the waif who opened it appeared a bit more civilized than the little savage who had answered the door at 417, rue Saint Jacques that morning.

"I only wanted to make sure everything is satisfactory, that you are quite comfortable."

"*Merci.*"

"*Bon.*" Edmond nodded. "And cleaned up, I see."

This time when Julia put her hand to her hair, her fingers slid through the strands effortlessly.

"Do I look all right?" she asked, placated by his approving look.

"Perfectly presentable. And tomorrow we will get you some new clothes."

"*Très bien.*"

"Until tomorrow, then."

Tomorrow and tomorrow and tomorrow....

It had taken more than one day to secure for the girl all of the articles of clothing a young lady considers necessary. Frocks, skirts, blouses, shoes, hosiery and, of course, lingerie. Julia might have competently selected her own underthings, but as soon as she saw that they made her Cousin Richard desperately uncomfortable, she insisted he view and consider every scrap of satin and lace.

Finally, after almost another complete week, Edmond and his charge boarded the ferry that would take them across the English Channel.

With the sweet forgetfulness of youth, Julia had left the horrors of her abandonment in Paris behind her. And she was also willing at last to acknowledge that, while Philippe's kiss had been very pleasant, there were young men on the other side of the Channel, as well.

On board the boat she ran back and forth from stem to stern, calling to Cousin Richard to look at this sea gull or that bit of flotsam. Cousin Richard truly believed he had observed all of the points of interest of any seabird or floating debris there was to be found in the strait between the two countries, yet he came each time the girl beckoned and attempted to appear fascinated.

It was the same when they finally landed on the British side of the Channel, and Richard was frankly relieved when the carriage they had hired finally pulled into Aspen Grove and Guenivere Edmond hurried out of the door.

"Oh, my dear, let me look at you! Has my son not given you anything to eat at all? Look at these bones, Richard," the woman scolded. "Let us see what we can do about padding some of those rough edges, shall we?" Mrs. Edmond's own bones were encased in a very comfortable padding, and now she put one plump arm around the girl's shoulders. "And tired... Heavens, child, you must be exhausted."

"I am a bit fatigued," Julia murmured. Her voice sounded rough and her eyes glistened at the spontaneous outpouring of motherly love. No one had spoken to her like this since her own dear mother faded out of her life eight years before.

Suddenly Mrs. Edmond was sweeping the girl along in front of her, telling her about the neighborhood and the house and passing along bits of family gossip.

"My niece, Beverly Simpson, was married in that sitting room. That is where Mr. Simpson proposed to her, as well. It was a lovely ceremony The room was positively packed. Even the Kimberlys from way over in East Grinstead came. Beverly still mentions the wedding in every Yule letter she sends. Lovely girl, lovely girl. And this is your room, Julia. Nothing too grand, but comfortable and homey for all that."

Julia looked around her at the airy little room. The walls, washstand, bed covering and curtains were all white, with a large southern exposure window that made everything glimmer in the sunlight. It was a room in which she immediately felt welcomed and at home. She could not imagine that the grave gentleman who had accompanied her from France had ever inhabited these quarters, and she wondered briefly for whom this very feminine room had originally been meant. But now it was, without question, hers.

Mrs. Edmond said something about her taking a few minutes to rest, and Julia might very well have answered her, though she could not recall what she said. She only knew that when Mrs. Edmond—Aunt Jenny—left, closing the door behind her, the girl sank down onto the bed's white coverlet, closed her eyes and did not open them again until the light coming in through the window had changed from gleaming white to a dusky rose, and shadows filled the room.

When she awoke she looked around her. She still was not entirely happy in her new home and her new homeland, but for dear Aunt Jenny and Uncle Charles's sake she was willing to give it the benefit of the doubt.

A smile tripped across her lips. The image suddenly came to her mind of the red blush mounting Cousin Richard's face when she held up the ruffly *jupon* and innocently inquired, "It is beautiful, is it not?"

And then she felt again his strong arms around her shoulders, arms that held her safe and secure. She heard again that deep laugh rumbling through his chest.

Perhaps she would get to know this England for her dear Cousin Richard's sake, too.

She heard the faint confusion of conversation outside her bedroom door and down the stairs. Shivering slightly, she remembered that what had awakened her was the coolness that had invaded the room. She pushed herself up from the mattress and swung her legs from the bed. Now hearing a faint laugh from the parlor she was suddenly anxious to join the warmth of the room and her new family, but when she opened her door she recognized Uncle Charles's voice and paused to hear what he was saying.

"Richard thinks that the girl lacked the proper supervision there. What was it you said about the place?"

"I said the girls were not safeguarded against the all-too-easy morals of the country," the young gentleman said with amusement in his voice. "Miss Brewster was frankly appalled when I told her the liberties that are allowed the students there and insisted we immediately transfer the child to this country and—though she did not say it in these exact terms—civilization."

So! It *had* been Cousin Richard who had so cruelly torn her from the happy shores of her homeland. If there had ever been any doubt.

She had allowed herself to forget how content she had been at Madame Chevous's, and her heartbreaking departure from that institution. The terrifying week when she had been alone and abandoned in Paris had momentarily dimmed, as had, heaven forgive her, the memory of Philippe and his passionate kiss of agonized desolation. Now, having destroyed her every hope for happiness, there was Cousin Richard recounting his exploits and sounding insufferably proud of himself and his Miss Brewster.

In righteous indignation, Julia flung her door open so that it slammed into the wall, and marched out into the hall, following the light and the sound of the surprised voices into the Edmond sitting room.

"Oh, my dear," Mrs. Edmond greeted her when she appeared in the doorway, scowling, her eyes burning angrily. "We were just discussing the merits of the school in which my son and Miss Brewster have enrolled you. Richard believes it will be much more suitable."

"Does he?" Julia asked coldly.

"Absolutely." Uncle Charles nodded. "Good English school. Fine education. Sound principles. All that sort of thing."

"And not so very far from London. Richard promises he can keep an eye on you." Aunt Jenny beamed.

Julia did not beam. Nothing was more guaranteed to keep her from beaming than the news that Cousin Richard would be keeping an eye on her.

"How lucky for me," she said. The major and Mrs. Edmond had both redirected their attention elsewhere—Major Edmond to a brass medallion of some sort he was polishing and his wife to her needlework—so they missed the sour note in her voice. Cousin Richard, standing in front of the little fire that was making only a halfhearted attempt to warm the room, looked at her curiously. Julia returned his look defiantly and was further exasperated to see that ridiculous mustache of his twitch treacherously.

Sulkily, she dropped into one of the chairs and grabbed a book lying on the table next to her. She was not particularly interested in Nehemiah Grew's treatise on *Comparative Anatomy of Stomach and Guts,* but she took what came to hand. What she was thinking as her eyes skimmed down the page was that it would be an *eternity* before she grew up and could assume control of her own life. It was a terrible thing to be thirteen with her fate in the hands of a monster like Mr. Richard Edmond.

What was it she had told herself about getting to know this England for her dear cousin's sake? She thought not!

Chapter Four

Milestone Fifteen

Days passed, as days do. Seasons came and went.

Christmases, Easters and summer breaks were spent at Aspen Grove with Aunt Jenny and Uncle Charles. Cousin Richard escorted her back and forth to school, and after a time it occurred to Julia that Charles Edmond delegated almost all of his business to his son, and for Major Edmond to have made the Channel crossing to meet her when her father died had been a momentous undertaking for the gentleman.

She also was vaguely aware that her Cousin Richard had completed his studies and now worked in London, in co-operation with Uncle Charles's erstwhile partner, Mr. Brewster, overseeing certain properties and investments they still had in common. Cousin Richard always remained perfectly friendly, and in time, Julia had reluctantly forgiven him for so rudely uprooting her from her native French soil and her first French *amour juvénile*. The vagueness of the girl's knowledge concerning her cousin was not because she refused to talk to him, nor that he kept his personal concerns strictly confidential, but only due to her own youthful self-absorption and his profound maturity.

In that conglomeration of time, which seemed so distant and indistinct to her now, Julia remembered one thing very clearly: her first meeting with Miss Rachel Brewster, the woman who, in her imagination, had joined her cousin to form the team of harpies who had laid waste to her young life.

She stayed that first month in Aspen Grove with her aunt and uncle, and then, the first of November, Cousin Richard once again swooped down upon her.

"We shall travel to London today, where Miss Brewster has graciously offered you a bed for the night. We will finish the journey tomorrow," he announced. "I am not sure how strenuous the trip will be and wanted to allow sufficient time on this initial trek." He smiled at his young ward, though, owing to the whimsical moods of a thirteen year old, he did not know what her reaction to his announcement would be. Today she returned his smile.

Her things were loaded into the coach Edmond had hired and the two of them departed. Her cousin gave the driver directions, and during the ride the two of them slept or watched the scenes changing outside the window or talked.

"Is Mademoiselle Brewster your sweetheart?"

"We are friends," Edmond corrected.

Which was as much as the gentleman would say about Miss Brewster.

Finally the carriage came to a stop and Julia jumped down, without waiting for assistance, to look at the town house before her. Mrs. Brewster, wife of Uncle Charles's former partner, had been a stage actress, if Julia remembered correctly. The house was flashy and ornate, agreeing with Julia's idea of what the home of a stage actress should look like, and appealing to the vibrant Parisian blood that flowed through her veins.

Cousin Richard came to join her in a more orderly fashion, and together the two of them approached the front door. A serving man in white wig and velvet coat answered the door.

"Ah, Mr. Edmond," the man said, opening the door wide and ushering the gentleman and his ward across the threshold.

"Richard? Is that you?" a feminine voice called out from the recesses of the halls that receded behind the serving man.

"It is I," he returned. "I have brought my ward, Miss Masonet."

"Show Miss Masonet and Mr. Edmond in, Lawrence," the voice called again, and the serving man, "Lawrence," Julia assumed, led them down one of the halls.

The room into which it eventually opened was dimly lit, and the young woman sitting upon the divan was a pale, almost ghostly shape in the shadows.

"You may light another lamp, Lawrence," she said. "I have been sleeping a little and allowed it to grow too dark in here, I think." She held her hand out toward the doorway and Edmond stepped into the room to take her hand and sit next to her. "You brought Miss Masonet with you?" she asked.

"I did. She is right here. Julia, Miss Rachel Brewster. Rachel, my ward, Miss Julia Masonet."

Now Julia took the hand Miss Brewster extended toward her and smiled.

"Enchantée."

She suddenly realized that Miss Brewster could not see her smile—that she was blind—but the young lady could hear the expression in her voice.

"Are you well?" Miss Brewster asked.

"Oui, mademoiselle," Julia said.

"C'est un plaisir de vous rencontrer."

Cousin Richard had reclaimed Miss Brewster's hand and now patted the white fingers that Julia had found to be very cold.

"Here now, I shall not be left out of this conversation," he playfully scolded.

"But, Richard, you speak French."

"Yes, I do indeed, but we brought Miss Masonet to this country to be English, Rachel. You must not undermine all of our endeavors."

"It seems we must speak English, Miss Masonet. I hope you will enjoy your new home and your new homeland. I am certain you will love your new family." Miss Brewster turned her head in Cousin Richard's direction and one did not need to see to know there was a brightness of emotion in his eyes.

Miss Brewster had a maid show Julia to the room that had been made up for her. Cousin Richard stayed to sup with them but left for his own rooms shortly thereafter, warning Julia that they would be leaving early the next morning.

Miss Brewster, familiar with her own house, moved from room to room gracefully, with little hesitation and almost no false steps. Julia was gratified to see that her cousin did not smother the lady with attention and refrained, though she suspected it was with an effort, even the offer of help very often.

The next morning Miss Brewster received the girl in her bedroom to exchange their farewells, sending her greeting to Edmond down with Julia.

The remaining distance was traveled very quickly, and they arrived in Barnet while it was still in the forenoon.

The Hampton Academy for Young Women delivered all that Uncle Charles had promised by way of fine education and sound principles. Miss Dansforth, the extremely correct single lady who oversaw both, was the epitome of propriety. Madame Chevous had been short and squat, swathed in black robes like a Muslim matron and crouched over her cane, with those fascinating long, coarse hairs growing out of her chin. Miss Dansforth was tall and erect, possessing far too much self-discipline to allow anything unseemly to protrude from her person.

"Miss Masonet, what a pleasure to meet you," she greeted the girl when first they met. She pronounced Julia's name "Mas-on-ette," but she spoke with such inflexible authority the child did not dare correct her and might have spent the next four years answering to the wrong name if Cousin Richard had not spoken for her.

"That is Mas-on-ay, Miss Dansforth," he said. "The young lady's father was French."

Miss Dansforth raised one eyebrow. Having a French father evidently bordered on the scandalous in the schoolmistress's ordered scheme of things. However, Mr. Edmond was nice looking and well-spoken, and since he vouched for the girl, Miss Dansforth relented. A woman, could overlook much if a gentleman possessed tolerable good looks and acceptable manners. In fact, she could overlook lack of manners if his looks were tolerable enough.

"Masonet," Miss Dansforth said to the girl again, this time using the French pronunciation. "My name is Miss Elizabeth Dansforth. The Hampton Academy for Young Women offers a great deal, if one is willing to put forth some effort. But I am positive we shall have no difficulty with you, shall we?"

She offered her hand, and when Julia took the cool fingers and bobbed her little curtsy, she was not absolutely positive that she would give the headmistress no difficulty, but she fervently hoped not.

Her studies at the Hampton Academy were not demanding, and if she had been able to think consistently in English, she might have been placed at the head of her class. Perhaps, in light of juvenile rivalry, it was just as well that when Mrs. Fife told the students to spell *counterpane,* Julia thought *couverture,* and could not for the life of her spell either one.

The same bugaboo plagued her in mathematics, science, geography and music, and it was only because Julia Masonet was unusually intelligent that she was able to stay unremarkably in the middle of the class.

Her first Christmas with the Edmonds, after she had been at Hampton for only two months, was difficult. Uncle Charles and Aunt Jenny and even Cousin Richard, whom she was still mentally labeling as her horrible Cousin Richard at that time, all were perfectly sweet and considerate of her, taking her to their familial bosom, attempting to infuse her Yuletide season with joy.

Everything was so strange, though, so *barbare,* so pagan. At home—that is, in France—she and the other girls at Madame Chevous's would scour the woods for laurel and holly, even small stones and moss, with which to decorate the *crèche.* They made *santons* to people the manger. The girls made it a contest to see whose "little saints" were the loveliest, which would then be placed around the Christ child.

Papa would bring the *bûche de Noël,* and on Christmas Eve a glass of wine was poured over the log before they lit it.

In a grand procession, with the young people dressed as shepherds and shepherdesses, they would march through the streets to the cathedral, where, just at midnight, the organ, bells, harps and flutes would accompany the choir in singing "Adeste Fideles."

The next day, Christmas Day itself, there would be little gifts from *le petite Jésus*.

What did they here in this England?

They decorated trees instead of manger scenes. The closest they came to a church was the bell ringer who walked the streets in lieu of bells pealing in the abbey towers.

At midnight here, rather than "Adeste Fideles," they tried to convince Julia that the cattle all knelt in adoration of the newborn king. When Julia would have hurried out to the stable to see the miracle, the Edmonds all laughed and said how marvelously naive she was.

They would have her believe it was a gaunt old man called Father Christmas who brought the presents, not the baby Jesus.

And then, as they all sat at their heavy English meal of goose, roast potatoes, mince pies and plum pudding, a rabble of rowdies in masks and garish costumes burst into the house, sang a loud song she supposed had something to do with the season, then grabbed a handful of goose meat each and left. Aunt Jenny and Cousin Richard seemed to find it all hilarious, and even dear Uncle Charles was tolerant of them.

"They are mummers, Julia," Aunt Jenny told her, as if that explained everything.

When she finally crawled into bed in her little white room that night she could not help but feel, loud and raucous as the day had been, that something had been missing. *Le petite Jésus* had not been invited to this English party.

The next morning Julia wakened to find a small, neatly wrapped present on her nightstand. When she opened it she found a little New Testament, bound in soft leather. Penned on the fly leaf was a short dedication.

May the Good Lord always grant you the Comfort of His arm. Merry Christmas, Your Cousin Richard.

* * *

The winter chill departed; hints of green appeared here and there. The new growth grew more bold, brazen and then rampant.

Julia enjoyed spring in the English countryside, enjoyed the scenes, and like the emerald green that had washed across the fields, she also enjoyed the weather, which became mild and then warm, and then frankly and uncomfortably, hot.

During August when there were no classes at the academy, Cousin Richard took her to London to see a play and do a bit of shopping. That was one French characteristic she could not seem to throw off: a fascination for shopping. She begged her Aunt Jenny to come with her, instinctively sensing the Universal Law of Adventure—two sharing an adventure increased its enjoyment fourfold. Aunt Jenny could not be persuaded, however, and Uncle Charles was unapproachable on the subject. That left only poor Cousin Richard. By summer he had been advanced from "horrible" to "poor."

Actually, the three days were delightful. Cousin Richard was a very presentable escort and Julia was flattered to note the recognition and respect her cousin received at the theater, the restaurant, many of the stores they went into and even on the street.

She was fourteen that summer and had spent eight months in a Victorian girls' school. Now she would rather have died than let Edmond see any of the underthings she purchased for her rapidly transforming body, but his study and approval were required for every dress and bonnet.

"And what of this? Is it not *merveilleux?*" she asked eagerly, twirling around in front of Richard, sending the pale chiffon out in billowing waves.

"Is it not a bit . . ." He paused, well aware that telling the girl the dress was too mature would only make her want it more. "Garish?" he ended.

The girl stopped to study herself in the full-length mirror once more. Unconsciously she pulled the thin strap that had fallen back up onto her bony shoulder.

"Do you think?" she asked uncertainly. She would not have believed that a ruffly dress of a pale peach shade would be considered *voyant,* but her Cousin Richard usually had a true eye for that sort of thing. She was often told how well she looked when she wore the red shawl he had sent to school with her in the fall or the shirtwaist Aunt Jenny had given her, confiding as she did so that her son had insisted Julia have it.

She cocked her head the other way to study the dress from another angle. Perhaps he was right. Not the chiffon, then.

Even so, she would have had his arms and their coach piled high with boxes, but her cousin slipped momentarily back to horrible when in the end he insisted she purchase only two dresses and one meager little *chapeau.* Edmond realized the girl's rapidly transforming body would affect her over- as well as her underwear.

They made several calls on Miss Brewster while they were in town, but though Edmond regularly invited her to join them, she always refused and would only receive them in the safety of her own house.

Back in Aspen Grove, Julia chafed under the monotonous routine of *les Edmonds grands.* They insisted the household rise at seven o'clock, but that was the only urgency they expressed all day and Julia failed to see any point to the rule. After everyone was up, night visions banished, the morning invaded, Uncle Charles and Aunt Jenny would nap until noon. They certainly napped after noon. They called five o'clock tea "supper" and were in bed again by eight or nine every evening. True, Mr. Edmond had his Hereford cattle to see to, care for, read about and curse—though only mildly, in deference to his wife and now Julia—and Mrs. Edmond had a pretty little flower garden and kitchen garden she liked to putter about in during the summer, but the simple pleasures and tame pastimes that filled the older couple's lives seemed pale indeed to the young French girl.

It was during those quiet summer months that Julia was amused to find herself actually looking forward to the weekends and brief holidays Cousin Richard would take to come down to Aspen Grove. Imagine her being anxious to

see serious Cousin Richard? Recreation was indeed sadly
wanting if he was the high point of her summer.

Yet that was not to be wondered at so much. He always
came with a smile, with interesting stories from town and,
probably most gratifying, a listening ear and attention that
never seemed to wander or doze off.

When he had come to take her home at Eastertime for the
spring vacation the academy allowed its students, Cynthia
Fenstermacher had been standing with her.

"Who is that perfectly gorgeous creature?" the girl
whispered into Julia's ear.

"Where?"

"There." Cynthia pointed to her cousin, sitting atop the
carriage he had brought for her.

Julia was surprised and took the statement as proof positive that Cynthia was *sotte,* as she had suspected for some
time.

"That is only my Cousin Richard," she said.

That observation, however foolish, led Julia to concede
that Richard's mustache was not so very ridiculous and
might even, by some impressionable girls, be considered
debonair.

His visits during the summer, therefore, with his genuine
interest in her and his appearance, which she supposed was
agreeable enough, were too short and too widely spaced to
relieve completely her impatience with the Aspen Grove
home.

It was with relief that she saw the summer's end.

And so the days skimmed by and the seasons blended into
one another. September was here again, at last, and Julia
had been fifteen for two months. She was three inches taller
than she had been at thirteen, and she had been tall for her
age at thirteen. She still wore her black hair in the tight little schoolgirl chignon, though she supposed the girls in her
class would start wearing it more elaborately dressed this
year. Despite Aunt Jenny's best efforts when Julia was at the
Grove, the girl's bones remained starkly unpadded.

She stood at the back door of the house, anxiously
watching out the window for the bay gelding that always
drew Cousin Richard's phaeton. Visitors to the Grove could

hide under the carriage hood and deceive Julia, but the bay gelding was unmistakable.

"Did you get your woolen cloak? It's warm enough now, without a doubt, but you'll surely wish you had it come November," Millie said.

The girl nodded but did not turn to speak to the Edmond housekeeper. Millie reminded Julia of Marguerite, so she never had been able to warm to the woman. Millie was more than a servant in this house; she had been in the Edmond employ for so long that she thought of herself more as a companion to Mrs. Edmond than a servant, elevated above a number of menial chores. Aunt Jenny was intimidated by the woman, and though, as Julia suspected, Richard had little patience with Millie's airs, his mother would not hear of her dismissal.

So rather than packing Julia's things, or even helping the girl, the housekeeper only came to nag and scold, making demands like a stern taskmaster.

"And you make sure you take all your shoes or put them back into the closet. I don't want to be stumbling over them after you're gone."

Julia half turned, the impatient assurance on her lips that she had not left anything of hers, shoes, clothes, books or games, "strewn about," but before she could speak she saw the movement at the end of the lane out of the corner of her eye.

"Cousin Richard!" she cried, flinging open the door. She saw the riding crop extended in greeting from the shadows of the driver's seat. Merrily she bounded down the steps, black hair coming loose from the knot, reminding one rather unkindly of a scarecrow with knobby limbs flying in every direction.

"The trunks are all filled, everything is ready. *Il est temps de partir,*" she chattered, hopping around the carriage and the bay like one of the driven migrating birds that landed in the fields only long enough to seize a few grains in their beaks. "It is so *heureux...*"

"Fortunate," Richard supplied automatically as he climbed down from the box.

"So fortunate that you came early. We can be back in London by suppertime."

Richard reached in to the floor of the carriage and pulled out a valise.

"Not quite so precipitately, Julia. I have just come from town and was not planning to ride directly back this evening. Not only did I want to wish my parents good-day, but I thought I might even stay the night in my own bed."

For a moment Julia seemed crestfallen, but then her spirits lifted.

"Well, at least you are here now," she said, falling into step beside him. "Perhaps it will not be *quite* so dreary tonight."

Richard gave her a sideways glance and smiled a bit ruefully.

"Perhaps not," he said quietly.

Julia continued to chirp fretfully about the house until Cousin Richard finally loaded her things and lifted her into the carriage the next day.

"No more scrambling over the wheels, Julia," he cautioned her. "You are becoming a young lady and must learn to act like one."

Julia laughed and squirmed in his grasp until he almost dropped her.

"Julia!"

"Oh, all right. I shall be a proper lady. Though why you have made it your aim in life to see that I am perfectly boring I shall never understand."

"If that were my aim, I would be doomed to failure and frustration. Fortunately, all I ask is that you try not to be savage."

Julia laughed again as Cousin Richard jounced the reins peevishly and the carriage rolled down the lane.

By early afternoon they reached the Hampton Academy and Julia jumped from the carriage to join the gaggle of girls who really did appear to be a flock of noisy autumn geese, leaving Edmond to carry her considerable luggage into the hall.

Casual greetings were exchanged, and a confusing re-counting of adventures since last the girls met filled the air.

"The opera was perfectly grand..."

"I told him I was seventeen..."

"The green grapes were so sour they made one's jaw ache to eat them and Gregory slipped one into Lady Potts-worth's salad..."

"What a stunning new hat!"

"...dress!"

"...shoes!"

Suddenly the cacophony hushed and the girl next to Julia, Rebecca Aimes, whispered, "Who is that with Nyla?"

Julia turned to see Miss Jessop being handed from a carriage by not one young man but two. Two perfectly delightful gentlemen, who proceeded to escort Nyla Jessop to the envious circle of friends and acquaintances watching from the meticulously manicured lawn.

"What a pleasure to see you all," she cooed. "It would appear that I am the last to arrive. Though I might be forgiven." She glanced in either direction at the youths beside her. "I was not so awfully impatient to return, I suppose." The air filled with her silky laugh, a laugh women often produce when in the company of handsome men. It was echoed by several of the girls in the semicircle that faced the newcomers, with exactly the same timbre and tone.

"But I do not believe you know these gentlemen. May I introduce Mr. Thompson and Mr. Drummond?"

Miss Jessop released the young men, who bowed gallantly and smiled—dazzlingly—into the group of panting females.

"How do you do?" they said.

"Warmish weather we are enjoying, do you not agree?"

"The flower garden looks particularly beautiful this time of year."

"Bath was charming enough, I suppose, though we would have welcomed a more lively crowd," the girls replied, nudging one another aside to deliver their little comments vis-à-vis one or the other of the gentlemen.

Julia was not in the forefront and with the rest of the outer fringe was smiling and murmuring soft sounds of agreement, hoping, like the others, that she might be noticed and be able to take part in this all-too-rare diversion.

She would have been embarrassed, but not too surprised, to know that her tall, gangling form and the sharp features of her face had already been noticed by the boys. And dismissed. There were softer, prettier things around them, so there was no need to trouble themselves about only marginal game.

"Julia?"

It was Cousin Richard, and dutifully, albeit a bit reluctantly, she detached herself from the cluster to bid him farewell.

"I have left your things with Miss Dansforth," he said. Julia's impatience deepened. She would have to carry her bags to her own room, and Miss Dansforth made it clear to her last time that she did not appreciate her quarters being used as a holding station. Naturally Miss Dansforth would not tell Mr. Edmond that, but would save all of her injured dignity for Julia alone.

"Very well," she mumbled, her eyes darting toward the throng of young people as several of the girls laughed merrily over some witticism. From the chirping note of the girls' laughter it was either Mr. Thompson or Mr. Drummond who made the remark.

"I shall return for you on All Saints' Day. Mother thought she might have in the Millers and Lord Ramsgate to make it a rather jolly holiday." Richard's mustache twitched over one of his faint smiles.

The signal was lost on Julia.

"*Ça c'est merveilleux*" was her distracted reply.

Now Edmond glanced toward the group that so fascinated the girl.

"I am away, then," he said.

"*Adieu,*" Julia returned.

It did not matter that she was halfway turned when she spoke. Richard already knew her mind was not on this conversation. Julia still slipped unconsciously into French if she was distracted and not paying strict attention to what she said.

"Yes. Well. Let us know if you require anything."

"Je le ferai."

Richard started toward the carriage and released Julia at last. She had almost rejoined the group when she realized Cousin Richard had said something about returning for her sometime but she had not really been listening. At least not closely enough to remember the day he said. She hurried to catch him, but seeing he was about to enter the closed carriage, she took a desperate step, of which Miss Dansforth and Madame Chevous, and even very probably Marguerite, would have disapproved. She called to him loudly.

"Cousin Richard!"

Not only was she successful in catching his attention, but most of the young people behind her looked toward her and then the gentleman standing next to the commanding coach and four, whom she was evidently hailing.

"What is it?" he asked in a subdued voice as soon as the girl was close enough to hear him.

"When did you say you would come for me?" she gasped, winded after her hurried walk and the breath her call had required.

"All Saints' Day. November first."

"Of course." She nodded, offering him a smile of apology. "I suppose I was not paying strict attention," she said.

Edmond glanced over her head at her friends.

"I suppose not," he agreed. This time Julia was watching for the twitch of his mustache, but it remained perfectly still.

"I shall see you then," she said.

"Yes."

"Have a safe journey," she cautioned. Now, ever so slightly, the hair above his lip moved and the tiny crinkles that were beginning to show at the corners of his eyes deepened.

"I shall," he said.

Satisfied that her cousin, who was inexplicably eccentric sometimes, was her friend once more, she turned with a gay little wave and hurried away.

By the time she rejoined the cluster on the lawn, several who had been clinging to the anonymous outer fringe had been flung off, like tiny asteroids circling a planet with too

tenuous a gravitational pull and being hurled off into the
outer darkness of space. Julia found herself unexpectedly
near the inner circle, and then, more unexpected still, she
found Mr. Drummond's eyes focused, directly and undeniably, on her. Not being of a florid complexion, she did not
actually blush, but she lowered her eyes in confusion. Other
than her Uncle Charles and her Cousin Richard, there had
been very few men she had ever met who looked at her
squarely with full interest. She knew for a certainty that no
good-looking young man of contemporary age had ever
paid her as marked attention as Mr. Drummond appeared
to be paying her now.

"Miss Jessop failed to introduce us, I am afraid." It was
him. Talking to her. "I am Bennet Drummond, of South-
end. And you are?"

"Julia Masonet," she murmured very indistinctly.

The young man bowed toward her gallantly.

"Very pleased to meet you, though I do not suppose I
would ever be able to address you again."

Julia looked up sharply, confused and hurt. She was relieved to see an encouraging smile on his face.

"Because I did not actually hear the name," he said.

"Julia Masonet," she repeated.

"Ah, Miss Masonet. You are French?"

"My father was, *oui*. My mother was Sarah Parson of
Tunbridge. England."

"And was that gentleman your brother?" Drummond
indicated with a glance the place near the lane where she and
Cousin Richard had said their farewells.

"Cousin Richard?" She laughed.

"Your cousin, then?"

Julia laughed again.

"*Nullement,*" she said. "I merely call him cousin. He and
his father are my guardians. Mine and my estates." She
smiled nervously. She had run out of things to say, and she
really hoped the conversation was not about to come to an
abrupt end. Quite to the contrary, Mr. Drummond detached himself from Miss Jessop's entourage and offered his
arm to the dark-haired girl. Uncertainly she placed her hand
in the crook of his elbow. Like the rest of her body, the

bones in her hand were long and appeared to Julia to be large and clumsy resting against the dark sleeve. Mr. Drummond did not seem to notice and only pulled her along with him.

"This is a lovely school. Much more pleasant than the Barge."

"Le Barge?" Julia repeated with her accent, which she did not realize was charming.

"Bumbarage. The school Thompson and I attend. Other side of London."

"And Miss Jessop?" Julia asked, coming directly to the point.

"My cousin," Drummond said. "My *real* cousin."

Both of them laughed as Mr. Drummond led the girl around the corner of the dormitory, amiably conversing, pointing out this exotic bird and that tropical flower until Julia was convinced she truly had been living in a fairyland all this time and had been completely unaware of it.

"Your cousin is evidently quite taken with Julia," Beverly Walters said to Miss Jessop as Drummond and the girl disappeared around the corner of the building.

"Do you think? I am not so sure he is the one being taken," Nyla said, and then both girls laughed with a certain feline undertone that is also recognizable when females gather.

"You must write to me, Miss Masonet."

"Oh, really, Mr. Drummond. I do not know what to say."

"Say you will write to me."

"Yes…well, certainly. If that is what you wish. If—" she paused and dared look into his face "—if you will write to me?"

"Of course I will. Daily. Hourly."

Julia laughed. If the laugh sounded slightly disbelieving, it was not Mr. Drummond she doubted but her senses, possibly even her sanity. Nothing like this had *ever* happened to her before. Not even Philippe's passionate kiss, which, until today, for two years, Julia had kept enshrined as her most glorious memory.

Mr. Drummond had chosen her from all the girls at the school dangling themselves before him like plump and juicy clustered grapes. He had plucked her from the vine and spent the forenoon with her. He asked all about her mother and father and the Edmonds. He made polite inquiries about Paris and told her, in detail that bordered on grueling, of life in a boys' school. It sounded remarkably like life in a girls' school, but Julia did not stop to consider whether or not what he was saying was interesting. That he was saying it to her was interesting enough.

But now Letty Bramble had found them down by the brook that ran behind the academy.

"Nyla has been looking for you, Julia. She says it is time the two gentlemen were on their way." The girl, no more than ten years old, looked at the mature couple before her, eyes filled with wonder. The idea of male-female couples was not foreign to the girls, of course. It was only here at this girls' academy that it was so very remarkable.

"By gad, she is quite correct." Drummond scrambled to his feet and offered Julia a hand.

Julia, carried away by the romance and the setting, rose to her feet with a grace of which she was completely unaware. There was a soulful glimmer in her eye with the realization that this fairy-tale encounter had come to an end.

"You run along and tell Miss Jessop that Mr. Drummond is on his way, Letty," Julia told the little girl, who dutifully hurried back to the other couple.

When they were alone once more Drummond stood close to her and spoke softly.

"I have enjoyed this morning," he said.

"Oh, so have I!" Julia breathed tremblingly.

It was then that the young man suggested they correspond.

"I will write daily," he claimed.

Julia felt giddy and assured him she would, too.

"I must go," he said.

She nodded.

"I cannot go without taking something by which to remember you," he said.

Now he took her hand in his. Julia's pulse pounded. The locket she wore around her neck, the one Cousin Richard had brought to her last Easter, throbbed against the pale olive hollow of her throat. Mr. Drummond raised his other hand and brushed the feverish skin of her neck with his cool fingertips.

"What is this?" he asked.

Julia gulped convulsively.

She pulled the chain of the locket over her head and offered the tiny gold heart and chain to him.

"Will this remind you of me?" she asked timidly.

He took the necklace from her and kissed it.

"It is perfect," he said. "Like you."

They heard a "halloo!" from the other side of the building and Drummond gave her cheek a little peck.

"You remember me," he warned. And then he was gone.

She was glowing. She continued to glow for days.

"I am pleased that you and my cousin got along so famously," Nyla said after the boys were gone.

"Mr. Drummond is the handsomest boy in the world," she sighed. She was in a sighing frame of mind.

"He *is* nice looking," Nyla said.

"And bright."

"And bright," she agreed.

"I think he is terribly romantic," Julia said.

Nyla smiled a small smile.

"Terribly," she agreed.

"He insisted he have a memento of our morning. I gave him that tiny gold locket I wore and he said it was perfect. Like me."

"Did he?"

"Oh, Nyla, I am the luckiest creature in the world!" Julia cried, unable to contain herself any longer.

No, Miss Jessop thought to herself. That distinction belongs to my cousin.

Chapter Five

Three days after that, Julia received her first letter.

"My dear Miss Masonet," it began, which warm greeting caused Julia's heartbeat to increase several beats per minute.

> The Barge is the same. You remember me telling you about Mr. Trevor. Ghastly boor. Never made an interesting statement in his whole sorry life. Beastly luck, old Trev was made headmaster of my form. I shall have the devil's own time trying to remain conscious during his lectures. But it occurs to me that I can pass the time by writing to you.

Mr. Drummond's letter was a full four pages and referred, usually unkindly, to several of his teachers and classmates. Julia found it witty and charming. As witty and charming as he was himself. She sighed. She was still in a sighing frame of mind.

Her eyes skimmed quickly through the letter when she first opened it. She would, she knew in the days to come, memorize every line, every word. At the bottom of the page was a brief postscript he had attached.

> As desirous as I am for our correspondence to be steady, I find myself somewhat embarrassed at the moment as to notepaper. If I do not reply immediately, I hope you will understand that it is not that I do not wish to reply, only that, for want of materials, I am

unable to at the moment.

Yours, Bennet Drummond.

Hers. How *romantique!* And as for the little matter of
notepaper, she would enclose a tiny bit of silver when she
replied and tell him it was for their continued mutual enjoyment.

Which she did.

Dearest Julia, I hope you approve of the stationery I
selected for us. I thought of you as I purchased it and
hoped I had chosen something you would like as well
as I.

For myself, I cannot say that I enjoy the study of the
exact sciences as much as you evidently do. Quite honestly, as I think about it, I cannot name any of my
studies to which I particularly look forward.

Riding, though, and hunting. If one could include
those courses in one's curriculum, this schooling might
not be so very dull. Our exchange of letters promises to
brighten my scholastic year, though.

This time, Mr. Drummond's letter ran to three pages, and
with a schoolboy's assurance on a number of weighty topics that would have given the most insightful doctor of phi-
losophy pause. It was, in short, such a letter that only the
very young and very infatuated could have enjoyed. Julia
loved it.

"It was ambrosia to my soul," she would say to herself.

It was a week and a half before the mail contained another letter from the Bumbarage school. A two-page snip-
pet that said Dimsdale had a new cocker and Martins was
insufferable. The references meant nothing to Julia, who did
not remember Mr. Drummond ever mentioning a Dimsdale or a Martins to her before, and surely she remembered
every syllable that had ever dropped from his lips.

In another postscript the boy apologized for the untidy
appearance of the written page and bemoaned the fact that
he was running low on blotting paper and he wished he had

a better pen. Julia enclosed a few more bits of silver with her letter.

"Bennet?"
"Carlyle?"

Julia and Miss Jessop had both been summoned when the post arrived. Nyla was impressed by her cousin's attention span and the carrying out of his stated intent. Evidently he had been genuinely taken by the French girl. Acting on that assumption, she had put forth an effort to become better acquainted with the girl and found her to be pleasant, quick with unexpected flashes of biting wit. Nyla allowed her to be a worthy object of her goodwill and the two had become friends. Not best friends, not good friends, but advanced beyond the acquaintance stage.

Now each held an envelope, which they tore open immediately. Julia unfolded her paper and groaned softly.

"What is it?" Nyla asked.

"He is imploring me to send a likeness," Julia said, scanning again the first paragraph of the letter. "Oh, but how can I? I have one little miniature that was done when I was a child, but anything of more recent vintage is painfully accurate in its depiction."

"Is that not what one wants in a portrait?"

"Good heavens, no!" Julia laughed. "I paid a good deal of money for gentle lies. Both of the artists who have been commissioned to do my picture since I was a baby insisted on using harsh colors and gaunt lines."

"You do have rather dramatic coloring, Julia."

"I would not mind the black hair and the depiction of my skin at least one shade darker than it really is. But they go on and on about the *traits classiques* of my face, its striking bone structure. Then they proceed to represent me as death's-head."

Nyla laughed and waved away Julia's misgivings.

"Bennet has already met you and was taken by those classic features. Now he only wants to be reminded of the girl he found so fascinating."

Julia shook her head, no more convinced by Nyla's flattering words than she had been by the portrait of painters

There was just nothing soft or cute about her. And Mr. Drummond, without question, would prefer the soft and cute. They all did.

Julia bit her bottom lip thoughtfully. Now wait. Had not Cousin Richard dashed off a little pencil sketch of her this summer? If she remembered correctly it looked quite a bit like her, but, though he had a natural flair, Richard was not so studied an artist that he insisted the features be exact.

She would ask her guardian if he still had it and could send it to her—in a nice frame.

"It would be perfect if I could display it proudly, properly framed, but I am afraid I shall have to merely tack it to my wall," Bennet had said.

If it would help Mr. Drummond appreciate her likeness, she would certainly provide a frame.

Julia, I was touched by your request for the sketch I did of you. Certainly you may have it if you wish. I am sending it along, and yes, it is framed. In fact, I am sending it in the little gilt frame I put it in. Grandmother's portrait used to be in that frame, but she has joined Grandfather in the picture album now. I cannot help but be impressed by your appreciation of fine art, but do not expect an extra week in London at Christmas.

                                                    Richard.

Julia, Carlyle sends his best to my cousin Nyla, but things are so busy here right now he cannot find the time to write. I myself must insist on these little breaks in the monotony to preserve my sanity. This and the occasional wager we lads make provide my desperately needed recreation. . . .

That letter closed with a frank appeal to "my dearest's generous nature." The mention of the occasional wager with the lads was not accidental. Drummond, as it turned out, had been "beastly unlucky" this past week, and if she could see her way clear to help a fellow out, a pound or two would come in handy.

But whatever you decide is more than satisfactory. You
know that each word I receive from you is more precious than gold.

Your own, Bennet.

Now he was not just hers, he was her own. As she told
Miss Jessop, how lucky she was to have found such a noble
prince among men. She returned her own twelve-page letter of insignificancies, wrapped around a five pound note.

"What is that? Another letter from my cousin, I suppose." Not surprisingly, Nyla sounded sour. It had been
several weeks since the post had included anything from Mr.
Carlyle Thompson, and then it had been only two lines on
a single sheet of paper that said something about how he
really did not have time to reply to her at length, but he was
well and hoped she was, too.

"I believe so," Julia said. Actually, she had long since
come to recognize the hand and knew for a fact that it was
from her own Bennet.

"Still exchanging letters? Whatever do you find to write
about? Mr. Thompson and I ran out of things to say to one
another after two weeks."

"Oh, we talk about all sorts of thing. Bennet, that is, Mr.
Drummond, is well versed in a number of topics. But have
you heard from your mother lately? I do hope she is feeling
better."

Julia was quick to veer the conversation away from
Drummond's letters. It was more than a regard for Nyla and
her disappointing correspondence. It was the uncomfortable feeling she had recently that Mr. Drummond's continued attention was getting to be an expensive luxury.

Cousin Richard's letter did not help:

Julia, Mother tells me you have been writing for funds
again. The money is yours, of course, and you are certainly entitled to whatever emergency increases you require, but we are somewhat surprised that you have.

evidently spent more in the last three months than you
have in the two years since you came under our trust.

We are afraid that you are faced with some difficulty and still do not feel confident enough with us to
ask for our assistance.

Please, Julia, think of the Edmonds as your family
in fact and not only in the theory of the polite titles we
have insisted you give us. I will be happy to come up
and see you if you think it would help.

Richard.

She did not believe that Cousin Richard's presence would
help the situation. The very suggestion made her break into
a cold sweat. As he said, the money was hers, and sending
a few bank notes to her was not going to impoverish her account. She did not appreciate the Edmonds interfering in her
personal concerns. One might get the impression they did
not trust her judgment or believe her capable of overseeing
her own well-being. Which was ridiculous. She was in her
sixteenth year. Schoolmates of hers were making plans to
marry. She could certainly be trusted with some of her own
money. Cousin Richard no doubt also believed that his
control extended beyond her finances into her personal life,
her studies, her acquaintances and friends. His assumption
of control made her furious just to think about.

Her Bennet was the sweetest, most thoughtful young man
in the world! That was her next outraged thought. Somehow it seemed a logical progression, though she did not stop
to work it out right then. She only knew that she would
never allow Cousin Richard and his petty, tawdry fascination for her inheritance end this involvement.

I am sure another two pounds will be all I will need.
Please do not trouble yourself to come up on my account.

Julia.

Aunt Jenny, it seems I need another five pounds. Please
send it and do not say anything to Uncle Charles, and

especially not to Cousin Richard.

Dear Sir,
My name is Miss Julia Masonet. My mother, Mrs. Sarah Jane Parson Masonet, left me certain monies upon her decease, deposited, I understand, in your bank. Though I will not have complete control over that money and property until I come of legal age, I wondered if something might not be worked out between us where I could receive an occasional advance against the capital. I assume that we can keep such arrangements strictly between ourselves.

(Miss) Julia Masonet

Julia, I have received a most troubling communiqué from the bank. Apparently you, or someone claiming to be you, has been trying to elicit funds from your mother's account. I am coming up to see you and to rectify this matter. You may expect me a week from tomorrow.

Richard.

It was damp and gray. The sky was like an old, discolored washcloth wringing itself out onto the sodden ground. The sort of day that is cheery if it is on the outside and one is on the inside, in front of a blazing fire, a thick quilt across one's knees, a well-loved book in one hand and a steaming cup of hot cocoa in the other. Topped with whipped cream.

Richard Edmond was not inside. He was not even in a closed carriage. The phaeton the stable hand had loaned him was covered, but the rough cloth was old and torn and certainly not waterproof. The soggy washcloth of sky splashed water continuously onto the hood and from there onto his face and into his lap.

He sneezed miserably and shook the water from his hat.

He had not intended to tell his parents about this little excursion or about the puzzled letter from Mr. Killion at the bank. Mr. Killion had received a letter from someone who signed herself "Julia Masonet," requesting money from the Parson-Masonet account. Normally such an unauthorized and apparently bogus letter would simply be ignored, but Mr. Killion understood Miss Masonet was a French girl and perhaps was not familiar with the banking practices of this country.

From the tone of Mr. Killion's letter it was easy to surmise that what he meant by "this country" was the *real* world, as opposed to France.

Richard had written his first letter when his mother mentioned to him that Julia had requested money again and it seemed to her that the girl was spending quite a bit more than she ever had before.

Richard inquired exactly how much "quite a bit more" was, and was surprised himself by the regular request for one or five pound notes in the girl's letters his mother had shown him. Mrs. Edmond suggested he write to Julia to see if there was a problem with which they might help. He did so, his help was refused as unnecessary, and he forgot the matter.

He had honestly been pleased when the girl remembered the sketch he had done of her, and though sending it left a white patch on his study wall, he had been happy to do so. With frame, as Julia had specified.

He did not connect the desire for the framed sketch and the frequent requests for money, not even when Mr. Killion sent his letter reporting that the girl had applied directly to the bank for funds. Thank the heaven above, blue or gray, that Mr. Killion had not simply ignored the request. Julia was obviously in some sort of difficulty, and like a knight errant, Cousin Richard was on his way to save her. A knight errant not on a silvery steed in shining armor but behind a miserably shuffling old nag, both of them dripping wet by now and him beginning to exhibit the early symptoms of cold and influenza.

Julia was alone in her room. This was not the same as when Cousin Richard came to take her back to Aspen Grove

or down to London for a special treat. Then she would wait
by the door or even halfway down the lane, straining her
gray eyes to catch the first glimpse of him.

Now she was sitting in the straight-backed chair at the
foot of her bed, her eyes resolutely glued to the page of Holy
Writ in front of her. The book had, curiously enough,
opened to Lamentations 4.

"How is the gold become dim! How is the most fine gold
changed!"

She had been reading and rereading that verse for ten
minutes or more, so that the words had become a dull throb
in her head, when Letty burst through the door.

"Julia!" she cried, breathing in great gulps of air, evinc-
ing recent physical exertion. "Here you are at last. We have
been looking everywhere for you."

Well, they could not have been looking everywhere for
her, she thought, because here she was in her room, one of
the first places one might logically investigate. It was not as
if she had been hiding from them.

"What is it?" she asked.

"It is your Mr. Edmond come to see you. You must hurry
down. Miss Dansforth said you must not keep your cousin
waiting, although she seemed perfectly willing to entertain
the gentleman personally until you made your appearance,
however tardy that might be." Letty tittered and Julia shut
her book noisily and stood.

"Well then, let us get this over with. *Il s'est laisse faire à
l'abattage,*" she said resignedly.

"What does that mean?" Letty asked as the two girls left
the room together and Julia turned to latch her door.

"Like a lamb to the slaughter. Come along."

Her cousin stood dripping wretchedly on Miss Dansforth's fine imported rug. He still was not in front of a
blazing fire, he still did not hold a cup of steaming cocoa in
his hands, and he was definitely coming down with something.

"Ahhh-choo!" he roared as Julia came into the room.
Miss Dansforth backed away in alarm and Edmond mum-

bled some sort of apology, which sounded like the auction-
ing of a prized Aberdeen hog in Scottish Gaelic.

"Ah. Miss Masonet. Miss Masonet is here, Mr. Edmond," Miss Dansforth said brightly.

Cousin Richard lowered the kerchief with which he had
covered his face and peered dolorously at Julia.

"Julia, I believe we need to talk," he said.

"I cannot imagine what...that is, I was not expecting you
to...how very nice of you to come see me, Cousin Richard," she ended lamely. She was aware she sounded flustered. She was, but she was sorry she had given her cousin
such an advantage before they began.

"Miss Dansforth, might Miss Masonet and myself speak
in private?" he asked.

"Oh, by all means, Mr. Edmond," Miss Dansforth
gushed, then transforming her words into action, she bus-
tled in a tall, gaunt, spinsterly sort of fashion out of the
room.

The schoolmistress shut the door behind herself, trap-
ping Julia and her cousin in the room with a heavy silence,
a silence so palpable it almost constituted a third presence.
Julia became aware of the murmur of the rain on the other
side of the thick glass in the window. Somehow her mind got
directed to an intent concentration on the sound of the rain:
How long had it been raining? Were there puddles in the
lane by now? Would they be frozen over in the morning?
How long was it going to continue?

Edmond blew heavily into his handkerchief and Julia
jumped.

"What is going on here, Julia?" he asked, wiping at his
nose.

"What do you mean?"

Richard returned the kerchief to his pocket and looked
into her eyes with a disappointed look that nearly crushed
the girl.

"I mean this money. It appears to be slipping through
your fingers like that rainwater out there. And now Mr.
Killion tells me of a letter he recently received from a Miss
Julia Masonet, requesting an advance against her inheritance. Mr. Killion believed it might have been written by

someone other than the genuine Julia Masonet, but I do not believe that. Do you, Julia? Do you think it was someone else claiming to be you, trying to get money from your account?''

"It is my money," Julia said grudgingly.

"That is not the question, Julia." He spoke quietly and with a reasonable ring to his voice that annoyed the girl almost beyond words. "The question is, what is this sudden need you have for ready cash? Your tuition and boarding expenses at the school are paid. There are no other legitimate avenues for your expenditures here. We are not trying to deny you your legacy, but it is our duty to safeguard that legacy until you reach your majority."

Julia's lip curled ever so slightly in a sneer of distaste. It was all so cold-blooded with Richard. He had long since forgotten the passions of youth that could rule one's life.

"And more than that," he continued, taking a step toward her, narrowing the physical distance between them but failing to close the gap of understanding that, like a yawning chasm, separated the two occupants of the room. "We are concerned about you, Julia. Mother and Father feel helpless, having you so far from them. They want you to be happy, to be safe, and they have given me the charge to see that you are."

"I am safe," she said.

"And happy?" he asked.

"*Oui.*"

Richard narrowed his eyes and studied the girl carefully.

"Then I do not understand your sudden need for these additional funds."

"Am I to be denied all personal pleasure?" Julia lashed out suddenly. "Must every aspect of my life come under your scrutiny and meet with the approval of the committee?"

Richard took the step back again, obviously surprised and troubled by the girl's outburst.

"It is our charge to watch over you and to care for you."

"To care for my mother's money, you mean. It is that which you think of as a helpless brood of baby chicks. As long as it is safe and warm, nestled in your cozy bank, what do you care for me?'' Tears of fury and betrayal glistened in the girl's eyes.

''Julia!'' Richard sounded shocked, and what was worse, he sounded hurt. ''You cannot honestly believe that. We care for you. Mother and Father hold you as dear as if you were their own daughter. And I ...'' His voice faded.

Julia, consumed by her own self-interest, did not require a completion of his thought.

''Then why do you not trust me?'' she demanded.

''We do trust you, Julia. But that does not prevent our being concerned.''

''And demanding an accounting of every franc I am allowed.''

Richard stepped toward her again in another conciliatory gesture. This time his effort seemed to meet with more success as he noticed the fire dim in the girl's eyes. Actually, it was a combination of his unfaltering kindness and her own totally indefensible position that was cooling her anger.

He took another step and now stood directly in front of her. Close enough for him to hear the tremor in the breaths she exhaled.

''You know that is not true, Julia,'' he said quietly. ''We are aware that money is required for even the most innocent of pleasures in this life. And you are welcome to that. But this sudden, constant requirement of funds is unusual, and for our peace of mind, if you would simply explain the need we will gladly provide the money.''

He stopped and waited. Silence had once again taken its obtrusive position between them, even though they now stood close together. Julia fumbled distractedly with her little lace handkerchief. Richard did not rush her.

''I have needed the money for a variety of things,'' she mumbled down toward her hands.

''A number of things?'' Richard encouraged her.

''Stationery, pens, blotting paper.''

Richard nodded. ''For you?'' he asked.

''No. Actually—'' she gulped ''—they were for a friend of mine.''

"Very well," Richard allowed quietly. "But, Julia, the items you have mentioned so far would total one, perhaps two pounds. My mother tells me she has forwarded over fifty pounds to you in the last two months."

"My friend needed . . . to borrow a little money."

"Borrow?" Now Richard's eyebrows lifted.

"I am certain I will be paid back," Julia assured him, or perhaps herself.

"And this friend—a fellow classmate of yours here at the academy?"

Julia shook her head.

"A friend from France, perhaps? From your first school?"

She shook her head again. Richard had run out of ideas and waited for the girl to provide the missing explanation. Unwillingly, Julia nudged the silence aside.

"A cousin of one of the girls here. Nyla Jessop."

"You have been loaning money to Miss Jessop?"

"To her cousin."

"Her cousin."

"A certain gentleman I met when I returned to school this year."

"A *gentleman?*" There was no mistaking the irony in his voice. Obviously, according to Edmond's code of ethics, gentlemen did not borrow money from guileless school-girls. But he was careful to speak gently, not to anger or be-little the girl.

"A young gentleman. A boy. A student, enrolled in a school outside of London."

"And you have been loaning money to this young man?"

"He . . . he had certain personal debts. Personal and pressing debts."

Which Richard immediately and unerringly interpreted as gambling debts. And though he winced at the idea, he hoped he was correct, because gambling debts were, by compari-son, the least offensive of the "personal and pressing" debts a young man could incur while away at school.

"Am I correct, then, in assuming you would rather not disclose the name of this—gentleman?" he asked his young ward.

"Never," she affirmed, softly but determinedly.

"Mmm. I thought not." Richard half turned from her, his brow furrowed in serious thought. Julia watched him fearfully from under her lashes. Now he walked to the window and looked out upon the colorless lawn. One expected grass to be either live green or dead brown; this blended with the dishrag gray of the sky.

"What..." Julia's throat closed hoarsely around the word, but she had attracted Richard's attention. "What about the money?" she completed on her second try.

"The money?"

"My money."

"Oh. Of course. I brought this with me." He took a small rectangle of paper, folded several times, out of the deep pocket of his greatcoat. He held it out toward her, then bounced it impatiently in his fingers when she failed to take it from him. "It is a bank draft for twenty pounds. I brought it with me in the event there was some immediate need. It is yours."

Julia took the paper from him at last and studied it carefully as if she had never seen a bank draft before.

"Mine to do with as I please?" she asked uncertainly.

Richard turned from the window to look at her. He did not answer her immediately, and when he finally did speak she was not sure of the answer.

"Yours is a fine and generous nature, Julia. I would not change that for the world. Though one must unfortunately always be wary of the importuning of others." She appeared to be still waiting for a decision, so he nodded. "As I said, the money is yours." He glanced out of the window and then removed the watch on its gold chain from the watch pocket of his vest. "I ought to pay my respect to Miss Dansforth before I go, then I must be off. I shall tell Mother and Father that we spoke and all is well with you."

"You will not tell her...?"

"I will say there were certain unexpected expenses here at the school. And, of course, you are a young woman. That excuse holds great sway with other women and seems to cover a multitude of sins. As long as I am satisfied, Mother and Father will let the matter drop. It is a fact of law and

Tender Journey

life, though, that I or my father must issue you funds from your estate until you come of age." He nodded toward the bank note she held. "But you see that we are not parsimonious with your money, Julia."

"Thank you, Cousin Richard. For this—" she held up the note "—and your discretion."

Now it was Julia who came to stand directly in front of Richard.

"You have always been so kind to me, dear cousin. And I do love you for that." She put her hands on his shoulders and raised herself on tiptoe. She kissed him lightly on the cheek and then laid her own soft cheek against his prickly one, his shaving not attended to because of his unanticipated morning ride.

"Julia," he said, beginning to raise his arms to embrace the slender form she held against him.

"A brother in very fact could be no more thoughtful of me," she said.

He dropped his arms again and pulled gently away from her.

"Take care of yourself, Julia," he said.

"I thought that was your job," she answered.

He smiled a thin smile. "Not entirely. Though I am sure it seems so to you."

He was gone then, and Julia was left alone in the little room, holding the money and considering the chalky taste of a hollow victory.

Chapter Six

Dear Miss Masonet,

Enclosed you will find a sketch we here at the Bumbarage Institution assume is yours, since it has your name on the back. Mr. Edmond has instructed us to return the drawing to you.

Several weeks ago this institution was contacted by your guardian, Mr. Richard Edmond. We were not aware of any gambling taking place in the dormitories and have put a stop to it. Although Mr. Edmond did not instruct us to interrupt your letters to Master Bennet Drummond, he did suggest we monitor the correspondence.

Now, however, the whole question has become academic due to the fact that Master Drummond no longer attends the Bumbarage Institution.

We apologize for any inconvenience this correspondence may have caused you, but as we have already explained to your guardian, Bumbarage cannot be held accountable for any money that may be owing you from Master Drummond. For that you must contact the young man personally.

With warmest regards, et cetera,
(Mr.) Thomas Quilling,
Headmaster, Bumbarage Institution.

Julia looked at the fresh young face of the girl in her cousin's drawing. She would never have that look of innocent trust again. Bennet Drummond had taken her locket, her picture frame, her coins and her cash. And that look.

A single tear dropped from her lash onto the letter in her hand. She would not be contacting the young man personally. And the only inconvenience involved was a broken heart.

The Train
Birmingham

The soothing jounce of the car altered its rhythm. Julia opened her eyes to find the afternoon shadows deeper, the coach much darker than when she had closed them.

I must have fallen asleep, she thought. She remembered thinking of her meeting with her horrible Cousin Richard, and then vivid flashes, evidently scenes from a dream, had carried her back in time.

She shifted in the seat and became aware that the train was slowing. She felt totally disoriented and pulled at the cord over her head to summon the steward.

"May I help you?" The steward's head gleamed like a polished plum, his dark hair smoothed straight back from the forehead and molded around his small, narrow skull with the help of some highly scented unguent. The head popped around the frame of the door when Julia rang and might have been disembodied for all that Julia could tell.

"Are we stopping?" she asked.

The head nodded.

"We are coming into Birmingham," he explained.

"How long will be the delay?"

"Only long enough to take on another passenger or two. Oh yes, and I believe there will be a disembarkation."

"Only to Birmingham?" Julia said softly, not really directing her question to the steward, who did not bother to answer. "When will we get to Gretna Green?"

"Not until tomorrow morning, miss. It will be a long night for you in here." The eyes in the head shifted back and forth, up and down, inspecting the coach and its single occupant. "You might have been more comfortable in a sleeper, miss, if you are bound all the way to the Green."

"I shall be quite comfortable where I am, thank you," she told him, convincing neither of them.

"Very well, miss. Can I get you anything?"

Julia smiled a small, warm smile, which made the steward wish she would ask for a sarsaparilla or a sandwich or his firstborn child. Instead she shook her head.

"Nothing, thank you."

"If you do need anything . . ." The eyes glanced up to the service cord. She followed their direction and nodded.

"Yes, I will ring."

The head inclined, revealing the back of a neck, and a hand appeared at the edge of the door to pull it shut, suggesting that there was indeed a full body attached.

Once again Julia found herself alone. She moved closer to the window and, resting her arm on the narrow sill and her chin on her arm, she looked out upon the scenes of the approaching city life. Buildings, vehicles, animals, people flashed by the window in denser and denser concentration. The sound of the city began to infiltrate the walls of the coach, even rising above the sound of the train.

But Julia was not seeing the scenes or hearing the sounds outside the window. Her eyes were focused on scenes much more distant. Details of leaves on trees and plants in fields, even rocks and stones on the city streets became distinct as the train slowed and pulled into the Birmingham station. Her memory locomotive, the one taking her through her life again this night, was stopped at a station, too. She was seeing herself when she was seventeen, able to distinguish all the details: hear the voices; detect what others called an accent and she called the sound of home; smell the paint and thinning fluid; feel dazzled by the glint of sunlight. For just a moment she felt once again the vibrancy of a seventeen year old's vision and passion.

Chapter Seven

Milestone Seventeen

"*Oh, ma chère, c'est merveilleux! C'est prodigieux!*"

Monsieur le Professeur Davenôt took a step back from the canvas and studied it thoughtfully, tilting his head first to the right and then to the left. He did not actually hold up his squared thumbs and forefingers to frame the canvas, but that was the only gesture missing.

François Davenôt was a recent addition to the faculty of the Hampton Academy for Young Women.

"From Paris," Miss Dansforth solemnly added at the end of his introduction. A soft "ooh" whispered through the room.

Professor Davenôt had been engaged and imported as an art instructor for some of the older girls, the ones who showed promise or interest, or whose parents had provided enough additional funds to ensure that their daughter's work showed promise and that *Monsieur le Professeur* would be interested.

He came from a garret in the Latin Quarter of Paris, a district thick with artists—indeed, what district is not thick with artists in Paris? The stationery on which he answered the inquiry, though, had as its letterhead, L'université de Paris, Place de la Sorbonne. When he arrived, his shabby dress and ragged goatee were afforded an artist's allowance. His ravenous appetite was attributed to his artistic temperament, as well. He was abrupt with Miss Dansforth and his fellow teachers, and positively licentious with his pretty young pupils. In short, he presented the ideal image of a French art teacher, and the Hampton Academy faculty and student body thanked their lucky stars every night that they had been able to secure Monsieur Davenôt's employment.

Julia had somehow survived the loss of Bennet Drummond. She heard from him one more time after receiving the picture and letter from Mr. Quilling. It was a brief, impersonal little note that said he liked his new school because it included horsemanship as a regular class and he hoped she was well. His address was included in the letter, but he did not express any particular urgency about hearing from her; although to give him credit, he also did not ask her for any money. Julia kept the letter under her pillow for only two days before she resolutely threw it away.

Mr. Drummond was forgotten.

Cousin Richard did not get off so easily.

That Edmond had made some surreptitious investigations was obvious from Mr. Quilling's crushing epistle. Probably Miss Dansforth had been able to provide him with everything he wanted to know, though Julia could not help but suspect Nyla Jessop as having volunteered information, as well, and the friendship between the girls cooled.

There were other girls at the academy who liked the self-effacing French girl and did not like Miss Jessop, so Julia was quickly absorbed into another circle. Nor did it take her long to feel the relief from the constant drain on her financial resources. Taken all together, her estrangement from Mr. Drummond caused her no lasting ill effect; it was, in fact, beneficial, though that was more difficult for her to acknowledge.

But for all Richard Edmond could tell, he was solely responsible for the total ruin of the girl's life and the collapse of her every dream.

He wrote but she would not answer. Aunt Jenny was allowed to make inquiries, but any reply concerning Cousin Richard was short and cold. She was prepared at Christmas to impale him on her sharp retorts and the daggers that would shoot from her eyes. But Edmond was on the Continent on business over Christmas, so her vacation was miserable without her victim, and then, the rogue, he brought her a darling little spaniel bitch that she could not help but fall in love with, and which she immediately christened Cousine.

Before she knew what was happening, they were speaking again, and then they were laughing, and one day, when she had come to Aspen Grove for Easter, they began to talk and laugh about Bennet Drummond. Actually Richard's laughter was more at her expense, but, better than buried, the hatchet that had threatened their friendship was examined and ridiculed.

At sixteen Julia did not stop to consider the disharmony her ill will toward Cousin Richard had brought to her life. With the faulty vision of youth she saw only that now she was happy and therefore she was responsible for her happiness and Cousin Richard was to blame for her unhappiness.

With harmony restored, she glided smoothly to her seventeenth birthday and then her final year at the Hampton Academy.

Her interest in theoretical science was still strong, but Mr. Willow did not exactly stoke the fire of her enthusiasm. Mr. Willow taught indifferently, relaying information that was, for the most part, though not invariably, factual. He relayed such information in a dry voice, a voice that one wanted to pour water upon and keep in the cool shade, a voice that made his students clear their throats until they were scratched and irritated, at least those of his students who were still able to remain awake during his lectures.

Being a romantic young woman, that, of course, would not have mattered to Julia had Mr. Willow been attractive or semiattractive, or if he had any one physical attribute that could have been imagined as attractive. But Mr. Willow was short and thick, with a grizzled halo of gray hair wreathing his bald crown. He wore glasses, had prominent yellowish teeth and a complexion roughened by pockmarks. And his breath was always foul.

Anything Sir Isaac Newton or Johannes Kepler might have had in store for her edification suffered greatly in the instructional process.

Enter Monsieur le Professeur François Davenôt.

Davenôt was not a young man, but he was younger than Mr. Willow. He also had that certain devil-may-care attitude of an artist and a rebel. He was above concern for his personal appearance or the *rigueurs* of social amenities. He was, in short, a stunning romantic ideal, and Julia was not the only young woman at the Hampton Academy who was smitten by the new art teacher and found herself suddenly fascinated by painting.

"Julia says she is studying painting this year," Mrs. Edmond told her husband and son one morning at the breakfast table shortly after their ward had returned to the school for her final year. Aunt Jenny had received the letter from Julia with the morning post and was sharing its contents with the men, generously augmented by comments and discussion.

"Is she now?" the major asked, buttering a slice of bread, which he topped with a thick layer of Millie's plum jam.

"I am surprised. She has never shown an interest in painting before," was Richard's comment.

"Yes, well, it appears she is very interested now. She talks about pigments and canvases as if she were the teacher rather than the student, pointing out the qualities of this and the advantages of that."

Curious, Richard held out his hand, into which his mother placed the letter currently under discussion.

"I am striving for a certain harmony of design and color in my work," began the paragraph that Mrs. Edmond indicated to her son. "Monsieur Davenôt insists that we paint out-of-doors in an effort to capture the essence of the sun in our painting."

"She has not mentioned this Monsieur Davenôt before. What is he like, Richard?" Mrs. Edmond asked.

The young man shook his head as he returned the letter to his mother.

"I am sure I do not know," he said, turning his attention to his own slice of buttered bread. "I have never met a Monsieur Davenôt at the school."

"Sounds French to me," Major Edmond contributed.

"He seems to have made quite an impression on our girl, wherever he is from," Mrs. Edmond said.

Richard did not say anything, but he no doubt agreed with both statements.

Taking advantage of the warm September sun, Davenôt's students were sprinkled across the lawn in back of the main building of the Hampton Academy for Young Women. Each wore a long sweeping skirt and simple shirtwaist, topped by a protective pinafore. Each also wore her hair loosely piled on top of her head, and an expression of intense study and concentration on her face. The scene was charming and might itself have been a painting by Millet.

The girls were trying their hand at landscape painting.

"But more than that," Professor Davenôt told them. "Strive to infuse your paintings with something of yourselves. Your own *humeur,* your own *sentimentalité.*"

The admonition accounted for the grave concentration the young women were all devoting to the trees across the field. Producing a fairly recognizable image of a tree on the canvases before them was not as difficult as producing that image with something of their own mood, whatever it was *Monsieur le Professeur* meant by that.

The enthusiastic approval he was expressing was for the canvas in front of Julia.

"Ah, magnifique!" Davenôt said, having already declared it to be marvelous and extraordinary.

Wilma Peterman and Dora Baxter, the two fellow artists situated nearest to Julia's easel, came to stand in back of her and study this tree that Davenôt so highly praised. It looked like a tree to them, though not as much like a tree as the tree Wilma had painted. But Dora sensed an exotic flavor to the painting, perhaps suggested by the faint tinges of purple here and there among the leaves, perhaps by the voluptuous form of the tree itself.

"Of course, definition is not possible working with watercolors, so you must concentrate on lightness. Lift the brush—thus!" Davenôt had taken the brush from Julia's hand and now illustrated his words with an airy pass across the canvas that left a stain behind rather than a stroke.

"*Compris?*"

"Oh, *oui,*" Julia replied, seeing the difference but not really sure how to produce it herself.

"*Bien,*" Davenôt said, walking away a few steps and then turning quickly to be surprised by the girl's canvas at another angle. Suddenly he clapped his hands sharply, attracting everyone's attention. "*Maintenant, mesdemoiselles,* we must all endeavor to see *la vie* that surrounds us through a poet's eyes. I want to see the tree as only you see it. Class is over for this day. *Je suis fatigué.*" He waved his hand languidly and the girls dutifully picked up their easels, palettes and canvases to carry them back to the building. Miss Dansforth had designated the cloakroom near the back entrance as the artists' room. Each young woman took her tools to the location that had somehow become her own in the dark little room. Monsieur Davenôt had imperiously requested that a bucket of clean water be kept near the door and a bucket of water had faithfully been provided ever since. Now, like maidens of the Far East around the village well, the girls surrounded the bucket and scrubbed at their brushes.

"Oh, I shall never get this green out from under my fingernails," Cynthia Fenstermacher lamented.

"Rachel, is your Mr. Crenshaw driving out again this week? Miss Dansforth was unpleasantly surprised when your parents gave their permission for you two to step out together."

A general titter followed that remark.

"Julia, we had no idea we had as a schoolmate an artistic prodigy."

Julia smiled faintly as she began to vigorously shake the water from her brush.

"It was only a trick of the light. You know how Monsieur Davenôt is sometimes."

Now there was a general murmur of consensus. Each of Monsieur Davenôt's pupils believed she enjoyed a unique insight into the art instructor's personality.

"Did you see the gown Isabel brought back with her this year?" Beverly Higgins asked softly in scandalized tones. "She *claims* to have worn it to a ball this summer, but if she wore it outside of her bath it was absolutely indecent!"

Several of the girls agreed with Miss Higgins and the conversation moved on to a discussion of the faults and foibles of absent friends, which is often the trend when women, young or old, gather.

Julia was relieved that the spotlight of attention had so quickly passed by her, and now, as the other girls expressed their disapproving views of Isabel's ball gown, she was free to carefully store her painting utensils and to consider her artistic ability and Monsieur Davenôt's appreciation of it.

The Edmonds were justified in their surprise at her sudden interest in art. She was surprised herself. Being by now a self-aware young woman, she knew exactly why she had joined the art class; it was the same reason all the other girls had joined the art class: Monsieur le Professeur Davenôt was so very *intrigant et beau,* because *le professeur* had that devilish goatee and that gaze, which was generally acknowledged in the dormitory to be intense. What Julia was surprised by, though, was her genuine flair for art. She knew instinctively what Davenôt was talking about when he told the class they must try to get the "essence of the sun" in their pictures. She did not know yet how to produce that effect, but she knew what she was trying to learn, which put her head and shoulders above most of her classmates.

She smiled as she leaned her easel up against the wall of the cloakroom. To think that she had reached the hoary age of seventeen without realizing she had the Soul of an Artist. But she knew that now. She knew because Monsieur Davenôt told her she did.

Chapter Eight

It all proceeded so easily, so naturally. Like the frog in a pan of cold water placed over the burner, Julia was only vaguely aware the water was getting warmer and really did not know when things were too hot and she ought to jump out.

Besides, Julia was no more than a tadpole in life's—and love's—treacherous waters.

"Mademoiselle Masonet," he said to her at the end of the class period a few weeks later. "To complete your canvas you will need to work in a room with a good east-west exposure. Where the light and shadow have depth, *drame,* a life of their own."

Julia was giving the instructor her full attention, but a loud clatter at the end of the room interrupted him. They both glanced, Monsieur Davenôt impatiently, toward the sound and saw Rachel Ornsby fumbling to retrieve the easel and paintbrushes she had dropped.

"You need to work in a room with an east window," Monsieur Davenôt continued, "and *no* distractions."

Julia nodded ever so slightly.

"It is a bit—distracting working in here," she said.

"With them," he completed for her. "We must approach Mademoiselle Dansforth in the matter. Surely there is one room in this mausoleum that is unused and in the east wing."

He did it so subtly, putting the distance between Julia and her schoolmates: "them" and "those girls," never "those *other* girls," suggesting by the pronouns he chose that Julia was different, apart, *above* the rest of the girls. No one, least of all a seventeen year old, is immune to that sort of flattery. Unconsciously, Julia started referring to the rest of the students as a collective and distinct "them." Even when she thought of them it was always "those girls," nor was it long before those girls became "those children."

It was the middle of October when Monsieur Davenôt and his pupil approached Miss Dansforth.

"Julia needs a studio," Davenôt began without prelude, without an employee's attitude of servitude, without, in fact, common civility. It further testified of the man's French artistic genius to the fading English spinster.

"A studio?" Miss Dansforth spoke carefully.

She did not want to ruffle the teacher's sensitive feathers, but neither was she in the habit of giving preferential treatment to her students. Consciously, that is. Miss Dansforth was extremely human and subject to the myriad weaknesses of the species. So it was true she allowed Miss Peterson a great deal of personal liberty for the sake of Mr. Randall Peterson, the girl's widower father, who paid Miss Dansforth a cool attention the schoolmistress interpreted as suppressed longing. And Nyla Jessop was something of a skilled manipulator who had found some of the head teacher's susceptible strings—Miss Dansforth's conceit that her profile was classic and her knowledge of Greek literature was encyclopedic, to name only two—upon which the girl played to advance her own interests at the school. But consciously Miss Dansforth believed she was perfectly non-preferential in her treatment of the girls and did not like to set an unfortunate precedent. Monsieur Davenôt had, however, an extremely energetic personality that was difficult to resist. Julia might have warned her of that, if either of the ladies had been aware of how completely they were controlled by the painter.

"A *private* studio?" the headmistress asked, allowing a careful note of uncertainty in the question, which she hoped would discourage and not outrage the art instructor. She was not successful. Both females quailed under Davenôt's resulting tirade.

"*Naturellement*, it must be a studio *privé*. Mademoiselle Masonet is an *artiste*. She must have quiet, seclusion, the chance to look within herself and search her very soul." He spoke with fire and conviction. "She must also have a window facing the east. Our ultimate goal is the quintessence of light."

He put his arms around the girl's waist and drew her to stand next to him in front of the teacher. Miss Dansforth was not at all sure she liked to see that, but the man was French, which she supposed accounted for everything.

"Very well," she sighed. "There is a room above Mrs. Kimber's geography classroom that has not been used for years. You may use that, though," she added in a cautionary note to Julia, "you will have to clean it out yourself."

Miss Dansforth, after all, did not treat any of the girls with preference.

There was an accumulation of several years' worth of dust in the room but other than that it was ideal as a studio. Monsieur Davenôt viewed it with austere approval.

"*Bien.*" He nodded. "This will do. There is not a skylight, but a true *artiste* must represent life as he finds it." He turned to the girl who stood behind him.

"Oh, *oui, Professeur*. It seems, though—" a slight shiver passed through her thin shoulders "—a trifle chilly, *n'est-ce pas?*"

"Bah!" Davenôt dismissed the girl's paltry objection. "If a cold studio is as much as you ever have to suffer, you will never be a great artist."

He stepped farther into the room, turning to inspect it.

"*Bon! Entendu! D'accord!*" He indicated the open space, the dimensions of the window and finally the long cupboard against the wall. "You can keep your implements in here," he said, but as he flung the doors open he released a cloud of dust, which in turn triggered a series of sneezes. Davenôt sneezed with a wild abandon that was typical of his temperament. Julia looked on with alarm, which might have become panic if Davenôt had continued his prodigious roars much longer.

"Something must be done about this dirt," he said at last, his eyes red and watering. He blew his nose with the same gusto with which he sneezed, and then continued to wipe at his face with his big red handkerchief as he turned slowly to give the room one last look.

Julia spent the next week cleaning the studio alone. She could not ask any of the teachers for help or Hilda, the cook, or Mrs. O'Rourke, the round, red-faced Irishwoman who did up the laundry for the Hampton Academy and its young ladies. She also did not feel as if she could ask any of her schoolmates. She might have last year, when they had all been closer, but now, this year, the other girls seemed so cold.

So alone she hauled the buckets of water, mops, brooms and cleaning rags up the three flights of stairs and sloshed water across the floor, up and down the walls and over the eastern windows. She was not terribly efficient in her labors, this being rude, manual labor at which she had never had much practical experience in her seventeen years of life, but her desire to please *le professeur* was sincere, so her work was diligent anyway.

In a week's time the dust had been drowned and cleared away and the windows admitted even more light, which highlighted the streaks across the panes of glass. With a physical exhaustion that was new and surprisingly gratifying, Julia took the buckets and mops back down to Mrs. O'Rourke's laundry room and brought up her easel, palette, brushes, and completed canvas and several bare and half-completed ones.

The light was streaming through the window, and while admiring her handiwork, Julia began to watch the play of light on the floor and walls of the room and then to wonder how it would highlight an apple, and one of Hilda's pitchers of cream, and perhaps a few of those bright orange chrysanthemums still in bloom against the south wall of the academy.

Another shiver stirred her bony frame, bones still devoid of almost any insulating tissue. But that was all right. All of these hardships contributed to the Soul of an Artist.

* * *

"What does Julia say today?" Richard Edmond asked his mother. A study of the sunlight that illuminated the Aspen Grove morning room would have fascinated the budding artist. The glass vase and silver letter opener glittered harshly, but a more comforting ray fell across Mrs. Edmond's shoulder onto the letter she held against her lap.

"She says she is working in a room Miss Dansforth has given her for a studio. Monsieur Davenôt says she will be working in oils soon."

"Nothing about some dangerous experiment she hopes will not blow Hampton sky-high, no mention of one of Sir Isaac Newton's fascinating theories?"

Mrs. Edmond shook her head.

"Only her art class," she said. "And Monsieur Davenôt."

"Really? I did not think our Julia would ever lose her interest in the sciences."

"Young women change, Richard."

"Well, certainly young women change," he replied impatiently. "It is only that ever since we first knew Julia she has been spouting numbers and laboratory discoveries at us like a fire hose."

"When she was a toddler her mother wrote that she could count before she could say her letters."

"Then . . ." Edmond began, but his mother cut him off again.

"But young women of Julia's age often find their attention redirected." Aunt Jenny smiled faintly as she glanced down toward the letter filled with descriptions of Professor Davenôt's wonderful skill as a teacher, his brilliance as an artist, his insight, ability and how very fine he looked with his tousled hair and rakish beard.

"You mean they fall in love?" Richard asked quietly.

Mrs. Edmond looked up, the faint smile still on her lips.

"Oh, not in love always," she said, "but certainly attracted. Every schoolgirl flirts with her male instructors. It is nothing more than that. Indeed, what harm can come of schoolgirl infatuation?"

Richard returned a smile that was not as faint yet at the same time less sincere than his mother's.

"Indeed," he said.

The weather was too chill by the end of October for Monsieur Davenôt to take his class out onto the lawn. Now the half dozen or so easels were circling an orange and a chipped bowl sitting like a mystic pagan idol in the center of a shaft of sunlight that entered the high windows in the public reception room, which was the current stronghold that Davenôt and his implacable host had assailed and claimed as their own.

"*Non, non,* you miss the shadow here. See how dramatic it becomes? Now you try." Monsieur Davenôt watched Miss Baker smear a daub of black paint beside the yellowish oval on her canvas that was evidently meant to represent the orange, just as the black was theoretically the shadow cast by the fruit. Finally the teacher sighed heavily and turned to the next canvas.

Julia, on the other side of the room, glanced frequently at the objects on the table and coincidentally at Davenôt. There was unquestionably something compelling about the man.

His soul burns, Julia thought to herself now, as she had countless times in the past few weeks since the dark phrase first occurred to her.

While the words were still running through her mind Davenôt glanced across the room and caught her eye on him. Hastily she looked down and applied herself diligently to a study of the fruit and bowl that had been confiscated from Hilda's kitchen.

"*Belle.*"

Julia jumped, startled by the teacher's sudden materialization at her elbow.

"*Merci,*" she responded automatically. Before Monsieur Davenôt's advent at Hampton, Julia had been almost completely Anglicized. Now, if she did not stop and make conscious effort, she responded in French. And she was beginning to think in French again.

Monsieur Davenôt squinted his eyes critically at her canvas and took a step back. He sighed again and Julia looked behind her with concern. Monsieur Davenôt's sighs were theatrical and not meant to be ignored.

"Qu'est-ce que c'est?" Julia quickly inquired.

"This. That. They are all wrong. *Artificiel.* There is nothing of *you* in this."

Now Julia looked forlornly at her disappointing canvas, which only a minute before she had been admiring.

"I am sorry. I do not know what..."

"Oh, there is nothing you can do here. You are doing the best that you can. Carry on."

The teacher moved on again and Julia attempted to put something of "herself" into a painting of an orange and a bowl.

After the art class Julia shared with the girls downstairs, she would usually take her easel upstairs to the studio to work another hour or more—depending on how long it took Monsieur Davenôt to look in on her and pronounce his judgment on her day's labors.

Today he accompanied his student up the stairs and leaned against the wall, watching as she positioned her canvas on one side of the room and the sprig of holly, the only thing left with any color in it on the school grounds, on the other.

"One thing is as good as any other," Davenôt told her, tearing the cluster of waxy leaves from the stem. "We are not studying color, we are searching for depth, light and shadow."

With the sprig in place, Julia put a daub of dark green on her brush and looked over her shoulder for the teacher's approval. Davenôt was not watching her, however. He was looking up toward the window. The sun was past its zenith now and the room was already beginning to take on dark shadows. The Frenchman's face was darker still in the shade, yet his eyes glittered beneath his brow and the hair grown long across his forehead.

"The chestnut trees are just beginning to turn golden," he said.

Julia followed his glance up to the windows and then looked back at him questioningly. There were no chestnut trees out that window. There were not many chestnut trees in this part of the country at all.

Davenôt's lips stirred and his features softened into a reminiscent smile.

"The countryside out of Paris is glorious this time of the year. The leaves of the trees are like large coins, *monnaie d'or* being offered to the heavens as a tithe." Now he actually chuckled. "And the lanes, *mon Dieu!* They are filling with the nuts. Sunshine and sparkling air and children laughing outside the open windows."

He lowered his eyes from the closed windows, the windows that showed only the gray English sky, which would remain gray for another two or three months. A scowl had replaced the smile. Now the sound he made was not a chuckle but something approaching a growl.

"They cook their vegetables here until they are *bouillie,*" he said.

Julia, though confused by his mood, was forced to agree with her teacher about English cooking. Although she had come to accept England as her home, she still wondered why, if they truly admired French cooking as much as they professed, they continued to cook in their sloppy, heavy fashion, boiling their vegetables until, as Monsieur Davenôt said, they were mush.

"*Oui,*" she murmured.

"Julia, there is a place near Fontainebleau, a little village called Barbizon. Do you know it?"

"I have never been there, but I have heard of it."

Davenôt nodded. His gaze was now fixed on the floor of the cheerless schoolroom.

"A number of artists have left the *cité* to paint in Barbizon, where the air is clean and the subjects simple. Animals, landscapes, peasants. They are searching for the same things I am looking for, that you struggle for. A grasp on truth and life." He paused. Into the void fell the sound of thumps against the windowpanes. It had started to rain. Again. Davenôt shook his head. "It is not enough. I believed when I came that the money would be sufficient, tha

I would allow myself to be made rich by these ignorant *Anglais* instead of starving with my work in Paris. But it is not enough.'' Now he looked up at the spellbound girl in front of him.

Julia had been fascinated by the art teacher's reflective tone of voice. This was not the *affreux Monsieur le Professeur* who towered over his students with furious demands. This was a lonely, homesick man who missed the blazing chestnut trees of a Parisian autumn.

"Come with me, Julia," he said.

"What?" She honestly did not understand his meaning.

"Come with me to Barbizon. Let us continue our search together. Let us learn with Rousseau and the others in the country. There we will become one in mind and body. Two persons with but one soul, and that the soul of beauty."

He was still not the *terrible professeur,* but now his eyes blazed and the echoes of his voice rang in the room and urged her even when he stopped speaking.

She was not aware they were standing so close to each other, but he put his hand out and grasped her thin arm, pulling her, stumbling, to him. His eyes burning, he lowered his lips onto hers. He kissed her fiercely, grinding the rough hairs of his goatee into her soft chin and cheek. He forced open her lips with his and his breath was like the blast of a furnace. She felt the burning tip of his tongue between her lips, in her own mouth. In a flurry of fevered caresses he moved his lips from her mouth to her cheek, her neck, pulling the soft white skin between his teeth. She gasped as he lowered his face to the bulging mounds of her bosom. His intensity frightened her but she could not pull away.

"You will come with me?" he whispered, his lips at her ear. He held her to him tightly and she gasped again as he began to trace the folds and ridges of her ear with his hot tongue.

"I...I..." she stammered. Julia felt like a leaf, like one of Davenôt's golden chestnut leaves, thrown helpless and without will into a twisting cyclone.

"We can slip away together into the night. In two days *la vieille fille* will pay me, and we shall have enough money for the boat and a loaf or two of the good French *pain crous-*

tillant one can buy for a simple copper coin. Nowhere else on earth do they make bread like that, and it is available to beggars on the streets of Paris. The music, the *arôme*, the vibrancy of the people. I can see it all now, and you at my side. And then, at night, in my garret where the stars will look down upon us with envy, you and I shall make love. You will be asleep, but I will turn to you and I will kiss you thus." He kissed each of her eyelids and then, gently this time, her lips. "You will murmur little protests, but they will not be *sincères*. I shall not take them seriously, but I *will* take you." He pulled her against him and covered her lips and face with kisses that suggested the passion of his promise. "You will come with me. *D'accord?*"

Julia's gray eyes filled her face, the pupils enlarged in the dim room, making them look even darker and larger. Her breath came in short pants, her bosom rose and fell. She gazed at him, understanding nearly washed away by passion and fear.

"*D'accord?*" he repeated urgently.

"*Oui.*" Her lips moved to form the soundless word.

He released her and swept from the room. Julia put one hand on the forgotten easel to steady herself. She knew that in the strictured, *bourgeois* world of Miss Dansforth and the Edmonds what she was contemplating would be condemned. But was it not inevitable? Did she not possess the Soul of an Artist?

Chapter Nine

"Nothing from Julia again today?" Richard Edmond asked, coming up the walk to greet his mother at the door she had opened for the postman. Mrs. Edmond checked through the few envelopes she held in her hand and shook her head.

"I am afraid not, my dear. Why? Were you expecting something in particular from our girl?"

"Not any particular thing, no, but *something*. She has not written for two weeks."

"You know Julia. If she gets caught up in her studies or some student intrigue, we may not hear from her for a month."

Edmond could not deny that fact, but it did not seem to comfort him.

Together they went into the sitting room, where the major sat dozing. Mrs. Edmond sat in her favorite chair to peruse the mail, but her son remained standing, his arm on the mantel, his head against his arm, gazing down into the faintly glowing coals. Suddenly he stood erect and turned restlessly.

"Is something troubling you, dear?" Mrs. Edmond asked, squinting up from the writing, which was growing more and more indistinct with the arrival of every post.

"What? Eh? Eh?" Major Edmond roused himself sluggishly at the sound of his wife's voice.

"It is Richard. He seems high-mettled this evening."

"Something is amiss." Richard spoke toward the wall, but loudly enough for his mother to understand his words, if not their meaning.

"Amiss? What is amiss? Is something amiss, did you say?"

"With Julia."

"Because she has not written? But I told you..."

"I know what you told me, Mother. Nevertheless, I tell *you* that I feel uneasy."

Mrs. Edmond, watching her son, saw him take two brisk passes in front of the fireplace and then give his head a determined nod.

"I must go," he said.

"To London?" Mrs. Edmond asked.

"To the academy," Richard corrected, halfway through the sitting room doorway.

"Tonight?" Mrs. Edmond cried.

"What? Eh? Eh?" Major Edmond mumbled again.

In his room, Richard flung a few things into a traveling bag with the careless vigor that is the hallmark of a man packing. Mrs. Edmond, with furrowed brow, was still watching the doorway he had quitted when he filled it once again, carpetbag in hand.

"Are you taking the carriage?" she asked him.

"No," he replied, not stepping into the room but putting the bag on the floor and feeling in several of his pockets for watch, latchkey, purse. "I shall be going a-horseback. Much quicker."

"Richard, what is it you suspect? What are your intentions?"

Finally he stopped his tugging and pulling and tried to give his mother a reassuring look.

"I suspect nothing, Mother. Julia has never given us cause to worry and the Hampton Academy is perfectly respectable."

"Then why...?"

"I have no specific concern or aim. I only know that I cannot feel easy until I have been to Barnet."

"Would not a letter do?" his mother asked fretfully, very alarmed by now despite Richard's calming words and reasonable tone of voice.

"I need to go myself. Besides—" he stooped to pick up the carryall again "—this will be quicker. Do not disturb Father right now. Tell him I have gone to see Julia and will be back tomorrow or the next day."

"He will wonder why," Mrs. Edmond called softly after her son, who had turned to go.

Edmond did not answer her. The best he could do was murmur "I wonder why myself" as he closed the front door behind him.

The moon was full, lighting the night with secondhand silver sunlight. The road was deserted, the weather just chill enough to be invigorating without being uncomfortable. His horse was a fine four year old with a strong, steady pace and indefatigable endurance. Nevertheless, even traveling in those most favorable conditions, the ride took all night. He did not arrive in Barnet until eight-thirty the next morning and did not reach the Hampton Academy and Miss Dansforth's receiving room until a half hour after that.

"Good heavens, Mr. Edmond!" the schoolmistress exclaimed as she came in answer to his impatient ring. "Can I get you something? Are you ill?"

Edmond shook his head, smoothing back the hair that had fallen around his face and running his finger solicitously across his mustache in an attempt to civilize his appearance.

"It has been rather a long ride," he said, "but I am perfectly all right, thank you. I have come to see my ward."

"Miss Masonet?" Miss Dansforth asked uncertainly, not placing full confidence in Mr. Edmond's words and not at all relieved by his efforts to tidy himself, which efforts may have smoothed his hair and assured him his mustache had not blow off, but did nothing to straighten his clothes, wipe the grime off his cheeks, the dust off his boots, or dispel the musky, untamed scent of equine perspiration that exuded from his person and had by now filled the room.

"Yes. Certainly. Miss Masonet. If you please." His first word was loud and urgent, but with an effort, and by degrees, his voice returned to its calm, reasonable tone by his "If you please."

Miss Dansforth opened her eyes very wide but did not actually take a step backward at Edmond's outburst.

"I will send one of the girls to summon her, Mr. Edmond. Are you sure you would not like a very small tumbler of sherry?" she offered again.

Edmond smiled. "Well, perhaps a very *small* tumbler," he said.

Miss Dansforth's trepidation was markedly eased. It coincided with her view of the world that any virile young man would consider no hour too early for a robust drink. Of course, in Miss Dansforth's view of the world two tablespoons of sherry in a tiny crystal glass constituted a robust drink.

Miss Dansforth left, after indicating the sherry, and went to call Julia. Edmond had time to swallow the touch of restorative and wipe his face with his handkerchief in a further attempt to repair the damage of his nightlong ride before the door opened again.

When the door to the receiving room did open, it crashed open and Julia burst into the room, a smile on her lips, her dark eyes sparkling.

"Did you get the mon...?" she began gaily, and then she recognized the figure in the middle of the room. "Cousin Richard!" She drew herself up short and her fine olive complexion darkened, which was as close as Julia ever came to a blush.

"Julia," he returned. Then, abruptly, he too stopped, struck by how bohemian the girl appeared at times. Now a case in point. "You are looking well," he finished rather colorlessly.

Julia was looking better than "well." Strands of her black hair had come loose when she ran down the stairs at Letty's announcement that there was someone to see her in the front hall. Now those strands coiled around her cheeks and trailed behind the unprincipled knot at the back of her neck. Her figure had reached almost its full maturity by now, a fact that sometimes took Edmond by surprise, for he tended to think of the girl in her thirteen-year-old persona when he had not seen her for a while. As she stood at the door, breathing heavily after her exertion, the gentleman became uncomfortably aware of that figure.

The students and female teachers at the Hampton Academy all wore white shirtwaists and long gray or black skirts. Rather than severe or forbidding, Julia's ensemble looked like simple peasant dress. With a colorful bandanna she might have been part of some wild Gypsy band.

Richard cleared his throat.

"Your studies? Going well, I trust?"

"Well enough. What are you doing here, Cousin?"

He cleared his throat again. There it was then. The question. What *was* he doing here? What could he tell the girl when he had no idea himself?

"I had business in town," he said.

"I thought—that is, you did not say anything in your letters. You usually tell me—"

"It was unexpected," he said.

Now Julia glanced behind her and pulled the door shut. She stepped into the room and motioned to the chairs.

"Shall we sit?" she asked.

"I hope I did not come at a difficult time," Richard said, following her example and sitting in one of the chairs, which was typical of the Hampton Academy in that it was very straight-backed and very uncomfortable.

"Not at all." The girl gave her head a kindly shake, and with that familiar gesture became once again the confiding friend she had been for years instead of the wild creature who first rushed into this room. "You took me by surprise. Nothing more. But it is a very pleasant surprise. As you must know."

There was a loud clock on the fireplace mantel of this room, the sonorous ticking of which filled the silent moments. It also made one acutely aware of those silent moments, and Richard tried not to let many *tocks* rebound off the walls before he thought of something to say.

Tock. Tock.

"Mother and Father send their greetings."

"They are well?"

"Perfectly."

Tock. Tock.

"And you?" he asked.

"Very well."

Tock. Tock.

"Do you still find your fellow classmates agreeable?"

"As agreeable as ever," Julia confirmed, not confessing to more friendship than she was allowing herself to feel these days.

"Miss Dansforth? The rest of your teachers?"

"*Bien.* That is, they are all in tolerable good health, as far as I know. But you spoke to Miss Dansforth yourself, did you not?"

"Yes. Certainly. She seemed fine."

Tock. Tock.

"Well, tell me, Julia, how are your art studies coming? Your letters have been of nothing else and I am eager to see some of your work."

"Are you?" It was like surprising a thrush's nest; suddenly there was a chirp in the girl's voice, an eager glimmer in her eye. She fairly preened her feathers at his suggestion. "Come with me." She jumped to her feet and held out her hand. "My things are up in the studio."

Richard took her hand and dutifully followed her up the three flights of stairs. Now he did not need to cudgel his brain for something to say. The dark bird in front of him chattered and twittered all the way, talking about pigments and depth and wonderful qualities of light. She complained about her technique with an insincere note, so Richard knew he was supposed to refute her, but not having seen an example of her technique, he did not know what facet of it he could compliment.

"Monsieur Davenôt had me using watercolors outside to begin with. He said it was important to paint from life, to capture moments and moods." She turned to him seriously. "Watercolors are faster, lighter." She fluttered her hand like a restless wing. "The whole process is much quicker."

They had reached the east wing of the third floor by then, and as Julia opened the door in front of them, Richard made sounds of agreement in his throat. Although his own study of art had not been extensive, he knew as much as anything Julia had told him so far. "Now Monsieur Davenôt has me working with oils. More intense, but perhaps less demanding. That is, the same demand for speed is not required with oils. What do you think? You must be *candid*. I have a great reliance upon your eye, Cousin Richard."

It was a sprig of holly in a brass bowl. Richard did not need to look at the subjects sitting atop the table near the window to recognize them. It was a very fair representation. Julia had achieved a certain degree of dimension and intensity that was very pleasing. Perhaps even promising. Richard continued to study the painting as Julia chirped away.

"It is not finished, of course, and I am sorry. Monsieur Davenôt said I must only paint in the early afternoons, so the shadows would always be the same. I was never able to work long enough on it to complete it." She stood next to Richard, looking at the picture intently until she became aware that he was looking at her quizzically.

"Is something preventing you from finishing it now?" he asked.

"Oh, no. Certainly not. Of course I will complete it." Without meeting his eye she turned from him and hurried to the few canvases leaning with their painted sides against the opposite wall. "These are some of my early things. Watercolors." She held one up and looked at it critically. "Not terribly good, I am afraid. Though at the time I was convinced they were destined for renown." She smiled and turned the watercolor of a meadow and distant line of trees toward him. Even this that she spoke of disparagingly looked quite passable to Richard. Not only were the trees and meadow perfectly recognizable, and depicted in a delicate wash of watercolors that many a more practiced artist does not achieve, but there was also something illusive about the painting that raised it above the anonymous wilderness of such amateur attempts and identified it exclusively as the work of Julia Masonet.

"I like it," he said, nodding his head with considered approval.

Monsieur Davenôt often stood so close to her shoulder that she could feel the heat of his body, exclaiming, *"C'est fantastique! Extraordinaire!"* And without a doubt, his approbation and enthusiasm pleased the girl. But her cousin's simple phrase sent a glow of warmth through her being that was deeper, though quieter, than the tingling sparks of Davenôt's praise.

"Do you?" she asked, smiling gratefully.

"I do." He leaned the picture against the wall and stood back from it, cocking his head to one side. "It is a view of the scene through your eyes. The meadow and trees are familiar, but there is more here than I ever see."

Julia glowed, even though her cousin had not complimented any particular point of the painting, had not lauded the textures, the colors, the faithful replication of the scene. But he saw, she believed, and appreciated her intent.

With the same excited pride of a child demonstrating his mastery of a cartwheel or snapping of the fingers, Julia placed all of her paintings side by side against the wall next to the first one. Like some revered art connoisseur, Edmond walked slowly past the display, his hands clasped behind his back, nodding gravely. Occasionally he would stop and point out something or ask a question of his ward. Very probably, he knew what pigments to combine to achieve that shade of yellow or the direction of the light that produced this shadow, but he allowed the girl to answer his questions loftily and said, "Is that so?" with just a touch of wonder in his voice.

When the review was completed and Richard had passed favorable judgment on all of her work, he once again stood back to consider the whole array.

"Naturally it is not my prerogative to lay claim to any of your work, Julia," he said. "But Mother would be delighted with any one of these paintings. You know your aunt. She would display it prominently and point it out proudly to everyone who stepped across the Aspen Grove threshold." He looked down seriously into her eyes and raised his eyebrows imploringly, the hair above his lip hiding any hint of humor. But Julia was not fooled.

"If I refuse I see I would break your heart," she replied, laughing. "And you know I would never hurt you, cousin." She looked back at the canvases she had spread out for his inspection and so did not see his expression falter. "Which do you think Aunt Jenny would like?" she asked.

The scenes were watercolor landscapes of the familiar country that surrounded the Hampton Academy. There was the stand of oak trees across from the main dormitory and the rise of ground that sloped up behind the village of Barnet, besides the meadow and the distant grove in Julia's first two paintings. But after only a few silent moments of study, Edmond stepped to the display and selected the first landscape Julia had done.

"That one?" the girl asked, surprised that after seeing her later, more studied work, he would select that first feeble attempt. "But *le professeur* had not the chance to teach me anything when I did that."

"That is its charm, I believe," he said, holding it before him as he spoke, studying it again. "This is our Julia. Which is very probably the title by which it will be known at Aspen Grove." He turned his head to look at her innocently. "You do not mind, I am sure," he said.

She smiled her defeat. "Oh, very well!" She laughed.

He put the canvas down, apart from the others, and rejoined his ward in front of the display once again. In a gesture of casual camaraderie he put his arm around her shoulders.

"And then later, of course, if you find yourself once again in so generous a mood, you may give one of your more mature works to your Uncle Charles," he said.

"And what of you, Cousin Richard?" Julia asked, glancing up at the tall figure beside her. "Would you like one of my paintings, as well?"

"I do not believe so" was his surprising answer. Julia's expression turned to one of disappointed surprise.

"No?" she asked.

"What if I were to choose one of these—" her guardian waved his free hand toward the wall "—and with your next painting you produced the quintessence of artistic beauty to my eye? I would be denied a lifetime of satisfaction by making too hasty a selection." He smiled playfully and shook his head. "No, when you return to Aspen Grove with your full complement of work, then, if I may, I will choose something of yours for myself."

There was a stiffening of the girl's shoulders under Richard's arm and a quiver, ever so slight, in the smile she returned to him.

Cousin Richard's words had rekindled all of the guilt and uncertainties she had managed to lay to rest in the day and a half since her teacher had made his proposal. Her reluctance had been further overcome by additional passionate encouragements and assurances from François.

She glanced up furtively at Richard when she thought of Davenôt's Christian name, as if her cousin could detect the unspoken familiarity of which he most certainly would not approve. He was studying again the painting he had chosen for his mother, a look of thoughtful scrutiny in his eyes. When he concentrated like that, his blue eyes took on the color of a troubled sea. Julia was fascinated by the depths in those eyes, so close to her, and she considered fleetingly what colors on her palette would be required for that hue and how she could convey the deep thought the image suggested.

But the questions were fleeting, washed away by a wave of unhappiness that caught her unawares.

She knew he was right; Aunt Jenny would love the painting and would display her first, uncertain dabbling in watercolors, proudly announcing to any and everyone who darkened the Edmond doorway that her ward had painted the picture. But would she ever be able to do that? Dear Aunt Jenny, who was so forgiving and understanding, could she ever understand, would she ever forgive Julia for running away with an artist and living with him in a French art colony?

The time Richard stood with his arm around her shoulder, silently contemplating the simple landscape he had chosen for his mother, was no more than half a minute, yet in those thirty seconds Julia saw the life she was about to choose spread out before her. There would be those moments of breathless excitement with Davenôt, and perhaps even her own achievement as an artist. Her work *might* attain reputation and recognition, she *might* realize a stunning potential as an artist, and, too, she certainly might hope that François Davenôt would marry her eventually, that together they would become a formidable name in the art world.

As uncertain as her success as an artist was, though, there was no question that the step would ostracize her from English society, that her name would be spoken in hushed and scandalized tones, that the Millers, the Brackens, the Fentons and other of the Edmond friends and acquaintances would shake their heads and murmur to one another that it was too bad about the Edmonds, but the girl *was* French, and what else, really, could they have expected?

"I wish I knew where the gilt frame was that was around my grandmother's portrait for so long. It would be perfect for that painting." Richard's words pulled Julia roughly back into the present. After her glimpse into the future she was momentarily confused by Cousin Richard's question and surprised—and relieved—to feel the strength of his arm still holding her to him.

He looked down into her eyes with a half smile of dismissal, a smile that held no accusation, nor even any recollection his question had brought to mind.

"Perhaps not, though. I think it would probably have been too small."

Julia did not reply. Now she was admitting to herself that she knew where the frame was to which her cousin was referring. Or at least she knew what had happened to it: it had gone to pay some of that ridiculous Bennet Drummond's gambling debts, she was sure. What a dunce she had been over him. She could only pray that her dear, generous cousin would never remember what had happened to the frame. He could not help but think ill of her if he ever found out what a foolish mistake she had made. And she never wanted her Cousin Richard to think ill of her.

She raised her hand and grasped the fingers lying on her shoulder. Richard looked down on her in surprise.

"What is it?" he asked, genuine, though mild, concern in his voice.

"I want you to always be proud of me, Cousin Richard."

"And I always shall be, Julia," he said, giving her a gentle hug before he removed his arm from around her.

She felt cold when he did. The coldness was only partially external. In a chilly splash of reality, she realized that if she took the step she contemplated, Cousin Richard would not always be proud of her.

Richard left her side and gave her displayed paintings one final, sweeping glance.

"Your work is very fine, Julia. And your schooling appears to be coming along famously. I do not know what had me so worried. I am like a fretful mother hen." He laughed and looked back at her, inviting her to join his laughter. She smiled but did not do so, for any attempt at laughter would have sounded forced and insincere. "I promise to wait to hear from you at Christmastide before I come again."

Richard rolled up the canvas he had chosen and stepped to the door. Together they went down the stairs, Richard making small, harmless comments on the weather, the condition of the school, telling her Aunt Jenny was as lively as ever, though his father appeared to be failing a bit.

"And Rachel? Miss Brewster? She was well when you left London?" Julia asked.

"Very well. I will tell her that you inquired after her."

Like the old friends they were, they exchanged tiny bits of news that would have interested no one but themselves as Julia accompanied him to the stable, where his horse was feeding and recuperating after the long ride of the night before.

"You are not returning to Aspen Grove today, are you?" she asked him.

His laugh had a faint note of fatigue in it.

"Not today, no. I shall return to my rooms in London for a day or two. Though there is nothing urgent to which I must attend, I will perhaps use my time trying to convince

Miss Brewster to go out to dinner with me or attend a concert." He smiled faintly and shook his head over Miss Brewster's stubbornness, failing to notice his ward's look of bewilderment.

"I thought you had come to town on business," Julia said, puzzled.

Richard took her hand in his, her slender hand with its long, sensitive fingers.

"I may as well confess that my primary object was to see how you were. We miss you at the Grove, Julia. Perhaps we get unduly anxious at times. Take care of yourself, dear cousin. Remember that your Edmond family cares for you."

He bent his head and kissed her very lightly on the forehead.

"I will," the girl whispered hoarsely.

Her eyes glimmered as she watched Richard climb wearily onto his saddle. He had made a great effort to assure himself that she was well. She told him that she was, but was she? And how was she going to repay his effort?

Chapter Ten

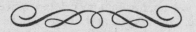

"Well, did you ever! I never dreamed—would not have imagined—that such a thing could ever occur. Not here at the Hampton. Oh, Mrs. Fife, whatever will I say to the girl's people?" Miss Dansforth paced distractedly back and forth in her private sitting room. The other woman, Mrs. Fife, who introduced the Hampton Academy young ladies to a very tame selection of classic literature, shook her head in commiseration, selecting, as she did so, a tempting chocolate bonbon from the silver tray on Julia's writing desk.

"I am sure I do not know. I fear the reputation of the school has been indelibly damaged by this."

Mrs. Fife was evidently not aware of what Miss Dansforth was hoping for by way of consolation. Her prediction of the injury done to the school did nothing to comfort the headmistress.

"We should have known, we should have known," she moaned. "One simply cannot expect anything better of the French. And to think I engaged him to come here, I paid him to be with our young ladies. I was *pleased* by his inclusion on the faculty. Oh, Mrs. Fife!"

"A scoundrel. An unmitigated scoundrel," Mrs. Fife agreed, licking the melted chocolate from her fingertips.

"And the girl! Have I not always said it is a mistake to give them any preferential treatment? I have tried, truly I have, but they take such advantage of one, insisting on this special favor and that consideration until they are marching all over one and one's most adamant reservations."

"Indeed."

"Then, the reins loosened, *they* have no restraint. It would seem they have no intelligence at all. Why would she not stop for the tiniest moment and consider what something like this can mean? What on earth could possess a young woman to do such a foolish thing?"

"She will be ruined," Mrs. Fife announced.

"Of course she will be ruined. She is ruined already. She has destroyed her future, even should Monsieur Davenôt have the decency to marry her eventually."

Mrs. Fife sniffed derisively at Miss Dansforth's naive hope.

"And her family. Consider what she has done to them. They will be condemned, whispered about and pointed out to each new acquaintance as having raised a wayward girl."

"A loose woman," Mrs. Fife augmented.

"They will no longer be accepted by former friends and families. They will be shunned by polite society. Just as if it had been they who had acted so heedlessly, so shamefully."

"And that is to say nothing of what she has done to your good name," Mrs. Fife said, critically looking over the dish of chocolates again.

Miss Dansforth collapsed onto the divan opposite the literature teacher, broken by Mrs. Fife's final straw.

"I am ruined!" she wailed.

"Perhaps not, my dear. The girls here all know the circumstances, certainly, and will doubtless tell their families. But we may still hope the story will not spread the entire length and breadth of the kingdom."

Miss Dansforth groaned under the weight of still yet another of Mrs. Fife's leaden straws.

"And in time your part in the whole sordid affair may be forgotten."

"I *had* no part in it."

"You did hire the fellow, Elizabeth."

"As an art instructor, not as a philanderer. How could I have known he would seduce one of my girls and entice her to run away with him? It seemed so fashionable, so very *distingué*, to have a French art instructor at the Hampton Academy, just the thing for the older girls who wanted to enter society truly accomplished! Fools! Fools! They are all fools! *We* are all fools!''

Mrs. Fife was nodding and selecting another chocolate, which she hoped was not a camouflaged caramel, when a soft knock was heard at the door.

Miss Dansforth wiped at her eyes and pushed a stray hair under the white cap she wore.

"Come in," the headmistress called. The door opened carefully, but the pale girl did not speak until she was all the way in the room and had half closed the door behind her.

"Cynthia and I have been through everything, Miss Dansforth. I am afraid there is no question. She is gone and has taken all of her things with her."

"It is as we feared, then," Miss Dansforth said.

"If there is anything I can do, Miss Dansforth..."

"No. Nothing. Nothing is to be done. Davenôt is gone, as well?"

"Yes."

"This could destroy the school." Miss Dansforth shook her head. "Well, all we can ask for now is your discretion. You and the other girls. Nyla has made a grave error, true, but you will be mindful of her family, will you not, Julia?"

"Certainly, Miss Dansforth."

Julia backed quietly from the room, leaving the distraught headmistress in the care of Mrs. Fife's tender mercies.

The Train

The train jerked into motion, pulling Julia's hand away from the window and startling her into wakefulness once again. She shivered. In the few minutes they had stopped at the Birmingham station, the sky had grown black and cold had invaded the coach with insinuating tendrils that now clasped her shoulders and wrapped themselves insidiously around her fingers and toes. She shivered again, then stood to pull down a blanket from the compartment over her head.

The blanket was a rough wool and scratched at her delicate neck, but heedlessly she pulled it snugly up around her shoulders. As the steward had warned her, this would be a long night. The rhythm of the train, which had soothed her to sleep earlier, now jerked her from sleep every time her mind began to find refuge. She peered into the darkness and considered once again, as she had often in the past years, from what an unspeakable fate her cousin's visit that day had saved her. She still painted a little, but Davenôt had taken her driving force with him when he and Nyla ran away together. Julia was a passable artist and might have become very good, but looking back with a more mature eye, she knew now that she never would have been great.

She was stunned, naturally, when the teacher and his student left. Everyone at Hampton was. But since she had believed herself the only object of her teacher's erotic attention, her shock had an added dimension.

"I cannot come with you, François," she told him the very evening of Cousin Richard's visit.

"Consider, *ma chère*. Our dreams..."

"Are only that."

"And our *désir*. Is that only a dream?" He trailed his finger along her cheek and neck. She caught at his hand and held it, hoping to warm her fingers against his flesh.

"A very lovely dream, if that is what it is."

"How can you turn your back on your destiny?"

"How can I betray those I love?"

"Bah!" he snorted scornfully and turned from her impatiently. She had been very young and very impressionable then and fancied herself very much in love. If Davenôt had not turned from her but had held her in his arms and pleaded with her urgently, her will would undoubtedly have collapsed. But by some happy chance he gave her the time and distance she needed to strengthen her resolve.

"I cannot," she said again, then pleaded, "forgive me."

"What is it you wish me to forgive?" he asked. "You are forsaking an opportunity that will not come your way again. Forgive yourself, Julia Masonet."

He left her alone in the little studio, her pictures still displayed for cousin Richard against the wall behind her. She did not see the art teacher again and was not aware of his intentions until Cynthia Fenstermacher burst in at break-

fast the next morning, exclaiming that her roommate, Nyla
Jessop, was gone. Had run off with Monsieur Davenôt!

Had that always been his plan? To take both Julia and the
other girl with him, a *ménage à trois* that would share a vision of art and who dared imagine what else? Or had Nyla
been his alternate *amoureuse* in the event that Julia failed
him? Or was his flight with Nyla completely spontaneous?

Julia was never to know. Scandal had indeed descended
on the academy, and though the girls looking for a school
might have been lured by the whispers, their parents were
shocked and became leery of Hampton.

Nyla Jessop was not heard of again. She did not achieve
fame as an artist, and neither did François Davenôt, though
the Barbizon school itself did contribute to the world of art.
Nyla's family was from up north and Julia did not know if
their position in society was altered. It may not have been;
Nyla may have returned to them. Julia fervently prayed for
that happy resolution, hoping for every good to come to the
girl who saved her from a dismal fate, who took her place
in the sacrificial flame of Davenôt's passion.

Julia did not return to the Hampton Academy for Young
Women after that year. Her studies were completed and she
had reached a certain degree of maturity. Julia herself reck-
oned that her advanced years and all of the jading experience she had encountered within the confines of a girls'
school qualified her for the title of *dame âgée* by the time
she reached eighteen.

Ironically, that very summer the Higginses invited Julia
to join them and their daughter Beverly on the Continent for
a few weeks. She saw the Louvre in Paris, the charming city
of Brussels and the magnificent art of Florence.

Yet, as thrilling as that was for a young girl, as fond as she
was of Beverly and as pleasant as the Higginses were, those
were not the scenes that were spotlighted in her memory.

As the train sped along, those whirlwind days rushed past
her memory like the blurred images that streaked past the
windows of the coach. She was young and vibrant, intelligent and at last beginning to feel not so very "horsey," as
she always had. Aunt Jenny and Uncle Charles were dim,
consenting images during that year. Cousin Richard was not

often at Aspen Grove, seeing, as he was, to business in town, monitoring the Brewster-Edmond investments, of which he was the primary guardian now, with Mr. Brewster semiretired himself.

He did return to the Grove for a week at Christmas and occasional weekends, when he would serve as Julia's escort to balls and parties, as he always had done. A smile crossed her lovely face as she sat in the dark coach, her head against the cushion, her eyes closed, seeing before her the lights and dazzling colors of one of those Christmas fetes. She did not remember the place, though the Tunbridge society was limited and it must have been at the Brackens or Fentons or another one of the Edmond neighbors. Her Cousin Richard had just returned to the Grove that afternoon, and though tired, she knew now, he agreed to accompany her.

"And dance with me, cousin," she said, laughing into his face, bubbling with the excitement the prospect of a ball brings to every young woman. "I will not have you off discussing your dreary business all night with the other old, stout gentlemen who do not like to dance anymore. I shall save one set for you and you must be very gallant and allow me twenty minutes."

Richard smiled and brushed at the sleeve of his jacket.

"By all means. If you will allow me one set I shall do my very best not to embarrass you. If you think I am presentable after my long ride today?"

Julia looked at him critically and then stepped directly in front of him. With a serious expression she raised her hand and smoothed the collar of his shirt and brushed back the hair from his temple. She dropped her hand to his shoulder and nodded her head ever so slightly.

"There now. Any woman could feel quite honored to be seen with you. You may tell Rachel for me that she would not need to be embarrassed if she were to join you some evening. I wonder that you do not bring her down to the Grove with you some weekend, but how lucky for me that you did not think to do so tonight."

"Ah, yes. Was that not a lucky thing?" he asked. Julia smiled and Richard smiled, and if other thoughts were running under their words they were well hidden and resolutely dismissed.

The ball and what other partners she may have had that night were of a grayish tint, but like one of Rousseau's brilliant paintings, Julia saw her cousin claiming his set, sweeping her onto the dance floor, turning her in a breathless waltz.

The whole picture was lovely, the memory one that, with the watercolor of the meadow and trees, she wished she could frame and hang on the wall in the drawing room at the Grove. Her smile wavered and she felt a catch in her throat. A tear dampened the lashes of her eyelid. The tear, she realized, was not only for a year of gaiety that was past forever, or the grief that was to follow, but for a single set of dances she had saved for her dear, dear Cousin Richard one Christmas.

Chapter Eleven

Milestone Nineteen

Uncle Charles was not so very old by a mere consideration of accumulated years. He was only five years older than
Aunt Jenny, and Aunt Jenny was an active, healthy woman.
But his years in the military, years that tone other men and
give them vigor, depleted Major Charles Edmond. Instead
of five, he looked fifteen years his wife's elder.

Winter drizzled into spring. Julia was busy, caught up in
her own world, which to the young is the whole world.
When she was not spending a week here and a week there
with friends in the neighborhood, she was painting in her
room or out under the trees when the weather turned warm.
She did not know now if her Aunt Jenny was really always
caring for Uncle Charles or if she had excluded Mrs. Edmond from her life. The question was painful and one that
Julia had learned to suppress.

Spring shook itself off and dried itself out and summer
spread its skirts across the countryside. But with the advent
of summer, Julia was finally forced to notice her uncle's
failing health, and with that came another staggering realization that man is mortal and his sojourn in this life too
brief.

On the afternoon of August 19, a month to the day after
her nineteenth birthday, Uncle Charles, sitting with head
drooped upon his chest near the open French windows,
gasped. Julia was sketching out a scene from the vantage

point of the windows on the other side of the room. Her
uncle occasionally wheezed and half snored when he dozed,
and Julia would not have given his sound a second thought.
But Aunt Jenny looked across at her husband sharply and
hurriedly put aside her needlework. By the time Mrs. Edmond stood, Julia sensed her urgency, and like a series of
daguerreotypes, Julia put down her sketchbook, and Aunt
Jenny bent over Major Edmond's white head, Julia stood,
Aunt Jenny dropped to the chair next to her husband, Julia
took a step toward them and Aunt Jenny raised her face,
streaming with tears.

The sun was shining on the two old people, making Aunt
Jenny's tears sparkling rivulets against her pale cheeks and
wreathing Uncle Charles's silvery head with a halo of light.

It was another warm, sunny day when they buried Uncle
Charles in the little cemetery on a rise of ground outside
Tunbridge. All of the Edmond neighbors came to bid the
major a last farewell. It was a solemn, fond gathering that
stood at the graveside while the pastor said the prayer and
offered his words of comfort to Mrs. Edmond. Julia stood
on one side of her aunt, lending her arm as a support.
Cousin Richard was on the other side, like an onyx pillar in
his black weeds, his tall black hat held in the hand that
dangled at his side. His mother leaned more heavily on her
son's arm, but she grasped both supporting arms that
flanked her.

Many of the graveside mourners returned with the Edmonds and their ward to Aspen Grove, where Millie, still in
casual service to the Edmonds, served dainty sandwiches
and tea, and the gathering broke into little groups who quietly discussed the ills of old age, the outlook for the crop
markets and Disraeli and Sir Robert Peel's latest altera-
tion.

After a while, large empty spaces began to appear between the sandwiches on the tray, and some of the gentlemen began to hanker for cooler, more comfortable attire
and a drink of something stronger than lemon tea. Quiet
words were spoken to Mrs. Edmond and the neighbors returned to their homes and the private affairs that would save

them from too long considering the grief of an old woman who had shared thirty-five years with a man she loved.

Julia carried the trays of sandwiches from group to group, offering delectables and receiving condolences. She smiled softly and moved with a grace that was at last becoming natural for her.

"Mrs. Miller, will you not have another sandwich? This is chopped ham and I believe that is chicken."

"Mr. Davenport, I could heat up your cup of tea if you would like."

"Lord Ramsgate, I know my aunt is grateful to you for making this trip."

Lord Kirby Ramsgate had come down from London with Cousin Richard when Richard received word of his father's death. Younger than Aunt Jenny, older than Cousin Richard, in the days of turmoil that followed, Ramsgate had been a stable, stalwart presence in Aspen Grove. Richard returned to town to bring back most of his things, since, for the time being, he would stay at the Grove with his mother. Lord Ramsgate remained with Mrs. Edmond and Julia while Richard was gone and lengthened out his stay once the younger man returned. Quiet evenings passed, evenings that would have seemed so empty without another man in the house. Ramsgate was not Uncle Charles but he was someone, a comforting addition who sat reading or playing backgammon with Richard or whist with the Edmonds and Julia.

He was unfailingly solicitous. He asked after Aunt Jenny's health every morning, and he and Richard seriously discussed international issues, as men do everywhere, as if they had the power to change them. He made appreciative noises over Julia's paintings and Julia inquired after Duchy, the gentleman's horse, and Derby, his Irish setter, and Ramsgate Hall.

Lord Ramsgate answered her every question slowly and completely, conveying the flattering impression that there was no one more important in the world than Julia Masonet and no question more worthy of his gravest consideration than hers.

Lord Kirby Ramsgate was the owner of a large tract of land in the southern end of Wessex County. He was a tall, slender man, his hair shot with silver and heavy, very black eyebrows above his deep-set eyes. Rather than forbidding, his dark brows and generally serious expression suggested deep thought and invited confidences that one felt would be guarded as safely as if couched solely within one's own bosom.

Not surprisingly, Ramsgate accepted his political responsibilities very seriously and seldom missed a session of Parliament. Though not often heard in the House, every question received his thoughtful attention. He was respected by his peers and was often asked to sit on one important panel or another.

He had married the Honorable Winifred Dunsmore when he was five and twenty, obeying the wishes of his parents and her parents. Winifred had been a cold, haughty woman who treated her husband with perfect civility, even, perhaps, considering her personality, with fondness. She was exactly what the young man was expecting in a wife, and she performed her duties as mistress at Ramsgate Hall flawlessly. Ramsgate considered it nothing less than his bounden duty, his part of their sophisticated understanding, to offer her his every advancement and recognition as gratification for her vanity. It was a small price to pay for servants who attended to their labors faithfully and silently, his house running like a well-oiled machine, his staff, as far as he was aware, never changing in the eight years of their marriage. Winifred saw to all of the details of the customary annual ball and the necessary dinners for politically influential neighbors and visitors from the city. At the beginning of each winter Ramsgate hosted a hunting house party with anywhere from ten to twenty-five guests who stayed at the Hall, sometimes for a month. Lord Ramsgate had only to greet his guests when they arrived and join them for dinner most evenings. He was not even required to take part in the hunt if he did not wish to, although he usually did, if the gentlemen knew what they were doing and would not make a shambles of the hunt or his property.

Every other duty fell to Winifred's lot and she held the reins of Ramsgate Hall in proud and tight control.

Theirs had never been a marriage of love, but if ever there was a marriage of convenience Ramsgate recognized his as supremely so. In fact, the only untimely, inconsiderate, common thing that Winifred ever did, perhaps in her life, was to die of pneumonia in midwinter of the ninth year of their marriage.

Lord Ramsgate was intensely sorry for her loss. He might not have missed her silent presence at the other end of the dining room table, the occasional polite questions about his well-being or his business in town, or even the less occasional courtesy visits to her bedroom. But he did not enjoy overseeing the endless minutiae of running a country manor or his social requirements. His marriage had certainly been convenient, but despairing of finding another woman as capable as Winifred, who would, like her, cause him no trouble, and even being aware as he was of his place and duties in society, still he had never remarried. Instead, he hired a competent housekeeper who was herself a widow and—he made inquiries to be certain of the fact—in excellent health, with a family history of longevity. For his part, he spent most of his time in his rooms in London, summering on the Continent when it became absolutely necessary to relocate.

It had been six years since Winifred Dunsmore Ramsgate's death the year Uncle Charles passed away. In those years, Lord Kirby Ramsgate had filled his life with friends instead of a marriage partner, of whom one of his favorite was young Richard Edmond. He and Richard had become acquainted while the lad was still in school, and now, with Richard in town so much on business, the two men saw a great deal of each other. They spent time together at their club, often they went to dinner together, even, when Edmond was not attending Miss Brewster, they would "take in" a musical review. Nothing was more natural than for Lord Ramsgate to return to Aspen Grove with Edmond and lend him the support and sympathy of an older brother during his time of grief.

Julia, along with the rest of the Edmonds intimates, had been introduced to Lord Kirby Ramsgate years before, and the tall, quiet gentleman was a familiar guest. Perhaps it was the shared grief, perhaps the additional time she spent in his company in the days following the funeral, but the young woman finally came to know the Lord Ramsgate of whom her cousin was so fond and to appreciate the qualities of unfailing courtesy, selflessness, erudition and gentle humor the man possessed.

"Lord Ramsgate, tell me what you think. Are the ruins down by the mill there Saxon or Gaul? My Cousin Richard says they are Saxon, but by their lines and structure they would appear to suggest a more European origin."

Ramsgate looked up from his book at the young woman who stood gazing out the library windows. The windows faced south and were directed to the mill, but the ruins were not visible from the house. Nevertheless, Ramsgate put down Plato's *Republic* and came to stand next to Julia to look out the window with her.

After he had made the effort, the best he could offer Julia was to consider the descending lawn and shake his head soberly.

"I really do not know, Miss Masonet. Being well-informed on current events is only achieved by sacrifice of historical study. I could answer any question at all you might choose to ask about Ramsgate Hall—one's family history is rather pounded into one's head at an early age, assuring that it will never escape. But my range of historical knowledge hardly expands past the Ramsgate property lines." He smiled slightly and bent his head to catch the next words of the young woman at his side.

"It is not a question of any gravity," Julia admitted. "A more docile female would readily concede the point to her well-informed, more mature guardian. But you know my Cousin Richard. He will not allow anyone's opinion but his own, and I am afraid it tends to make one contentious."

Ramsgate nodded his bent head and Julia's eye was caught by the glitter of light off the silver strands of his hair and his prominent nose, which somehow lent authority to everything he said.

"Would you mind awfully if I sketched your likeness?"
Julia asked him abruptly, then wished she had held her
tongue or at least slowed it down just a bit. "Your profile is
so very distinctive. I know you would make a fascinating
subject," she added, hoping her words would do something to justify her interest and soften the demand. Instead, Lord Ramsgate raised his hand self-consciously to his
nose.

"A legacy from my mother's father," he said. "As I understand it, the union was always considered equal on both
sides. Grandmother brought to it a great deal of personal
wealth and Grandfather brought his nose." He chuckled
good-naturedly and Julia made soft little sounds of nega-
tion. Ramsgate straightened, raising his head a good four
inches above Julia's. He struck a heroic pose and then
looked down on her with black eyebrows raised playfully. "I
am certain you are correct, Miss Masonet. The Ramsgate
profile is, without a doubt, distinctive. If the sketching of
it will add to your artistic experience, then by all means you
may render my likeness."

Julia turned eagerly to the door.

"I shall run up to my room this very minute and get my
paper and pen. You may return to your book, but you must
sit in this chair so the sun will be on you."

"I tend to doze in the warm sunlight, Miss Masonet. I
may very possibly be sitting in that chair with my eyes closed
for the next several hours."

"Better and better," Julia said.

"Yes, well, I cannot guarantee that my profile will continue to be noble when I sleep."

"But it *will* be distinctive."

"Granted," Ramsgate said with a laugh.

Julia hurried from the room to get her drawing tools. As
she paused to gather her pen and its various nibs, she realized that her heart was pounding. Pounding more force-
fully than the climbing of one flight of stairs would seem to
justify.

The sketching of Lord Ramsgate required two long afternoon sessions. The gentleman might have had things of

more importance to which to attend, but one would never have suspected it from his patience and interest in everything Julia did.

When she initially returned to the library, Ramsgate was not asleep but arranging his chair and hers so that she would be in the most favorable position in relation to the light coming through the window. He looked up when she came in and then promptly sat in his chair, assuming a haughty expression with chin raised and eyebrows drawn fiercely together.

Julia laughed. "No, no, that will never do."

"Not distinctive enough?" he asked.

"Not Lord Ramsgate enough," she corrected. "I am not drawing a likeness to be reproduced on some Roman coin but rather that of a kind, gentle man. Not a national hero but a personal hero." Julia stopped and drew in her breath sharply. There had been a waver on that last word that caught her completely off guard.

Ramsgate was looking at her and smiled.

"A hero. Fancy that," he said.

Julia scrutinized his smile. Had he heard the emotion in her statement? Was there a question in his look? Did he understand? Did *she* understand?

She sat in the chair opposite him, fixing her pen, unstopping the inkwell, fussily smoothing her paper. When at last she looked up again, Ramsgate was still looking at her.

"Is this satisfactory?" he asked with a wave of his hand that included her chair, his chair, his position and that of the sun in his question.

"Perfect. Now you must go back to your reading and not give me another thought."

"Easier said than done," Ramsgate replied. "Plato requires too much concentration to rivet one to the written page, certainly not when lines are being drawn on another page that will soon create one's own image. I will not make you nervous if I watch, will I?"

"Frightfully. I have only painted trees, fruits and crockery before now. They do not inspect one's work. Drawing a cognizant being will be extremely unnerving, I fear."

"If you want me to return to my reading with no other thought of you, then you must think of me as a bowl of grapes," Ramsgate said, picking up the book he had laid down when Julia first asked her question concerning the ruins. Quickly he found the page he had been perusing and then, despite his profession of fascination for Julia's work, was soon lost in the philosophic questions in the work before him.

He sat silently reading for an hour, glancing up now and then when he turned the page, following the progress of Julia's work. The clock in the receiving hall was just striking three, the muffled chimes filtering in to them, when the door to the library burst open.

"There you are!" Richard cried triumphantly, as if the two of them had been craftily evading his most diligent search. Ramsgate looked up and nodded.

"Having myself preserved for the ages, old man," he said.

"Ah well, that explains and justifies your cloister, I suppose. Let us see if the ages will be happy with their legacy." Richard stepped to the side of Julia's chair to study the portrait. Not a caricature, certainly, but Julia had emphasized Lord Ramsgate's most outstanding features, his nose, his pitch-black eyebrows, enough to make the likeness that of the peer and a bit more.

"Do you like it?" Julia asked, raising her head to look at the man next to her, her pen poised above the inkwell. Richard glanced toward Ramsgate and then down at the drawing again.

"I do," he said. Julia flushed with pleasure and returned her attention to her work. "She has captured you, Kirby. This is a likeness one should send to one's closest friend or paramour. Someone one knows well. Someone who would say, 'Yes, old Ramsgate is like this sometimes.'"

Ramsgate raised his eyebrows curiously.

"What is it you have put down on that paper, young lady?" he asked.

Julia smiled but did not stop her work.

"Lord Kirby Ramsgate, I hope," she said.

Richard, though he claimed other intentions, interrupted the session and in a moment Julia put the sketch pad aside and began cleaning her pen.

"Do not let me stop you," Richard protested. "Carry on, carry on."

Julia continued to wipe the ink from the nib of her pen and her fingertips.

"I cannot 'carry on' if you are going to insist Lord Ramsgate comment on, look at or decide about everything you have encountered today, Cousin Richard." She smiled at him forgivingly. "Besides, as you have pointed out a number of times, Lord Ramsgate has been held captive long enough for one day. We can complete this another day."

"If young Edmond here can find something to occupy him tomorrow, I shall return to continue my reading. I am starting on the Dialogues now and the Apology of Socrates. That work contains a favorite line of mine. 'Young men of the richer classes, who have not much to do, come about me of their own accord.' It is true. Twenty years ago his work attracted me like a lodestone. Now his work is familiar and I have reached that period of life when familiarity is comfortable, and comfort is the primary goal."

Ramsgate was standing by this time, deliberately stretching first one long leg and then the other.

Richard scoffed at the claim and invited Lord Ramsgate to join him in an inspection of the kennels to loosen the rest of his cramped muscles.

"And breathe some fresh air," Cousin Richard continued. "You are becoming delusional in this closed room, which accounts for your claim that comfort is your primary goal in life. Do not be ridiculous. Let us be up and away." He started toward the door but Ramsgate stopped to smile down at Julia.

"Now it is your cousin who draws me like a lodestone, Miss Masonet. Can you forgive our desertion of you?"

Julia laughed and waved the two gentlemen away.

"After a lifetime of association with Cousin Richard, I have come to accept the fact that he is unswervable once his eye is upon a goal. Take a biscuit down to Duchy for me."

"A very reasonable young lady, your ward," Ramsgate said to Richard, who had paused by the library door. "I will meet you with your sketch pad here at two o'clock tomorrow afternoon."

The two men left the library and then the house. Julia could hear their progression from room to room as they loudly discussed the advantages and disadvantages of various breeds of hunting dogs. Even outside the house and on the pathway down to the kennels Julia heard her cousin's distinctive laugh, and her lips automatically curved into a smile of appreciation, without hearing Lord Ramsgate's amusing sally.

She was a long time at putting her drawing things away. Her mind replayed the last hour, repeating every word and look of Lord Ramsgate's. Such reveries are pleasant enough, but their dangers are twofold. One cannot help giving added importance to certain exchanges and discounting other remarks altogether.

Chapter Twelve

Lord Ramsgate sat listening to Julia. His book of the works of Plato lay shut against his leg, his finger between the covers holding the page.

"I do not miss the academy," she was saying. "The days spent there were certainly fruitful, but they are all behind me. There is a wide world before me now. What is it?"

The girl's question was in reference to the smile that settled on and around Ramsgate's lips.

"I was only remembering when I felt that way about the world before me. As if I had unlimited time to see it all and make my mark in it."

Julia shook her head impatiently.

"You talk as if that were a hundred years ago," she said.

"It might as well be. It was a time before you were born, which is almost incomprehensible to a child of eighteen summers."

"Nineteen," she corrected automatically. "And it is not incomprehensible to me, nor is it so very long ago."

"On that, at least, we are agreed," Ramsgate said.

Julia glanced down at the finished sketch she held. Ramsgate had already seen it and made his comments about it, comments that admired her work while ridiculing her subject.

"And I would say that in the years, brief and few as they might have been since you made your resolutions, that you *have* made your mark upon the world," she said.

"An infinitesimal mark at best."

Julia sighed in exasperation.

"I can see there is no reasoning with you today. When you insist on being contrary you are as bad as Cousin Richard, and no opinion will do but your own. Very well, say what you like about the length of your life and its small accomplishment, but I think you are a noble man who has achieved much in a very few years."

Ramsgate laughed his deep, slow laugh and now closed his book for good and all and laid it on the table at his elbow.

"Oh, Miss Masonet, what a tease and a vixen you are. What do you want of me that you would flatter me so shamelessly?"

"That is not fair, your lordship," Julia protested. She truly was hurt that he would not accept her sincere praise, but now her lips twitched treacherously. "But as long as you brought it up . . ."

Ramsgate laughed again.

"You have taken undue advantage of me, Miss Masonet. What I believed was simply a sitting to have my portrait drawn, you have turned into an exercise in twisting an old gentleman about your little finger."

"Not . . ." Julia began, but Ramsgate held up his hand in concession.

"A mature gentleman. What is it you require of me now?"

Julia smoothed at the lap of her dress, a mannerism she used when she was hesitant or uncertain of herself.

"It is only that Cousin Richard has promised to take me to London next week and I hoped you might be persuaded to join us."

"Richard knows London quite as well as I do, Miss Masonet. But I am sure you know that, after your years with the Edmonds."

"Oh yes, we eat at the best places and see the finest shows, but a party of three would be ever so much more jolly."

Ramsgate shook his head. "I am sorry," he said, "but it is absolutely incumbent upon me that I go down to the Hall. Tenant complaints that need to be seen to, repairs I understand must be made, and Mrs. Flauerty writes that the chickens are not laying again. I do not suppose I can do anything to induce the hens to lay, but Mrs. Flauerty, hardy trooper that she is, seems to have met her match in that flock of poultry. If I can do nothing else I can shake my head solemnly and assure her that Saint Francis himself could do nothing with those birds.''

Julia had voiced a disappointed little cry when Ramsgate began his refusal of her invitation, and now she sat with such a stricken face that Ramsgate could not help but laugh a little at her.

"London, dear girl, will not be half so forlorn as poor old Wessex the last week in October. And the Hall is like a mausoleum. I really do not know how Mrs. Flauerty abides those great empty rooms all year long, but of course she has her own apartments, which are cozy and familiar.'' Ramsgate paused and raised his eyes to look thoughtfully out of the long windows on the other side of the room. ''It is different with guests in the house who fill it with noise and gaiety. How long it has been since those poor old walls rang with laughter.'' He looked back down at Julia and smiled. ''The walls really did ring in those days.''

Julia sat listening like a little boy hearing some wondrous tale of pirates and lost treasure.

"They will ring again," she said with determination.

For a half moment it seemed that Ramsgate was almost fired by Julia's enthusiasm, but then he shrugged his shoulders.

"It requires a great deal of time and effort to manage a house party. More time and effort than I am willing to devote to it.''

"I could do it for you," Julia offered eagerly. Ramsgate would have dismissed her proposal with a smile, but the young woman would not let him. "I would love to make all the arrangements. I do not know your friends or neighbors or whoever it is you would like to include, but you could give me a list, and then, naturally, I would have to go down to Ramsgate Hall and consult with your housekeeper. If there has not been a party in the Hall since she came to your employ, we two would have to work very closely together. I trust she could take care of the menus, or at least offer suggestions with her greater knowledge of what would be available in the country at this time of year. And I, well, certainly I would not be the hostess. *You* are the host in your own home, but I would be the power behind the throne."

"You make it sound so feasible, my dear," Ramsgate said, interrupting Julia and slowing her headlong flight of fancy. "Richard! Come in here my boy and save me and Ramsgate Hall from your ward's impetuosity."

Richard, whom Lord Ramsgate had seen passing the library door, returned and entered the room.

"I thought you two were still incommunicado, that the library was *terrain défendu* to the unwashed masses," he said.

"My picture is completed, or at least Miss Masonet says it has reached a point of such perfection that another stroke of the pen would ruin the entire effect. For myself, I find it looks too much like me to be really pleasing and wish the girl possessed a little less integrity as an artist."

Richard stepped toward Julia to study the finished sketch, but Ramsgate rose from his chair and stopped him.

"The portrait is quite delightful, but now your ward proposes invading Ramsgate Hall and making me—heaven forfend!—a contributing, convivial member of my community."

Julia still sat in her chair and the two men loomed together over her, Lord Ramsgate with an unconvincing scowl on his face and Cousin Richard with a look of confusion on his.

"What our friend is protesting against so strenuously is a house party at Ramsgate Hall that I have volunteered to supervise for him," she said sweetly.

"You see what the girl does?" Ramsgate asked Richard. "She makes it all seem so reasonable, so simple, even—if you can imagine it—delightful."

"A house party at the Hall? A hunting party?" Richard mused, ignoring Ramsgate's ravings. "Granted, your birds would not be in any grave danger from me, but one does like to get out and blast away fruitlessly at things now and then."

"And we would ask other of his lordship's friends and neighbors down for the week. All the gentlemen could hunt or fish and all the ladies could enjoy themselves. There would be cribbage and whist in the evenings, generously augmented by performances of guests skilled in some pleasing art, as, I am certain, everyone of Lord Ramsgate's acquaintances surely is."

"And when would this week of grand festivities take place?" Richard asked.

"We were talking about the last week of October," Julia told him.

Richard nodded. "Yes, yes, I could arrange it. But would that give you enough time, Julia? I assume you realize there will be endless details to which you will have to attend?"

"Lord Ramsgate's housekeeper would help me."

"Wait a moment . . ." Ramsgate began.

"I really think a very respectable party could be gathered at this time of year," Richard said, cutting him off.

"Oh yes, very respectable. And though I am hardly an authority on the subject, the deer or grouse or whatever it is you intend to tramp noisily after should be running about the parkland in great droves, is that not true, your lordship?"

"If I might . . ." Ramsgate tried again.

"Well, up and about then, Julia," Richard urged. "Things like this do not arrange themselves. I will have to go back up to London right away then, and I am afraid I will not be able to take you with me. Do you mind awfully?"

"No, this will give me plenty to do," Julia reassured him. "And then I *will* have to go down to Ramsgate Hall early in October." Now she stood and started gathering her art supplies. "So much to do and so little time," she said distractedly. "I do wish you had given me more warning, Lord Ramsgate."

She and Richard hurried from the room together, leaving Ramsgate to stare at the empty doorway dumbfounded.

What, exactly, had happened here?

"Julia will need that list of names from you today, Kirby," Richard said, looking into the library again, disturbing Ramsgate's confused reverie.

And that is how Ramsgate Hall finally came to host another house party after so many years.

* * *

Julia was thrilled and excited and very nearly plowed under by the twenty-third of October. She was so eager to spend a few weeks at Ramsgate Hall, to have further, daily contact with Lord Ramsgate, that she plunged headlong into the project without having any idea of the depth or temperature of the water. She found it was scalding hot and nearly fathomless.

Lord Ramsgate, helplessly carried along on the tidal wave of Julia's enthusiasm, provided her with one of Winifred's old guest lists. Sir Percy Lyons was dead now, and Reginald von Simmons had embarrassed himself at the gaming tables in Monte Carlo and might as well have been dead, but Ramsgate went over the remaining names, and as far as he knew, anyone else on the list could be asked. He suggested Miss Masonet not try to orchestrate a week with twenty guests and Julia gracefully ceded the point.

Ramsgate left for Wessex and young Edmond agreed to bring his ward down to the Hall the second week in October to oversee the final arrangements. They all decided—or rather, Julia and Richard Edmond decided and Lord Ramsgate offered no objections or none that he was allowed to complete—that all the preliminary work could be directed by correspondence. A day or two after Ramsgate's arrival at the Hall, Jake presented him with a letter at the breakfast table. The serving man brought the envelope to him on a silver tray and offered no reply to Ramsgate's murmured, "Ah, Tunbridge. This must be from Miss Masonet concerning her house party."

Dear Lord Ramsgate, after agonizing for days over the list you gave me, I have chosen the following people to make up your house party: Alfred and Dorthea Tindel, Mrs. Therese Watterly and her daughter Grace, Mr. Jeremy Dice, Dr. Terrence Crane, Mr. and Mrs. Burton Buxton and, of course, Aunt Jenny, Cousin Richard and myself. As we discussed, the only duty it is absolutely vital you assume is the writing and sending of the invitations. Your friends and acquaintances would be extremely confused to be invited by a total stranger to a hunting party at Ramsgate Hall.

Ramsgate reread the names of the guests upon which Julia had decided. The Tindels were a couple not so very much older than himself but who had known Ramsgate's father, the former Lord Ramsgate. They and Dr. Crane were old friends from down near Southampton, and his lordship was relieved to see their names included. He remembered mentioning something about the Tindels, and possibly the good doctor, too, when he first showed the list to Miss Masonet. The girl, he realized, was doing everything within her power to make this endurable for him.

Mr. Jeremy Dice was a younger man, rather well-to-do, his father having made a great deal of money in some mercantile trade or other and then having left the entire fortune to his son. Dice struck one as being arrantly idle and flip, but the lad was no fool. He invested his money wisely, hoping for a healthy return on the marriage market. Dice and young Edmond were acquainted—if Ramsgate remembered correctly, he had introduced the two—which no doubt was the reason for his inclusion in the party.

Mr. Dice and Richard accounted for Miss Masonet's choice of Mrs. Watterly and her daughter Grace. Mrs. Watterly was a widow, a rather handsome widow, in possession of a comfortable living and an unmarried daughter of an age and station that might interest either one of the young men. The Watterlys were acquaintances of Ramsgate's from the old days. Ramsgate had known the Widow Watterly when they were both children and had fancied himself heartbroken when she left to marry Sigfried Watterly. He recovered very quickly and then married Winifred, and, when the Watterlys took a home in the country nearby, they had appeared regularly at Winnie's "do's." Ramsgate had not seen the Widow Watterly since her husband's death more than two years ago and found himself unexpectedly pleased to see the Watterly name on Julia's guest list.

Yes, he nodded his head, rather handsome. And the daughter—he glanced at the name again—Grace would no doubt enliven the party for Dice and possibly even young

Edmond, as well, though the lad was already more or less committed elsewhere.

With Mr. and Mrs. Burton Buxton he was not familiar. Neighbors of his who had the Kentworth Manor on lease. They had moved in since Winnie passed away and Ramsgate virtually quitted that part of the country. But as they were neighbors of quite long-standing, it was entirely appropriate they should be included on the guest list.

Miss Masonet had chosen her assembly wisely, and with only a small wince of irritation, he brought out his pen and stationery and posted the letters of invitation.

"Now, Mrs. Flauerty, let us keep Tuesday's menu and Saturday's menu flexible. If any of the gentlemen actually do kill something or land any of Lord Ramsgate's trout, we can include the trophies of their hunt on those days. The fish will not keep so long, I imagine, but we could have a few fish on Thursday, as well."

Julia and the Ramsgate housekeeper sat together at the large kitchen dining table, studying the menus for the coming week. It was Friday night and Lord Ramsgate told them people would start arriving tomorrow afternoon.

"You shall have one more morning, Miss Masonet, to check every detail for the thousandth time. Even the Buxtons, who do not live two miles away, would not think of coming before the late afternoon, and no one else will arrive until evening."

His words sent a shiver of nervousness down Julia's spine. When he said the girl had made a thousand inspections he was not exaggerating: bed linens, tea supply, firewood, cigar boxes, divan cushions, the London daily, the pianoforte and music room acoustics. Julia climbed up into the henhouse and down into the root cellar, across the lumpy mattress in the green room and through the narrow French windows off the small sitting room to see if they could be used as a practical means of ingress. She and Mrs. Flauerty decided they probably could not, while Lord Ramsgate smiled to himself at the smudged cheek and disheveled hair that were the results of the girl's latest inspection.

A dozen times a day she sought out Mrs. Flauerty with the latest crisis of monumental proportions, and the cooler head of the very capable older woman would prevail. Usually Julia herself had never presented anything but the calmest of facades to Ramsgate and the assurance that the mighty ship of the Ramsgate hunting party was on true course about to come safely into port. But Mrs. Flauerty had spoken with Lord Ramsgate twice. Once about the great oven in the cookhouse, which had not been used for ten years and appeared too dámaged to be of practical use now. Ramsgate inspected the oven, agreed that its days of contribution were passed and suggested that Timothy do all the cooking in the main house kitchen. Mrs. Flauerty warned that the house would smell of cooking, Ramsgate said that was not so very bad an odor, and Julia was told not to worry about the oven, that Timothy and the girls could manage "Not to worry" was an easy bit of advice to offer but not to heed.

The other problem Mrs. Flauerty had taken to Lord Ramsgate behind Miss Masonet's back was about some evident thievery that was going on below stairs. Lord Ramsgate asked if the housekeeper suspected anyone. She did One of the new girls hired for the hunting party. Ramsgate raised his eyebrows. Mrs. Flauerty nodded, and the girl was let go. It is possible that in her state of nerves Julia did not even notice the change in the serving staff.

It had all come down to Friday night now. Julia reiterated her suggestion for the Tuesday, Thursday and Saturday menus, which, surprisingly, she had only warned Mrs Flauerty of twice before.

"Certainly, miss," the housekeeper said now. "I have told Tim to plan on fish and possibly game during the week. He is prepared for either or neither."

"The tea cakes?"

"Iced and ready."

"Silver?"

"Polished."

"And Timothy promises not to drink the whole time the guests are here?"

"He does, miss, and he apologizes again for the incident on Tuesday. He attributes it to nerves." The rascal, Mrs. Flauerty added to herself.

"Yes, I can certainly understand that," Julia said.

Actually, the cook had done nothing more offensive than dance a simple little jig in the kitchen Tuesday night when Julia told him the pudding had been delicious and she hoped he would serve it for the house party. The young woman giggled, the cook laughed somewhat louder, Mrs. Flauerty had come to check the disturbance and certain accusations and subsequent pledges had resulted.

"Really, miss, you must not worry. I do not know how you could have done any more. It will all come off famously, I am sure."

Julia smiled gratefully and stood up from the table.

"I do hope you are right, Mrs. Flauerty. But I have the strangest feeling some great catastrophe is about to happen for which I am totally unprepared."

"Now, now, miss. There is not a thing for which you have not prepared. You and Timothy are both letting your nerves get the better of you."

Julia smiled uncertainly, willing to grant Mrs. Flauerty's point but nevertheless unable to calm the unaccountable trepidation she felt about the coming week.

But I need not fear, she told herself as she climbed the stairs to her room, the room with yellow appointments and windows that faced the east so that one awoke in a dazzle of sunlight every morning. She did not need to fear because dear Kirby Ramsgate was there to help her through any trial she might encounter.

She fell asleep with a smile on her lips, and echoing through her mind was the phrase "Dear Kirby Ramsgate."

Chapter Thirteen

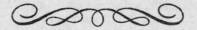

"Ramsgate, old man, it has been how many years since we did this? Too many, too many. You look about a day older, except around the eyes. Loneliness there. It creeps up on a man, Kirby. Ought to do something about that."

The speaker was Dr. Terrence Crane. He was the last of the guests to arrive, and his carriage drove under the Ramsgate arch as the sun was setting in the west, behind the hills that flanked his lordship's property.

Dr. Crane was a bluff old gentleman who had been Ramsgate's friend for years, though he had not, as he occasionally claimed, personally delivered him "mewling and puking in his nurse's arms."

He handed his hat and topcoat to the serving man, Jake, and followed his host into the main floor parlor. The rest of the party was gathered in that room, engaging in fitful conversation, at least two of them about to be bullied into a card game by Mr. Burton Buxton. Dr. Crane was introduced to everyone in the room. The other guests may all have met with guarded reactions and even guarded prejudices, but Terrence Crane was much too old to worry about presenting the proper image. He had always been too keensighted to be misled by others' images, so his impressions came the closest to giving a true measure of the occupants of the room.

Ramsgate took him by the arm and led him first to a brocade settee, on which was seated a refined-looking woman of the pallid English hue and middle years.

"Mrs. Watterly, may I present Dr. Terrence Crane. Crane, Mrs. Watterly and her daughter, Miss Grace Watterly."

The doctor inclined his head toward the woman and the slight girl, with hair that reminded him of dried bulrushes, at her side. Because his own head was crowned by long white locks, he did not feel that anything more than a polite nod was required from him. Dr. Crane had mellowed. When his head had been crowned with short brown hair he quite often had not offered as much courtesy.

"A pleasure to meet you, Dr. Crane," the woman said. "I have heard of you from his lordship."

"The pleasure is mine, madam. And if Ramsgate has been giving reports of me, I suppose a general apology is in order." They all laughed and Ramsgate and Mrs. Watterly made the appropriate disclaimers.

Ramsgate, in recalling the Widow Watterly, had remembered her as handsome, then rather handsome. What Crane said to himself was—Damned fine-looking woman. Healthy, firm build, bright eyes, even teeth ...

He also bent toward young Miss Watterly, though the judgment he passed on her was not quite so favorable.

Has her mother's eyes, all right, but that jaw probably came from her father along with his bad temper, I suppose. Too proud for her own good. Not enough money to tempt even the poor pups in this room to look past those pinched raised nostrils.

"And these young men being lured by the card table are Jeremy Dice and Richard Edmond."

"Mr. Dice. Come down for a bit of shooting, have you? Mr. Edmond and I have met before, I believe."

"Indeed we have, sir. I remember it well. A very pleasant meeting it was."

"Good memory, and knows how to pay a pretty compliment. Not too flowery but pleasing to one's ego because it is understated enough to be believed. Very good, Mr. Edmond."

Now all the gentlemen chuckled, with various estimations and critiques running through their minds. But Dr. Crane's thoughts were not only sure-sighted, they were also the least self-absorbed: Young popinjay, this Dice, looking for the most pleasure to be had for the least personal effort. Amusing enough, certainly sociable, generous, too, as long as he is not actually asked to pay the check. I may have been wrong. Miss Watterly's pocketbook may be bright enough to dazzle Dice.

Edmond now, the doctor mused, sturdy fellow. Have always liked him. Ought to be married but, ah well, cannot push the lad, I suppose.

"You know the Tindels," his lordship said.

"Alfred. Mrs. Tindel. If Ramsgate had told me you would be here I would not have dragged my feet so about coming."

Crane and the Tindels had known one another too long for any hidden thoughts to run under their conversation. What they said to each other they meant, and nothing more.

To get a fuller impression of the Tindels one should refer to Julia's first meeting with them. They had arrived just before Dr. Crane and Ramsgate presented them first to the Edmond ward.

They exchanged their greetings, with Julia smiling and thinking, What very pleasant-looking people. Not pleasing looking. He is rather too short and bald and she too...rectangular to be really pleasing *looking*, but one can tell from their handshakes they are happy people who try to make others happy.

Which might have been a very evenhanded description of the Tindels but for Julia's muddying the water with her final thought: No wonder dear Kirby is so very fond of them. He has a faultless eye for character.

But the Tindel introduction to Julia had been a half hour before, and now Ramsgate pulled the doctor away from his old friends to complete the formality of the exchange of names.

"Dr. Crane, my neighbors, Mr. and Mrs. Burton Buxton. They are leasing the Kentworth place, two fields across from me. You know the place?"

"Yes, of course. Fine house."

"Drafty," Mrs. Buxton complained.

"Expensive as hell to heat," Mr. Buxton added loudly. Mrs. Buxton winced at his profanity, Mr. Buxton guffawed. Dr. Crane's ruminations can be imagined. But he consoled himself with the hope that the Buxtons would be too awed by Ramsgate's estate, title and impeccable manners to become too obnoxious. Mr. Buxton withdrew a gray handkerchief from someplace behind him and blew into it coarsely. Dr. Crane had little hope for any saving grace to be found in the Buxtons.

"Mrs. Edmond, Miss Masonet, my old and dear friend, Dr. Terrence Crane. Doctor, Edmond's mother and his ward, Miss Julia Masonet."

"Mrs. Edmond, I understand his lordship has been staying with your son since his father's death. You have my sincerest condolences." Dr. Crane bent deeply over Aunt Jenny's hand. Mrs. Edmond, who had been cajoled into joining this party very much against her better judgment and every tenet of decency she held as true in her little Victorian bosom, was touched by the doctor's words of sympathy.

"Why, thank you, Dr. Crane. This loss is a recent one and still very painful to me."

"I am sure, I am sure," Crane said.

"And we must not overlook our little Julia," Ramsgate said, lifting the tone of the conversation, though not roughly, out of its melancholy depths. "It is she to whom all credit for this week's gathering must be given. She teased me unmercifully until I relented, and just look how famously it has all turned out. This may be the last time I give you credit for the party, Miss Masonet. I suspect I shall want to garner all of the praise myself for this week."

"Lord Ramsgate exaggerates on a number of points, Dr. Crane." Julia laughed, offering the older gentleman her hand, but directed her next remarks to Ramsgate. "And *you* may be wise to postpone your claim of responsibility until the *adieux* at the end of the week, sir."

"Mademoiselle Masonet is an extremely circumspect young lady, Crane. It seems our fine English schools have ground all of the French impetuosity from out her bones."

"Not at all, Dr. Crane," Julia said. Ramsgate and Julia were both addressing their remarks to Crane, but the conversation they were carrying on was between the two of them and quite exclusive. "The one thing *mon père* inculcated into my being was *insouciance*. What English schooling did teach me, however, was to accept the consequences of my thoughtless acts."

"Do not be fooled. Miss Masonet is only jealous of the honor this week will surely bring her."

Dr. Crane smiled back and forth at his friend and the young lady. But while Ramsgate and Julia were talking to each other, Dr. Crane was talking to himself.

By gad, his thoughts ran, the girl is in love with old Ramsgate. Look, you can see it in her eyes when she looks at him, how she leans toward him when they talk, the little lilt in her voice she saves only for him. Ramsgate, you blackguard, how do you do it? I know you do not set out to capture the heart of every young thing you meet. It must be those damned black eyebrows and that silver hair, although my head is every bit as venerable as yours, more so, and you do not see any young girls pursuing me. Granted, she is not the delicate, filmy sort of lass that foolish young men are prone to pant after like a pack of hunting dogs after a fox. And perhaps if she were the center of fawning male attention she would not find our elder statesman so very intriguing. But no, she is a thoughtful one, this Miss Julia Masonet. The attention she is paying him is not merely the result of frustrated vanity. And her vanity need not be frustrated anyway. With only a touch of sobering experience, she will mature into a stunning woman.

"Come along now, Terrence." Ramsgate pulled again at the doctor's arm, bringing an end to his internal monologue. "The ladies have already refused Mr. Buxton's suggestion of cards, but I know you enjoy a lively game, and they only wait for a fourth."

Ramsgate and the doctor exchanged a look, the one pleading, the other accusing, that suggested that, as far as the Buxtons were concerned, Dr. Crane had not been alone in his opinion.

"Yes, yes, come and join us, Crane. I'll not have Mrs. Buxton as a partner. Learned that lesson years ago. But you and I can show these young rascals a thing or two." Mr.

Buxton eagerly indicated the empty chair across the table from himself, and Dr. Crane had no choice but to take the seat with as good grace as possible.

"Very well," he said. "But if Edmond and I were to be partners, then you would see some notable card playing."

"Ha, ha!" Buxton roared. "And do you think we would allow you two to join forces? You are probably in collusion, have been since old Ramsgate sent his letters. No, Dice here and myself will keep everything on the up-and-up. Deal the cards, boy. Let us get this game under way."

Dr. Crane, who really did like a good foursome of cards, also gave up his hopes to have young Edmond for his partner with relatively good grace and settled down to serious play. Buxton was loud and generally annoying, but he was a fair card player and it is easy to forgive a man who will follow one's lead and save the odd hand with a trump. In only a few minutes the good doctor found himself smiling now and then at some of Buxton's beefy witticisms.

Ramsgate, relieved to have his one difficult guest occupied, even at Crane's expense, turned back toward the room and its fairer contingent. Ramsgate had nothing against a game of cards, but he could not understand why men would hunch over a small table, exhaling cigar smoke into one another's faces, when one could engage one or more of these lovely creatures in conversation. Judging from the eyes that followed his lordship from the table and the wandering attention Buxton had to reclaim roughly now and then, Ramsgate was a little hasty in his assumption that the other gentlemen all preferred to be at the game table.

As a matter of fact, Ramsgate's preference for the room at large was something of a departure for him, although if confronted with that suggestion now he would stoutly have denied it. It had been too long since he had been surrounded by a room full of comely females, all eager to hear what he had to say, watch him as he moved about, agree with all of his observations. In truth, he did not remember ever having been in such a situation before. Certainly he was never the object of female adoration when Winifred was alive, and since his wife's death, he had never courted female attention.

"Kirby, Mrs. Tindel and myself were just wondering if you have not changed this room somewhat. New furnishings? Opened that window on the east there?"

"Nothing new for years. The latest thing I can recall is this wall panel, which Winifred selected herself."

"Well, it has been a while since we were here. The memory tends to get a little tenuous, I suppose."

The Tindels returned to their quiet study and discussion over the appointments in the room, and Ramsgate was allowed to continue on his passage.

"Is the fire warm enough for you, Mrs. Edmond?"

The lady smiled up at him.

"I am perfectly comfortable, Lord Ramsgate. Thank you."

"Aunt Jenny is attempting to teach me candle wicking," Julia said, explaining the attention both ladies were devoting to the bit of white material and long coarse threads in the young lady's hands. "It is a lovely art, the mastery of which I am beginning to despair of." The young woman displayed her efforts and then leaned forward and spoke in a more confidential tone. "The evening seems to be a grand success. Even Mr. Buxton seems to be enjoying himself."

At that moment Buxton threw a card on the table and let forth with a great bellow of triumph and a loud laugh. Ramsgate glanced toward the table.

"Mr. Buxton's enjoyment does not seem to be the one in question there," he softly returned to Julia. The girl ducked her head to hide her appreciation of Ramsgate's remark. "But yes, it would seem you have done yourself and old Ramsgate Hall proud, Miss Masonet. To say nothing of old Ramsgate himself."

Like a grand potentate passing regally through the peasant throng, scattering shekels among the eager crowd, Ramsgate paused to distribute the bounty of his attention and then moved on. Julia was awed and delighted by the favor she interpreted from his words. Mrs. Edmond was rather amused by his posturing but could see he was doing it unintentionally, that he was only extremely pleased by this gathering of friends.

Mr. Buxton brayed once again.

And casual acquaintances, Mrs. Edmond added to herself.

"Mrs. Watterly. Miss Watterly. I see you watching the gamesters, Miss Watterly. You would have a much better view closer to the table, and I suspect the gentlemen would not object to a fascinated audience."

"I do not know..."

"We have you now, Dr. Crane," Richard was heard to say, and the noise Buxton made was not triumphal.

"My daughter has little use for cards, Lord Ramsgate," Mrs. Watterly said.

Dice and Buxton laughed. Mr. Dice made some remark that caused Mr. Buxton to laugh even louder, and Dr. Crane said, "Just deal the cards, Mr. Dice. An analysis of your opponents' failings and the failings of your opponents' progenitors is not necessary after every hand, though if it were, much might be said of the invertebrate, mucilaginous characteristics of your own."

Miss Grace, her eyes still on the players, absently stood.

"Will you excuse me, Lord Ramsgate?" she asked, starting to make her hesitant, seemingly undirected way toward the card table without waiting for Ramsgate's leave.

Mrs. Watterly watched her daughter for a moment, then looked up to Ramsgate with an ironic smile.

"However, my daughter can appreciate the masterful play of cards with a detached interest, I suppose." The woman laughed a soft, melodious laugh and indicated the place on the divan next to her so recently vacated by her daughter.

Ramsgate, before so conscientious of his duties as an impartial host, now sat down beside Mrs. Watterly without a moment's hesitation.

"I understand there is at present something of a turmoil in the House of Peers, Lord Ramsgate," Mrs. Watterly began, her speaking voice as low and melodious as was her laughter. "This Anti-Corn-Law League is making itself heard in political circles."

Ramsgate raised his eyebrows in surprise.

"They are campaigning for an abolition of the tariff on imported grain," he replied. "The P.M. does not like it."

"Mr. Cobden and Mr. Bright make some valid points, however," Mrs. Watterly said.

Ramsgate leaned back against the cushion of the divan and considered the woman, perhaps even her words.

"It is unusual to encounter a female who is well-informed on political questions, Mrs. Watterly," he said.

"Perhaps you have not been looking, Lord Ramsgate. Or listening. There are women of insight and interest in every gathering."

"I would beg to differ with you, but you speak as if from a position of authority. I am willing to allow your claim if you refer to gatherings of which you are a party."

Mrs. Watterly smiled but shook her head. "That will not do, sir, as a placation for my outrage." She did not look or sound outraged. "Intelligent women crowd your social scenes, but most disguise that fact for fear you gentlemen will find it too off-putting. Do you find it off-putting, Lord Ramsgate?" Mrs. Watterly asked, raising her own eyebrows slightly.

"Not at all. Not at all. I find it refreshing. It does not speak well of my skill as a conversationalist, but I find it so much easier to discuss intelligently an intelligent topic of discussion."

Alfred Tindel had been importuning Julia about something, and now the girl laughed protestingly and stood.

"Oh, very well," she said. "I will *sit* at the piano, if your wife will agree to play a charming little duet with me that I was taught at Hampton."

The two women sat side by side on the little bench in front of the instrument and Julia began to play the simple chords, which Mrs. Tindel more clumsily duplicated. Mrs. Edmond and Alfred Tindel, who had come forward to stand by the piano, laughed and applauded and the card players increased their volume to make themselves heard. Ramsgate spoke to Mrs. Watterly, raising his voice, as well.

"Perhaps I could read to you a circular I just received on the Corn League. If we repaired to my library we would not even have to shout at one another." He stood and offered his hand to the lady.

She accepted his assistance but warned, "Unless we disagree violently with one another, your lordship."

Their exit from the room went unnoticed. The card players argued and laughed, and the piano players and their audience *plunked* and applauded. However, in only a minute or two, Lord Ramsgate and Mrs. Watterly's absence was noted, and when they returned twenty minutes later they were met with a variety of greetings, from Tindel's broad wink to Miss Watterly's puzzled look. One reaction neither of them saw was the tightening at the corners of Julia's lips and the furrow in her brow.

The card game was almost over, but even with the closeness of the scores and the uncertain outcome, the cards were still not receiving everyone's full attention. Dr. Crane saw Ramsgate and Mrs. Watterly return. He also saw the friendly pat Mrs. Watterly gave the gentleman's arm before she released him to his duties as host once again, which gesture escaped several in the room, though not everyone. And he saw the first hint of pain, like a misty fog, wrap Julia in its icy vapor.

Dr. Crane was not the only card player who saw it all, and even Dr. Crane, compassionate humanitarian by profession and inclination, did not feel the corresponding ache that Julia's reaction engendered in one of their hearts.

Chapter Fourteen

Cousin Richard originally accompanied Julia to Ramsgate Hall. Julia and her bags and trunk and carryall and several hundred lists. Edmond was inclined to number them closer to a thousand lists, but he was exaggerating. A little.

He stayed at the Hall only one night before returning to Aspen Grove. He hated to leave his mother alone even for that long, but Mrs. Edmond pooh-poohed his worry and insisted she would be quite all right, and just who did he think had been providing all of the care in this house for the last several years?

Edmond suggested Millie and Julia, but his mother pooh-poohed those suggestions, as well, and he supposed she was correct.

Julia was nervous about the arrangements she had to make for the house party, but the onerous responsibility was a small price to pay to be alone with Lord Kirby Ramsgate for an entire week. And her expectations were fully realized. Ramsgate was helpful, caring, interested in her and what she was doing. He warned her that he could not be much help, yet he was always offering his assistance and often providing it to help solve difficulties Julia had never foreseen and had no idea how to solve.

"Julia," he kindly told her the evening before the guests arrived, "one shoots grouse and pheasants but hunts ducks. Something to do with stalking and lying in wait, I suppose. And for goodness' sake, remember not to wish anyone good luck when he starts out. It is something of a superstition held by hunters and fishermen. They believe it spoils their luck.''

''That is perfectly foolish,'' Julia scoffed.

''Foolish or not, I would hate to see you and one of my guests come to blows, which is a grave danger if you violate any of the shooters' mystic taboos.''

Ramsgate offered his warning in light tones, but Julia took it to heart and was glad she did when Mr. Buxton arrived and displayed what the girl saw as definite pugilistic leanings.

She consulted with Ramsgate on everything, though she had promised not to bother him. Yet he never appeared to be bothered or out of patience with the girl.

In the evenings, when she had worn poor Mrs. Flauerty almost to a frazzle, Julia would join Ramsgate in his heretofore private den, to which he welcomed her kindly. They would sit, Lord Ramsgate reading and Julia going over a menu or list of guest rooms or merely gazing into the fire.

''How terribly domesticated we have become,'' she would say to him, and he would smile and nod. But she would hug the rest of her thought to herself as she watched him read. Occasionally he would look up to find her eyes on him. Then he would put aside his book for a moment and make some comment about her dress, or the fine color in her face, or ask if the fire was warm enough or too warm.

We are like a comfortable couple, Julia would think to herself. Here we sit, night after night, at ease and at home with one another. Yet he comprehends my look as easily as I comprehend his. That if it were proper, if we *were* married, or even if Mrs. Flauerty would only go to bed, we would not have the length of the room between us. Perhaps we would not even have shirtwaist and reading jacket between us. She blushed at the thought and smiled slightly. Naturally, it was when the color was still in her cheeks and the smile still on her lips that Lord Ramsgate chose to glance up.

''What is it?'' he asked.

''Nothing. I was only worried about next week, hoping everything will go as planned.''

Ramsgate tightened his eyes critically. "You do not look worried," he said.

Julia smiled again but did not bother to refute his statement. If she did not look worried it was possibly because she did not feel worried. She only felt very much in love.

For six nights they shared that quiet hour, sometimes two, in his lordship's den, and Julia knew Lord Ramsgate no longer saw her as a child, as the ward of his young friend, but as a woman, as the woman who loved him. She also knew, from his looks and the tone of his voice, that he was beginning to love her.

She brushed her black hair until it gleamed like the glossy wing of a raven. She softened her deep voice and practiced walking with a smooth carriage instead of the ungainly shamble she had assumed when she outgrew her classmates by a head or more. Lord Ramsgate was tall and proud and imperious in the way he stood and walked, inspiring Julia to at last be proud of her own tall, commanding frame.

When Richard Edmond returned with his mother to Ramsgate Hall at the end of the week, he saw a remarkable difference in his ward, though he doubted anyone else saw the change. At last, at long last, she seemed to have thrown off the terrible shadow of inferiority that had encompassed her in her school years. This was the same independent, unselfconscious girl who had greeted him in her empty Paris apartment so long ago.

"You look well, Julia," he told her. "Better than well, you look happy."

"Oh, Cousin Richard, I *am* happy," she said. "But come in, come in, say hello to Lord Ramsgate, then let me tell you what I have done."

She hurried her guardian and Ramsgate through their greeting, and after kissing her Aunt Jenny on the cheek, she left the little lady to his lordship's stewardship. Fortunately, Ramsgate was conscientious in his stewardship and saw to Mrs. Edmond's comfort while Julia chattered away to her cousin.

"The rooms are all ready. Mrs. Flauerty and I have been through everything. Penny and Sybil have simply *flown* this week, this whole month Mrs. Flauerty says, getting the Hall cleaned and in order. And Timothy is prepared to include any of the gentlemen's fine catches in his meals. He is a clever fellow who will make the most potpourri sort of meal seem perfectly planned and harmonious.

"I told you who we invited? Yes, well, we have heard back from everyone—except you and Aunt Jenny, you thoughtless beast. I could only hope you would not desert me in my most desperate hour."

"Never," Richard told her quietly, but she hurried ahead, barely stopping to hear the word and none of the timbre that ran under it.

"Everyone is coming. Not one refusal. But how could they? A Ramsgate hunting party is not to be sneezed at." Julia spoke her last sentence loudly, for Ramsgate's benefit, and his lordship looked across the room at her fondly.

"Certainly not, dear girl. I hope if I have taught you nothing else, I have taught you that," he said.

"I have learned by lessons well from you, Lord Ramsgate," she vowed. Ramsgate nodded complacently. He did not hear the deep, underlying ring of sincerity in Julia's voice. Richard tried to tell himself he had not heard it, either, but looking at the two of them, he knew the ring had been there, and Ramsgate was supremely unaware of it.

Cousin Richard was not allowed to worry that fact, the way Julia accused him of worrying so many of the problems that faced him. She grabbed his hand in hers and pulled him up beside her.

"You must come and see!" she cried.

"What must I come and see?" Richard asked the girl, and then turned to Ramsgate. "What is it?"

"Just go along with her," his lordship said. "It will be something marvelous, I can assure you of that. Miss Masonet has been dragging me hither and thither through this place all week long to show me marvelous sights. Now it is your turn to be amazed." Ramsgate waved his hand in mock weariness at the two of them, but when they reached the sitting room door he called a bit of advice to the lad. "And admire whatever it is the girl has done. It really will be quite fine and she needs to hear that once in a while."

The look Julia directed back to the older gentleman was little short of adoring in its gratitude. Richard realized with a guilty start that Lord Ramsgate, in one week, had sensed a need of their ward that he and his mother had only casually and intermittently met over the years. Certainly, Julia was accomplished and bright, and the Edmonds had always assumed she sensed their quiet appreciation, which was as flamboyant as proper Englishmen were trained to be. But Miss Masonet was of a more demonstrative heritage and doubtless she had missed the words of praise she would have heard in her own home. Richard was ashamed of this thoughtlessness and vowed to be more vocal in his approbation.

He found the present opportunity ideal for the carrying out of his pledge. Julia hurried him up the stairs to the little, more informal parlor known as "the ladies' parlor" in Ramsgate Hall.

Julia explained the room's name and its use in past years as if she were a born resident of the house. Richard listened and smiled and even made little approving noises of which Julia may not have been consciously aware, but which made her eyes shine and deepened the curve of her lips.

"Now, though, I had Mrs. Flauerty and the girls bring up some books and Lord Ramsgate's field glasses and some heavier stationery. I believed this room would be an ideal place for smaller, more intimate gatherings of an afternoon or evening. What do you think?"

"I think you have been very industrious, Julia, and by your labors have managed to make Ramsgate Hall, already the pride of the country, even more agreeable." Edmond turned all the way around to view every part of the little room. "Yes, with a little fire in the grate it would be very cozy, even of a winter evening. Much easier to warm than the big open parlor downstairs."

"That is what I thought. And Lord Ramsgate already said he liked it very much."

"Then you did not need my approval," Richard said, dismissing his opinion. But Julia would not allow that.

"Of course I needed your approval," she said. "Not even his lordship's judgment can replace that of my dear Cousin

Richard." She hurried to the bookshelf to point out a book
about the heavens and heavenly bodies she had specifically
instructed Penny to place in this room. Cousin Richard, she
knew, would be very interested in it; in fact, it was with him
in mind that she insisted on its inclusion here. But for all of
her mindfulness of her guardian and what she imagined to
be complete knowledge of his life and preferences, she did
not see the look that crossed his face at her words or guess
its meaning.

Her aunt and cousin had been the first guests to arrive.
Julia *was* well enough attuned to Cousin Richard to know
he had timed his arrival on purpose so she would have an
advocate in her corner. They neither one needed to have
worried. Lord Ramsgate was a thoughtful host and the list
of guests he had given Julia included only affable people.
Even the Buxtons, she supposed, did not try to be horrid; it
was only a natural flair they both possessed.

Mr. and Mrs. Tindel arrived shortly after Aunt Jenny and
Cousin Richard, then Mr. Dice, then the Burton Buxtons.
While they were still being introduced and loudly making
their arrival felt, Mrs. Flauerty told Lord Ramsgate that
Mrs. Watterly and her daughter were just coming up the
drive. Ramsgate, who had patiently waited for his other
guests to disembark and summoned Jake to help with the
baggage, left the room at Mrs. Flauerty's alert to greet the
Watterlys personally.

Dr. Crane was the last guest to arrive, and his introductions have been noted.

Shortly after Lord Ramsgate and Mrs. Watterly's return
to the party in the library that evening, Mrs. Flauerty announced that dinner was ready, and if the guests would repair to the dining room, a light supper would be served.

Timothy's idea of a "light supper" included chicken Va-
lenciennes, asparagus with a rich, lemony sauce and some
sort of chocolate confection that was heavy and absolutely
irresistible.

By happy chance Mr. Buxton was a serious diner and applied himself to his plate with a single-mindedness at meal-
times. Around the table quiet, friendly comments were

exchanged as the rest of the guests made tentative efforts to become acquainted.

Julia sat with Grace Watterly on one side and the preoccupied Mr. Buxton on the other. Rather than disturb sleeping, or eating, dogs, Julia allowed Mr. Buxton his silent communion with his plate of chicken and asparagus and turned to Miss Watterly. Her conversation was almost as unsuccessful on that side.

"Did you and your mother have a pleasant ride over to Ramsgate Hall?" she asked by way of a ground breaker.

"Mmm," Miss Watterly murmured. The ground remained whole and unmarred.

Julia cut a bite of chicken and chewed it slowly, delaying the moment when her mouth would be empty and she would have to speak again. Briefly she admired Mr. Buxton and his two-handed eating technique, which guaranteed he would never be faced with the same social dilemma.

"And have you known Lord Ramsgate long?" she asked when the obligation fell upon her again.

"Mmm," Miss Watterly murmured again, this time with even less distinction in her voice, so Julia really had no idea what her answer was.

"Oh?" she encouraged.

Miss Watterly broke a small piece from her thin slice of bread and buttered it deliberately as she gave her cool answer.

"Lord Ramsgate knew my father before he died. Naturally I have known him all my life, and I assume he has known me all mine."

"I see," Julia said with her fork in a small stalk of asparagus, which she twirled back and forth through the lemon sauce around the edge of her plate. "How delightful for you, then. I think Lord Ramsgate is quite the handsomest man I know."

"Really?" Miss Watterly asked, allowing more genuine surprise to creep into her voice than she had in some time. "He is nice enough looking, I suppose, but I really thought your guardian would have claimed that distinction."

Julia laughed good-naturedly and Miss Watterly tilted her head curiously.

"Certainly Cousin Richard is presentable," Julia attempted to explain. "But he *is* my guardian." Evidently the logic that was so clear to Julia in that statement escaped Miss Watterly. However, Miss Watterly had demonstrated more interest in another female than she had bothered to express for years. Understandably, she was drained by the effort and turned her attention to the very small bit of chocolate dessert now before her, to pick apart every one of its several layers and examine it critically.

Julia saw that she had lost the young lady's attention and decided to let it go without a fight. Besides, she found that if she chewed softly and concentrated she could hear Lord Ramsgate's quiet words to his neighbors, which, meant for her ears or not, were vastly more interesting than Miss Watterly's inspection or Mr. Buxton's ingestion of the food.

"The Edmonds own a delightful cottage near Tunbridge," he was saying now. He sat between Aunt Jenny and Miss Watterly's mother. Miss Watterly's mother was evidently a more animated conversationalist than her daughter. The little Swiss clock in Aunt Jenny's boudoir with the milk maid who came out the wooden doors with a pail in either hand every hour was a more animated conversationalist than Miss Watterly.

"I have been to Tunbridge. Only last year, as a matter of fact. It is a delightful part of the country," Mrs. Watterly said.

"The wind can be fierce this time of year, September and October. But overall we have enjoyed Aspen Grove," Mrs. Edmond said, answering across Lord Ramsgate.

"Aspen Grove?" Mrs. Watterly asked.

"The Edmond homestead," explained his lordship.

"Lord Ramsgate tells me he has some family living near Tunbridge," Mrs. Watterly said.

Julia looked across the table, directly at the small group. Lord Ramsgate had never told *her* he had family in Tunbridge. Not this week, and not any time in the years since Cousin Richard first introduced his friend to the family.

"From over in East Grimstead?" Mrs. Watterly asked. Ramsgate nodded.

"A branch of the family of the ordinal number variety. Second or third cousins, I believe."

"Is that right?" Mrs. Edmond said. "I was not aware of other Ramsgates in our part of the country."

"Thornapple is the family name," Ramsgate said.

"Well yes, we do know the Harmon Thornapples. You might have told us they are family, Lord Ramsgate." Aunt Jenny's voice had the mildest reproach in it, which was as much reproach as Aunt Jenny's voice ever contained.

So. Lord Ramsgate had never told Aunt Jenny about his Tunbridge family, either.

Mrs. Watterly's soothing voice floated across the table toward Julia.

"I merely mentioned that I knew the Thornapples and asked if there was not some connection there. His lordship was obliged to acknowledge the relationship."

Ramsgate laughed. "You make it sound as if I were ashamed of my relations, Mrs. Watterly. Before she has you believing poor Harmon is a black sheep and persona non grata in the Ramsgate house, let me assure you he is guilty of no more heinous crime than having a forgetful lout for a cousin."

Julia's concentration was interrupted by an unexpected question from Miss Watterly. The question itself was commonplace enough, it was the unsolicited asking of it that was unexpected.

"What is it your guardian does, Miss Masonet?" she asked.

"Cousin Richard? He deals in investments."

"Investments?"

"The London Exchange. Buying and selling. That sort of thing."

"Indeed. I understand one must be very clever to succeed on the Exchange. Is your cousin very clever?"

Julia followed Miss Watterly's gaze to the other end of the table where Richard was sitting on the other side of Mr. Tindel, who sat beside Mrs. Buxton. The two gentlemen were speaking earnestly, evidently delving into some serious question. At that moment, though, Mrs. Tindel, on his other side, asked about the latest London trend as to buttons on evening gloves, and Cousin Richard turned to her with as thoughtful an expression, evidently as well-informed on that subject as national finance.

"Why, yes, I suppose he is." Julia smiled in answer to Miss Watterly's question.

Another ripple of laughter drew Julia's attention back to Lord Ramsgate and his party. Cousin Richard was dismissed and Miss Watterly was left to dab thoughtfully at her lips with the linen napkin before she pulled it through its ring beside her plate.

The meal over, the diners stood. Lord Ramsgate caught Julia's eye on him and smiled his congratulations. The first hurdle had been met and topped.

In the main parlor again, Julia hurried to his side, invited by his smile, enfolded in his warm congeniality.

"I think we have a success on our hands, Miss Masonet. I forgot how much I truly enjoy opening my home to guests. Or perhaps I did not ever know before. What a shaft of sunlight you have brought into my life." He smiled down at her and the smile she returned could have been the shaft of sunlight to which he referred. Surely, in that moment, he was like the sun to her and filled her entire sky. And in his sky, he was not completely unaware of Julia's little star, which twinkled determinedly in the night.

The next day, Lord Ramsgate went out with the gentlemen to hunt.

The women stood in the receiving hall to see the brave warriors off. Mr. Buxton had a wicked-looking shooting piece and Mr. Tindel had one that looked as if it had come down to him from the last century. The whole party laughed over it, but Mrs. Tindel averred that her husband had brought down countless quail with the gun.

"My wife does not exaggerate," Alfred Tindel told them. "What she does not tell you is that the birds come down, but only long enough to mock me before they fly away again."

Richard had the firearm that had been his father's, though neither of them had ever been great hunters, and Lord Ramsgate and Mr. Dice were without weapons.

"You must think of us as native porters who will carry your harvest of game," Ramsgate said. Mr. Dice held up a small canvas bag and everyone laughed again.

With a holiday air the hunters departed and the women went upstairs to their rooms or the little parlor. Julia was tired and lay down for a brief nap. When she woke the morning shadows had shortened enough to warn her it was nearly noon. She had not meant to sleep so long, and splashing a bit of the tepid water still in her bowl onto her face, she reprimanded herself for being so careless of her duties as a hostess. Lord Ramsgate, as landowner and master, was unquestionably the host, but since the house party was originally her idea and its reality due primarily to her efforts, she had assumed the role of hostess. Then, on the second morning, to desert her ladies for so long, what would they think of her?

How mortifying it would have been to her youthful self-importance to learn that they, like Lord Ramsgate, thought of her more as a star than the sun.

She rushed into the sitting room, full of apology, only to find an apology unnecessary as the women were all occupied and perfectly happy. Mrs. Tindel was mending a hole in the elbow of one of her husband's shirts.

"I am sure the Ramsgate servants are fully capable of sewing and mending, but none of them knows that the patch must be doubled to make it last longer, or that Mr. Tindel will not even recognize it as his shirt if I do not put one signature green thread in the seam I sew," she explained to Mrs. Flauerty when she asked for the shirt and a bit of white damask for the patch.

Miss Watterly was reading a popular, scandalous novel she extracted from a certain recess in her travel bag.

Mrs. Buxton had not retired to her room for a nap but sat in the large stuffed easy chair sleeping, her head back, her mouth open, issuing faint snores and snorts occasionally.

Mrs. Watterly was quietly talking with Aunt Jenny. Mrs. Edmond looked toward the door and Julia's entrance and the girl was pleased, and a little surprised, by the smile on her aunt's face. It was certainly a familiar expression; Julia could remember when Aunt Jenny smiled all the time. But since Uncle Charles's death, and even for quite a period before that, she had not smiled often.

"Come and join us, Julia," she said now, holding her hand out toward the young lady. "Mrs. Watterly was just telling me about another hunting party she attended with her late husband and the row that ensued over a partridge, no larger than a balled fist, I think you said?" Mrs. Edmond turned to the other lady for confirmation.

Mrs. Watterly nodded and held her own doubled hand up for Julia's inspection.

"Not as big as that," Mrs. Watterly said. "And the gentlemen would not speak for the remainder of the week. I believe they have partially, or at least publicly, made it up since, but only because they serve in the same branch of municipal government."

Julia widened her eyes and cocked her head as she took the place at Aunt Jenny's side.

"What happened?" she asked.

"Sir Suthern claimed it was his ball that killed the bird. Mr. Trevor Haag said no metal touched the bird, it was stunned by the noise and Haag's dog pounced upon it and broke its neck. The unlucky fowl lay in a sort of state on the dining room sideboard all afternoon until the cook insisted it be thrown out, that the flies were becoming noxious."

All three ladies laughed together, and then Mrs. Watterly rose to let Mrs. Edmond and her ward talk in private. Mrs. Watterly stepped to her daughter's side and asked how she was enjoying the book. Grace jumped, startled by her mother's question and proximity, fumbled with the book and stammered some sort of reply.

Mrs. Watterly smiled and told her it was all right.

"I have enjoyed my own share of light romance," she said. "I do not think of it as dissipation, but more as exercise for my imagination."

She left her daughter to return to her reading and sat next to Mrs. Tindel, admiring her work, asking after Mr. Tindel and inviting whatever Mrs. Tindel wanted to tell about her family. And what is more, she appeared to be absolutely fascinated and delighted by Mrs. Tindel's report that her youngest son, Clemen, was excelling famously at his school.

Mrs. Watterly agreed with the proud mother that Master Tindel was very probably the brightest scholar to have ever attended Bigalow's.

Julia asked how Aunt Jenny was feeling. Was she tired after the trip? Did she not think Ramsgate Hall beautiful? Did she like the room Julia had chosen for her?

Aunt Jenny felt fine, though a trifle worn-out by the journey; Ramsgate Hall *was* a beautiful old house, and she loved the room with its ivory and rose colored trim.

"And the flowers—late autumn azaleas, are they not?—are beautiful."

Julia looked surprised. "I wish I *had* thought of flowers, Aunt Jenny, but they were not my idea." A low, soft laugh came from the other side of the room where the other two women sat talking. "Perhaps Mrs. Watterly had them brought in," she suggested.

Mrs. Edmond nodded her head. "Very probably," she agreed. "What a charming woman she is. How lucky that you thought to invite her."

"She does make a very congenial addition to my party," Julia allowed.

"Oh, not just for that. For Lord Ramsgate's sake."

Julia laughed a little and Mrs. Edmond looked at her.

"What are you laughing at?" she asked.

But Julia simply erased her smile and shook her head. How could she tell her dear Aunt Jenny how fruitless were her matchmaking schemes? Lord Ramsgate was already spoken for, his heart already claimed.

A great ruckus was heard at the front door. Julia jumped to her feet and hurried out of the parlor to stand at the balcony railing that overlooked the front receiving hall. In a moment Miss Grace Watterly and her mother joined the young lady, but by then Julia was already calling down to the begrimed hunting party.

"Were you very fierce and terrible?" she asked.

Mr. Buxton held up two trussed quails and the rest of the gentlemen pointed to them, immensely proud to have done their part to free the neighborhood from the pall of fear the ravening creatures had spread over the countryside.

Julia laughed and Mrs. Watterly cried "Bravo!"

"I thought you and Mr. Dice were to be the game carriers," Julia reminded Lord Ramsgate.

"Buxton would have none of that," Ramsgate said.

"If he could not kill them, he certainly wanted to carry them," Richard goaded.

Mr. Buxton sputtered, but it was all perfectly good-natured and Julia was pleased that the strangers she had sent out this morning had come back friends. She took Miss Grace by surprise when she looped her own arm companionably through that young lady's to show that the womenfolk had spent their morning as constructively.

"Come up and regale us with your tales of prowess," she urged.

"I can see from here that the gentlemen would all like to freshen up a bit first," Mrs. Watterly said. "We will contain ourselves for a few minutes more and meet you at the luncheon table."

Miss Watterly disengaged her arm and said she would be in the parlor, but Julia and Mrs. Watterly stood together, side by side, at the top of the stairs, watching the gentlemen as they disencumbered themselves of their hunting gear and relinquished the birds into the custody of Jake, who would take them to Timothy, who would serve them fresh and hot—with some pungent sauce, Julia hoped, because she did not much care for the flavor of quail—in another hour.

When the rest of the gentlemen had dispersed to various washbasins, Lord Ramsgate, dismissing Jake with a final word, looked over his shoulder at the watchers on the balcony. He raised his hand cheerily, a look of great pleasure on his face.

"I will be right with you," he promised.

Julia returned his look of particular happiness, her heart fluttering to think she had brought that smile to his lips, and would for the rest of his life.

Chapter Fifteen

The week was like a fairy tale, like one of Perrault's beautiful stories of fancy. The houseguests were always pleasant—putting the broadest interpretation possible on the word for the sake of Mr. and Mrs. Buxton—the meals sumptuous, the hunting enjoyable and even, occasionally successful. The ladies, being ladies, courted the disagreeable possibility of discord, but the air was always quieted usually by Mrs. Watterly's gracious presence. Therefore they, too, spent the days alone together quite enjoyably.

On two evenings Lord Ramsgate had musicians come in to play for the dancers. The second time the musicians came it was Thursday night, the last night of the hunting party. On Friday morning bags would be packed, farewells said with polite little references to "doing this again" and "looking one another up in town," and the carriages would depart. But on Thursday night Lord Ramsgate asked four more of the neighborhood couples and their grown children to join the party at Ramsgate Hall, turning the final dance into something of a ball.

Nothing too terribly untoward happened all week, though at the time Mr. Buxton stepped on Dr. Crane's spectacles and broke them, and when Grace Watterly complained loudly that she thought someone was stealing from her—she misplaced her little coin purse, which she found again not two hours later—it had seemed tragic enough. But feelings were soothed. Dr. Crane had the good grace to laugh off the incident and Mrs. Watterly took her daughter aside, after which Miss Grace kept her unfounded suspicions to herself.

Mr. Dice and her Cousin Richard did not "hit it off," which was her intent when she included Mr. Dice on the guest list, but, surprisingly, Mr. Dice and Mrs. Tindel struck up a very happy friendship. They played backgammon for hours, insisted they always be partnered in the four- or six-handed card games, went for several long walks together around the Ramsgate estate, and often, in the quiet evenings, when everyone else was dozing or reading, peals of laughter would roll forth from the corner of the room where the two of them sat talking together.

"I might find it in my heart to be jealous of him," Mr. Tindel told Dr. Crane, "if it were not for the fact that Mrs. Tindel calls him Jeremy. A woman calling a younger man by his given name can only mean one of two things. If she does it in private it means they are intimate with one another. If she does it in the hearing of her husband it means that not only is there no intimacy, there is not even any interest."

For his part, Cousin Richard acted the male counterpart of Mrs. Watterly's happy influence. Where Mrs. Watterly would seek out Mr. Buxton and share a few minutes, or even an hour, of conversation with the man, a task no one else seemed willing to undertake, Richard would sit with Miss Grace Watterly and jolly her out of whatever bad humor she happened to be in at the present moment.

Mrs. Watterly was acerbic when she talked to Dr. Crane, matching his sharp wit, making the old gentleman smile in his admiration of her. With Mr. Tindel and Jeremy Dice she was much more gentle, softening the cutting edges of her repartee. She made them smile, as well. Nor was she a woman who was more congenial with men than with members of her own sex. All of the women liked Mrs. Watterly. Aunt Jenny's enjoyment of this forced vacation was enhanced a great deal by the private discussions she had with the other widow of the party. Mrs. Watterly not only told amusing stories to divert Mrs. Edmond from her sorrow, but also let Aunt Jenny talk about her husband and shared a few tears with her.

Mrs. Watterly somehow found out that Mrs. Tindel had been something of a celebrated songstress in her younger years and might very well have made a profitable living by employing that talent. What was so remarkable about Mrs. Watterly learning that fact was that at the end of the week she knew it and Jeremy Dice did not.

Mrs. Watterly endeared herself to Julia by giving her all due credit for the success of the party and praising the young woman's efforts. And Mrs. Watterly also grew to be on such friendly terms with Mrs. Buxton that the two ladies were calling each other Therese and Mildred by Thursday evening.

"Therese," Mrs. Buxton said, "do you think this bracelet would look well with my gown this evening?" Mrs. Buxton held up a grotesque conglomeration of tarnished silver and huge yellow stones, probably topazes, but if they were, they were very inferior topazes.

"I am not sure, Mildred," Mrs. Watterly said. "It might be a little too—heavy."

Cousin Richard perhaps did not put forth as much real effort as Mrs. Watterly—he never warmed to Mr. Dice and frankly avoided Mr. Buxton—but his presence was as calming as the lady's, his wit as gentle, his presence at any time as welcome.

Even as preoccupied as she was by thoughts and the physical reality of Lord Ramsgate, Julia was aware of what a popular favorite her cousin was. She was amused by the way Miss Grace Watterly suddenly brightened and turned a cheery face to the doorway whenever he came into the room. And she was strangely touched when Mrs. Buxton lit up like a candle the same way. Yet when Mrs. Watterly sought out her cousin or took him aside to enjoy one of her friendly tête-à-têtes, it did not please her at all.

But as the week came to a close and Lord Ramsgate announced his intentions to turn their final evening at Ramsgate Hall into a ball, all the petty differences that may have accumulated during the week were wiped away in an instant. Miss Watterly even forgot herself so far as to squeal the tiniest little bit.

"Really?" she cried. "Oh, I do not know that I have brought anything with me to wear."

Miss Watterly and her mother had arrived at Ramsgate Hall with a trunk, two commodious traveling bags and one modest-sized valise, full of clothes. The valise was Mrs. Watterly's.

Thursday, which might have been spent in dolorous meditation as the guests prepared to part company, was filled instead with excited activity. Mr. Buxton and Mr. Tindel went out shooting one last time in the morning, but even they returned early in order to be refreshed and ready when Lord Ramsgate's musicians and additional guests arrived.

A ball was not exactly what Julia had planned for this last night, so she insisted Lord Ramsgate join the last-minute planning session with herself, Mrs. Flauerty and Timothy.

"It is your doing. Now come and help sort out the happy turmoil you have caused," Julia said, grabbing his hand and pulling him toward the kitchen.

"I am not good at this sort of thing, Julia," he protested, smiling and dragging his feet.

"You are very good at quelling revolt. At least I hope you are, since that is what we are threatened with when we tell our housekeeper and your cook that there will be a ball with twenty hungry people here tonight."

Taking his medicine, Lord Ramsgate accompanied the girl and was amazed to find himself enjoying a discussion of the countless details that had to be addressed in order for his casually announced ball to be realized. And, predictably, his ideas and contributions were very valuable.

The disclosure that there was to be a ball that evening did not come as a complete surprise to Mrs. Flauerty. Although no one had bothered to inform her until Thursday morning, Miss Watterly had made some comment to her mother the night before about which shoes she should wear to dance in when Penny was in the room turning down her bed. And Mr. Tindel, pouring himself a brandy at the sideboard late that same night, laughingly asked Lord Ramsgate if his wine cellar was so well stocked it could meet the demands of hunters *and* dancers in one week. Jake was waiting to turn down the lights when the gentlemen left the dining room.

The guests believed they had been absolutely mute on the subject, yet chance words were spoken, ladies asked to have their hair done, the gentlemen all wanted extra shoes shined and special coats brushed. All of which was reported to Mrs. Flauerty by her invisible minions.

"Yes, sir." She nodded serenely to Lord Ramsgate when he told her they had decided to invite a few of the neighbors to their dance that evening. He spoke with greater care than he usually took with the serving staff, inspired by Julia's trepidation, which had been, in turn, inspired by six years in the same house with Millie. But Mrs. Flauerty was not Millie, and instead of outraged accusations, she merely asked Lord Ramsgate at what time his guests would be arriving.

"Not before eight o'clock," Ramsgate said, turning to Julia with a "you see?" expression.

Timothy was summoned. He did not take the announcement so well, but with Lord Ramsgate looming over him there was little he could do but sullenly receive his instructions.

Julia gave Ramsgate her own "you see?" look.

The planning took a little more than an hour and then Mrs. Flauerty and Timothy hurried away to begin their work. After they were gone Lord Ramsgate sat at the bare dining room table with Julia, conveying, as he always did, the impression that there was no place else on earth he would rather be, and no one else he would rather be with.

"Your house party has gone marvelously, Julia," he told her. "After sitting here with you and Mrs. Flauerty this morning, I begin to suspect how much effort you expended to make it so."

Julia beamed at his words, and the glow in her eyes and on her cheek suggested the added happiness it gave her to be alone here with him.

"I never thought of it as an effort. I honestly enjoyed every moment of it."

"Even Miss Watterly's unnerving diatribe?" he asked, one eyebrow raised.

"Perhaps not Miss Watterly's unpleasantness, no." She smiled.

"Or Mr. Buxton's..."

"Or the Buxtons," Julia admitted, and both of them laughed out loud.

"You seem to have a flair for this sort of thing," Ramsgate said, looking around him at the empty room. Julia saw the same friends and neighbors gathered, the same meals prepared and served, the same entertainment provided that Ramsgate was seeing. "The late Lady Ramsgate arranged for and was hostess at countless such social assemblies here at the Hall. Yet as wonderfully skilled and experienced as she was at her duties as hostess, your party has had an added warmth I do not remember in other years."

"It was you..." She hesitated before she finished the sentence. "Kirby. You have been so thoughtful, making everyone feel so at home in your home."

"Rather than exchange the only cross words that have ever come between us, let us agree that we are both equally responsible for the success of your endeavor."

"Of *our* endeavor," Julia corrected.

Ramsgate smiled and conceded.

"I hope you shall continue to be such a charming hostess. And I hope Ramsgate Hall will see many more of these festivities. The rooms have been too long empty, do you not think so, Julia?"

"Too long," she repeated softly, her heart pounding wildly, tears of joy threatening to break their dam.

"The house ought to be lived in, opened and aired. There ought to be a beautiful woman sitting at the other end of this table." He looked toward the opposite end of the long, formal dining table as if he could see the woman there now. Then he looked back into Julia's shining eyes. "I think you agree with me there, too," he said.

"I do," Julia whispered.

Now Ramsgate took one of the young woman's hands between his own. Julia drew in her breath and let it out slowly, tremulously.

"The week has been very special to me, Julia," he said, gazing earnestly into her eyes. "I have found happiness I never thought I would, and I have you to thank for that."

There was a knock at the door and Richard Edmond opened it.

"Ramsgate?" he asked, peering around the door. Julia and Lord Ramsgate still sat together at the table, Ramsgate still holding the young woman's hand. Richard stopped.

"What is it, man?" Ramsgate asked after a long moment of silence.

"Mrs. Watterly has a question about where the musicians are to be situated with the additional guests."

Ramsgate stood, still holding Julia's hand with one of his.

"I must go to her at once," he said. But he did not leave before smiling down at Julia and tightening his grip before he released her hand. Then he hurried out of the room, leaving Julia to look after him with an expression of transported joy on her face, and Richard to look at Julia with an altogether different expression. His, in a grimmer reality, might have been sorrow, but Julia could not see that.

"Kirby thinks he has done something terribly clever this evening, I daresay. Well, someone ought to inform his lordship that gentlemen of advanced years do not enjoy being caged by tight coats and—ye gods!—*ruffles.*" Dr. Crane pulled petulantly at one of the folds in the material that pushed relentlessly against his chin.

"Dr. Crane, please. I cannot get this tied if you do not hold still."

It was Jeremy Dice who was attempting to perform the requested service for the doctor. Crane had come looking for Edmond, but finding young Dice instead and acknowledging the fact that Dice's cravat, if nothing else, was always faultless, he asked that gentleman to tie the formal tie that stiffening joints would no longer allow him to master.

At Dice's injunction, Dr. Crane dropped his hand and raised his chin, but before Mr. Dice had a chance to make even one pass with the two ends of the tie, the doctor was speaking and wagging his head from side to side again.

"Where is Edmond anyway? Lord Ramsgate preoccupied the way he is, someone has to assume the duties of host."

"I believe that is what he is doing," Dice said, trying to match the movements of Crane's head and shoulders with his hands.

"He might have told someone—*ouch!*"

"I *am* sorry, but you must hold still."

Dr. Crane decreased his mobility a fraction. "And what are we to do for dinner, I might ask?"

"Mrs. Tindel said there will be a full buffet spread for the guests."

Dr. Crane humphed his low opinion of *that* proposition.

"Grass from the lawn and flowers from the hibiscus bush are not my idea of dinner," he said.

"Timothy has been roasting a full ham and several of Lord Ramsgate's chickens," Mr. Dice said, giving the completed bow a final pull that Dr. Crane considered a good deal too enthusiastic. "There, now. A knot good for an entire evening of strenuous frivolity."

"At least," Dr. Crane squeaked, moving his neck in an attempt to get some breathing room.

It was almost eight o'clock then and preparations were being completed in every part of the house. Sybil and Penny were getting final approval from Mrs. Flauerty on their appearance. Timothy was burning himself on a roasting pan he was removing from the oven. Alfred and Dorthea Tindel were dressing, exchanging tidbits of news with each other accumulated in a full day of being apart. Mr. and Mrs. Buxton were pulling down the bunched sleeve of a coat and pulling up the bodice of a dress that was too tight and too low cut. Their final adjustments were made in stony silence, the result of twenty-five years of being together.

Aunt Jenny was fretting. Though in somber black with only a dab of white lace at her wrists and neck, she still was fearful that her presence at a ball would be unseemly. Julia was assuring her distractedly.

Every sight, every sound, every touch was perceived by Julia as if through a gauze netting. Everything was muted by the love coursing through her body.

He had held her hand, smiled into her eyes and confessed the joy she had brought to him. Was it the same as the joy she felt? It must be. She remembered the softness of his smile, the pleasure he took in everything around him. She knew exactly what he was sensing.

She hummed a little air as she leaned toward the looking glass to make sure there was no shred of the plum she had nibbled, just before coming upstairs to get ready, caught between her teeth.

Mrs. Edmond smiled indulgently.

"All is right with the world when a young woman attends a ball," she said, then sighed, catching a glimpse of her own dark image in the mirror. "But there is joy more glorious than a dance with a handsome gentleman, and sorrow more deep than the fiddler's last tune."

"It is only a dance," Julia said, turning to her aunt with a look that suggested it was a good deal more than that. "We shall all have a wonderful time, and you will make a dozen new friends, as you always do."

"Then you do not think it will be too..."

"Absolutely not," Julia said, cutting her aunt's uncertainty short. Whatever it was Aunt Jenny was hesitating about now, it would not be "too" anything.

The musicians arrived at a quarter to eight and at eight o'clock the bows were drawn across the strings. At five after eight the Tudburys arrived. By eight-thirty the Bradshaws and the Devlins, with their three daughters, were there. At eight forty-five Timothy brought out the ham and two of the chickens and placed them in the center of the breads, cakes, pastries, mustards, pickles, fruit punch, roasted nuts, baked squashes and Yorkshire pudding already on the table.

Dr. Crane, who had sampled most of the food, nodded his approval when the meats arrived as if he had been teetering on the very brink of starvation.

The doctor felt he deserved some sustenance. He had danced the very first set with Miss Masonet, explaining that he must dance early in the evening while his vigor was strong and the call of the liquor cabinet was still weak.

Julia declined Mr. Tudbury's invitation for the second set, having to see to matters in the kitchen—Jake had dropped one of the puddings, which explained why there was only one on the table for twenty guests—but she accepted Mr. Buxton's surprising request for the third set.

By then the room was full and the air strong with the scent of baked ham, toilet water and perspiration, a combination that was not altogether unpleasant.

She circulated through the room, greeting the new guests who kept arriving to augment the party. Mrs. Devlin looked surprised when she stopped to offer a few words of welcome, and the Eurichs were completely confused when she met them at the door and instructed Jake to take their wraps. Julia smiled to herself over their reactions. Soon, very soon, they would understand why she was putting herself forward as if she were the mistress of this house.

Lord Ramsgate did not have a chance to dance with her, but she understood that. He had to make introductions, send orders and instructions down to the kitchen and dance with all of the women who had not been in this house since Lady Ramsgate oversaw her final dance here nearly seven years before. Julia did not allow herself to fret over his lordship's abandonment of her. They would have a lifetime to dance together. Their marriage would be one grand ball.

At nine-thirty Dr. Crane stepped outside for a breath of fresh air, which acted on the alcohol in his system, and sitting down on the grass "to rest for just a moment," he did not return to the ballroom until Jake came out looking for him, after the specially invited guests had all left and congratulations were only being offered sporadically by the party remaining.

At nine forty-five one of the fiddle players broke a string and Julia accompanied him to the kitchen, where he was able to make imperfect repairs. The quartet of musicians was not in tune for the rest of the night, but someone—either Jeremy Dice or Mr. Buxton—had laced the fruit punch with some strong alcohol, and no one really blamed the players if the music sounded a little queer.

At ten o'clock Cousin Richard asked her to dance.

She started to explain that she was too busy right then, that Penny was about to bring up another plate of sliced bread and Timothy needed to bring another chicken, too. But Richard would not release her arm and told her they really ought to dance. Now. Julia was shaken by his intensity. It was the first thing that completely penetrated the haze that had surrounded her since Lord Ramsgate released her hand and left the dining room that morning.

"Certainly, Cousin Richard. You are in the legal position to force your demands on me, but I will *dance* with you without recourse to Monsieur Naft." She smiled at him and was further shaken when he did not return her smile but soberly accompanied her to the dance floor and silently led her through the steps of the solemn quadrille.

At ten-fifteen the music stopped and Lord Ramsgate called for the attention of the room. Julia's heart caught in her throat and she started to take a step toward him, but Cousin Richard, holding her hand in a firm grip, would not release her.

"Friends and neighbors, it is only right that you should be here tonight. Ramsgate Hall has not been the site of such a gathering for too long." There was a cheer, but Ramsgate quieted it. "There is a reason the Hall has been so drear. For too long there has been no mistress to cheer it—or me." Lord Ramsgate paused for a moment and took the hand of the woman who stood at his side. A handsome woman, familiar to everyone there. Mrs. Devlin and Mrs. Tudbury nodded over this appropriate denouement, which should have come about three years ago.

"But there soon will be. If Therese will have a rascal like myself."

The smile on Mrs. Watterly's lips was an unmistakable acceptance of Ramsgate's unorthodox proposal, the duties of the Ramsgate Hall mistress and his lordship himself, with all of his stubbornness, idleness and deplorable shortsightedness.

The musicians struck up an only slightly off-key rendition of "For He's a Jolly Good Fellow." Amid the singing and laughter that ensued, only two people in the room were aware of Julia's gasp. She felt, and Richard saw, the blood leave her face. She was suddenly weak and the hand that at ten-fifteen had been an annoying detention, at ten-eighteen was her sole means of support.

"Julia?" he asked softly.

She turned on him a look of such innocent betrayal he thought his heart would stop.

"I must . . . I must . . ." she stammered dazedly, and without finishing or having any idea what she was saying or where she was going, she turned and wandered through the throng that was pushing forward to beam on the couple at the front of the room, who were already beaming on the crowd. Somehow in the confusion the girl got turned around and pressed along, and when she heard her name and looked up, she stood directly in front of Lord Ramsgate and Mrs. Watterly.

"Well, Julia, you, at least, were not surprised by my announcement. But let me thank you again for bringing Mrs. Watterly here this week. I understand I have been a blind fool for four years now and needed your impetus to finally open my eyes." Ramsgate smiled down at the lady at his side, but Mrs. Watterly was looking at the young woman with mild concern.

"Are you all right, Miss Masonet?" she asked.

"Julia was just saying how close the room has become. If you will pardon us, we will step outside for a breath of air. Best wishes to you, Ramsgate, old fellow. And the best of luck to you, Mrs. Watterly. You will need it." It was Cousin Richard, his arm about Julia's waist, holding her steady, while with his other hand he shook Ramsgate's hand and pressed Mrs. Watterly's fingers.

The happy couple turned to more well-wishers and Richard guided the girl through the maze toward the dark doorway and the blast of chill air that rocked her like a slap in the face.

Just as the fresh air had reacted immediately with the alcohol Dr. Crane had drunk, when Julia breathed in the cool breeze she at last exhaled a shuddering sob. Tears were suddenly streaming from her eyes and Richard guided the girl, now unable to see through the tears, to the garden bench under the willow tree.

The torrent of words that might have fallen from her lips in defense and explanation were unnecessary. Richard sat beside her and held her trembling frame, and the only thing she whispered was "I thought it was me."

The Train

The memory faded and Julia opened her eyes again. It had come and gone in a flash: the longing, the love, the desperation and the humiliation. Now she sat with head tilted back, gazing up at the ceiling overhead and the indistinct designs and irregularities she could make out in the dark coach.

This strange journey she was taking through her lifetime tonight suggested questions she never had considered before.

She had always assumed Richard's visit right before she was to run away with Professeur Davenôt had been purely coincidental, that his request for a dance just when Lord Ramsgate made his shattering announcement was merely chance. Seeing it all again, though, in the theater of her mind, remembering the look in his eyes, the tone of his voice, she wondered if his succor had been as accidental as she supposed.

In the dark she shook her head faintly. It was only because it had been dark and moonlit and he had been such a pillar of support. She was attributing more to his actions than he had intended. Much the way she had enhanced Lord Kirby Ramsgate's casual looks and friendly words into near declarations of love—and alone, in the dim train car, she blushed at the thought—she was attributing more to her guardian's caresses than had ever been there. It had only been the night and her devastation and his offer of comfort.

It was only two years ago and she remembered her unrequited love for Ramsgate clearly. Painfully. Cousin Richard sat with her under the willow for an hour or more that night. Once he told her everything would be all right, but she did not believe he said anything else. Just sat with her and held her and waited for the night breeze to cool her burning shame. She did not believe her shame would ever cool, just as she could not think that everything would be all right. But she was wrong on both counts.

Eventually the tremble of her shoulders ceased. The tears fell slower and then did not fall at all. Cousin Richard held her next to him with a strong arm around her shoulders, his chin touching the top of her head. She could hear him swallow once in a while, the sound traveling through his throat and down into his chest. Somehow, she remembered, she began concentrating on that, and straining to hear his heartbeat against her ear, and that which she did not believe would ever happen again happened. She smiled.

"Are you all right?" Richard asked. He must have felt the motion of her lips against his chest.

"Yes," she said, nodding her head wearily.

For the first time since he had put his supporting arm around her as she faced Lord Ramsgate and Mrs. Watterly, Cousin Richard pulled away from her.

"Are you going to *be* all right?" he asked, looking into her face.

"I really loved him," she said. It was not a direct answer to his question, but she did not know what else she could tell him.

"You speak in the past tense," Richard said. "Do you mean it?"

She smiled again, very faintly.

"Eventually," she said.

The night breeze rustled the willow under which they sat and involuntarily Julia shivered. Richard tightened his arm around her. It was like a spark in a pile of dried tinder. For a moment he looked into her eyes and then bent his lips to cover hers. They tasted faintly of salt, a flavor he tested and savored against his tongue. She parted her own lips to breathe his breath. He returned her sudden ardor, pressing against her lips fiercely, pulling her closer and closer to him. He raised his head and lunged toward the milky softness of her earlobe and neck. In a moment of blessed forgetfulness, she relaxed her head and allowed herself to revel in the sensuality of his mouth and teeth and tongue against her sensitive skin. With her hand she guided his head as he ex-

plored the hollow of her throat, the rise of flesh where the
bodice of her dress dipped low. With his hand he raised her
bosom to meet his hungry lips.

Julia gasped.

Suddenly he drew himself up and she opened her eyes to
find him gazing at her with an expression of alarm.

"What is it?" she asked.

He backed away from her. She felt for the moment as if
she were diseased.

"I cannot..." he began. His voice was dazed. He turned
from her, but she put out a hand and grasped his, keeping
him on the bench with her, preventing him from rising.
Preventing him from fleeing, which is what it appeared he
was about to do.

"Julia, you must forgive me, although what I have done
seems unforgivable."

"What have you done?" she asked.

"Taken advantage of you like this. You need my compassion and understanding, not my unrestraint, not my
madness."

"Cousin Richard—" He winced at the title she gave him.
"You have given me your compassion and your understanding. The madness was as much mine as it was yours."

"It is not only you I have injured," he said, shaking his
head, passing his hand across his forehead.

She smoothed her hair, her skirt, then stood and held her
hand out to him.

"Let us talk no more of this right now," she said softly.
"If I was weak you gave me strength. I can face the world
again."

Richard rose to stand beside her.

"But can I?" he murmured.

When they returned to the Hall, everyone but Mrs.
Flauerty and Penny and Sybil had gone to bed. Quite correctly, Julia Masonet had been forgotten in the joy of the
evening.

Just as she had assured her cousin, eventually the pain of
Lord Ramsgate's injury to her faded until, like a tissue of
mist, it evaporated completely. But unlike her silly crushes

on Philippe, the grocery boy, or Mr. Drummond, or even her passionate infatuation for François Davenôt, she had really been in love with Lord Kirby Ramsgate.

When Dr. Crane met Miss Masonet he thought a touch of sobering experience would mature the girl into a stunning woman. Her heartache for Ramsgate lifted, but it left behind a sober, beautiful woman.

A woman who at last saw Mr. Richard Edmond as something other than her guardian. With even more wonder and awe than she had afforded Philippe's kiss so many years before, she recalled the tingling sensation of Richard's lips against her own. She was full of questions, confused and unsure of what any of it had meant. But Richard would not answer her questions, he did not speak of his caress, or the moment the two of them had shared.

Aunt Jenny and Cousin Richard and she all returned to Aspen Grove the day after the ball. Edmond stayed the weekend in Tunbridge, but on Monday he returned to town as if nothing had happened.

In the two years since, though business took him to London often, he spent a good deal of time with his mother at the Grove. Their shared moment of longing and compassion was never discussed, and no reference to it was ever made, no matter how obliquely. At the same time, Julia was always very careful to ask after Lord Ramsgate, so his name would not become verboten in the Edmond home. Her guardian, she knew, was relieved by that. He would have shielded her from the friendship, but he did not want to divide his life and the people he cared for and Julia did not require that of him.

Besides, though she learned not to love Lord Ramsgate, she would always be fond of him, and she liked Lady Ramsgate very much. Her interest was genuine, her pleasure real at news of them.

A year later, for her twentieth birthday, she insisted Cousin Richard bring the Ramsgates to Aspen Grove for a modest little celebration.

"I can think of no two friends with whom I would rather commemorate my birthday," she said.

Richard nodded. "Yes," he said, "and it has been so long since Ramsgate has been here. Not since…" He stopped and looked at her.

"Not since last summer," she completed for him. "After Uncle Charles died. Right before his house party."

"No, not since then." He paused. They were in the small, cozy parlor, the one in which his mother kept all of her keepsakes. The walls and shelves seemed at first glance a disharmonious clutter, yet the room was instantly homey and familiar to anyone who set foot in it. Mrs. Edmond had been ill for a day or two and her son had come down in midweek to see that all was well. It was she who had mentioned Julia's upcoming birthday and suggested a celebration of it.

"And would you mind, I wonder, if I invited one more guest to your party?"

"Certainly not," Julia smiled. "Whom do you have in mind?"

"I thought I might ask Miss Brewster to join us."

"Oh, do you think she would come?" Julia beamed.

"I think so." He paused again. Mrs. Edmond and Julia were both working on bits of handiwork, and when the silence lengthened, both looked up at Richard expectantly. His statement had sounded like an introduction instead of a conclusion. He was standing and directed his next words to his mother.

"This will come as no real surprise to you, Mother. I know it was what my father expected—wanted. I have asked Miss Brewster to marry me."

Aunt Jenny made a little cooing sound and held her hand out to her son. Mother and son embraced and Julia looked on and smiled. But at her cousin's words she felt as if something had been torn from her bosom, leaving a great gaping hole.

They all came and stayed a week. Lady Ramsgate was wonderfully gracious. Her conversation was quiet, though always interesting, and she saw to her husband's comfort and happiness in everything. Ramsgate was occasionally thoughtless and already took his wife and her gentle attentions for granted, but though he seldom expressed it, she truly had brought more joy to his life than he ever expected to find.

Julia could see the deep satisfaction they both had in their marriage and it pleased her. Lady Ramsgate made him happy. As much as she had loved him, as happy as he could have made her, Julia knew she would not have made him happy. Not this happy.

Miss Brewster also came. It was a heroic step for her to take, so careful was she of her blindness, as if it were a fragile baby chick that must be cared for and coddled always. But with Richard's arm she braved the outside world, the world outside her bedroom and the dim sitting room into which she had welcomed Julia that first time. Julia and Aunt Jenny welcomed her now to their home and introduced her carefully to the limited range of this slightly broader vista.

At night the party would sit quietly in the parlor—Mrs. Edmond and Lady Ramsgate watching as Richard and Lord Ramsgate played chess, Julia and Miss Brewster talking, or Julia and Lady Ramsgate reading aloud. Occasionally during the days, Richard was able to cajole Miss Brewster into coming with him on walks about Aspen Grove. Julia was often invited to join them and together they guided Miss Brewster around the property, the two of them describing the scenery and telling amusing anecdotes of the people in the neighborhood.

At the end of that week, after her cousin lifted Miss Brewster into the closed carriage that would convey the entire party back to town, he turned to her and took her hand in his. Richard had avoided touching her for a full year, since that night in the Ramsgate garden. Now he took her hand and pressed it firmly between both of his.

"Thank you, Julia," he said. "Thank you for both of us."

She smiled but did not trust herself to speak. The carriage drove away, taking Lord and Lady Ramsgate and Richard Edmond and his fiancée and Julia's heart, torn and divided between them all.

* * *

The train whistle blew, jarring Julia's reminiscent thoughts. They must have just passed the crossing at Uttoxeter or Stoke-on-Trent or Congleton.

The train would pass through Manchester sometime early in the morning. She wished vaguely that the train was faster, could get her someplace quicker, but now she did not know where she wanted to go. Or rather she did, but this train could not take her there.

Just as the last year that she had hurried along so impatiently had not brought her to the destination of which she had been so certain.

She shifted uncomfortably on the seat and thought of the feather mattress on the little bed in her white bedroom at the Grove. The bed she slept in every time she came home from school, the room to which she returned when Uncle Charles died, the mattress that had held her safely in the dark hours, though not as safely as Cousin Richard had held her in her darkest hour.

It was a beautiful room that any little girl would love. She wished the next little girl to call it her own would be . . .

The blanket slipped from her shoulder and fussily she pulled it up again.

If only I could sleep, she thought. The quicker this night is over the better.

It was the same old refrain. She sighed. How many times had she wished for time to pass, only to find that what she had rushed through might have been very pleasant if she had taken time to enjoy it.

Now she put her feet up, tucking the blanket around them, and reclined awkwardly on the short bench.

Not quite the same, she told herself. She could not imagine anything in this trip ever becoming a pleasant memory.

If only I could sleep, she thought again.

Chapter Sixteen

Milestone Twenty-one

The little parish that included Aspen Grove did not belong to Tunbridge proper, yet for years the Edmonds and their neighbors had been without a local pastor, journeying into Tunbridge or down to Wells in search of spiritual guidance. Julia had never felt the lack as keenly as her Aunt Jenny. Partly because Julia was younger and the drive was always more of an adventure for her than a hardship, and partly because she had never, in her heart, stopped thinking of the Englishman's religion as *barbare*, stemming from her first Christmas on these shores.

She still took her faith in and devotion to *le grand Dieu* very seriously. It was the Church of England she did not.

But one day, after her twentieth birthday, as Autumn was beginning to whistle in the lane outside their house while he painted his trees and gathered his nuts and waved goodbye to the summer birds, a knock was heard at the front door.

Millie no longer served in the Edmond home. She was still alive, but she was old and tired and one morning last winter she sent her niece down to do the laundry. Millie found that Glenda could do the work—evidently she was satisfied with the girl's sour disposition—and not a week later she sent down word that Glenda would be assuming her place permanently.

The Edmonds were never consulted on the matter, so instead of finally throwing off the ill-natured inefficient influence in the Aspen Grove cottage, they merely replaced it with a younger version. A woman who would serve them for years and years and only get gloomier as the days passed.

"A Mr. Worthington," Glenda announced.

The Edmonds and Julia had been sharing a quiet hour after lunch. Cousin Richard had been able to spend the week, but he would be going back up to London on Monday. He seemed more reluctant to leave the Grove after each visit now. Julia found that strange. Cousin Richard and Miss Brewster still were not married. Though formally engaged for almost a year, each hesitated over the next decisive step. First Cousin Richard would put forth an unavoidable delay and then Miss Brewster claimed some impediment or other, back and forth. At the present time Rachel Brewster was nursing a cold and Cousin Richard was waiting for a market report on a herd of New Zealand sheep, though what bearing that would have on his marriage was a cloudy question. And now, instead of rushing back to London and Miss Brewster's tender care, Richard had put off his return an extra day, as he often did; a day, or two, sometimes three.

Aunt Jenny was perfectly healthy, but Julia was willing to admit his disinclination to leave his mother alone with their ward—and how that word was beginning to annoy her, in a way it had not since she was thirteen and first met her horrible Cousin Richard. Mr. Fenton and his wife were only one field away, but still, when Richard was gone, the two women were in the house alone. Except when Glenda was there. Which she was with dreary consistency. Like now.

"Mr. Sidney Worthington," the girl repeated.

Aunt Jenny drew her eyebrows together, trying to recall a Mr. Sidney Worthington, while Cousin Richard and Julia exchanged puzzled looks. Unlike Mrs. Edmond, they were very sure they had not heard of the gentleman before.

"Ma'am?" Glenda asked, ending the pause for reflection.

"Show the gentleman in, Glenda," Aunt Jenny directed.

Glenda turned and nodded down the hall. Footsteps were heard. In another instant the serving girl moved to one side and was replaced in the doorway by a young man.

Richard stood. Worthington stepped through the doorway, fumbling in his watch pocket, which pocket did not contain a watch, for his name card, which evidently the pocket did contain. By the time he and Richard met in the middle of the room, his search met with success and he was able to present the card—albeit bent and slightly soiled—to Mr. Edmond.

"Mister..." Richard paused and glanced down at the card. "Worthington? To what do we owe this pleasure?" he asked.

The young man smiled. He had a very agreeable countenance, with a supplicating smile that held in its gentle curve his primary goal in life: not to give offense. He was shorter than Edmond, no taller than Julia, if as tall. He had red hair and freckles, which made one think he was but a lad, though in truth he was twenty years old.

"I only recently left the seminary, ladies, sir—" Mr. Worthington directed his wistful smile at them all "—and have received, as my first humbling assignment, the stewardship of this parish."

"Ah," Aunt Jenny murmured with satisfaction.

"*Pastor* Worthington, then," Richard said.

"No, no, let us remain as familiar as possible. Mister is surely as much title as I want or deserve."

"Well, *Mr.* Worthington, it is a privilege to meet you. I know my mother is pleased. It has been many years since we have had a local curate to bring us spiritual comfort. Mrs. Edmond has missed that. Mother—" Richard turned to Aunt Jenny "—Mr. Worthington. Mr. Worthington, my mother, Mrs. Guenivere Edmond."

The curate stepped to Aunt Jenny's chair and took her hand.

"Welcome, Mr. Worthington," Aunt Jenny said. "We have missed you."

Worthington's smile wavered, fearful that he had unwittingly caused distress, but Aunt Jenny smiled and patted the hand that held hers comfortingly.

"And this is my ward, Miss Julia Masonet." Richard stood next to Julia's chair. Mr. Worthington took a sharp turn from Mrs. Edmond's chair and fell into a bottomless pit. He did not actually stumble and trip until Miss Maso-net looked up at him and smiled. It was fortunate that he had come to stand where he meant to be, because when she raised her face it was as if he had been turned to stone.

"Mr. Worthington," she said. Her voice was soft and low. Even after all those years in an English school it had the trace of an accent. "We are honored to have you in our home."

Mr. Worthington stared dumbly.

"I daresay Mr. Worthington is visiting all of his parish-ioners," Cousin Richard said. "Very commendable of a new vicar."

Mr. Worthington blinked.

"It has been so long," Aunt Jenny said behind them. "Where are you staying, Mr. Worthington? With one of the local families?"

At last Mr. Worthington swallowed and turned back to Mrs. Edmond.

"I am afraid not. But Mr. Bracken has a little house on his property. It once was inhabited by his gardener or gamekeeper, I believe."

"The Bracken gardener?" Richard asked. "That is more of a shed than a house, Mr. Worthington."

"It satisfies my small need. And—" his smile returned and deepened "—it will not be difficult to heat thoroughly in the winter."

"You must take care. It *will* be difficult to keep the whole thing from going up like a tinderbox," Richard warned, shaking his head.

"Cousin Richard, might you not meet with some of your neighbors and arrange for more suitable lodgings for our new curate? The light of dedication cannot warm a person through an entire winter, and if only for Aunt Jenny's sake, we do not want to soon lose our Mr. Worthington, now that we have found him." Julia turned to her guardian to make her earnest entreaty. Mr. Worthington felt a warmth settle around his shoulders like a woven shawl when she spoke for him. When she spoke to him. When she spoke.

"The Millers have an old henhouse," Edmond said, then apologized to the young churchman. "I do not mean to in-

sult you, Mr. Worthington. But Eli Miller was always more
careful of his chickens than Bracken ever was of his
groundskeeper."

"The old school?" Mrs. Edmond offered. Her son nodded.

"Perhaps. Though it, too, has stood empty for a number
of years and would need repair. But you need not get too
comfortable in your present abode, Mr. Worthington. We
will find you something more worthy of a churchman,"
Richard said.

"And match our words of welcome with deeds," Julia
said. "Which is exactly what you would admonish us to do
in your sermon Sunday." She smiled once again into the
young man's freckled face and Sidney Worthington actually felt his knees wobble.

Such was Curate Worthington's introduction to his parishioners and love.

He came from a home that had teemed with children,
most of them redheaded, though his sister Deborah and
brother Harold were both flaxen blond and clear com-
plected. Worthington did not begrudge Deborah her delicate beauty, but his envy of Harold's face and form was the
first sin with which he had to contend.

Two brothers had gone into the church before him, and
most probably another brother would follow. Harold had
married well and early, but his mother-in-law was a shrew
and his children were all as redhaired and even more freckled than any of his brothers and sisters. The Good Lord
forgive him, but that secretly pleased Sidney.

His belief in the teachings of his church was not apostol-
ically strong, but his desire to serve his fellowman was sincere, and the calling his other brothers had felt themselves
pushed into was the one Sidney would have chosen anyway,
had the choice ever really been his.

For four years he had dedicated himself to study and
training, the years between sixteen and twenty, the years
when other young men are dedicating themselves to a study
of young women. When he looked down on Miss Masonet
that day it would be no exaggeration to say that he had never

looked on a woman before. He had certainly never looked on a raven-haired woman with bewitching gray eyes and skin of an exotic, olive hue.

When Edmond escorted him to the door and showed him out, the young man stumbled home, dazed by thoughts and feelings that were new to him.

He did not complete his scheduled rounds that day. He had meant to call on the Fentons and the Davenports, arriving at the Brackens', he hoped, at suppertime. Instead, he returned to the little shed Mr. Bracken had so generously given over for his use and collapsed onto the straw-filled pallet that was his bed.

He tried to convince himself to be sensible. Who was he? The fifth son of a poor English farmer. The fifth of six sons and two daughters. He would be a very conscientious curate who would watch over his parish, whatever his parish, like a mother hen. But he would rise no further. He had no ambition, no brilliance, no drive, no determination.

When he left the seminary he supposed that someday he would marry a solid country maid who would care for him and his home with an able hand while he cared for his congregation. He would not look for anything more in her than capability. His brother Rudolph, his oldest brother, the first of the Worthington boys to go into the church, left the seminary with that same design, and Selma, his wife, was a perfectly pleasant woman. Nathan, on the other hand, married a woman who he thought was the same sort of girl and she turned out to be a fishwife. She screamed at her husband, she screamed at her children, and she and her mother, who lived with Nathan, screamed at each other.

Sidney Worthington, therefore, was prepared to approach marriage with a philosophic eye. He hoped for the best, naturally, but he was prepared to honor and care for whomsoever the Good Lord put in his way as a marriage partner. What he was not prepared for was to have his life disrupted and his heart stolen by a glorious vision.

He tossed fitfully on the thin mattress, trying to keep his thoughts in check, reminding himself that he was a Shepherd of God, that Miss Masonet should be of no more interest to him than any other member of his little flock. But

Worthington was young and in love for the first time in his life and he could not heed the council that men of venerable years and vast experience so often ignore.

"I believe the good pastor admired you, Julia." Richard Edmond spoke teasingly as he and his mother and the young lady sat down to the supper Glenda had prepared. Millie and her niece may have been ill-humored, but they were both excellent cooks. If it were not for that fact Richard undoubtedly would have dismissed Millie years ago, even over the objections of his mother, and so saved himself the unpleasantness of dealing with the younger version. But if the way to a man's heart is not through his stomach, certainly the way to a man's tolerance is.

Now steaming on the table was a roast duck, browned potatoes, a yellow squash from the kitchen garden, and if he was not mistaken, that was a cobbler he smelled in the kitchen.

Julia looked up at her guardian's words and shook her head in dismissal of them.

"Do not be foolish, Cousin Richard," she said. Julia, despite the changing evidence of her looking glass, still thought of herself as the rawboned scarecrow of her adolescent years and could not think of such a claim as anything but foolish.

Aunt Jenny, for her part, was shocked at her son's flippancy regarding the delightful young curate.

"Richard!" she scolded. "Mr. Worthington was polite and making an effort to become acquainted with the neighborhood. You must not undermine his good intentions with your imagined elaborations."

Richard chuckled as he sliced off one of the bird's crisp brown legs and put it on his mother's plate.

"That Mr. Sidney Worthington was taken by our Julia does not undermine his Christian endeavors. Indeed, I believe it was Saint Paul who said, 'Whatsoever things are pure, whatsoever things are lovely, whatsoever things are of good report, think on these things.' The man would be forsaking his teachings if he was *not* favorably impressed by Julia."

"Oh, Cousin Richard," Julia protested, embarrassed by his flowery praise.

"Richard!" his mother repeated.

He dropped the subject. He could see the women were not to be amused by it. But he knew what he knew.

He pulled one of the steaming portions of squash onto his plate and broke through the tough skin to the meat underneath.

"I will ride over to talk to Mr. Bracken and Eli today. I do want to resolve Mr. Worthington's living arrangements before I am called back up to town. It looks like it will be a glorious day. Care to join me, Julia?"

Julia looked up from her plate with a look of solemn pleasure. When she was younger she used to laugh and smile often, with little or no provocation. Now her smiles came slowly and her laugh was a rarity that Richard missed and sometimes set out deliberately to elicit.

"I would be pleased to accompany you, but you must promise not to tease me anymore," she warned.

"Oh, Julia, you have always wanted to deny me one of my most signal pleasures. But very well, I shall attempt to be on my best behavior, though you know how hard that is for me."

Julia murmured a gentle little laugh and Richard left the table to hitch up the phaeton feeling very pleased with himself.

"Mr. Edmond, you cannot mean my old henhouse. That is where the chickens roosted and covered the floor with—well, what chickens cover the floor *with*."

"That can be swept out, Eli. And the walls washed down. I am sure that Mr. Worthington only wants to know if your chickens were warm in the wintertime."

"I kept new hatched chicks in there in February. Never lost a one to the cold. But this is a churchman, Mr. Edmond. How can I ask him to stay in a henhouse? It just does not seem decent to me."

"What is not decent is Mr. Worthington spending another night in that little lean-to Bracken calls a gardener's hut."

"I don't know..."

"Judging by your own lovely home, I believe Mrs. Miller could have the little building as clean and snug as any room in Londontown by this afternoon." It was Julia who spoke now, making her first contribution to Cousin Richard's negotiations.

Deborah Miller, who had been, like the younger woman, silently listening to the discussion, beamed in pleasure and looked around her at the very comfortable home she kept for her husband and the two children still living there.

"The place always was too good for chickens, Eli," Mrs. Miller said. "If you were to take that little stove out there while I cleaned it up some, nobody, not even your fine Mr. Worthington, would know it was not our own gardener's hut. And a sight better than the one on Bracken's property."

Eli Miller continued to hem and haw, but now that the enemy line had moved into his own camp, the battle was lost.

"You can tell Mr. Worthington he can move in tomorrow morning, Mr. Edmond," Mrs. Miller said.

Over the first hurdle, Richard and Julia returned to the carriage to face the next one: the redoubtable Woodward Bracken.

Mr. Bracken owned a piece of land. It was no larger than the property at Aspen Grove, but it included a rise of ground that Bracken called a "mountain." For some reason that hill and the title he gave it made Mr. Bracken believe that he was a Very Fine Person. It might be argued that Mr. Bracken's claim to prominence was no less valid than the man whose political ambitions have raised him to the heady position of borough alderman, or his neighbor, whose grandfather was a pinchpenny usurer who passed the trait and a box full of money down to his descendants.

Bracken rather liked the feudal idea of his own churchman quartered on the Bracken land, and he was not pleased when Mr. Richard Edmond suggested he, the churchman, be relocated.

"I am sure that what was good enough for my groundsman is quite good enough for a mere lad of a curate straight

out of the seminary," Bracken told Edmond when he spoke
of "better quarters in the neighborhood."

"What was good enough for your groundsman would not
be good enough for..." Richard began angrily, but Julia put
her long-fingered, slender hand across his own.

"My cousin is concerned about Mr. Worthington's avail-
ability to his parishioners. Granted, we are a very small
parish, but your gardener's lodgings are a bit secluded and
not easily approached, as the leader of a congregation's
must be."

"The place is not hidden away. Folks can find it easily
enough."

"Yes, that is true," Julia agreed. "But that suggests the
other, more serious problem, of people from all over the
country crossing your lands, your own grounds. You can
imagine what that would mean." She paused for a breath to
give Mr. Bracken's imagination time to catch up with her.
"Of course..." And now Julia stopped to smile her sweetest
smile into Mr. Bracken's red and puffy face. Though a
woman unconscious of her own stunning beauty, Julia did
use her charms with an intuitive skill. "The old schoolhouse you so generously built on your own land is in an ideal
location. Since it is no longer in use, we wondered why you
did not offer it to Mr. Worthington, until we considered the
expense of the renovations, which would be minimal, com-
bined with the unseemly attention such a project would
draw."

With the ease of swatting a fly, the young woman had extinguished Bracken's anger and turned his thoughts toward
the building, sound enough, still on the Bracken properties, but facing the public road—adjacent to, he noted, "the
mountain." He also agreeably considered the awe and admiration of his neighbors if he were to undertake such a
charitable project.

"It could not be readied in anything less than a month,"
Bracken said reflectively. The little shack Lenny, his one-
time groundskeeper, had used had required no such attentions. Not because it was in any better repair than the
schoolhouse, but, as Miss Masonet said, it was secluded, out
of sight, back behind his own home. The school was out on

the public thoroughfare, or at least as public a thorough-fare as the little neighborhood boasted. People would pass it and say to one another—in an admiring tone of voice—"That is where the Bracken minister lives." It must be a jolly little house, welcoming to church members and altogether representative of Bracken quality. And importance.

"I am sure Mr. Worthington can be comfortable with the Millers for that long. He would be out of your way and would give your workmen free range."

"Yes, yes. True enough."

"He is a dedicated gentleman and never says any but the kindest words for the generosity you have already shown him. But perhaps moving to the old school that you have refurbished into a comfortable parsonage will give the rest of the parish an opportunity to say the same things," Julia coaxed and soothed in her soft, gentle voice. Bracken nodded sagely and Edmond very wisely kept his expression neutral, though at times it was a struggle to quell his smiles over Julia's skillful manipulation.

"Now see here, Edmond, if you had explained it to me as carefully and completely as Miss Masonet has done, we might not have had that little flare-up of tempers there. The ladies always can see it better than two headstrong men, though, can they not?"

"Indeed," Richard returned ironically, careful, too, to keep the ironic note very soft.

They all exchanged harmless little bits of news about their homes. Edmond's mother was very well, thank you. Molly Bracken was over her toothache but now one of the boys had sprained his ankle. If it was not one thing it was another.

Mrs. Bracken brought in some lemonade, which, as the afternoon cooled, Julia wished was hot tea, and, as the afternoon lengthened, Richard wished was something stronger. Nevertheless, they drank it, Julia offered to stop at Mr. Worthington's place on the way home and tell him of the plan, and Mr. Bracken and Mr. Edmond shook hands warmly, which had not at first appeared to be the way this interview would end.

* * *

"*You* are a vixen and an imp, Julia Masonet. If your voice was the least bit shrill, people would call you a termagent. Instead, you speak softly and grown men collapse helplessly at your feet."

Julia looked solemnly at her cousin, but Richard saw the twinkle in her eye and the twitch at the corner of her mouth.

"And you know it, you scamp."

Julia's smile broke. "I know that if I had not been there, poor Mr. Worthington would have stayed in the gardener's hut, if he had been allowed to stay at all."

"As a man of business I have prided myself on my tact, but I bow to a greater authority." Richard did offer a little mock bow before helping the girl up into the carriage.

By taking the circuitous route behind the Bracken home and past the farm outbuildings, they came a few minutes later to the tiny shack Bracken euphemistically called his groundsman's hut. There was not a window opening in any of the walls, but Worthington was nevertheless out the door and greeting Richard and Julia before the phaeton came to a stop.

"I am honored by your visit. Deeply honored," he said, believing he was speaking to both of them, though his eyes never left Julia's face for an instant. "I did not know how prompt one is in the country to return calls, else I would have . . ." He waved his hand vaguely, because there was no ending to that sentence. There really was not a thing he could have done with his abode to prepare for guests, and with his meager supplies and primitive facilities he could not have offered them any eatables whatever his forewarning.

"I hope our visit will be even more welcome than you imagine," Richard said, looking down on the young fellow. But as he watched Mr. Worthington watching Julia, he did not believe that anything he could say would make this visit any more welcome than it already was.

"Miss Masonet, you do not find the afternoon ride too cool, I hope?" Worthington asked anxiously.

"It was somewhat warmer when we began," she said.

"Could I offer you a cup of tea? It would only take a moment. . . ."

"We will deliver our news and be on our way, Worthington. Get Miss Masonet in front of her own fire, that is what is best for her."

"Of course, of course," Worthington quickly agreed, sounding like a little boy whose first proffered bouquet of wildflowers has been ridiculed. The tone cut straight to Julia's heart. Richard was even touched and he was a mature gentleman viewing this whole production with an indulgent eye.

"Cousin Richard, I really do feel that a cup of tea would do me good. If it would not trouble the curate too much?"

Life sprang to Worthington's eyes. He insisted it was nothing, would take no time, was lovely to be allowed the chance to be hospitable, was a treat to have guests in his humble abode, assured them that once inside it was actually very cozy—which Edmond had no trouble believing; he only wondered if the three of them could actually fit in there—and offered, tremulously, his hand to help Miss Masonet down.

Julia took the curate's hand and stepped gracefully from the box. She might have been the queen herself as Worthington showed her the path and pointed out the autumn foliage that still clung to its stems. If he had had a red carpet he surely would have rolled it out for her. Lacking that, he would have laid his cloak at her feet to step upon, if he had had a cloak other than his poor little jacket.

"I believe that, given a few more days to tidy up, the room will be quite satisfactory," he said, opening the door to the gloomy den.

Julia went in—Richard admired her for not hesitating at the doorstep—and her cousin followed. There was one chair before the plank that was evidently serving as table, desk and all-purpose work area, but Worthington pulled a wooden box from under his cot for Richard and insisted he would stand himself, that he would be busy with the tea anyway.

"I will put a few shelves over here," Worthington said, lighting a fire in the cubbyhole of a stove, "and they will fill my modest storage needs, I am sure."

"You must not make yourself too comfortable here, Mr. Worthington," Richard said. "You will be reluctant to move."

"Move?"

"We have been visiting your parishioners today. My mother would be appalled to at last have a local curate, only to find him lodged in a place like this." Richard looked around the room and Worthington followed his gaze.

"It is unprepossessing, I admit..."

"It is hideous," Richard corrected.

"But I assure you it is all that I require. I would not want to lose my position over something so paltry as—Spartan living quarters."

"Your humility becomes you, but perhaps so deep a humility is not necessary in this instance," Richard said.

Worthington drew his brows together in his effort to understand the other man.

"What my cousin is trying to tell you, Mr. Worthington, although not terribly tactfully or successfully, is that we were determined to arrange better living quarters for you, not another position," Julia said, hers once again the voice of reason.

"Good heavens, no!" Richard exclaimed. "My dear mother would have you move in with us before she would let you go, now that she has acquired you."

"I am not sure..." Worthington said faintly, the tea, for the moment, forgotten.

"We spoke with Mr. Miller first and he will have a— building on his property readied for you tomorrow," Julia said. She did not specify exactly what sort of building it was, but her Cousin Richard was not so careful of the younger man's sensibilities.

"It is the chicken coop we talked about this morning, Mr. Worthington. A sound, warm, roomy chicken coop, which Mrs. Miller will have cleaned with curtains on the windows and fresh straw on the floor when you arrive."

"I do not know what to say," Worthington said hesitantly, honestly at a loss for words to express his feelings about the dubious favor done him.

"But you must not make yourself too much at home there, either," Julia reassured him. "We also spoke with Mr. Bracken and suggested that, with a few repairs, the schoolhouse no longer in use on *his* property would make an ideal parsonage."

"What Miss Masonet suggested was that a curate in a comfortable home on a very visible part of his land would be seen as extremely admirable of Mr. Bracken. And Mr. Bracken likes to save money, but he loves public admiration."

"I will not have you belittling Mr. Bracken, cousin. He is going to prepare a comfortable home for our Mr. Worthington, for which he deserves gratitude and a good deal of that admiration of which you are so stingy."

"Very well, Julia. Woodward Bracken is a prince among men, an angel in disguise. Do you not agree, Mr. Worthington?"

But all that Worthington had heard was that someone was an angel, and there was no question in his mind who that angel was.

Chapter Seventeen

Cousin Richard did return to London, called away on business he could no longer ignore. Julia was correct; he did not hurry away from the Grove to be with Miss Brewster, but hers was certainly the first door upon which he knocked when he returned to London.

It was not Lawrence, the serving man, but Mr. Clyde Brewster himself who answered the summons and showed Richard into the sitting room, where his daughter was practicing the miniature pianoforte, a relic from his wife's stage days.

"Richard? Is that you?" Rachel asked, lifting her hands from the keyboard as he entered the room. If she had not been playing she would not have needed to ask.

"Returned at last. Is all well with you?" He put his hands on her shoulders and bent over her to plant a light kiss on her cheek.

"You were away longer than you planned," she said.

"Neighborhood doings."

Miss Brewster had stood up from the bench and now made her way around it with her hand extended slightly.

"Chair," Richard said, warning her of the piece of furniture turned at an unfamiliar angle and too low for her hand to encounter before her shin did. She stepped around the chair and waited until she was safely settled on the divan before she spoke again.

"Neighborhood doings?" she prompted.

"Ah, yes," Richard replied, reminded of their interrupted conversation. "It seems we have a new pastor for the little parish that includes the Grove and the surrounding area. A Mr. Worthington.'' He chuckled softly. Rachel raised her head and turned her ear toward him.

''Something?'' she asked.

''Mother and Julia would not hear of it, but the undeniable fact is that the good Mr. Worthington has been smitten by our Julia.''

''Has he now?''

''Well, who could blame him?'' He smiled. ''You know Julia.''

''Of course,'' she replied softly. ''And what do you think of Mr. Worthington?'' she prompted again.

''He is a very pleasant gentleman. He is, I believe, a genuine Man of God. Sincere, charitable, humble, self-effacing, much more concerned with the welfare of others than his own. He is, in short, such a rarity as to be almost unheard-of in the world today.''

Miss Brewster nodded. ''Then it would appear to be a good thing if he is 'smitten' by Miss Masonet. And how does she feel about him?''

''They have only just met,'' Richard said.

''You suggest that the gentleman has had time enough to make up his mind about your ward.''

''Yes, well...'' Richard waved his hand vaguely, and though Miss Brewster could not see the gesture, it was not as lost on her as might be supposed.

Back in the little community just out of Tunbridge, the Millers welcomed Mr. Worthington to his new lodgings, the little shed made as homey as possible, though still smelling faintly of chicken droppings, which odor Mrs. Miller had been unable to eradicate entirely.

''I do hope you can be comfortable here,'' Mrs. Miller said as her husband opened the door for them. ''It does not seem altogether proper to offer you a henhouse, but my husband has always been careful of his animals, so you've light and a sound room, no matter what the other shortcomings.''

"It is lovely, Mrs. Miller," Worthington said before he stepped through the door, and then, "It *is* lovely," he repeated, once inside.

Mr. Miller turned in a full circle of inspection, nodding his approval.

"Like I told young Edmond, never lost a chick in here. And the missus has cleaned the place up right well. With the door open you hardly notice the smell at all."

"Eli," Mrs. Miller scolded.

"Can't say how it will be in the winter, though closed up and a fire burning." Now Miller shook his head doubtfully.

"Well, ah, you see," Worthington began, his inoffensive smile resting tremulously on his lips. "I believe Mr. Bracken will have the repairs finished on the schoolhouse before it gets too awfully cold."

"Schoolhouse? You are moving in there? If that was always Bracken's plan then this whole thing was kind of a waste, I'd say," Mr. Miller said indignantly, just as Worthington feared he would.

"I do not believe that was Mr. Bracken's original intention. He only agreed to make the improvements when Miss Masonet and Mr. Edmond informed him that you and your wife were providing me with *much* better accommodations than Mr. Bracken allowed me. And I will not be able to move into the school for another month."

"A month, you say?" Mrs. Miller asked. "Husband, if Mr. Worthington is gone by the last of October you can get those birds you talked about. Now that we've sealed the chinks in the walls, you could raise a winter brood that would be ready to sell by Christmas."

"You see how well it all works out?" Worthington encouraged.

Mr. Miller agreed gruffly.

Feelings were soothed and Mr. Worthington moved his small store of personal belongings into the cozy little shed. The Millers lived only a mile from Aspen Grove, and Worthington barely had his possessions dumped onto the narrow bed fitted in the space where chickens had formerly

oosted before he set out for the Grove to give his favorable
report on the new living quarters.

"It is all perfectly pleasant. Mrs. Miller has cleaned it as
well as she possibly could, and though Mr. Miller says the
stove has not been used for a score of years, he cleaned that,
too, and says I should have no trouble with it. I really cannot thank you enough, Miss Masonet, Mrs. Edmond, for
the wonderful improvement."

"Do not thank me, Mr. Worthington," Aunt Jenny protested. "It was the doing of my son and Julia."

"Miss Masonet." Worthington turned toward the young
woman and bowed deeply.

"My cousin is not here, Mr. Worthington, to receive your
gratitude, but we shall certainly tell him you are pleased
when he returns," Julia said. "Actually, he would want an
eyewitness accounting. Would I be too bold if I asked to see
your new room?"

"Miss Masonet! I would be thrilled! Honored! Would
you? I did not dare ask, but if you think you would like
to..."

Julia laughed and stood, hoping to cap Mr. Worthington's gushing fountain of gratitude.

"Absolutely, Mr. Worthington. Allow me to fetch my
wrap," she said.

In moments, Mr. Worthington was off across the inter-
vening mile again, this time floating above the ground, Julia at his side. Walking.

Julia approved of everything. She noticed the clinging
owl scent, but being in no position to change the situation,
she ignored the smell completely and endeavored to make
the young man feel easy as he showed her around the place,
what there was of it.

"Mr. Miller's cookstove. Quite adequate, do you not
think?"

"I do."

"The table. Makeshift, but better than the rough board I
was using."

"It appears to be serviceable."

"Mr. Miller put in those shelves, there, against the wall.
You see how neatly they hold my books and things?" Mr.

Worthington was demonstrating their utility as he hur
riedly picked the few books and tins from the middle of hi
bed where he had left them and placed them on the shor
shelves. They held all of the curate's things with room t
spare.

"And this, of course, is my bed." The young ma
stopped, a blush putting red in his cheeks to match his hair
Contrarily, it made his freckles stand out.

"It is comfortable?" Julia asked, also delicately ignor
ing his embarrassment.

"Oh, yes. Try it. Or no. That would not be...but it is ver
comfortable. Narrow. Firm. Not hard. Well, yes, hard, bu
not uncomfortably so. Very comfortable...I would say."
Flustered, Worthington turned from the source of his un
ease and indicated the window. "My window," he said.

"Did Mrs. Miller put up the curtain?"

"I believe she did. But of course she would have to, sinc
I did not. And probably Mr. Miller did not, either. It ap
pears to be an old sheet."

"Is it?" Julia stepped to the small square of partitione
glass. She took the thin material between her fingers. "Yo
are probably correct, Mr. Worthington. I assumed it was a
old window covering. How clever of you to identify th
material."

"I only recognized it because that was what the curtain
in the Worthington home were usually made of." Now h
was embarrassed by the poverty of his home.

Julia stood away from the window and tilted her head t
critically view the effect of the material.

"Whatever the source, I think it makes the whole room–
homier. Do you not agree? What a thoughtful touch."

Worthington had completely overlooked the little scra
of cloth that was hung across the window, but seen throug
Miss Masonet's eyes it suddenly became the finest thing i
the room.

While he was admiring the wonder of his curtain, Juli
was noting his eating area and the very small supply of co
mestibles he seemed to have on hand.

"Now, Mr. Worthington," she said, "you must retur
with me to Aspen Grove for supper tonight. Aunt Jenn

would never forgive me if I were to enjoy the pleasure of your company all afternoon and not share that pleasure with her this evening. And, too, we will want to send back some of our surplus garden vegetables and a little salted pork. When my Cousin Richard is away I am afraid we simply founder there at the house. Glenda has not learned to lessen the amounts she cooks when Mr. Edmond is in London and it is just Aunt Jenny and myself at the Grove.''

She spoke very matter-of-factly, as if this had already been discussed and she was only reminding him of a promise he had made.

He nodded uncertainly. This solved his quandary as to where and what he was to eat, tonight and for the next several days, until he conducted his first church meeting and made other arrangements with the good people in his congregation. And though he was extremely pleased and flattered to have Miss Masonet care for his need, he did not want to be a burden. Not on those shoulders, those lovely, silken shoulders. Worthington drew himself up short and again blushed.

Julia smiled a smile that was nothing less than radiant.

"Très bien," she said. "And you must tell us all about your family, and your studies, and your aims.''

Now it was Worthington who radiated. His life had been pleasant enough to that point, his family loving, his schooling easy, his choice of a livelihood natural and, he hoped, fulfilling. But in twenty years he had never been as happy as he was at that moment.

Mrs. Edmond was delighted to have the new curate join Julia and her for supper and to have the chance to get to know him.

Worthington told about his family and growing up in a house with eight children. Some years had been lean, but Ruth Worthington, Sidney's mother, somehow kept food on the table, and his father taught them how to work.

"It was my father who gave us all the red hair. For the longest time I thought it was the mark of stern discipline and unfailing endeavor. Then, when I was a lad of ten or twelve, it finally occurred to me that I had red hair, but *I* was not stern, and I certainly did not enjoy working all the time. If I and my brothers have some of Father's industry it is because he taught it to us, not because he gave us red hair."

"Do you think?" Julia asked quite seriously. "I have wondered that myself. I find that I am intolerant and demanding at times. The Edmonds did not teach me that, nor did Miss Dansforth or even Madame Chevous, my schoolmistresses. My own father, on the other hand, was very intolerant and demanding and I have blamed him for all of my faults of character."

Julia sat on the sofa in the sitting room, across from Worthington's chair. It was after supper and the curate and the two ladies had retired to this room to visit. It was not late, but the autumn dusk was arriving earlier and earlier, hurrying the year along to its cold, dark conclusion. When they first entered the room Julia put a wick to the fire Glenda had laid and lit the lamps. Now the deep rose of her dress caught the glow and wrapped her, and Worthington, in a gentle warmth.

Nothing about her suggested even the most minor flaw of character.

Worthington said something along those lines, omitting his observation on the glow of her rose gown and the gentle warmth he felt in her presence.

After a while, for propriety's sake, the young man was forced to leave. Julia did not forget her promise of food and sent with him a very large basket filled with everything she and Glenda could find in the kitchen or pantry. Worthington protested, Julia pooh-poohed, and Glenda saw a week's supply of food walk out the door.

Before he left the young man asked her, in a tone of voice Edmond undoubtedly would have described as "desperately hopeful," when he might see her again.

"I often go walking of an afternoon," she told him. " will turn my steps toward the Miller home and perhaps we will meet then. If you are about."

Oh, Sidney Worthington would be about. Of that there was no doubt. His smelly little chicken coop could burn to the ground, but he would be on hand to join Miss Masone on her afternoon walk. On that he would have, and she could have, bet his life.

Julia's afternoon walks with Mr. Worthington became, in a very short time, an established habit.

Julia would tell her Aunt Jenny that she was going to get a breath of air. Sometimes she left at one o'clock, other days it might not be until three o'clock or later. It did not matter. Worthington met her where the two pieces of property met and together they would traverse the neighborhood.

Often they went along the public road to the schoolhouse being remodeled, viewing the building and work under way on it. The thought occurred to Worthington that the living space was unnecessarily large and that by dividing the one large room and making a modest addition, the remaining area could serve as a meeting house.

Julia was charmed by the idea and insisted they talk to Mr. Bracken. As Mr. Worthington could have warned the old gentleman, when Julia was charmed by an idea, everyone would be charmed by it.

"What have we gained, pardon me, Mr. Worthington, to have our own spiritual leader when we still must travel to Tunbridge to attend worship service?" she asked Mr. Bracken.

Bracken hemmed.

"The work is going forth and these slight changes would not be difficult and would hardly postpone the day of Mr. Worthington's occupancy."

Bracken hawed.

"You are perhaps uncomfortable with the idea of a humble layman erecting a House of God, but Mr. Worthington and myself will not publicize that fact, though since it is near the public thoroughfare and located on your property, we cannot promise that knowledge will not become generally known. I am sorry."

Bracken balanced his chin on his steepled forefingers and approvingly studied the contrite girl.

"One cannot always avoid the public eye, I have found," he said.

"Especially when performing acts of Christian kindness," Worthington added.

All three of them nodded solemnly.

Not surprisingly, Worthington and Julia left that meeting with Mr. Bracken's permission for a congregational meeting hall to be added to the little school building.

But not all of their walks had such tangible developments. Often they left the pathways and wandered over the fading countryside. They talked about weather and the land, people and politics, books they had read and stage plays they had seen.

"I would not have thought a seminary student would be encouraged to attend the theater," she said.

"We were not—exactly—*encouraged* to attend," Worthington said, but quickly added, "Neither were we—exactly—forbidden to go."

"And therefore you . . ."

"We went occasionally. We saw some fine Shakespearean productions and a number of uplifting dramas with a religious theme."

Julia was looking at him with close attention and he sheepishly admitted, "And we saw a few frivolous comedies. I enjoyed them."

Now the young woman smiled and Worthington returned a smile of happy absolution.

Worthington often talked about his family and the home he had imagined he was happy to be away from at last. Julia rarely spoke of her early years. She mentioned that she was an orphan, which the gentleman had already surmised, since she was introduced to him as "the Edmond ward." She also said her mother was English and her father French. Worthington did not pry for further disclosures; in fact, even in love with her as he was, he did not notice her reticence but reveled, instead, in her listening ear and her sympathetic demeanor.

Julia was not being secretive, nor was she ashamed of her early life, but she had learned caution and reserve from Mr. Drummond and François Davenôt and Lord Ramsgate, and besides, those years spent in France and the experiences and emotions of that time were all in French in her mind. Not only were they foreign to anything Worthington had ever encountered, but she would have had to translate to tell him of them.

Instead she listened to and enjoyed stories of his life, his struggles, his ambitions—modest though they were.

It is said that acquaintances talk about things and friends talk about feelings. Julia and Mr. Worthington progressed steadily past the countryside and the neighbors to likes and dislikes and then emotions that ran deeper and closer to the heart.

Worthington spoke of his desire to bring a shaft of light into the world.

"Nothing grand, nothing noteworthy. I do not care if I never leave the little radius of land and families in this parish. But I want to make my spot an easier place. It is not a pompous conceit, is it?"

"It is a noble aim, Mr. Worthington. The world would be a dazzling globe if we each brightened only our own life and the lives of those we touched."

Like her failure to speak of her past, Worthington did not notice that most of the secret goals and desires discussed were his.

As a child and a young woman—being now of the wizened age of twenty, Julia looked behind her with a contemptuous eye—she had wanted nothing so much, and nothing more, than to find love and be happy. Now she wondered if that was enough, if it was a worthy ambition. Would it not be finer to bring happiness to someone else's life? Were the two goals mutually exclusive?

She did not tell Mr. Worthington that. The thoughts were not well-defined in her own mind, but the ideas were new, sparked by Mr. Worthington's words and example, witnessed on their long walks together.

Cousin Richard was in London for a month. He wrote regularly to both his mother and Julia, telling them of his business, of Miss Brewster and her father, of the sights with which Julia had become familiar through the years. He wrote often, like a man who would rather be where the letters were going than from whence they were sent.

And all the while he was in London, Julia was with Mr. Worthington.

Richard returned to Aspen Grove a month and a week after the three of them shared tea in the little hovel Worthington had originally occupied. He looked tired and slept soundly, the first good night's sleep since he left, he told them. The next morning he was able to listen to the problems and complaints that had arisen during his absence. They continued until lunch.

After the meal he went downstairs to his study, quiet and deserted at last. He sank into the deeply padded chair in front of the fireplace and stared thoughtfully into the flames.

His reverie was disturbed by a noise at the front door. It was Julia come down to get her cloak.

"Is it not a little brisk for a walk today?" he asked.

"Mr. Worthington and I always go for a walk in the afternoon. I find it invigorating."

Richard looked at her closely.

"Yes," he said, "your complexion is looking very fine. You have more color in your cheeks than I have seen there for some time."

She returned his look with a critical eye.

"And your poor cheeks are bloodless. You insist on covering your lips with that mustache, but I suspect that hairless, your face would be positively wan. Would you care to join us in a little healthful exercise?"

Richard smoothed the hair above his lip and raised his eyebrows.

"I have heard that exercise does stimulate one's system. It was Dr. Harvey, I believe, in his famous treatise on blood and its circulation, who said..."

"Are you eventually going to agree to come, and could this dissertation be as easily delivered as we walked?"

He stood and offered his arm.

"I should be delighted. And certainly my health would be benefited." He disengaged her hand to pull on his own cloak, it really being quite brisk out-of-doors. "If you do not think Mr. Worthington would mind?" he asked.

"Pas du tout," Julia said. She also unconsciously slipped into French when she was not *comfortable* with the truth of her words.

Richard understood her "not at all," and also her unwitting slip.

"Mr. Edmond! I had not heard that you were returned. What a delightful surprise you could join our walk," Worthington enthused when he saw Edmond with Julia. *And* he sounded perfectly sincere. "How did you find London?" he asked.

Richard suppressed the smart reply of "By following the road from Tunbridge through Sevenoaks and into the city."

"Damp and chill," he said. "I had planned on toasting in front of the home fire, but Julia tells me I need color in my cheeks. It has become a little confused as of late who is watching over whom in Aspen Grove."

"Miss Masonet is a very caring soul," Worthington said.

"I have been more inclined to call her bossy, but I will allow your verdict to stand." Richard laughed.

Julia smiled, wishing they would change the subject. Worthington, for his part, wished they never would and would have extolled her charms halfway to Tunbridge, but Richard called their attention to a little rivulet that ran down the hill and asked if that was there when he left.

"We did not come this way yesterday," Julia said. "But as far as I remember that is new with these last rains."

New streams of water were hardly a wonder in the rainy autumn of the English year, but the conversation was diverted.

"I understand you were asked to speak Sunday in the Tunbridge chapel," Richard said. "Were you successful?"

"I do not know how one would judge the success of a sermon. The congregation seemed attentive enough, though I do not suppose they heard anything they have not heard a thousand times before."

"Mr. Worthington was very good," Julia said. "Aunt Jenny said she has never heard the subject of covetousness presented so well."

"Or succinctly. Pastor Fischer advised me to use only ten minutes. And Pastor Fischer's advice takes second chair only to the Holy Commandments." Mr. Worthington laughed uncertainly, fearful he had overstepped the bounds of propriety with his witticism. Uncertain until Mr. Edmond laughed a full laugh and clapped him on the back.

"I have been struck by Pastor Fischer's sermons the same way, and he is not even *my* superior. I would be relieved to have a mere mortal delivering my Sunday address," he said.

"I am as mere a mortal as you shall ever hear," Worthington said.

"Cousin Richard, Mr. Bracken has volunteered to construct a meeting hall connected to the parsonage," Julia said, reminded that Edmond had been away at that juncture.

"Is that so?" Richard asked. His fellow walkers both nodded and he turned suspiciously to his ward. "Volunteered?"

Julia opened her deep gray eyes wide and assumed an expression of spotless innocence. Richard laughed again, very softly this time, careful not to frighten away the smile playing at the corner of her lips.

Their footsteps had led them away from the Bracken property and the building they might otherwise have passed. Going toward the setting sun, the cart trail they followed joined the main road into Tunbridge. Worthington and Julia usually turned onto the meadowland at that point, meandering slowly back toward the Edmond home.

Today Worthington stopped at the crossroads and tugged his thin jacket tightly across his chest.

"It has grown quite chill. Perhaps it would be wise to call an early halt to our walk today."

Julia looked at him in surprise, but Richard nodded and pulled at his own heavy cloak.

"The blood is absolutely racing through my veins. If my system were stimulated one whit more, I fear I would lose consciousness altogether," he said.

The trio turned back toward Aspen Grove and the Bracken property. Traveling east now, they were walking directly into a chill breeze and were forced to walk quickly and silently to stay warm. All six cheeks were rosy red when they arrived at the dividing property line.

"Perhaps it is too late in the year for our walks to continue," Worthington offered before they parted.

Richard stood quietly at Julia's side, not offering any comment, his face carefully neutral when the young lady glanced quickly at him. When she turned back to Worthington her expression was flatteringly disappointed. The young curate was thrilled, almost compensated for the cessation of the idyllic strolls by that look.

"Do you think?" she asked.

"I am afraid so. I would never forgive myself if you were to catch a chill because of our time together." It was a common phrase, never to forgive oneself, but Worthington meant it literally.

Julia offered her hand, which Worthington took, distressed to find the delicate fingers cold.

"We insist that you come regularly to the Grove to dine, then, Mr. Worthington. I have enjoyed our discussions and am reluctant to give them up completely. And, too, I know my Aunt Jenny would love to see you more often. Do you promise?"

"By all means, Miss Masonet. It is hardly a rigorous sacrifice you are asking me to make." He patted her hand fondly before he released it. It was a grandfatherly sort of gesture and seemed strange to be made by a very young man with bright red hair, freckles across his nose and his cheeks like two plump cherries.

They went their separate ways then, Worthington crossing the field that would eventually take him to the chicken coop on Eli Miller's farm, Richard and Julia starting down the lane that led to Aspen Grove.

Worthington was always warmed by his time with Miss Masonet, and today his hands, which had held hers, were tingling. He began to sing one of the familiar seminary hymns in a clear tenor voice before he was completely out of earshot.

Richard and Julia walked in silence until the strains faded away.

"Mr. Worthington is a very pleasant fellow," he said.

"Yes, he is," Julia agreed.

"And steady."

"Very steady."

"He seems to be a churchman who takes his calling very much to heart. But perhaps you know more about that than I?"

"He has spoken feelingly on the subject. He acknowledges the responsibility of his calling and yet he does not think of it as a burden so much as a privilege."

"Just as I imagined," Richard said. They were walking so close together that their shoulders often brushed, but he did not offer her his arm. Mr. Worthington always insisted she take his arm and solicitously helped her across any spot of rough ground they happened upon. Richard walked briskly, forcing her to hurry along beside him, choosing, it began to appear purposely, the most deeply rutted side of the lane or the stretch with the most loose and largest stones.

"And you have walked together everyday for the past month?" he asked, breaking the silence between them again, though their walk was not silent in the descending dusk. The breeze had freshened just since they turned onto their lane and now was growling ominously through the trees.

"We have rambled *leisurely*," Julia gasped, short of breath.

Richard looked around. Julia had at last been forced to fall behind and now stopped completely, breathing heavily, her hand at her side. He returned to stand next to her. When her breathing slowed he finally offered his arm for her support and so he would not outdistance her.

As they walked, much slower now despite the cold, Julia spoke thoughtfully.

"Our discussion of Mr. Worthington seems to have signaled that added stimulus of which you were fearful."

Richard shook his head but did not meet her eyes.

"I cannot imagine what you mean, Julia. I only wanted to hurry home to my hearth and the warm fire I trust Glenda is keeping at a healthy blaze for Mother."

"I was mistaken, then," Julia said.

"You were," he agreed.

There was no playful banter today suggesting that Mr. Worthington admired Julia. The subject, in the month that Richard had been away, had ceased to be a playful one.

Now they finished their walk in silence. At the house they both hurried to stand in front of the fire, which Glenda had let die down. Richard prodded the coals and stoked it so that in a minute it was roaring as loudly as the wind through the trees that gave the house its name.

Aunt Jenny had questions for them and a fine scolding for being out in such weather and leaving her until it was almost dark. They answered the questions and accepted their lashes, and humble, self-effacing, mild little Mr. Worthington never left either of their thoughts.

Chapter Eighteen

It was another Christmas. Her eighth in the Edmond home, her last as the Edmond ward. By next Christmas she would be of legal age. And who knew what would happen between now and then? Not only would this be the year when she reached her majority, but it was a pivotal year in her life. She felt it. She knew it.

In the eight years since that first tumultuous Christmas in England, she had grown accustomed to Father Christmas, the bell ringers, the *primitif* mummers who invaded their quiet home on Christmas Eve. She even looked forward to the day when Cousin Richard would drag in the fine little tree he had chopped down and Julia would wind around it the ropes of popped corn and cranberries she had strung.

She had learned to laugh and sing with the rest of them, and eat the roast goose and listen skeptically when Cousin Richard told of Christmas wonders. But she was always careful to spend a little while alone with the leather-bound Testament that had been her guardian's first Christmas gift to her when she joined the household, a lonely and frightened child. It was worn now and fell open to favorite passages.

This year their little family celebration had been augmented. Mr. Worthington was warmly invited to join them for the entire week, which invitation he warmly accepted, and Miss Brewster and her father agreed to take Christmas dinner with them, as well.

"We would not have Mr. Worthington spend Christmas alone, would we, Julia?" Richard said, explaining the rather protracted stay he had suggested for the clergyman.

Julia was certainly quick to second Richard's invitation, touched by it, but at the same time she was strangely troubled. She knew Cousin Richard well enough to know that he was often wearied by Worthington's sincere, though admittedly monotonous, discourses on brotherly love and Christian duty. They were sentiments one expected, even desired, to be delivered from the pulpit, but Mr. Worthington spoke of little else even in casual conversation with Mr. Edmond.

Worthington had no knowledge of, or interest in, the business and political affairs that filled Richard's life the other six days of the week. And though pleasant—heaven preserve us! the man was nothing if he was not pleasant—Worthington did not have the avid interest, the searching mind that would have encouraged the older man to act as his guide and mentor.

Yet it was Cousin Richard who insisted Mr. Worthington join them for two or three evenings every week, and now he asked the curate to join their Christmas celebrations.

"I had hoped to see my own family during the season, but it appears that will not be possible. Christmas alone can be dreadfully unhappy. Thank you. It is so good of you to think of me, to be mindful of someone in need. Your spirit of love and compassion is tremendously uplifting to me." Worthington smiled and Richard smiled, and as well as she knew both of them, Julia could not tell if either smile was insincere.

So young Sidney Worthington was with them the whole week before Christmas. The parsonage and meeting hall had been completed in early November and the curate had long since moved into the comparatively luxurious living quarters and made himself at home. But, Richard insisted the younger man lock up the old school building and spend the holiday with them.

"We will ride over in the buggy Christmas morning for service, but until then you must simply enjoy the Yuletide," he said.

It did not take much convincing. Richard's speech was one sentence more than was necessary.

Worthington ventured out with Richard onto the little hillock covered with fir trees to hew down the Christmas tree. It was the young curate and Julia who decorated it, where in other years Richard had given his ward a helping hand in lacing the ropes through the upper branches.

"Come and help us, Cousin Richard," Julia coaxed, but her guardian smiled and shook his head.

"You are doing very well with the help you have, Julia," he told her. "My two hands would only clutter up your work area. You know I am no good with such fancywork. You are the artist and this year we will allow Mr. Worthington to be your servant."

Mr. Worthington nodded his head eagerly. He could imagine no more paradisiacal existence than to be Miss Masonet's humble servant.

On Christmas Eve they opened the gifts they had wrapped so carefully for one another. Aunt Jenny gave them all knitted mufflers. Aunt Jenny gave them knitted mufflers every year. This year, the one Mr. Worthington received was shorter than the others. Mrs. Edmond, caught unawares by their Christmas guest but determined the curate not be overlooked, had only the week Worthington was there to work on it.

Cousin Richard's gifts came from London shops and were quite grand. Aunt Jenny received a silk scarf in an oriental design of red and black. She fingered the smooth, rich material appreciatively but was not altogether certain the symbols on the cloth were not paganistic.

For Julia he had a delicate crystal swan and even Mr. Worthington received a small prayer book.

Julia gave each of them a painting. Mr. Worthington's was only one of her old pictures done while she was in school, and she felt a little embarrassed to give it. She had done much better work since.

Aunt Jenny's was painted this year and depicted the apricot tree in full bloom. Mrs. Edmond had remarked one day last spring that the tree was a beautiful sight, would it not be lovely to have spring all year? Julia gave her what she could.

Cousin Richard's painting was something of a departure for her and not really her work at all, or at least not exclusively her work. She had found, only a few weeks earlier, while Richard was away in London this last time—when she was not out walking with Mr. Worthington—a box of childhood mementos, things Aunt Jenny had tucked away in an old trunk and sent up to the attic. There were papers and handwork from the Hampton Academy, and even Madame Chevous's little school. Aunt Jenny, the dear, had also saved some of Julia's earliest drawings, and smiling as she looked at the crude work, she was sure Aunt Jenny loved these as much as her most recent, polished pieces.

With the rolled and discarded canvases on which she had made her early drawings, no doubt included because Aunt Jenny believed it was her work, was the sketch of Julia Cousin Richard had done those long years ago. As she pulled it from the box and studied it, a flush of shame warmed her cheek. She had deceptively requested this from her guardian for Mr. Drummond, who had promptly sold the gilt frame and left the picture behind.

Dear Miss Masonet, enclosed you will find a sketch we here at the Bumbarage Institution assume is yours, since it has your name on the back. Mr. Edmond has instructed us to return the drawing to you.

Julia remembered, word for word, the humiliating note Mr. Quilling had sent telling of Drummond's desertion. She almost hurled the sketch into the wastebasket, but she paused for a moment, remembering how impatient Cousin Richard had been with her while he drew it.

"Sit *still,* Julia!" he barked at her innumerable times. If she remembered correctly, she never did obey him. She squirmed and giggled and chattered incessantly, which was the foolish way she used to act with her guardian.

The girl in the picture looked young, infantile. Julia could not remember ever being that young. Yet Cousin Richard, in his untutored style, had captured something of the woman she was to become. It was the eyes, and the shadow on the cheek.

Julia held the drawing away from her and then carried it downstairs, where she could study the drawing and her image in the mirror at the same time.

The idea came to her then. By deepening the shadows and filling in the white patches that represented her skin with a dusky watercolor tone, darker than her skin shade, more like the color of her skin shaded, she could make the basic drawing more three-dimensional, more lifelike.

Working back and forth from her mirror image and the juvenile drawing, she managed to age the portrait around the timeless quality Richard had given the eyes. The picture she gave Cousin Richard that Christmas Eve was not as beautiful as the young woman herself, but it portrayed both the child and the woman that was Julia.

Cousin Richard said nothing when he pulled back the tissue paper. His silence was not obvious in the room, filled as it was with Aunt Jenny's surprised pleasure and Mr. Worthington's ecstasies, but Julia was aware of it and watched him carefully to gauge his reaction, even while accepting the compliments from her aunt and the curate.

Finally he looked up at her and nodded ever so slightly.

"Have I finally achieved the 'quintessence of artistic beauty'?" she asked, recalling his words on that fateful visit.

He smiled.

"Perhaps you have," he said. " 'To my eye.' " He completed the quotation Julia did not think he would remember.

But then Worthington claimed her and did not release her for the rest of the evening. The painting she had given him was the most beautiful he had ever seen, he would hang it in a place of honor always, he would never forget the joy of this Christmas. Julia tried to stem his tide, but his enthusiasm continued to flood. She pointed out the flaws of her work, but he would not see them; belittled her effort, but he would not listen; assured him the recipient was more than worthy of the gift, but that he would not have. In amused defeat she finally allowed him to have his way.

Miss Brewster and Mr. Clyde Brewster arrived on Christmas Day. The Brewster carriage was large and warm and, like the Brewster residence, reminiscent of the late Mrs. Brewster and her colorful career and flamboyant taste. There were two tufts of red feathers that bounced alongside of the driver, the red matching—originally, before the rain, sleet and smoke of a single London season—the red of the interior of the coach. The seats were not of leather, but of a velvet finish that matted down quickly and unattractively. There were brass appointments and ornate carvings on the doors, sides, wheel hubs, driver's seat and lash and lash holder near the driver's boot.

Her father assisted Miss Brewster down and led her carefully to the front door, guiding her so fearfully it was not to be wondered if Miss Brewster considered her affliction with the utmost gravity.

"Rachel, sir, welcome to the Edmond home. Let me take your wraps. Go right into the sitting room, there. My mother is there with Miss Masonet and Mr. Worthington. I will see if your coachman needs any help with your things."

It was Richard who greeted them at the door and indicated the direction they were to take. The Brewsters joined the party in the sitting room and introductions were made.

Richard was fully aware that his mother did not really like Mr. Brewster. He had always been a part of her husband's life that she had never shared, and he was loud. Mrs. Edmond considered him coarse and could not understand why her husband had held him such a good friend. But now with her dear Charles gone, Brewster was a physical link to him, a tangible reminder of him, and Mrs. Edmond was surprised by how much she was looking forward to a visit that any other year she would have dreaded.

"Miss Brewster, sit down there, with Julia. And, Clyde, what a delight to see you," she was saying when Richard came through the doors. Her son was surprised and pleased by the pleasant and sincere tone of his mother's voice.

The strangers had all been introduced to one another and now Worthington joined Julia and Miss Brewster on the divan. That left no place for Richard but in front of the fire, excluded from both conversations. He rocked to and fro on his heel, listening to random remarks on either side of the room.

"Miss Brewster plays the piano, Mr. Worthington. It is a delight to hear her, though I warn you, it may not be easy to convince her to honor us," Julia was saying.

"Old Aspen Grove is holding up all right, I see. 'Course, it has been a time since I have been here. Quite a time," Brewster told his mother. Mrs. Edmond smiled and nodded her head but offered no explanation for the length of time it had been since his last invitation to the Grove, because any explaining could not be done delicately.

Young Edmond himself said nothing, just stood before the fire, hands behind his back, observing his family and guests with a serious expression Julia could not change to a smile, regardless of how often she looked up at him or how sweetly she smiled herself.

Glenda had insisted she have some help "if there's to be a mob here," so Richard had engaged two girls from the neighborhood for the week, and it was not a half hour until one of them, little Tansy, old Seamor Reynolds's girl, came to the door and announced, in her finest drawing room voice, which Julia was certain she had been practicing for a week, that "Dinnah is served!"

"You live in London, Miss Brewster? My, that must be thrilling."

Rachel Brewster smiled faintly. "I find all places to be thrilling, Mr. Worthington."

Sidney Worthington blushed a deep red and made an apologetic sound in the back of his throat. Miss Brewster's smile grew more definite.

"It is quite all right, Mr. Worthington. Please do not let me make you uncomfortable with my little teasing."

"Oh no, no, certainly not."

Miss Brewster held her hand toward the young man and Mr. Worthington took it uncertainly.

"It is a defense of mine. But I realize I need not defend myself against you."

Dinner was over and the diners had repaired to the familiar sitting room. Mr. Brewster was sleeping in front of the fire and snoring quite audibly. Another time Mrs. Edmond would have found that extremely offensive. Now she looked on it with an indulgent eye, reminded of occasions when Charles had laid his head back in that same chair and dozed off himself. Actually, underneath it all, Mr. Brewster was not so very unlike her late husband as she had always imagined.

For her part Mrs. Edmond was listening to the two young couples talk, offering comments when they were sought, but not interrupting otherwise.

"Mr. Worthington and your Miss Brewster seem to have hit it off quite nicely," Julia said quietly to her cousin.

"That is fortunate," Richard said.

Julia looked at him quizzically. "What do you mean?" she asked.

"Well, when Miss Brewster and I are married, then, of course, there will be Mr. Worthington. We certainly would not want the two of them to be at odds, now would we?"

Julia still did not understand her guardian's meaning completely. She did not see the inevitability of Mr. Worthington "being there" if—when—Richard and Rachel were married.

Worthington looked across the room at her and smiled.

"I believe I have Miss Brewster convinced to play for us," he announced to the room.

"Why, you silver-tongued devil!" Richard returned. "I have been trying for years to get Rachel—Miss Brewster—to play in public. How did you accomplish such a formidable feat in twenty minutes?"

"He did it by *not* asking me to play in public, but to play for him and four or five other friends and family members," the young woman explained, laughing.

She raised her hand, and while Worthington, sitting beside her, was still confused by the gesture, Richard was in front of her, lifting her hand, guiding her to the piano.

"A little Bach, I think," the girl said, finding her finger position on the unfamiliar keyboard. As she began to play, Richard returned to sit next to Julia.

"She is very good," that young woman whispered to him softly.

"And she has very keen hearing," Richard whispered back, not softly at all.

Miss Brewster smiled as she played but did not falter or lose track of the intricate counting and fingering of the prelude.

At the end of the piece Mr. Worthington, predictably, applauded, enthusiastically, vowing he had never heard anything finer in his life, and from Mr. Worthington it was not empty praise; it was the honest truth, every time.

Richard escorted the lady back to her place on the settee. The curate relinquished his place and went to sit with Julia.

"He is perfectly delightful," Miss Brewster said. Richard was looking across the room at the other two young people, unconsciously straining to hear what they said. Miss Brewster's quiet words, unlike Julia's, would not be overheard.

"What?"

"I said he is perfectly delightful. And I think you were quite right."

"About what?" he asked, but he knew.

"He is in love with her."

"Ah."

"And Miss Masonet?" Miss Brewster asked.

"Miss Masonet?"

"How does she feel about him?"

"Do you not know?"

"I am insightful, Richard. Not clairvoyant."

"Neither am I," he said. But he did not sound as ignorant as he wished he did, or as ignorant as he wished he was.

Later in the evening they played a few hands of cards and a silly little word game Worthington had taught them, which he remembered from his home. A group of carolers came to the Edmond door. They were invited in, where they sang for the party and then were refreshed with hot punch and cold meat.

Finally Mrs. Edmond announced that she was fatigued. She stood; Richard, Mr. Brewster, roused from the nap a blazing fire always seemed to summon, and Mr. Worthington all stood. Worthington would have reseated himself, but

Edmond declared that it *had* been a long day and Miss Masonet suggested they all retire.

Worthington watched as the raven-haired girl left the room, guiding Miss Brewster. Taking the warmth with her. Worthington sighed.

It had been the most glorious week of the young man's life. Not only had the festivities been gayer, the lights brighter and the gifts more lavish than anything he had ever experienced in his crowded home or the austere seminary, but he had spent the entire time at Julia's side. Edmond, the fine fellow, invited him to take that place at the table whenever they sat to dine, and seemed desirous that he always stay near his ward. Often Cousin Richard released his usual chair so Worthington could sit close to the girl.

Miss Masonet, for her part, was beautiful, naturally, and very quiet, which was also natural. For the Julia Masonet he knew. She had listened to him with interest, answered his questions softly, and when the carolers came on Christmas night she joined their songs with a rich alto voice, harmonizing beautifully with Miss Brewster's clear soprano.

Listening to them, Worthington had no doubt whatsoever that the choirs in heaven would sound like that. In fact, heaven could be no more a joyous place than Christmas in the Edmond house, with Miss Masonet at his side.

"'For I was an hungred, and ye gave me meat: I was thirsty, and ye gave me drink: I was a stranger, and ye took me in.'"

The hour was late, the house finally quiet. The other members of the house party had taken to their beds and been immediately asleep. The week had been full, the day hectic. Julia's bed was warm and the room, except for one candle on the nightstand, dark. Julia wished she, too, could sleep, but she clearly heard the clock down in Aunt Jenny's sitting room strike one, just as she had heard the twelve *bongs* one hour ago.

She sat up and opened the book of Scripture, searching for the peace and comfort she sometimes found there. Instead she found these words, which troubled her even further.

It was not strange or miraculous or even remarkable that the book fell open to the twenty-fifth chapter of Saint Matthew. In the years since her father's death, when the Edmonds had opened their home and hearts to her, she had read the thirty-fifth verse countless times, her eyes often dimming with tears over the words that seemed to have been written for her.

But tonight the verse had a different meaning, spoke of someone else.

Cousin Richard had opened Aspen Grove to another lost soul. And although he could not really enjoy the young man's company, one would never suspect that from his unfailing courtesy, his thoughtfulness, his friendly demeanor. But what was more, he brought the two of them, Julia and Mr. Worthington, together. He insisted they spend time with each other, arranged for them to be alone, made certain they sat together. If Mr. Worthington was not there, Richard spoke well, and often, of him.

At the same time Cousin Richard was drawing away from her. She felt the distance between them, knew that it was growing, could tell that it was her guardian's design that it should.

When he left for town last September and was away for a month it was the longest time he had been gone from the Grove since Julia had quit the Hampton Academy. She was not sure it was not the longest time he had ever been away on business.

Before that trip he spent every available day at Aspen Grove with his mother and Julia, sometimes, she suspected, at the expense of his London dealings, certainly at the expense of enjoying Miss Brewster's company. Since that trip, since she and Mr. Worthington had become so well acquainted during their long walks together, Richard went up to town at the first of every week, staying two or three days, often until the weekend, occasionally through the weekend. They might not see him until the middle of the next week.

But even when he was home, at the Grove, he no longer sat with the two women for those long evenings. He would read for a few minutes and then rise and bend over his mother's chair to give her a kiss on the cheek.

"I am going to my study," he would say. Or "up to my room," or "outside to make sure everything is sound before I leave again."

Often in "the old days," Julia would bring her book or her sewing or her drawing and sit beside him, even on the floor at his feet, in front of the fire. They would discuss her book or his, and he would tell her of things that happened in town and she would tell him the unimportant, inconsequential things of life at Aspen Grove. Things one tells one's family because only one's family would be interested.

Aunt Jenny used to have them sing to her, old favorites, familiar hymns, even rollicking folk songs—which Aunt Jenny had long ago accepted as paganish. Cousin Richard would sing the melody in his strong baritone voice and Julia would try the harmony or a soft countermelody in her alto.

They had not sung together since . . . She did not have to stop and reckon the time. They had not done any of those things since September.

Her eyes dropped to the verse of scripture again.

"I was a stranger," the words said. Mr. Worthington was familiar to the little community by now. His sermons, delivered each Sunday in the little meeting hall that had been added to the school building, were uplifting and admired by his congregation.

"Very well put, Reverend Worthington," Mr. Fenton would say.

"You brought tears to my eyes," his wife would add. Mrs. Fenton was a tender soul who clung to the churchman's every word, often beginning to cry with his "Good Sabbath to you, my brothers and sisters."

An invitation to dinner always followed his message, for Sunday evening and one or two nights during the week.

He had blessed two babies, officiated at one wedding and offered the graveside prayer for old Mrs. Grayson.

"Naked, and ye clothed me: I was sick, and ye visited me: I was in prison, and ye came unto me," the next verse said.

Mr. Worthington wore the mantle of the church nobly and had done all of that for his fellowman.

But "I was a stranger." The words echoed in her mind. They did not apply to Mr. Worthington. He might have lived here, a neighbor, all of his life.

It was Cousin Richard who had become the stranger.

"Mrs. Edmond, Mr. Edmond, I cannot tell you how much I have enjoyed this Holy Season you allowed me to share with you. I have been deeply touched by your generosity. If I were able I would offer you some recompense, but if no earthly reward, you will surely garner heavenly blessings, which are better by far."

The young man shook Richard's hand heartily and Mrs. Edmond's hand gently. He stooped and pulled his large traveling case into his arms. He said "Nonsense!" when his host offered to order the carriage for him, but fortunately he had been overruled and now the small wagon stood waiting to take him back to his very comfortable abode.

"The pleasure has been ours, Mr. Worthington. What a happy idea of my son's that you should join us," Aunt Jenny said.

"And we shall expect you for dinner on Saturday, as usual," Richard reminded him.

Worthington laughed. "I shall only have time to put my things away before I return," he said.

Julia stood in the doorway watching the departure, but now Cousin Richard motioned for her to step forward. She obeyed him, as she always did, not even aware of the little thrill of pleasure his gesture and his "Come join us, Julia," gave her.

She stepped quickly to his side, a smile beginning at her lips, when Richard placed his hand on her arm and pushed her away from him, toward Mr. Worthington.

"Why don't you ride over to his house with our guest, Julia?" he encouraged her. "Mr. Worthington has suggested that he hates to see the week come to a close and then we heartlessly send him away by himself." Richard smiled, evidently not seeing the faint light of surprise in the girl's eyes, surprise and hurt.

"I will not hear of it!" Worthington said, but he sounded as if he would, in fact, be very willing to hear of it.

Julia absorbed her cousin's gentle propulsion into her own smooth carriage and walked without pause with the young man to the curricle.

"By all means, Mr. Worthington. This will make our farewell as painless as possible," she said.

The curate may have been trying, but he could not disguise his happiness with the plan. He pushed his bag behind the seat and offered Miss Masonet his hand up into the cart. While she settled herself he came around to the other side, pulling at his coat, hoping his hair was combed smooth in case he dislodged his hat getting into the little carriage. But Miss Masonet was not watching the young man's excited figure. She was looking at Mr. Edmond, who met her dark eyes with his clear blue ones for a moment and then turned with his mother back into the house before Worthington was on the seat next to her.

The curricle was very small, pulled by the old gray nag. It would be easy for Julia to guide the horse back to the Grove, and certainly the ride was gentle. The horse plodded along at an extremely leisurely pace, and still Mr. Worthington pulled back on the reins now and then to slow their journey.

"I feared this Christmas would be a stark and lonely one for me," the gentleman said. "I never imagined it would be the happiest one of my life."

"Oh, Mr. Worthington, your compliments are very pretty, but I fear they will make our hearts sinfully proud. You should be more careful with your hyperbole."

"I do not exaggerate," Worthington said, and there was no mistaking the sincerity of his voice. "Words can never express my gratitude for the joy of this past week."

Julia stared out at the roadway coming toward them.

"Then I am pleased that my guardian thought to invite you. You made a happy addition to our little family," she said.

Worthington sighed happily and Julia continued to look straight ahead. She saw this twentieth year of hers as a pivotal period in her life; she recognized this slow buggy ride as one of those turning points.

Their month of long walks while Cousin Richard was away had been a time of getting to know each other. It was at first impersonal and grew to be more intimate only tentatively at best.

In the time since then, despite her guardian's prodding and herding the two of them together, their relationship had not deepened. Julia had purposely kept it in stasis while she attempted to understand it, and them, and her Cousin Richard.

But this ride, Mr. Worthington's next words and her response would mean something. Would change the course of their association. Perhaps their lives. How did she want it to change?

"Miss Masonet," Worthington said. His voice was very soft, but Julia could still hear the tremble in the words. "The joy I have known this past week cannot—completely—be attributed to Mr. Edmond. Much as I appreciate—as I have on countless occasions fervently thanked the Lord for—his invitation, he might not have even been there this week. Your aunt could have been absent. The delicious meals unpalatable, the walls bare. Nothing could have changed my joy, as long as you were there."

Julia drew in her breath and turned her eyes at last toward the young man beside her. Her expression was soft, her eyes dark, eiderdown pillows.

"Your presence has been very dear to me, as well, Sidney." The curricle swayed back and forth to the horse's slow, heavy steps. It was very quiet in the lane. There was no animal life about, the breeze was not blowing, the rain was not falling. The carriage swayed and the horse lazily swished her tail. The sound of Mr. Worthington's swallow reverberated in the silence.

"Do you know that I love you, Julia?" he asked. His lips formed their habitual pleasant smile, but there was fear and the question of his life's happiness in the smile and his words.

"I do," she said.

Worthington pulled on the reins, then jounced them, turning his attention to the horse and the roadway as if their progression along it suddenly required the most careful maneuvering.

"And?" he asked, hanging tightly on to the reins, his breath suspended, the knuckles of his hands white.

"And do I love you?" She completed the question for him thoughtfully. "I do not know."

The young man turned to her then and tried to gather more knowledge from her face than he had from her answer.

"One usually knows when one is in love, Miss Masonet," he said.

"I am not in . . . not in a *legal* position to make that decision."

That clarification was hardly satisfying.

"Not in the legal position?" Worthington asked.

"If I were to love you, if I could accept your love, if we decided to marry, all that must wait until this summer. Until I am twenty-one and of legal age."

"Your guardian would surely give you leave to marry before then. I know Mr. Edmond. You would have only to ask. He satisfies your every whim. Surely he would not deny you, frustrate you, in something as important as love."

Julia's smile was ironic.

"You do not know my guardian as well as you think," she said. "No, I would not want my marriage to you to be dependent upon Cousin Richard. It is for that reason that I have consciously made no emotional commitment, Mr. Worthington. Other than a very sincere friendship. I can only ask you to wait."

"I am ready to devote my life to you." Worthington's apologetic little smile was on his lips. "It seems a trivial question to ask how long you want me to wait."

The soft murmur in the air was Julia's laugh.

"Until my birthday. The nineteenth day of July. I only ask for half a year, Sidney. Not your whole life. And I *will* try to love you."

Worthington was not happy. He loved this woman and wanted to take her into his arms there and then and cover her face with kisses. He wanted whispered phrases and promises to pass between them as they planned the rest of their days together, and their nights. He did not want to return alone to his rooms tonight. He did not want to wait for seven months to know her decision, like some prisoner on the gallows waiting and praying for a reprieve. He did not want her to suggest that learning to love him would be a chore.

But he had no choice.

Even as slow as the horse had traveled, as haphazard as Worthington's guidance had been for the most part, they were now in front of the renovated schoolhouse. The white cloths across the windows were real curtains, ones that Julia brought to him the day after he moved in. The door was shut but not bolted. There was nothing in the building or that Worthington owned that he would not have given away for the asking.

"You can drive the carriage back yourself?" he asked.

"I can manage," she replied.

"I will see you again?"

She smiled and held her hand down to him as he stood beside the wagon.

"We will expect you at Aspen Grove on Saturday for supper," she told him.

He took her gloved fingers and held them to his lips for a long moment.

"I will try, Sidney," she whispered.

"Mr. Worthington is returned to the parsonage, then?" Richard asked.

"He is," Julia affirmed.

"And is everything well there?" Aunt Jenny said.

"From all outward appearances. Nothing seemed to be disturbed or out of place. I, of course, did not go in."

"Of course," Richard said.

Julia looked at him, a furrow between her brows, and then put her hand to her forehead.

"It has been an exhausting week," she said.

"Has it, my dear?" Aunt Jenny asked. "I thought Mr. Worthington was a delightful addition to our family party, but I suppose seeing to the needs of a guest can be tiring. And then, with the Brewsters here today, too, it was hardly the same close family group as in years past. Perhaps another year we ought to keep Christmas alone, just the three of us, Richard.''

''Oh no, Aunt Jenny. The holiday was very nice. Mr. Worthington was perfectly agreeable and no trouble at all. And Miss Brewster will very soon be part of our family. It is only that I am a little tired.''

''Richard, you should have escorted Mr. Worthington back to the parsonage yourself instead of sending Julia,'' Aunt Jenny scolded her son. She had been mildly disapproving of sending the gentleman and her ward off together in the first place, and now Julia was fatigued.

''I thought she might enjoy the ride,'' Richard said, not precisely defending his actions but willing to explain them to his mother. ''She and Mr. Worthington seem to be such great friends.''

''Yes,'' Julia said. ''We are. Great friends.'' She sighed softly and turned toward the stairway. ''I think I will lie down for a few minutes.''

''By all means. Now that it is just the family again I am sure after a restful nap you will find yourself restored. You will see that everything here at Aspen Grove is exactly as it was before our little Christmas house party.'' Aunt Jenny smiled fondly at her ward and son.

They both loved her dearly and returned her smile with little phrases of agreement. But in their hearts, in both their hearts, they knew that could not be.

Chapter Nineteen

Pastor Worthington delivered a sermon on New Year's Day that people were talking about the length and breadth of the county the next day. Some people said it was the most stirring they had ever heard. Others said that Mr. Worthington's ideas were a deal too worldly and vain for a man of God. Mr. Bracken nodded his head and patted Mrs. Fenton's hand in full understanding when she said, with tears in her eyes, that Mr. Worthington gave her hope no other preacher ever had. Bracken also shook his head in full accord when Mr. Eldon Davenport said young Worthington was treading uncertain ground. Mr. Bracken was very pleased with either response, since both brought attention to him and his colorful protégé.

Mr. Worthington's controversial subject was joy, his contention being that every man is responsible for his own. The Edmonds, including Miss Masonet, sat together on a bench close to his pulpit, and Julia was not the only member of the congregation who believed the minister was speaking directly, and exclusively, to her.

"And how can we attain that joy, that happiness that is rightfully the lot of us all? By giving joy away. By caring more for the good of others than for our own good. By opening our hands and our hearts. Happiness is not a gift from God but a prize we can win for ourselves."

As a result of his stirring words Mr. Worthington found his evenings fully engaged for the next week. He did not get a chance to speak to Miss Masonet about his sermon until the following Saturday. Now it was two weeks since his declaration of love for the young woman. In that time he had seen her, spoken to her, inquired after the Edmonds if they were not there, offered some uplifting piece of wisdom if they were. But he had not been able to sit down alone with her and talk.

Just as Julia saw the moments she was allowed with her Cousin Richard as changed, her quiet talks with Mr. Worthington could never be the same. Julia Masonet was not a stupid woman, as if to comprehend Mr. Worthington's transparent fondness for her required great deductive reasoning. From the beginning Julia could see the young man's inclination for her, and whether she returned his feelings or not, the admiration another might have for one always recommends that person to one, if for no other reason than a respect for their impeccable taste. But until this time, the partition of spoken words had not been raised between them.

Now their conversation was strained, with underlying meaning in every word they spoke to each other.

"How are you, Miss Masonet?" did not only mean was Julia well, but how was Julia feeling—toward the curate? Had she made her decision? Would it be favorable toward him?

When she said, "Very well, thank you," besides the fact that she was not ill, she was also confessing she was very fond of the gentleman, which was making an eventual decision easier for her.

Mr. Worthington still accepted his standing invitation to join the Edmonds for dinner Saturday evening, but now the conversation did not have the same spontaneity of previous engagements. Mrs. Edmond was certainly as hospitable as ever, though she must have sensed the constraint at the table. Julia and Mr. Worthington tended to make short replies, offered rare comments and seldom looked one another fully in the face but rather glanced at each other out of the corner of their eyes or under lowered brows like two guilty children.

"Well, Mr. Worthington, your sermons seem to be making quite a name for yourself and Mr. Bracken. I suspect you do not revel in all the attention you are receiving, but you fulfilled Bracken's fondest dreams," Richard said brightly. Any stimulating repartee was being supplied solely by the gentleman who sat at the head of the table.

"I only spoke what I sincerely believe," Worthington said.

"There is your departure and the wonder of your address. Do you plan on pursuing that radical course, or will you slip back to the familiar sentiments and sermons we have heard so often before?"

"I teach what I am called upon by the Spirit to teach. I would not call that radical."

"Certainly not," Julia said.

"Of course not." Richard smiled. "You *are* a breath of fresh air in our little community, though, Mr. Worthington."

After the meal, in the sitting room, Worthington was hoping for the chance to sit alone with Miss Masonet. She had made it plain that she could not hear any further protestations of love until she came of age, but just to sit with her in semiprivacy would be blissful.

But, perversely, Mr. Edmond, who was usually so thoughtful, who seemed to be actively promoting this match of his beautiful ward and the local curate, insisted on grouping the four of them together, required Mr. Worthington to go over some points of his notorious sermon again, to speculate on topics for future sermons, to exchange news about other parish families. All Worthington really wanted to discuss was how beautiful Miss Masonet was and what pleasure merely being in her presence gave him.

"And tell us, Mr. Worthington, for my mother's ease of mind, are you well settled? Your house comfortable? Position satisfying? Having at last acquired our own pastor, we would hate to have you leave us."

Worthington looked toward Julia, his lips attempting a nervous smile.

"I shall certainly stay through the winter and spring," he said. Then he turned toward Mrs. Edmond. "In fact, I am perfectly happy here and will not *seek* another assignment."

As Mr. Worthington was assuring Mrs. Edmond, Cousin Richard studied Julia. If he, too, was looking for some sort of assurance, it is hard to say whether he found it in the earnest expression of her face and those deep gray eyes she turned on him.

By the end of February the cold had eased. It was still gloomy and rained, at least a little, almost everyday, but the rain had a purpose now other than chilling one to the bone, whether one was out-of-doors in the damp or inside behind the walls that could not keep out the vaporous cold. Now in the moments, which were becoming longer and longer, when the sun shone, it often revealed bright green patches of grass. In the last week of February an intrepid daffodil broke through the soil of the garden box outside the big window of the Aspen Grove sitting room.

Julia was still on that window seat, looking out in the direction of those long spears of green, which would, in a week or two, be topped with a vibrant yellow crown.

"Spring will soon be here. If we are to take yon Monsieur Jonquille at his word, it is here now."

Julia was startled from her reverie and faced her guardian in surprise. It was the middle of the afternoon, in the middle of the week. Cousin Richard was not expected until the weekend or even later.

"I did not mean to frighten you, Julia," he apologized.

"Not frighten. You could never frighten me, dear cousin. I did not expect you, that is all."

There was a question in her words.

"There are things I suppose I should be seeing to in town, but at times I feel I must get back into the country or go mad. It stopped raining this morning and I knew the lawn and garden would look just like that." He motioned with his chin out toward the lawn, which had greened since his departure on Monday.

"You never have enjoyed the bustle and energy of the city," she said.

The first time she came to Aspen Grove she would have found that incomprehensible. Madame Chevous's school was outside of Paris, true, and she learned to like that well enough, but she was a daughter of Paris and she believed true life, full life, was only to be found in the teeming city.

Like many another belief she held when she was thirteen, she had changed her mind about this place and about what constituted a full life.

"It is not as much a matter of disliking that place as it is missing..." He paused, and in the unexpected silence Julia glanced over her shoulder to find him looking not out the window but down at her. Surprised in his gaze, Richard redirected his eyes to the broad pane of glass. "Missing this place," he finished.

Julia turned to sit straight in the seat and patted the empty cushion beside her.

"Come and sit and tell me all about your noble victories out in the wide world, cousin," she said. "It has been a long time since you regaled me with such thrilling tales. I used to picture you as a Roman commander marching off at the head of a great company of men to some heroic battle when you left here. And then you would return and sit with me on this window seat, telling me stories of the challenges and successes you had met with while away. And I knew I was right in my image of you. Your presence somehow comforted me with the knowledge that the world was once again safe for humanity. Do you remember those times?" Now she smiled up at him and indicated the place next to her again. With a deep sigh Richard sat. Julia put her silken, long-fingered hand over the back of his.

"You are tired?" she asked.

He turned his hand over, catching the girl's hand in the palm of his own. It looked like a delicate brown bird snuggled in its nest.

"A little," he replied.

"Business? The ride down?"

"Both, I suppose." The bird stirred in its nest. Richard found himself holding his breath, but it did not fly away. It only turned a bit and rested more securely in the nest of his hand.

"Home is the place to come when you grow weary of the world." she said.

"Home. Yes," he said, distractedly. He did not watch the soft bird of her hand, he did not want to frighten it, but he was lost in a consideration of how light it was, how fragile. He could close his fist and crush it, but the wonder of her hand was not its frailty but its cleverness, its ability, the warmth of its touch.

"Was all well with Miss Brewster when you left London?" she asked, and then it was the nest that left the bird. Richard pulled his hand away from Julia's, plunging it into the pocket of his jacket as he leaned back against the window and extended his long legs out in front of him.

"Rachel went into town yesterday. She rode in the carriage with her maid and actually went into the dressmaker's shop. She says Mrs. Crandell was stunned." He chuckled so faintly it was almost to himself. "She says I am a terrible influence on her, that it was never her intent to become a world explorer."

Now Julia laughed a little, too, but her poor hand was abandoned and had grown cold. She balled it into a fist and hid it in the folds of her dress.

"And Mr. Worthington?" Richard asked her. "He is well?"

"He is well."

The two of them sat very quietly for a few moments, then Richard turned to look out the window.

"It looks as if it will rain again," he said. Then, watching the lawn begin to dim as clouds filled the sky, he murmured softly, thoughtfully, "Things have changed since the old days when we sat together in this window."

Julia was not sure that he meant for her to hear him.

Mr. Worthington brought her a handful of crocuses the second week in March. He was not specific when he told her where he got them, but the only crocuses up and blooming of which Julia was aware were the ones in Mrs. Bracken's flower garden.

Julia accepted the flowers gratefully and hid her smile in the blooms she bent to sniff. She could picture dear Sidney sneaking under the Bracken window in his sober dark coat to snatch a few of that lady's prized flowers.

She was not surprised when the sermon the next Sunday was on the eighth commandment: Thou shalt not steal. She knew he was not being hypocritical but rather was calling himself to repentance.

"I cannot join you for tea on Tuesday," he told Julia and the Edmonds after meeting. "I have promised to help dear Mrs. Bracken in her garden."

It was a bitter penance he had imposed upon himself, and his duty and willingness to accept it touched the young woman at least as much as had the flowers, which were faded by now and would soon be thrown out.

Mr. Worthington did come for supper on Wednesday and again on Saturday. His regular meals at Aspen Grove had been increased to twice a week, which did not count his frequent afternoon teas, his calls to inquire after the ladies alone during the week, and the visits Julia returned, usually on the weekends with Richard.

He consulted regularly with Julia about his Sunday sermons, soliciting her ideas for text, reading to her his early drafts, revising anything she thought needed revision.

Julia could not help but be flattered. She enjoyed their discussions and was extremely pleased to hear her suggestions, often her own words, come across the pulpit in young Worthington's earnest delivery.

She enjoyed her discussions with Worthington, too, because Cousin Richard was drawing further and further away from her all the time. Being unable to talk with him about books and bonnets, poetry and paint, or any other subject that might occur to her, would have left a gaping hole in her life if it were not for the ubiquitous Mr. Worthington. But Worthington was there, giving her his undivided attention, giving to her all the time she wanted. Making it clear that he was at her most impulsive disposal, twenty-four hours a day. And if their conversations never touched on those lighthearted, amusing subjects that used to make her laugh with Cousin Richard, Mr. Worthington did give more serious consideration to her ideas, at times unnervingly to her every word, than her *cher* Cousin Richard ever had.

And to bring her flowers, Mr. Worthington was willing to relinquish afternoon tea with her and spend the day at Mrs. Bracken's strident beck and call.

What sacrifice had Cousin Richard ever been called upon to make for her?

Easter fell on the second Sunday of April that year. This would be Mr. Worthington's first Easter sermon, and to say that he was a little nervous about it would be like saying the Black Plague made people a little ill.

"I cannot make up my mind about which text to speak to," he said.

The knock came at the door early Tuesday morning, early even for Mr. Worthington. Julia answered the summons herself, and after a distracted salutation, Worthington preceded her into the sitting room, where he now stood looking out the window. It was the bay window that presented the scene of the lawn, now bright green, and the sunny spring flowers.

"Cannot make up your mind?" she asked. "I thought you decided upon the verse from Saint John. 'I am the resurrection and the life.'"

Worthington shook his head, but not with any force of conviction.

"That is so—expected, on Easter. Half of the preachers in the kingdom will be speaking to 'I am the resurrection and the life' on Sunday. More than half. Three-quarters. Nine out of ten."

A smile entered Julia's eyes but never crossed her lips.

"And you have grown accustomed to the recognition an unusual position brings you."

"It is not that," he replied seriously, not recognizing the light in her eye. "It is the more profound consideration I want my parishioners to give the message."

"What could be more profound than the resurrection of *Notre Sauveur?*"

Worthington's look was little short of scandalized.

"Nothing is more profound than that," he said. "But will hearing familiar thoughts on a familiar passage make my congregation realize that?"

He sat at the writing desk and pulled forward the family Bible. All these things in this room were familiar to him by now. He thumbed through the pages, skimming over the archaic text.

"'What good thing shall I do, that I may have eternal life,'" he read, glancing up at her.

"Perhaps," she said, but she came and sat next to him. Together they bent over the closely printed words.

He stopped turning and pointed to another verse in Saint John. "This one?" he asked.

"'And I give unto them eternal life; and they shall never perish, neither shall any man pluck them out of my hand.' Maybe," Julia said.

Worthington began to turn the pages again. In Saint John 13 his eyes were drawn to a verse that had been underlined. "This is it," he said.

"'A new commandment I give unto you, That ye love one another, as I have loved you, that ye also love one another.'" Julia read the words aloud and then nodded. "It is one of my favorite verses," she said.

Worthington noted the reference. "I knew you would be my inspiration, Julia," he said, then he looked up and gazed at her intently.

Sitting so close to him, Julia could hear him inhale and exhale, could see the thin breast of his dark jacket rise and fall with each breath.

"You would be the inspiration of my life," he said softly.

Julia ducked her head to hide the tears that sprang to her eyes at his fervent words.

"I am sorry," he said softly, closing the book of Holy Writ and standing it next to the other books on the desk. "You have requested time, and to speak of my feelings now is unforgivable."

She looked up at him, her tears gone and a smile on her lips.

"I think it is forgivable," she said.

Mr. Worthington's Easter sermon was centered around Saint John 13:34, and like his New Year's address, it was talked about a great deal.

"Very moving," Cousin Richard told the preacher after the meeting. "And unusual. I was expecting something on the resurrection and the life, that traditional verse. You must have been inspired."

Mr. Worthington looked past Mr. Edmond to the young lady standing behind his shoulder, nearly hidden by its broad expanse.

"I believe I was," he said.

Richard drew aside and allowed Julia to step forward and offer her low words of commendation. He did more than draw aside. He turned completely, stepped away, mingled with the departing congregation.

On a Wednesday in the middle of May, Cousin Richard returned to the Aspen Grove home with a very large valise in tow. He usually came for the weekend with nothing more than he could carry in a small carpetbag.

"I have come for the planting season," he announced to the three women who stood staring at his luggage in surprise, his mother, his ward and Glenda.

"Oh, Richard!" his mother cried, flinging her arms about his neck, tears in her eyes.

Her son returned her fond embrace, laughing a little contritely.

"Mother, you would think I had been stolen by Gypsies when a babe and we had been searching for one another all of our lives. I am here every week."

"Almost," Julia corrected. Richard looked in her direction.

"Here now," he said, disengaging himself at last from his mother's arms. "You make a fellow feel something of a rotter, however gratifying it is to be missed."

Glenda, for her part, smiled a tight little smile. Unlike the other two women, she clearly viewed Mr. Edmond's return in its true light. It would be a month of an extra mouth to feed, a man's stomach to fill and a man's mess to clean up. But it was only for a month, she consoled herself, breaking several more eggs into the pan for breakfast when she returned to the kitchen. She could bear it for a month, she supposed. Though she was aware that the roast she had planned on feeding the ladies for the remainder of the week would all be gone by tonight.

Richard did not farm his own land, but he leased the fields that surrounded Aspen Grove. He therefore felt some responsibility to take notice of them once or twice a year, at planting and again at harvest. When his father was alive they had taken a much more active interest in agriculture, some years retaining a field or two for their own crops. Like life in the country in general, Richard preferred the idyllic tilling of the earth and sowing of seed to the tense psychological warfare that was known euphemistically as "getting ahead" in the city. But first there were his father's investments to oversee, and then his own, and now, when he might have retired from the turmoil of the city to his country lands, there were . . . other things that kept him away, that kept him in the city.

But he would allow himself these few weeks. He could bear it for a month.

"And what are the plans for the day?" he asked an hour later, after he was washed and breakfast was over. He had eaten what Glenda gave him and then requested two more slices of bread.

"We have no plans, Richard dear. The time is at your disposal," Aunt Jenny said.

"I will not have that," he protested. "I know you both well enough to know that life continues whether I am here or not. I am a member of this household, not a guest."

"Well, actually, I planned on having Glenda plant the rest of the flowers. It is late in the spring, I know, but Mrs. Bracken just sent over some gladiolus bulbs that need to be put in the ground."

"Very good," he said. "And you, Julia?"

"I . . . I have sketched out the scene from the sitting room window." She looked away from him. "You know the one," she said with a lightness in her voice that seemed forced. But whatever significance she attached to his holding her hand that day as they sat on the window seat and his quiet words of missing the Grove and—whatever else it was he missed here, Edmond was evidently determined to ignore the incident himself, much the same way he had put away the memory of that kiss they shared so long ago at Ramsgate Hall. "I was going to start on that in oil," she continued. "However..."

"No howevers. I insist you set up your easel. After I check on Mr. Fenton's progress in the east field I shall come out and view your work."

"I thought I would paint it from inside, as seen through the bay window. It is a favorite retreat of mine."

"I know," he said. Now Richard spoke softly and Julia was guiltily thrilled that he *did* remember the moment, that it meant something to him.

They separated from the breakfast table to their various pursuits. The side door was open and Julia could hear Aunt Jenny giving directions for the other flower box. She set up the easel, placed the canvas with the faint charcoal lines on it and put small daubs of paint onto her palette. The day was sunny and Julia realized she would not be painting this same scene on an overcast day. The green of the lawn's new growth was pale, rich. The young leaves of the oak tree were a little darker, and the green growth of the lilac bush, now in bloom, was darker still.

The variety of shades and colors should have had Julia's exclusive attention. But her mind wandered, her thoughts frequently on the length of time it was taking her Cousin Richard to inspect one very small field not a quarter of a mile away.

When she heard the commotion at the open side door she turned expectantly to the sitting room door, a welcoming smile on her lips.

"You are painting."

"I am, Mr. Worthington," she said, not aware that her smile had slipped the tiniest bit.

"Mrs. Bracken said she saw Mr. Edmond ride by this morning."

"She no doubt did."

"I was surprised to hear it. I thought I might step in and make sure nothing is amiss here that would call the gentleman back so suddenly. There is no problem?"

"Not of which I am aware."

"Mr. Edmond does not usually return so early in the week."

"No." Julia noticed a speck of green paint on her finger and wiped it against the pinafore she wore when she painted. "He said he has come for the planting."

"The planting?"

"The season."

"He has come to stay, then?"

"Only for a month," Julia said. She also was not aware of the note of regret in her voice at those words.

"I see," Worthington said. "He is out now?"

Julia nodded, raising her eyebrows and her shoulders, indicating her inability to supply any further information on her guardian, his immediate whereabouts or his intentions.

"And you are . . ."

"Painting." She turned to look at the easel behind her.

"May I see?" he asked.

The young woman smiled over her shoulder at the gentleman's hopeful little request.

"Please," she said, moving so he could see the few strokes of color she had applied to the canvas. "Though there is not a great deal to see."

"It looks beautiful to me already," the curate sighed.

Julia turned to the canvas in scorn.

"Do not be ridiculous. So far, it is nothing." She waved her hand in dismissal, then noting the droop to his smile, she elaborated, "Only a light green slash here, a bluish green there."

"And it will be?" he prompted, coming to stand very close to the young woman, to see the canvas and the scene she was viewing from her perspective.

"That." She indicated the window. He glanced through it then turned toward the room again.

"You do not know when he will be back?" Worthington asked, apropos of nothing.

Julia had been studying the sketch on the canvas and was reaching for the little bit of charcoal among her paints to retrace one of the faint lines. She looked instead at Worthington, confused by his non sequitur.

"When who will be back?" she asked.

"Edmond. Mr. Edmond." Worthington quickly covered his informality.

"Soon, I believe. Actually, I believed he would be back before this."

Worthington faced her again. They were standing very close, and before either of them was aware of his intentions, he put his arms around her and drew her to him.

"I wish you would let me speak to him, Julia," he said.

"I do not think that would be wise, Sidney," she replied breathlessly.

"But I love you so."

"I know."

"Then why..."

"You must release me. What if my cousin or Aunt Jenny should see us."

"I wish they would. Then you would have to tell them and this terrible wait would be over."

Julia pushed against him gently and he dropped his arms, though he refused to take the step from her she was encouraging.

"It is only two more months," she reminded.

Now his smile was both apologetic and weary.

"That was going to be my argument to you," he said.

"Argument? Surely I am not interrupting an argument between our revered pastor and my reserved ward." The voice was Cousin Richard's.

Hurriedly, in confusion, Worthington backed away from Julia.

Julia could not believe she had not heard Richard's entrance. She had been listening for it so carefully a few minutes before, yet she was as completely surprised as Mr. Worthington. She looked toward the curate and his red face with freckles prominently highlighted. Then she looked at her cousin again. How would he interpret what he had seen between the curate and herself? What *had* he seen?

"Not an argument, sir," Worthington began. Julia gave him a warning look. "Rather a theological discussion," he finished lamely, then quickly changed subjects. "I came over to welcome you home. Mrs. Bracken said you had arrived and I..."

"Wanted to see for yourself?"

"Was surprised," Worthington said. He looked toward Julia, but her dark eyes were black against the light from the window and he could not read anything there. He had the feeling that even if she moved away from the window and gazed directly into his own eyes he would not be able to read anything in hers. He cleared his throat and pulled at the lapels of his jacket. "Having tendered my greetings to you, sir, I must attend to other errands. But I will see you all again this evening. For supper," he reminded them, seeing the blank looks on both their faces.

"Of course," Julia said.

"Certainly," Richard seconded.

Worthington showed himself from the room, protesting that he knew the way out quite well.

Julia and Cousin Richard stood silently looking at each other for a moment, hearing Worthington leave the house, even hearing Aunt Jenny's farewells to him outside.

"I saw you standing together near the window," he said at last.

Julia blushed, but with the light still behind her she hoped he could not see that.

"He heard you were come."

"So he said," Richard reminded her.

"He came to make sure nothing was amiss that would call you back in the middle of the week."

"Is anything amiss, Julia?"

"Nothing whatsoever," Julia answered flatly.

"I was surprised to see him, as well," Richard said. "Standing with you. At the window." The ending to his speech should have been unconvincing, since it had apparently been his every design to see his ward and the curate together at every opportunity. Julia did not notice the discrepancy.

"He asked to look at my painting."

"I see."

"Would *you* like to look at my painting?" She stepped to one side and indicated the easel behind her and the window behind it.

"I do not..." he started, then leaned forward to see her faint sketch better.

"I do not think you can see it from there," she said, encouraging him to come closer with a shyness that seemed out of place when she talked to her dear Cousin Richard, and yet one she could not throw off in the close confines of this bay window and the memories here.

He took a step toward her, and then another, until he was standing next to the girl in front of the window, in very nearly the same position in which he had seen Worthington and his ward from outside as he was returning from his inspection of the field. Except he did not have his arms around her waist, which was the position that brought him rushing into the house and into this room, his shortness of breath unnoticed only because the curate and Miss Masonet were both startled and confused themselves.

"This patch of grass is darker," he said.

"It is in the shade now," she explained. "I shall have to work at the same hour every morning to get it right."

"And quickly, before the lilacs fade," he warned.

"In less than a month even the sun will have shifted so the shadows will not be the same."

"I can see that. Even as familiar as that scene is to me, it is never the same, is it?"

"Never," she said so softly it was almost a whisper.

Richard had taken another step to stand even closer to her in order to get her perspective of the scene. Now he stood directly behind her, the lapel of his coat brushing her shoulder blade. Julia leaned back ever so slightly to rest against his chest. It was so strong, so broad, so... right. Richard, in the motion of a dream they both were unwilling to disturb, raised his hand and laid it gently against the front of her shoulder. With the barest increase of pressure it might have been called an embrace.

"Things change so quickly, do they not?" she murmured. "One believes they will always be the same, and then suddenly everything is different."

"What is familiar becomes unfamiliar," he said.

Whatever else they were discussing, it had ceased to be the picture.

* * *

Cousin Richard's month at the Grove slipped away from them, gliding from their grasping fingers to be lost in that yawning expanse of time past.

In the mornings he rode out to the fields and in the evenings he returned to sit with the two ladies, and usually Mr. Worthington. But not always. Some few nights it was just himself, his mother and his ward, in the same family circle that was so dear to them all, and grew to be ever more dear with each day, with every moment that threatened to irrevocably disrupt that circle.

But it was a dream. It could not last, and one morning the post delivered a letter from Miss Brewster. Her father had purchased for her, some years before, a cunning little machine of French design that produced raised letters on a page for her use. But it was an awkward contraption and Miss Brewster did not often take recourse to it.

Her letter to Edmond consisted of only two short lines. "Dear Richard," it said, "when are you returning? We need to talk. Rachel."

She was right. This was unfair to Miss Brewster. To Rachel. What was he doing here? What fancies was he spinning for himself? He had commitments; he had obligations. But he did not tell himself he was following his heart back to London.

"The fields are all in," he said at lunch, speaking more to his bowl of soup, which he wished had more chicken in it, than to either of the two ladies. "I suppose I had better return to London."

"Oh, Richard. Do you have to?" his mother said, her voice a perfect study in disappointment.

He smiled fondly at her. "I am afraid so, Mother. Business." His excuse was vague and unconvincing. He had been here at the Grove for more than a month, during a very active season of the London exchange, and never seemed pressed by business.

"I thought everything was in order," his mother said.

"It is."

"And will commerce cease if you are not there?"

He smiled. "It will not."

"Then why...?"

"Miss Brewster writes," he said.

There were no other protests, yet as fond as they all were of Miss Brewster, they were each of them sorry she had sent her laborious letter.

"I am sorry I cannot stay to see the finishing stroke on your painting, Julia." He turned to the young woman. Julia had been very quiet ever since her cousin made his announcement. Her silence was not the result of surprise. How could she be surprised? She knew he would be leaving, she even knew it would be Miss Brewster who called him away and not business. Still, she had been very quiet, not trusting her voice enough to express her own disappointment.

"It is almost finished," she whispered now.

"But it is not *all* finished," Richard reminded her.

"No," she said. "It is not all finished."

In the time Richard spent at Aspen Grove, Julia had made marked progress on her painting. Every time Mr. Worthington saw it he declared it was completed to perfection, but Julia insisted she had much to do on it yet.

The truth was, the painting had taken on a mystic quality for the girl. She believed, although it was not a thought she even admitted to herself, that as long as the painting was not finished things would not change: she would not have to reach a decision; she would not have to leave her life here all behind; Mr. Worthington would patiently wait for her until the stars fell from the heavens. She allowed herself to fantasize that Miss Brewster would somehow disappear from her cousin's life and Richard would remain safely and happily at Aspen Grove. As long as the painting was not completed.

But the painting was unfinished, and Richard said he would be leaving tomorrow, would be returning to Miss Rachel Brewster and his life away from here—and her.

That evening Mr. Worthington came to call.

The four of them, Julia, Worthington, Aunt Jenny and Cousin Richard, sat in the sitting room, commenting on the warm, though certainly seasonal, weather; what a delight it had been that Mr. Edmond could stay for a month; what a pity it was he had to leave so soon; and what they could expect the price of barley to be this fall, considering the unsteady market. Neither the women nor Mr. Worthington could make any intelligent contribution on that last question, but it was the sort of thing one is expected to discuss if one lives in the country on a farm. Mr. Worthington asked after Miss Brewster. Was she well when Mr. Edmond left London? What a remarkable woman she was, was she not?

Finally Mr. Worthington cleared his throat.

"Miss Masonet, it is such a lovely evening, I wondered if you would join me for a walk?"

Julia looked at him with an expression that might almost have been interpreted as panic.

"Now, Mr. Worthington? But we have been so enjoying the company."

"I thought we might take a private walk," he said.

Richard looked up sharply at the clergyman's phrase.

"My cousin is to leave again soon," Julia said. "I do not like to be away these last few hours he is here."

"Do not be foolish, Julia," Richard said. "You must not curtail your activity because of me. I thought we determined that when I arrived."

The beautiful world of clouds they had constructed here this month had been pulled to the earth with Miss Brewster's letter. Now Mr. Worthington's words made it vanish altogether. He had not been fair to Miss Brewster or to Julia. She had a life to continue, as well.

Julia looked to him with a stricken expression she could not disguise. If he had glanced up from his plate it would have broken his heart.

"It is my particular design that you return to spend more time with your guardian," Mr. Worthington assured everyone brightly.

"Run along, my dear. Richard and I are perfectly content to be with one another," Mrs. Edmond cajoled.

"You must go with Mr. Worthington, Julia," Richard said. "I could not forgive myself if you refused Mr. Worthington because of me."

Julia smiled weakly and stood.

"Very well, then," she said. "But we will return *very* shortly."

"Take your time, dear," Mrs. Edmond encouraged. "Take all the time you need."

Mr. Worthington did not need very much time at all. The two of them barely turned off the Aspen Grove drive into the lane before he began.

"I know I am anticipating your time schedule, Julia," he said. "But I received this letter from the bishop this morning."

He extracted a letter, folded several times, from his coat pocket. Julia took it and smoothed it, but before she could read a word of it, Worthington told her the message, quoting whole passages of the letter by heart.

"He says reports of my admirable ministry have reached him. He is pleased with my progress and is willing to offer me a somewhat larger parish near Northampton. 'That is not to say,' he assures me, 'that the work you are doing in Tunbridge is unneeded or unappreciated.' He leaves the decision with me."

Julia nodded her head, bent over the letter, following the message as the young man recited it. He was silent for a few moments, waiting for her to come to the "Yours in the Lord, Bishop Hunnington."

When she finished the letter she looked directly into his eyes. Julia and the curate were of the same height, and the dark eyes she turned toward him seemed to look past his own into the thoughts behind them in his mind.

"What will you do?" she asked.

"That decision is yours," he said. Julia dropped her gaze to the ground in front of where they stood, and Worthington elaborated, though he really did not need to. Julia understood him perfectly. "If you marry me I will be happy anywhere, and if you wish to stay near your home I will gladly serve in the community wherein we met for the rest of my life. If you do not marry me—" he turned his hands palms up and shrugged his shoulders "—it will not matter, though I suppose it would be easier if I left."

Julia shifted her gaze to look at the man's hands, stubby-fingered, only lightly tanned, the palms exposed in a touching attitude of defenselessness. She took a breath and he held his.

"You have been wonderfully patient with me and you deserve an answer." She spoke solemnly. A bird chirped cheerily over their heads, but the mood of the scene was not lightened. She stopped and took his two hands in hers.

"Mr. Worthington, I would be honored to be your wife."

Chapter Twenty

She sat pulling the brush slowly through the long, silky strands of her hair. It caught the candlelight and reflected a glossy, bluish black glow.

The motion of her arm never varied, never slackened. She might have been an automaton. Up and down. Up and down. Over and over.

She stared into her looking glass, not seeing the gleam of her hair, not seeing the face, olive-toned and exotic, so like her father's, but seeing something that was not there, another face. Seeing Mr. Worthington's transport of joy, hearing again his gasp of jubilation, feeling his fingers as they closed convulsively around her hand and drew it to his lips.

Up and down. Up and down.

"Miss Masonet! Julia! You have made me the happiest man alive!"

In the mirror in front of her she saw the young man again, his expression, his smile, the damp glimmer of his eye, and she believed she honestly had made him the happiest man alive.

He smiled, he *beamed*, he laughed out loud. He wanted all of the British Empire, including all the colonies, foreign possessions and isles of the sea, to be notified by that evening.

Julia would not allow that.

"You must not tell anyone."

"How can I contain my joy?" he asked.

"You must exercise some degree of self-restraint. That is all I ask."

"You are not ashamed of me?" The question was only half-joking.

Julia had smiled and shook her head.

"I am not ashamed of you, Sidney. You are one of the finest, most dedicated men I know."

"Is it because you still believe Mr. Edmond would prevent our marriage?"

"No," she said slowly. "No, I agree with you, he would be perfectly satisfied. But I would like to tell them myself. Aunt Jenny..." Her voice trailed away and she left Worthington to fill in any reason he cared to why it was necessary for Julia to break the news to her elderly aunt personally.

Her plan had been to tell the Edmonds—"when the time was right." Perhaps, she silently told the reflected eyes before her, the time would be right only after it was a *fait accompli*. She and Worthington could be married in Scotland, dispatch a happy note and return in a month or two to the humble parsonage on Mr. Bracken's land, or perhaps to the grander position the bishop had offered the curate in Northampton. It did not matter what they did, or where they lived, as long as she did not have to see Cousin Richard's face, hear his hearty congratulations, feel the "farewell" in his handshake when she announced her marriage.

There was a soft tap at her chamber door, and summoned back to the present, she looked at the brush in her hand in surprise and wondered dimly how long she had been brushing her hair.

"Entrez," she said, laying the brush on her dressing table and turning toward the door.

It opened, but only a little.

"May I come in, Julia?"

"Of course," she said. If she had still been turned toward her glass she might have seen the troubled look leave her eyes and a soft, tender expression enter them.

It was Richard who stepped from the dark hallway into the room, where the darkness was relieved only by the light of a single candle.

"You were so quiet this evening, I hoped you were not ill?"

"No, I am not ill," she said, turning back to the mirror.

Without waiting for an invitation, he sat in the chair next to the dressing table. It was a familiar chair to him, one in which he had often seated himself, more often than was proper for a gentleman to make himself comfortable in a lady's room. But Julia was not a lady. She was his...not his cousin, not his sister, and his ward for only one more month. He looked at her reflection in the glass and sighed faintly. Perhaps Julia *was* a lady.

"What is it?" She smiled back into the reflection of his face.

"Seeing you like this, with your hair down, it is hard to believe it is all over," he said.

"What is all over?"

"My charge. Your childhood. You are a woman, Julia. In three weeks you will be a woman of impressively independent means."

"My childhood has been over for some time," she said, reminding him of a fact she was afraid he often forgot, or perhaps never realized before.

"I know that," he said. "It has not been too onerous for you, I hope. Forced to answer to a man who no doubt seemed more like a tyrannical older brother than a guardian?"

She turned to face him directly and looked into his eyes, her own eyes shadowed by her black hair so that they, too, shone with a blue black gloss now.

"You have never seemed like a brother to me," she said.

"An ogre, perhaps?" He smiled and she inclined her head in a slight nod.

"At times," she admitted.

Now he chuckled. "Soon the ogre will be overthrown. And what will you do then?" he asked.

There was alarm in her voice. "Do?" she said.

"Travel? Study? Perhaps you plan on returning to Paris? You could pursue your painting in the heart of the art world." He was not offering the suggestions like exciting alternatives but rather like a list of unpleasant options.

"I will not be returning to France," she said. He could not disguise completely his look of relief. "My birthday will no doubt signal certain changes, though."

His look of relief faded, and now Julia might have been facing the other way, looking into her glass again, so alike were the expression of solemn regret on both their faces.

"And what will you do, Cousin Richard?" she asked him.

He forced a smile and forced it to look natural.

"I will continue to do what I have been doing, I should think."

"What of Miss Brewster?"

He paused for a beat.

"Miss Brewster and I shall be married very soon, I believe," he said, at last.

"Good." Julia nodded her head solemnly. "That is good."

"Yes, I think it is."

"And she is good."

"Very good. As is Mr. Worthington."

"Yes, he is."

Richard reached for her hand, which once again fluttered to rest in his palm.

"You have grown to be a beautiful woman, Julia."

Now her face lit in one of its teasing smiles, which had become so rare.

"Which, if true, comes as a great surprise to both of us, does it not?" She laughed.

He shook his head, though he returned her smile.

"I am not as surprised as you may think," he told her. "You will make—someone—very happy."

"And you will make Rachel very happy," she returned. Tit for tat.

It was quiet in the room. Mrs. Edmond had long been in bed, the house was closed, even the windows in here were closed so that none of the sounds of a summer night disturbed their conversation or the silence between them when they did not speak.

"Richard," she said, so softly it almost did not disturb the silence. "I have a question . . ."

"A question?"

"About us. About what has happened between us."

"Are you sure you want to ask it?" he said, a quiet warning in his voice.

"I need to know."

"It is too late to make a difference," he said.

"I am afraid I will always regret it if I do not know."

"There are some things in this life it is better not to know, some words it is easier never to have spoken."

"Richard . . ." There was a mournful pleading in her voice.

"It is too late, Julia."

"Is it?" she asked faintly. They had both been looking down, watching the bird asleep in its nest. Now the bird stirred and Julia looked up into his eyes. Her own eyes glimmered.

"It is," he said. Solemnly he raised her hand to his lips and kissed it. Then he released her hand, and Julia felt as if she were a bit of that drifting flotsam she had pointed out to her dear, dear cousin so long ago on the boat that had brought her to his home.

"I did not mean to disturb you. I only wanted to say good-night."

"Good night, Cousin Richard."

"And goodbye."

A sob clutched at Julia's throat, but she would not release it.

"I do not know how long I will be gone. I have neglected things for too long." He shook his head.

"Perhaps you do not want to return to business in the city," Julia offered.

"Perhaps you are correct. I have been thinking the same thing myself. I am thinking I could close my business in town and transfer everything to Tunbridge. But whatever I do, it will take me several weeks, I am sure. I may even miss your birthday. If I am unable to get away you must make arrangements to come up to town for a day. Your crotchety old guardian will have only that one last chance to lord it over his young ward.'' He smiled, but she could not.

"Something will be arranged," she said.

The morning leapt to the top of the eastern hills and crouched there, clutching the countryside with iron-tipped claws until, by the time Julia woke and was dressed, it held the land and its inhabitants immovable, mesmerized by the stifling heat of its baleful yellow eye.

"Richard was away before dawn," Aunt Jenny reported when Julia descended the stairs, wisps of hair already clinging damply to her forehead. "Which I suppose was very clever of him. Heavens, but it is warm." She fanned herself hopefully. "If you are hungry at all, Glenda can give you some porridge, or perhaps bread and milk."

"Cousin Richard has left?" Julia cried, ignoring completely the offer of food.

"I am afraid so, my dear. He said to tell you he was sorry to miss you, to tell you goodbye. But only think, Julia, he says he is going to move his business to Tunbridge, perhaps even farm some of the Grove. This may be the last time he will say goodbye."

Julia's throat tightened at her aunt's words and she did not answer.

Mr. Worthington came later in the morning. Mrs. Bracken had given him the report that Mr. Edmond left for town that morning, though Julia seriously doubted that the large, self-indulgent Mrs. Bracken rose with the chickens, even for the sake of a bit of neighborhood gossip she would pass on with great superiority to Mr. Worthington.

"Did you tell him?" he asked her when Glenda showed him into Richard's study. It was not the usual receiving room, but it was on the west side of the house and would be the coolest room until late in the afternoon, when the sun had prowled across the sky and sank to its haunches to glare in through these windows. It was also very dim in the room and Worthington did not notice Mrs. Edmond until his words had already flown from his lips and were fluttering about the room, unreclaimable.

"Tell what to whom?" Mrs. Edmond asked. "Richard? Tell him what, Julia?"

"Mr. Worthington has received a very favorable offer, Aunt Jenny. The bishop has suggested a parish near Northampton."

"Oh dear." Aunt Jenny sighed. It was too hot to be any more bombastic in her regret, though no matter what the weather, this gentle complaint was as much as Mrs. Edmond would ever have made.

"He has not yet made up his mind as to accepting it and he hoped to talk to my cousin." Julia did not actually say Mr. Worthington hoped to talk to her cousin *about* the bishop's offer, so she felt no compunction over the explanation she had given her aunt. Richard would have called it "a French absolution," which is what he had always called the half truths of her childhood. Now she spoke to Worthington. "Perhaps, after your walk, you would like a cool drink. Come with me into the kitchen and we will see what Glenda has left."

"Water will be fine, Miss Masonet," the gentleman said, following her out the door and down the hall toward the kitchen.

They were well out of earshot of the study on their way into the kitchen before Julia answered his original question.

"I did not have the chance," she said. Worthington drew a breath for protests that would have been as mild as Aunt Jenny's complaints, but Julia cut him off. "It does not matter, though. He will be away until the end of July, and by then you and I will be married."

"Without Mr. Edmond's leave?" Worthington sounded doubtful.

"Come the nineteenth we will not need his leave."

"This seems so—deceitful," Worthington said.

"Not deceitful," she told him. "Only simpler. And quieter. No great to-do in the neighborhood, people whispering and pointing whenever one or the other of us passes by. And heaven forbid we should ever pass by together."

"We shall be together a great deal in our lives," Worthington reminded her, smiling contentedly.

"Yes, but we will be married then and no one will give us another thought. It is only the about-to-be-married who are the topic of general fascination and comment. The never-married and the already-married evoke no interest at all."

Worthington, still not completely easy about their secrecy, continued to scruple; Julia continued to ease and soothe, which Worthington enjoyed as much as he questioned their actions. In time he ceded her victory, as they both knew he would, and rather than make any plans then, they returned to Aunt Jenny in the study and talked and laughed for the rest of the morning, discomfort forgotten, consciences salved, the road before them broad and straight. Sidney Worthington saw it strewn with rose petals.

Cousin Richard wrote regularly to report the progress of his affairs in London. He and Miss Brewster were making serious plans for their marriage, and he was also busy with plans for his financial move, the upheaval of his business life. Julia eagerly read each installment, his letters marking the stages of upheaval in her own life.

Rachel is an angel and has assured me she will wait patiently until I make final disposition of my business dealings here, but it appears that all can go forth in three weeks, perhaps four.

He wrote that news on July 2.

Mr. Worthington made arrangements to be away from his parish on "certain personal matters" the week of July 19. Another letter came from Richard dated July 5.

I have sold Father's shares in the mining and closed his account. They would not transfer those holdings via third party to the Tunbridge bank.

On the first day of the month Mr. Worthington told her that, in accord with her suggestion, he had written to Bishop Hunnington to accept the Northampton assignment, with the proviso that another minister take his place here near

Tunbridge. He told the bishop it would be a shame and an insult to leave vacant the parsonage and meeting house that Mr. Bracken had so charitably constructed and furnished for a local clergyman. Julia told him that she would not deprive Aunt Jenny of a daughter *and* spiritual comfort in one fell blow.

On July 9 Richard wrote again.

The partnership of Wayment and O'Leary has accepted my few investment clients. I fear my departure will have as lasting and far-reaching effect as withdrawing one's finger from a pail of water.

In that same post she received an answer to her letter to Monsieur Naft.

On the nineteenth day of July of this year, if you will sign the forms herein enclosed and return them to me, it will not matter where you go or where you live. Your mother's money and properties will be solely in your ownership, until such time as you marry. All legal ties with the Edmond family will be severed on that day.

Like taking one's finger from a pail of water.

By the eleventh of July, with only a week left until her birthday and the couple's elopement, Julia began surreptitiously to gather her belongings and pack the few things she would take with her. She knew she and Mr. Worthington could not take everything, but she assumed the Edmonds would forward the rest of her belongings as soon as the Worthingtons were settled in Northampton. So she packed only a few summer frocks. And her sketch pad, though she would not take her paints. Mr. Worthington loved her and was perfectly convinced she was the greatest artist in the world, but he had no inclination and could not knowledgeably appreciate her efforts or make helpful comparisons between her work and the work of the masters. She suspected that without shared interest her artistic endeavors would shortly cease altogether. Therefore, with a sigh, she closed her paint box and pushed it far under her bed. She half hoped that neither Aunt Jenny nor Cousin Richard would find it when they sent her other things.

July 12. I have begun to pack here in Farrington Street. I did not realize how much I had collected over the past eight years. There are valuable segments of my life here, things I will take with me whether I put them with my luggage or no.

Every evening Mr. Worthington came to spend at Aspen Grove.

"Ah, Mr. Worthington, how lovely to have you with us. Yet again," Aunt Jenny said. Worthington, consciously aware of very few things these days, did not hear the faintly weary note in Mrs. Edmond's voice. But Julia did and blushed. Her aunt, she knew, would not have grown weary of the young minister if he had conversed or given the appearance of hearing anything that was said to him, or even—Mrs. Edmond really was very indulgent and very fond of her pastor—had he seemed sentient during his calls. But he sat and gazed at Julia, who talked a great deal, no doubt in an effort to cover Mr. Worthington's silence. In fact, she talked constantly, never pausing for an answer to questions she may have asked, never stopping to consider if she had related this story or voiced that opinion before. Often she had.

Mrs. Edmond had no real objection to Mr. Worthington marrying her adopted niece, whom she had long since come to love like a daughter born of her flesh. He was pleasant and sincere, would always be a stalwart churchman and preacher, and he obviously drew his life's breath from Julia Masonet. But Mrs. Edmond had always wanted more— more substance in the man Julia married. Someone more like . . . She shook her head and told herself it was only a mother thinking such things, that her son was to marry Miss Brewster, that his father and herself had always considered it the ideal match. Dear Rachel needed someone as noble and good as her son, and Julia needed someone—with substance.

She could not regret that Mr. Worthington had not yet spoken to her, nor could she help hoping that he would not.

"I have made final arrangements for my departure, even going so far as to purchase a railway ticket," said Cousin Richard's letter of July 15.

Mr. Worthington whispered almost those same words to her that night when she opened the door for him, substituting "our departure" for "my departure" and placing an *s* at the end of "ticket."

Both mentions of a railway were very significant to Julia. She felt exactly as if she were tied to a train track with a massive, deadly locomotive bearing down upon her with blinding speed. It was inexorable, her fate was sealed, and more than once in that final week she woke in the night with sweat running down her back, short of breath.

The morning post of July 19, her twenty-first birthday, included a brightly colored card Cousin Richard had selected in one of the London shops. On the outside was an exquisite painting of a black and purple butterfly, so lifelike it might have floated to rest on the white pasteboard, slowly folding and unfolding its wings, before it flitted away again. Inside were two short lines.

"*Joyeux anniversaire,* Julia, I am coming home."

Julia hurried from the house and down the lane toward the Bracken property shortly after the mail arrived. Besides her birthday card, there was another letter to Aunt Jenny from Cousin Richard detailing his trip: when he was to leave; what he would be bringing with him; what would follow; what time they could expect him that evening. And that he had something to tell them both. Julia knew what it was. He and Miss Brewster had privately married. She would be returning with him.

When she arrived at the long building that faced the highway, half parsonage, half meeting house, she tapped at the door, glancing nervously from side to side, a conspirator arriving at a clandestine meeting.

"Miss Masonet! Julia! What is it?"

The opened door revealed Mr. Worthington in his shirt-sleeves. Although his calls did not usually take him out earlier than this, Julia was relieved to find him home.

He had been preparing a sermon. Not this Sunday's sermon. He and Julia would be but newly married this Sunday and no one would expect him to return to business as usual two days after wedding the most glorious creature in the world. Looking at the girl as she stood at his door, breathing rapidly, long, loose strands of black hair floating around her face and neck, her deep, dark eyes level with his own, he was not sure that with Julia Masonet as his wife, it would ever again be "business as usual."

"My guardian...that is, my cousin...Mr. Edmond, will be returning to Aspen Grove this evening. We must be away on the first train from Tunbridge," she gasped. She had floundered over the address she was to use for Richard Edmond now. As of this morning he was no longer her guardian, and he never had actually been her cousin. He had called himself her brother, but that was not true, either. The idea flashed into her mind that she could call him *mon ogre,* and if the moment had not been so tense she would have smiled at the title they both had found appropriate.

"Yes. Very well. That will not be difficult. But do not stand outside my door, Julia." Now Worthington looked over her head from side to side, completing the image of guilty intrigue.

She stepped into the house, and once inside he insisted she sit in the old, worn chair Mrs. Bracken had contributed for his comfort.

"Here is what we shall do," he said. He did not sit but paced to and fro in front of her, explaining the plan he had gone over and over in his mind hundreds of times since that blessed day three weeks before when Julia told him she would marry him.

"You return to Aspen Grove and privately carry to the front door any light luggage you are taking with you. I shall follow you directly, and when I arrive you may tell your aunt that I have asked you to accompany me on a drive. Will you leave her a letter of explanation, or will you write from Gretna Green?"

"I could not leave her—them—in suspense for so long. No, I shall certainly write a letter before we go."

"Very well, then, I shall wait an hour before I come, to give you the time to make your final arrangements. If we ride at a brisk rate we can still easily arrive in Tunbridge before the train departs. Will that allow you enough time?" He stopped directly in front of her chair and she looked up and nodded. "Excellent," he said. "We have not a moment to lose. Hurry along now and I will follow in an hour."

When Julia stood, Worthington took her into his arms and kissed her.

"You have made me happier than I had any hope of ever being," he whispered into her hair.

"I had better go," she said softly.

He released her and held the door for her. He could not see her go, though, without taking her hand one more time and squeezing it affectionately.

She returned the pressure and then left him, walking briskly, though not actually running, toward Aspen Grove.

It had been Mr. Worthington's first kiss, the first claim he made on her in all the time he had known her, in all the months he loved her, in the several weeks since she agreed to marry him. It was a pleasant enough kiss. Julia could tell, even from its brief duration, that it was a token of deeper affection than any of Monsieur le Professeur François Davenôt's urgent kisses, given with graver reverence than even Richard's passion on that dark night almost two years ago.

And yet, there was no fire in Julia's heart, there was no glow. She was very fond of Mr. Worthington, and his kiss was very pleasant, but any warmth in her heart came from her knowledge that Sidney Worthington was very happy and she was the cause.

It was not a negligible source of warmth and perhaps she was correct in believing that if her marriage to the young clergyman did not bring her breathless excitement it would bring her joy. But she might have wondered if the two were mutually exclusive.

"Where have you been, Julia?" Aunt Jenny asked when she returned to the house.

"Out for a little walk," she said.

"Your face looks flushed."

"I was walking quite briskly."

"Perhaps that is not wise in such warm weather," Aunt Jenny cautioned.

It was a homely bit of advice, but unexpectedly Julia went to her aunt's chair and bent and kissed the woman soundly on the cheek.

"Thank you, Aunt Jenny." To her surprise the older lady looked up into the girl's face and caught her rapidly blinking away tears. "I shall be more careful in the future," she said, straightening.

"I suppose we are both quite thrilled to have Richard returning," Mrs. Edmond said, explaining as well as she could Julia's outburst of sentiment. "I know I am as giddy as a schoolgirl. If you get a chance, I wondered if you would step into his room to see that it is all ready for him. Glenda has cleaned it, of course, but you know him so well. I want everything to be perfect when he comes home."

"Certainly, Aunt Jenny. I shall hurry up right now to inspect the room."

"There is no rush, my dear. He will not be here until this evening, so you have all day."

"Mr. Worthington asked if I would not like to join him for some of his calls today. Since I may be out all afternoon, I do not want to leave it to the last minute."

"No, we would not want that."

Julia fled the room under Aunt Jenny's once again surprised gaze. The girl felt tears threatening again and knew she would not have any answers for Mrs. Edmond if they filled her eyes and tumbled down her cheeks.

She would get the light valise inside her closet to put in the remaining toiletries and carry it down to the front door as Worthington had instructed her, all under the convenient guise of checking Cousin Richard's room.

In less than five minutes she had her brush and nightgown in with the few dresses she was taking and closed the door to the little white room she had claimed as her own when she arrived in this house eight years before, a child of thirteen.

She did not take any mournful last look around her because she would doubtless return to this room after she was married, when she came to visit, alone or with Mr. Worthington. She would return to check through closets and drawers and would find forgotten articles in here for years to come.

But when she stepped into Cousin Richard's room the realization struck her with a stinging blow that this was very likely the last time she would ever walk through that doorway. If and when she did return to Aspen Grove, she would come as a married woman. She would have no cause to enter a man's room, a man not her husband, a man who could never be her husband. By the time she returned to the Grove her cousin would be married, and this room would be the intimate retreat for him and Rachel. She would never again burst through this door with some bit of exciting news, like the day Stuart Miller shot himself in the foot and Mr. Miller had just ridden past the front door in the little buggy, hurrying his son into Tunbridge and the doctor there. She would never again, as she had when she was younger, sneak into this room early on a Saturday morning and fling herself onto the mattress and the bulging blanket that encased Richard's soundly sleeping form. How she had shrieked with laughter as he turned and twisted under her, trying to free a hand with which to tickle her unmercifully.

She smiled at the recollection, hearing in her mind his growl of outrage, which even in the gray dawn of a Saturday morning, when he had ridden on horseback the thirty-five miles from London the night before, did not really sound angry with her.

And never again would she sit on that chest at the foot of his bed, watching him write, or fix his cravat, or shine his boots, and discuss with him the weighty problems a child, a girl, a young lady or a heartbroken woman faced.

He was no longer her guardian and would not offer his quiet bits of wisdom, pulling on his mustache to hide the smile over her schoolgirl jealousy. He would not come to sit beside her to share her grief.

It was over. She had longed for this day of independence, and now that it was here, what had she gained?

She looked around the room carefully. Glenda was a sat-isfactory housekeeper. The floor was mopped and pol-ished, the bed was aired and made up, the curtains cleaned and hung across the windows, which did not even support little clumps of cobwebs at the corners. By tonight Richard would have his clothes hung in that closet, his coat across the back of the chair, his boots on the floor. He would put his books there, against the wall, his writing things on the desk. On his dresser he would put the flat shell he brought back from Dover the year he brought her the tortoiseshell combs. In it he kept his cuff links and shirt studs and his pocket watch if he was not wearing it. Julia remembered standing by that dresser, a skinny girl, tall for her age, and Cousin Richard putting the watch into her hand so she could wind it while he buttoned his vest.

And the room would smell like him. His leather boots, the horsey scent that clung to his riding things, the spicy soap he used.

She had grown from that bony scarecrow of a child to the stately, graceful woman who looked back at her from the mirror above the dresser. And through all of those years she had been welcomed into this room as a part of his life.

Now she was leaving. She would see her Cousin Richard again. He was not dying; she was not dying. She would re-turn to Aspen Grove and receive her Aunt Jenny's congrat-ulations and blessings. She and Mr. Worthington would sit in the parlor with the Edmonds, Aunt Jenny and Richard and his wife, at the dining room table; in time she would bring children here to meet their Grandmother Edmond and gruff Uncle Richard.

But she would never be in this room again.

She turned to go and her eye was caught by the pale square on the bare bedroom wall. A painting usually hung there. When he returned Richard would bring it with him and hang it in its place again. It was the picture she had given him for Christmas. The portrait of her to which they had both contributed.

The Train Tunbridge

Mr. Worthington called for her thirty minutes later. She was sitting with her Aunt Jenny, talking about former days spent in this house. Mrs. Edmond did not remember what got her started on the subject, but she was talking about Richard as a boy, some of the scraps he had gotten into, the sort of scraps little boys always get into. Julia wore such a solemn expression, though, and would only smile faintly at Aunt Jenny's merriest tales.

When the knock came the younger woman jumped so violently Aunt Jenny laughed and assured her it was not the police come to drag her away. In a moment Glenda came to the sitting room door and announced Mr. Worthington.

"You see?" Mrs. Edmond laughed again. "Your panic was all for naught. If the police would not drag you away, Mr. Worthington surely would not."

Mr. Worthington entered, exchanged nervous, disjointed greetings with the two ladies and then abruptly asked Julia to join him for a carriage drive.

"Out in your carriage today, are you?" Aunt Jenny asked. "You do not often arrive at our humble abode in such state."

"I do not like to hitch up the horse if the way is not far."

"Are you going a ways today, then?"

Worthington's florid, freckled face turned a bright red.

"Oh, no," he stammered. "Nothing like that. Nothing important. Only errands. Nothing else. Just going about the parish."

Julia interrupted to say that she was perfectly willing to join Mr. Worthington on his ride. At the front door, out of sight of the sitting room, before she bent to pick up the light bag waiting there, she called back into the house.

"Aunt Jenny?"

"Yes?"

"I left a little note for you in my room. You might read it when you get the chance."

"I will read it right now."

"Oh, it is nothing important. Do not hurry. Goodbye."

"Goodbye, dear. Hurry back."

Julia did not answer and a moment later the front door opened and closed.

On the ride into Tunbridge both of them were unusually quiet. Nervous and slightly embarrassed, feeling guilty about sneaking away like this. But Julia had left the letter, and as soon as Aunt Jenny read it everything would be out in the open. Or perhaps she would wait until her cousin arrived home and send him upstairs to get it. She would be a little uneasy about the length of Julia's absence if she waited until then, and Richard would read the note first to himself, upstairs, and then, disbelieving and probably slightly put out, he would bring it down the stairs and read it to his mother.

"You did not say anything to Mrs. Edmond, either?" Worthington asked, interrupting the scene playing before her mind's eye.

"Nothing."

"I thought you might tell her. I thought it was only Mr. Edmond's interference you feared."

"It was easier this way. And Aunt Jenny would have insisted on telling Cousin Richard."

"I see," Worthington said.

The ride into Tunbridge, even in the light phaeton behind the fresh horse, was a long twenty minutes.

At the station Worthington produced the tickets for the stationmaster, who took them without a word, never guessing that this was the train ride of a lifetime for the young man.

The bag he was carrying was even smaller than the one Julia held, and without assistance they mounted the narrow steps into the train and made their way down the narrow aisle to the private compartment Worthington had booked for the two of them. He was a poor clergyman and such a luxury had been a great extravagance on his part. But he would not ride to his marriage with the wonderful creature beside him in a noisy, smelly coach.

Julia was not blind to the sacrifice this must have required.

"A less expensive ticket would have been sufficient," she said.

"Nonsense," Worthington said. "You will always receive nothing but the very best from me. The desire of my life, from this day forward, is to make you happy."

Julia smiled and leaned toward him to give him a tender kiss on the cheek.

"You shall, Sidney. I am," she told him.

They took their places, and moments later the train staggered forward, like a man late to bed after carousing with friends, roused a half hour early the next morning by a wife in ill humor. Eventually its rhythm smoothed, but its speed barely increased. It struggled up every hill and wheezed down every incline.

The two passengers in the compartment, rather than chaffing excitedly like a giddy couple running away to be married, sat quietly side by side, Worthington nearest the window, pointing out interesting sights occasionally. Softly Julia began to hum and Worthington took her hand, holding it loosely as he listened to her nearly inaudible tune.

"We will have many children," he said dreamily. "And you will hold each in your arms and sing him to sleep with that song. Surely they will all look like you. God would not be so cruel to a child as to give him red hair instead of your beautiful black tresses."

"The color of a child's hair is not important, Mr. Worthington."

He chuckled. "No. If the child is yours, it will not matter what color his hair is."

He spoke fitfully and, as usual, Julia was thoughtful and silent most of the time. He loved her reveries, much as he loved everything else about her. She did not smile, but she did not often smile, so that was not unusual, either. In the silence of the train he wondered what she was thinking about. The thought struck him that Julia Masonet, who she was, what she was, what had made her the woman she was today, was largely an enigma to him. He wondered, too, if he would ever learn to know her. He could not imagine ever being entirely familiar with the exotic creature at his side. He was not sure he wanted to be. The thought troubled him and he started commenting on the rather uninteresting country through which they were passing to cover the disturbance in his mind.

London

The train dragged itself into London's busy railway station two hours after leaving Tunbridge. Worthington sighed, roused from a light doze, and asked if Julia wished to step outside, walk around a bit, get a breath of fresh air?

She smiled faintly and shook her head.

"Not in London," she said. "But you go out. Refresh yourself. From London to Birmingham will be a very long trip."

Worthington grimaced. "Perhaps I will," he said.

He believed he left her reluctantly, but he enjoyed the bustle on the platform. He bought an apple from a raggedy boy, a meat pie from a plump little woman, passing the time of day with each, learning their histories, becoming friends with both in the few sentences they exchanged.

He also sent a little beggar scurrying through the crowd in search of more delicate pastries than the heavy pies Mrs. Flynn—the pie maker—was selling.

The little fellow returned with two flaky rolls wrapped in a tissue paper. He tugged on Worthington's jacket just as the conductor was summoning his wandering flock once again. Worthington looked down, surprised. When he had put the coin in the lad's hand he fully expected it to be the last he saw of it or the child. The errand for light pastry was a cover for his charity more than anything else.

The clergyman took the bundle and gave the child twice what the rolls cost in recompense, then he turned to take his place at Julia Masonet's side. Where he had been. Where he would spend the rest of his life.

Out of the corner of his eye he glimpsed a form that seemed familiar. He turned, but the crowd was pushing toward him, a solid wall, and the familiar form, if it *was* familiar, was lost.

Back in the compartment Julia exclaimed with pleasure over the bounty with which Worthington returned.

"If you had asked I would have told you I was not hungry. But suddenly these things look delicious to me." She bit into the apple, which crunched loudly.

Once again the train was under way, and as if it had been filled with some potent elixir in the city's station, it now traveled at a respectable speed. At a soothing speed. Having had a bite to eat and the sun shining warmly, though not directly, on him, Worthington soon found himself irresistibly sleepy.

"Do you mind if I nap?" he asked.

"Not at all. You rest and I shall draw, and we will both arrive in Birmingham refreshed," Julia assured him. She pulled her bag from under the seat and drew the sketch pad from it. After groping deeper into its depths she also retrieved the bit of charcoal in the cunning little holder Cousin Richard had found for her in London. By that time Worthington's head was against the edge of the seat cushion, his eyes closed, his breathing deep and even.

Sidetrack
London—a month before

When Richard Edmond returned to London, the first place he went, even before leaving his luggage at his rooms, was the Brewster home. In the dusk of the early spring day the Brewster lamps were already lit, large, gaudy, burning twice as much oil as any other torches along the street, and only half as efficiently.

"Richard, is that you?" Her voice called to him from her sitting room, even before Lawrence had a chance to greet him.

He did not answer until he stood in the doorway of the room.

"Yes, it is I. But how did you know?" he asked, a smile in his voice as he stepped across the threshold and took the hand she held in his direction.

"I recognize your knock. Though it has been a while since I last heard it," she scolded mildly.

"I am sorry, Rachel. The planting, the tenants..."

"Your mother and Julia," she finished for him when it appeared he was reluctant to do so.

"Yes. The family. It was difficult to pull myself away." He spoke regretfully, then squeezed her hand to banish the ghost of regret. "But I am here now, with you. And I vow to be a more attentive suitor." He raised her hand to his lips and kissed it. It was a brave, sound kiss, as brave as his words and voice. And as convincing.

He asked how she was, how was her father, the house, news from the city. He told her about spring in the countryside, the crops he had seen planted, the repairs he had been called upon to make as a landowner. The hour grew late. Lawrence had lit the lamp in here when he arrived, which Miss Brewster sometimes did not have him light at all when she was alone.

Mr. Brewster was at his club. He did not often leave his daughter alone of an evening, but he knew young Edmond was to be there and so purposely left them alone. At least that is what he told himself he was doing, but it was undeniably refreshing to be out from the confines of those rooms that Rachel sometimes kept so gloomy.

During their long talk, Richard spoke much of his home, suggesting that he was going to remove himself permanently to his country estate and would Rachel mind that? He was sure she could not.

Absently she assured him she would be happy anywhere with him. But she was concentrating on the sound of Richard's voice, not just his words. There was a sadness there of which he was not speaking, something he was not telling her. It rang in every word he spoke, laugh he laughed, breath he took. And there, it was strongest there.

"Mother and Miss Masonet were very well when I left. And Mr. Worthington, you remember the curate? I saw him only last night. He asked after you."

"How good of him."

She could not see, it was true, but had she been *this* blind?

Finally Mr. Brewster returned. He was surprised to find Edmond still there, and Edmond and Miss Brewster were surprised to learn how late it was.

"We have been talking," Richard said, then was forced to admit, "No, actually, *I* have been talking, and your lovely daughter has, as usual, been listening. She is like another wily young lady I know who listens a great deal and speaks only to help a fellow out of some uncomfortable position." He turned to Miss Brewster. "That is your cue, Rachel. You are to interrupt here and tell your father that you have enjoyed the evening as much as I."

"I would if you would give me the chance," she said, smiling. "Mr. Edmond had a great deal to tell me, Father, and I enjoyed every syllable." Then she directed her words to Richard. "There. Did I come to your rescue properly?"

"Miss Masonet could not have saved me with a surer hand," he replied, laughing.

A shortened version of all of this farm news had now to be given to Mr. Brewster, and while the two men talked, Rachel considered what she had heard. What she had been hearing but had ignored for... how long? Months? Years?

As Richard's letters to Julia said, for the next few weeks he was involved in transferring his business dealings to Tunbridge, or severing ties in some instances, and he and Rachel spent most evenings together. He invited her to come with him to plays and musical reviews, to concerts, operas, even parties and "at homes"—all of the places to which he had invited her before, to which he had been asking her to accompany him for ages. Suddenly she listened to him and agreed and *went*. And, most surprising of all, certainly to herself, she actually enjoyed herself. There were awkward moments and thoughtless strangers, it was true, but there was also warmth and fun and life. Richard could not account for her sudden change of mind. It was almost as if she did not want to talk with him, did not want to be alone with him.

In the letter she sent him she told him that they needed to talk, but now she was willing to do anything he proposed rather than talk. He did not understand her. He had come in response to her letter, ready at last to set a definite date for their marriage, a date not too distant, in fact. He hinted that to her on a number of occasions, but she always changed the subject, telling him they would talk about it later.

He received a letter from his mother that said Julia and Mr. Worthington would surely make an announcement in the near future. Mrs. Edmond claimed she was delighted by the prospect, but she asked him how he felt. How could he feel? He was as delighted as his mother.

On the day the post brought that letter he told himself that it *was* later, and the time to talk to Rachel had come. He did not know what her hesitation had been, but he knew why he had delayed and now he knew there was no point to that any longer.

"Mr. Brewster, sir, I have come to talk to your daughter."

"Have you, now?" Brewster asked him, eyeing him with raised eyebrows. "And what has kept you from doing so before now?"

"I...I..."

"Well, never mind, son. Come in, come in. I believe, having answered the door and welcomed you in, my next duty is to make myself scarce." He clapped Richard on the back and ushered him to the sitting room. "Rachel, Mr. Edmond is here and I am off to the club."

Before the young woman could protest, her father had his hat and was out the door.

"Rachel," Richard said, sitting beside her and coming directly to the point. "Your father suggests that I have been a long time addressing this next question, but it has not, altogether, been my fault. Do not let us delay any longer, though. I am ready to marry you tomorrow, if you will have me."

"Richard," she said softly. "Oh, my dear, you are so brave. A hero in every sense of the word." Uncharacteristically she kept her hands strictly to herself, folded calmly in her lap.

"I do not..." he began.

"I am quite serious," she said, but she turned her head from him when she spoke. "You are, quite literally, my hero. At our parents' suggestion you agreed to be in love with me."

"That is not..."

"You have been patient with me, without pity. Understanding without cloying. You have urged me to fly when I refused to walk."

"You have not . . ."

"But I cannot let you do this. I *am* fond of you, but perhaps, like you, it is an emotion evoked by our parents. I have grown used to the idea that we were in love and would marry and you would care for me and I would be here to welcome you to your home—and your bed." She stopped and the embarrassing phrase hung in the air, drawing the blood to both their faces like a magnet.

"I have thought the same," Richard said. He sounded bewildered, but cruelest of all to Rachel Brewster, he sounded hopeful. "We will marry," he said, or more exactly, he asked.

She turned to him with tears in her sightless eyes.

"No, Richard. We will not."

"I thought you loved me," he said.

"I thought I did, too. Perhaps I was wrong. I know you were wrong if you believed you loved me."

But he did not tell her that he loved her. Instead, he extracted her hand from its clenched position in her lap and smoothed the fingers back.

"How did you know?" he asked. "I did not mean for you to know."

"Oh, Richard," she said, a sob catching in her throat. "You do not need eyes to see some things."

"Your sacrifice may mean nothing. Julia may marry Mr. Worthington whether we marry or not."

A tear fell from Miss Brewster's lash, but she smiled even as it slid along her cheek.

"I would not injure your self-admiration, Richard dear, but I think my sacrifice is not so grave as you believe it to be."

Now Richard smiled and drew her hand up to lay it against his cheek.

"And though you hardly need the assurance, I think if you return to Aspen Grove and actively pursue your ward, you will not find her such elusive game after all," Miss Brewster said.

"And you, Rachel my darling, what will you do? Will you draw the curtains and douse the lights and shut yourself up tightly in this room again? For if that is your plan, I will not go. I will never go." He still held her hand gently, but there was determination in his voice that Miss Brewster could not mistake. He had seen her enjoying herself for the first time in her life these past few weeks and he would throw himself, his happiness, Julia and kindly Mr. Worthington all onto the altar, without hesitation, rather than allow Rachel to relinquish the hold she had finally taken on life.

But the girl shook her head.

"I think I will go to Northampton," she said. "I have an aunt who lives in Northampton, a sister of my mother's who did not approve of dear Mother in the least. Aunt Martha has found the light of religion and has been trying for years to get me away, even for a few weeks, from this 'den of iniquity.' She will be good for me. Perhaps not as good for me as you have been, but she is a woman with a great deal of common sense and just a light sprinkling of compassion. It will be a delightful change, I believe." She laughed out loud now, thinking of her Aunt Martha and the contest of wills into which she was no doubt about to throw herself.

"Aunt Martha who, Rachel? I will not let you disappear entirely from my life."

"Would that not be better?" she asked.

"In some cases, perhaps. In our case I think not. We were in love because our parents instructed us to be. Let us see if we can be friends because we want to be."

"Very well. My aunt's name is Mrs. Martha Jefferies, wife of Mr. Paul Jefferies, church alderman first and tradesman in horses second. It was he who brought religion to Aunt Martha, though she took to it like a fish to water."

"Mrs. Paul Jefferies," Richard said thoughtfully, committing the name to his memory. "I shall write."

"Do," she said. "Tell me of the wedding."

"If there is a wedding," he said.

"There will be," she told him.

But she did not know Julia as well as she thought she did, and Richard refused to anticipate what Miss Masonet would do, or perhaps had done already.

The Train

Julia began her sketch absently, not consciously choosing her subject. She might not have been directing her fingers. But in moments she recognized the lines she had drawn. She was also unaware of the contented little smile that settled on her lips, the soft fog that entered her eyes. She bent her attention to more meticulous work and began to hum her tune again. It was a tune she had often heard at Aspen Grove, when she helped Aunt Jenny in the sewing room, when she sat on a trunk at the foot of a bed in a room where she had once been welcome.

The miles skimmed past the window of the coach. Julia's sketch became more distinct. Worthington groaned and turned so that now he faced her, though his eyes were still closed, his face lax in sleep.

Worthington did not know when Julia's song roused him. It was part of his dream at first. Then it was the sound of the train, and then it distinguished itself, and finally Worthington identified it.

He opened his eyes and the sight that met him very nearly took his breath away. He knew it always would. Julia was bent industriously above her sketch pad. But more than industriously. Happily. Contented. As Worthington's vision grew clearer he realized he had seldom seen such an unguarded, joyful expression on the young woman's face. Her deep, dark eyes were softened, her brow was clear and serene, and most surprising of all there was a smile on her lips, lips upon which, to his recollection, a smile rested so infrequently.

He might have hoped being here with him, on their way to be married, had summoned that beautiful expression, but watching her he knew that their journey, their journey's end, the train, the countryside and her companion in this compartment had all been forgotten. Every thought was upon the picture in her hands.

He dropped his eyes to the oversized book of heavy paper. There was no question who her subject was. The face was too distinct, the features too well rendered. He looked back to her face. She had never looked so beautiful to him before. When she looked up and saw him watching her, the veil would drop over her eyes and the smile would leave her lips. Just as the face on that paper before her was unmistakable, so was the unconscious look on her face. It was a drawing of Mr. Richard Edmond and in her eyes and on her lips was the look of love.

Worthington was surprised that the train did not stop or fall off the edge of the earth, that the sun remained in the heavens and his world did not come crashing down upon his shoulders. He took a breath and found he could breathe. He blinked his eyes and found they still functioned. And even then, at that terrible moment, he knew that as in love with the young woman as he was, his own face had never worn the expression he saw on hers now.

"You are in love with him," he said softly.

Julia started and hastily put the sketch aside. As he knew it would be, the face she raised to his was no longer suffused with love.

"You are awake," she said.

"You are in love with him," Worthington repeated. He did not need to indicate the pad for them both to know of whom he was speaking.

"Why certainly. You know how fond I am of my guardian. I have always loved him and Aunt Jenny," she said, purposely misunderstanding him.

Slowly he sat up straight and directed his eyes across the compartment. The difference in her expression was too painful for him to see, as lovely as her face was, as kind as her smile was.

"Yes, but you are *in* love with him," he said, speaking quietly to the opposite wall.

"I did not know I was," she said. "Not when you came to Tunbridge and loved me."

"But you knew when you accepted me."

Tears filled the young woman's eyes, but Worthington still refused to look at her and she took a breath to steady her voice.

"Yes," she said. "I knew then."

"Why?" he asked.

"Why did I tell you I would marry you? I knew I loved Mr. Edmond, but I have never been anything more than a younger sister to him. I knew that could never be, that he was to marry Miss Brewster and the two of them would be very happy. Would live happily ever after, as the fairy tales say. But I thought if I married you I could make you happy at least."

A pained smile covered his lips.

"Oh, yes," he said. "You could have made me happy. You *did* make me happy, Julia. But I could never have made you happy, could I?"

She extended her hand and put it warmly across his.

"I love you, Sidney," she told him earnestly.

"I know you do," he said, patting her hand gently. It was another absentminded, grandfatherly sort of gesture. "But you are not *in* love with me."

They sat in silence as the train swayed beneath them. Occasionally the motion brought their shoulders together. It was a contact that neither avoided, but its meaning had changed completely in the last quarter of an hour.

"I had better go," he said, reaching under his seat for his bag.

"Go? Go where? There is no place for you to go."

"There is a whole train, and then there is a whole world. There is much to do in it if I am ever to forget you."

"What *will* you do?" she asked.

"I will take the position in Northampton. The letter I received from Alderman Jefferies was filled with laud and admiration. I could not refuse the congregation now, even if I wanted to. But I will go, and I will serve with all dedication, and now—" he swallowed "—with all of my heart."

"We could still marry, Sidney. I promise to try to learn to love you, and I may in time. We could be—" she paused "—contented."

Worthington's smile was very bitter and he shook his head.

"Not contented, Julia. Marriage to you must be more than contentment." Now his smile softened, his whole expression changed to the one of compassion to which it was

so well suited. "I told you that my life's work would be to
make you happy. I will start by leaving you."

"I know you will go far," she said.

"I have not the ambition to go far," he told her, shaking
his head. To himself he said, *And as far as I went, it would
never be far enough.* "Go back to him," he said aloud.

Now Julia shook her head.

"There is no 'back to him,'" she sighed. "That book of
my life is closed forever."

But Worthington thought of Edmond, remembering certain expressions, certain lights in his eyes that the young
clergyman had ignored or misunderstood at the time.

"I think you are wrong," he said.

"I fear I am right."

The young man stood, and even in the unsteady footing
of the moving train, Julia stood with him. At last he turned
to look at her.

"May you find the happiness you deserve," she said.

"And may you find the happiness you left behind."

The look they exchanged was doubtful. Neither had any
hope of the realization of the other's wish.

He leaned toward her and solemnly kissed her cheek. It
was a dry kiss, moistened by the tear gliding down her
cheek. He picked up his bag and opened the door of the
compartment.

She stood alone. The life she had imagined, had prepared for, had walked away through that door. The life she
could never have, the best her life had ever been, was behind her on a little country estate, in the keeping of another
man she would never see again.

Manchester

Julia assumed Mr. Worthington disembarked when the
train stopped at Birmingham and either returned to Tunbridge or caught another train directly to Northampton. She
did not see him again after he left the coach and she wished
him the best. She had been prepared to spend her life with
him but she supposed he was right—a marriage between
them could never be satisfying as long as she loved some-

one else, and he knew she loved someone else. And, unfortunately, it appeared that she would love Richard Edmond, from afar, for the rest of her life.

Julia had seen Mr. Worthington's interest in people and hoped he could plunge himself satisfyingly into the duties of his larger parish. He was a young man and Julia, not able to imagine that she inspired the same devotion she was willing to give Richard, believed that in a very few years, or perhaps even less time, Worthington could forget her and find a sweet girl with whom he could share his life's work. They would meet in one of his services. She would admire his sermon and he would notice the fresh face of the maiden as she raised it to him, hanging on his every word. He would speak to her after the meeting. He would seek her out after every meeting. One day she would bring him a pound cake. The next week he would formally call on her in her parents' home. They would marry and have the fine, large family Worthington wanted.

It was a lovely projection, and Julia fervently hoped it would be the course of Mr. Sidney Worthington's life.

She wished the course of her own life were even that hopeful, with any possibility at all of eventual felicity. Now that she was in possession of her fortune, the world was open to her. All of the world except for Tunbridge, England, the only place on earth she wanted to be.

She could return to Paris. Richard himself had suggested she do that. She left the City of Lights when a child, innocent and ignorant, but she did not doubt that when she returned, a woman of means, she would find countless ways to plunge herself into forgetfulness. Or at least make the attempt.

And in a few weeks, or a few months—suddenly time held no importance for her—she would write to Aunt Jenny, tell her she was well, whether she was or not, and tell her that her elopement with Mr. Worthington had not come to pass. She would be very vague about the reasons for their separation and even less precise as to her whereabouts or her plans. Aunt Jenny would be hurt by Julia's evident ingratitude and desertion, but at least the girl could alleviate her worry.

She would travel. There was the rest of Europe and all of Asia to see. Just as she could purchase tickets and food, she had no doubt that her money could buy friends and traveling companions.

She would not return to Aspen Grove. She would not join her Aunt Jenny to watch Richard marry Miss Brewster and make a home with her. She could not look on in silence, smiling her encouragement, her approval, voicing hollow wishes for his marital bliss.

Nor would she allow herself to be manipulated by her erstwhile guardian anymore. She clearly saw now that Cousin Richard had orchestrated the relationship between herself and Mr. Worthington from the beginning, from that first call the clergyman made on the Edmonds. Richard had thrown them together, had encouraged the curate's suit at every turn. No doubt he looked upon it as another of the duties of his stewardship. He had always taken his responsibility very seriously. Julia was willing to admit that he had saved her from making a number of serious mistakes over the years, but with his recent actions, he had promoted the most serious mistake she would ever have made.

Not again, Mr. Edmond.

She was at last of age and she would attend to her own happiness—or heartache—herself. If she could not have him, she simply did not want anyone.

The journey of her childhood behind her, the bleak and lonely road of her adulthood stretched out before her, she closed her eyes and willed herself into a hopeless, exhausted sleep.

She awoke near dawn. She faintly remembered the stop in Manchester and then the lurch as the train started to move again. She feared she would dream when she slept, either sad dreams of Mr. Worthington and his pain or tragic dreams of Richard Edmond and a life that could not be hers. But she slept as if drugged. A heavy, woolen sleep that wrapped night visions in dense clouds and now clung to her mind, resisting her attempts to throw it off.

She moaned and turned away from the back of the seat to face the compartment and the padded bench across from her. With her eyes still closed she realized she was warm. That surprised her. The motion of the train and her own troubled thrashing should have caused the blanket to slip off her shoulders at least and most likely to fall to the floor. But it was snugly about her, as if it had been carefully tucked around her by a solicitous nursemaid.

She acknowledged at last that sleep was gone. With regret she opened her eyes.

She was not alone in the compartment.

Another form sat across from her. The light of the early morning was still a very dark brown and the form was indistinct. Nevertheless, she recognized it. She recognized the broad shoulders, the shape of the head, the build and carriage of the body. She could even distinguish the dark line of the mustache above his lip.

"Richard?" she asked softly in disbelief. This must be the dream that had evaded her all night.

"Yes," he said.

"You put the blanket around me."

"I did not want you to grow cold."

They both spoke quietly, reasonably, in matter-of-fact tones. It convinced Julia that this was indeed a dream.

"Mr. Worthington is gone, and Miss Brewster has released you," she murmured.

"That is correct."

"And at last you are here."

"I am." His mustache twitched and he reached across the space between the two seats to tenderly brush a lock of hair from in front of her eyes.

She closed her eyes and sighed. In the entire range of her fancy, this was the dream she would have chosen. Richard would be here with her, to save her—again. To claim her. A half smile moved her lips.

"I am glad you have come," she whispered, her words more like another soft sigh than anything else.

"So am I," he said. As the author of her own dream, she would have imagined him to say exactly that.

"I suppose you have come to stop me from making another grave mistake."

"Have I?" he asked.

That was perhaps not what she would have had her phantom cousin say. She opened her eyes the tiniest slit and saw his form, even more distinct this time, still sitting opposite her.

"From eloping with Mr. Worthington," she explained, though dream phantoms were supposed to be omniscient.

"And did I save you?"

"You are too late."

"Too late!" Richard's voice was loud, and if her sleep had not been so very deep, it surely would have awakened her.

"Hush now," she cooed sleepily. "He has gone."

"And why has he gone?"

"Because I did not love him. Just as you did not love Miss Brewster."

"But I did love Miss Brewster," her dream Richard said.

"Yes," she sighed. "And I did love Mr. Worthington."

"I see."

"But I was not *in* love with him. Were you *in* love with Miss Brewster?"

Richard raised the gray shadow of his hand and ran his fingers thoughtfully across his mustache.

"That is an interesting distinction," he said. "No, I was not *in* love with Rachel."

The images of this dream were so distinct. Julia could not throw off the feeling that it was all real. But of course it could not be.

"If this were not a dream I would ask you what you are doing here," she said. Even the hoarseness of sleep was leaving her voice. "I would want to know how you happened to be in my coach on this northbound train in the wee hours of the morning, instead of on your way south to Aspen Grove with Miss Brewster, who is Mrs. Edmond by this time. I would require a very sensible explanation from you. And that, of course, you could not give."

"If this were not a dream, I would tell you that Miss Rachel Brewster is able to see many things, things you and I have been blind to all our lives. She could see that she and I should not marry, just as you and Mr. Worthington should

ot marry. She tells me that you are in love with me. Tell me,
my precious ward, is she right?''

Julia's forehead creased as she frowned quizzically.

"What are you doing here?" she asked again, ignoring,
or at least not answering, his question.

"Well, I was at the train station in London, waiting to
atch the 12:05 home, to my mother and to you, to tell you
oth that Miss Brewster has broken our engagement. She
old me you would be pleased by that announcement, but I
vas waiting to see the expression on your face before I pre-
umed too much. But on the platform, waiting for the train
o Tunbridge, I saw someone I thought I recognized step out
nto the platform of the train *from* Tunbridge. It looked
ke Mr. Worthington.''

"It *was* Mr. Worthington," Julia said. She had closed her
yes again. She had been struck by the undeniable realiza-
ion that the car was getting lighter by the minute, that if this
as her fondest dream, it would be over any minute now.

"Yes," Richard said quietly.

"We were eloping." Julia sighed again, this time with a
ote of sorrow in the breathy sound.

"Ah," Richard said.

"You do not sound surprised," she said, then shifted
ncomfortably on the hard bench. "But why would you?
ou have done everything in your power to bring Mr. Wor-
hington and myself together since the day we met.''

"I was not—expecting an elopement. When I saw your
Mr. Worthington I was surprised. Surprised that he would
e away from Tunbridge. Surprised that he would be away
rom you." He paused for a moment as the engineer blew
he whistle. When he could make himself heard again he
inished his thought. "And then, of course, I realized he
vould *not* leave Tunbridge without you.''

"So you boarded the train to stop us.''

"I would not want to interfere," he said slowly.

Julia laughed suddenly and sharply. It was a harsh sound,
nd like Richard's bark of surprise when she told him he was
oo late, it had no business in a dream.

"Did not want to interfere?" she asked. "My dear Cousin Richard, you have made it your life's work to interfere in my affairs at every turn."

This conversation and her surprising companion had started out as purely phantasmagorical. But now, with the light becoming brighter and the haze of sleep lifting from her brain, it had all taken on a concrete substance. Richard Edmond really was sitting across from her in this railroad car. They really were discussing his aborted marriage plans to Miss Brewster and her unrealized elopement plans with Mr. Worthington.

Julia pulled the blanket from around her shoulders and sat up. She pushed another wave of thick black hair back from her forehead and looked at Richard with a troubled expression on her face.

"What *are* you doing here?" she asked.

"I told you. I was surprised to see Mr. Worthington at the London station and realized you must be with him."

"So you boarded the train to—"

"Make sure all was well."

She shook her head in dismissal of his claim.

"You boarded the train to stop us. But why would you want to stop us when you as much as arranged our marriage personally?"

"I did not arrange it. And I do not want to stop it. If it is what you want."

The young woman turned her head to look out the window at the passing countryside swathed in the pale gauze of sunrise.

"And once my life is neatly settled, *then* you and Miss Brewster will be married and move into Aspen Grove." She was sorry to see the morning come, sorry to discover that her beautiful dream was not real and that in this harsh reality of morning her Cousin Richard was still—her Cousin Richard. "But I am sorry, there will be no elopement," she continued. "There will be no marriage. Mr. Worthington has left the train and is on his way to a very fine living in Northampton. So what you planned to do or not to do about the elopement is of little moment," she said.

Richard nodded. "I saw him get off," he said. "I wondered..."

"You wondered what disrupted the happy little comedy you had so carefully directed? It seems it was not so very happy after all."

"He left you?" Richard drew his brows together and clenched his fists.

"It was a mutual decision," the young woman explained, too weary and heartsick to be amused by Richard's brotherly outrage and evident readiness to come to her defense.

"Then you do not..."

"Love him? No, I do not love Mr. Worthington. I already said that, I believe. I will not marry Mr. Worthington. But you must not let that prevent you from marrying Miss Brewster."

"I told you, Julia, Miss Brewster broke our engagement. She is going to Northampton herself, and she told me to come to you."

"What can you mean?" she asked.

Richard smiled and shook his head. "Are you awake now, my dear? I do not want to repeat this many more times."

"You really were on your way home when you saw Sidney on the platform?"

He nodded.

"So you boarded this train instead with every intention of...what?"

"When I saw Worthington at the station in London, I followed him onto the train and took a seat in the passenger car. It was located so that I could see through the door into the passageway. I watched this compartment, but I cannot say what I planned to do. I cannot say I had any plan at all." He smiled weakly. "I only wanted to be sure."

"Mr. Worthington would have been very good to me," she said.

"I know. And Miss Brewster is a noble, lovely lady."

"That is true. She would have made you a truly gracious wife."

"Yes, she would. And Mr. Worthington was willing to devote his life to you."

"He was. So you see, you need not have feared for me."

"No, I suppose not," he admitted.

"You and Miss Brewster could have lived in London or Aspen Grove, and Mr. Worthington and I would have lived together in Northampton, or any other parish to which he was called, he serving his congregation and I serving him."

"You would have been the ideal helpmeet for him."

Julia smiled across the compartment at him. "Miss Brewster could have made you a gentleman," she teased.

"If anyone could, I think Miss Brewster could have. Certainly she has taught me the meaning of meekness and patience."

"And Mr. Worthington is a good man, Richard, a man of high ideals."

"Indeed he is."

"I could have made him happy."

"I am sure you could."

It was silent in the train car for just a moment. Julia and Richard had been searching each other's face during that exchange, but now Julia turned to look out the window, afraid to see the expression that would cover his handsome face at her next words.

"But I would have made him happy without being happy myself," she said. "Much the same way that you tried to make Miss Brewster happy."

"I do not know..." he began, but she went ahead with her thought as if he had not interrupted her.

"To sacrifice one's life for someone else is a noble theory, but how many of us frail mortals can give or accept such a sacrifice without feeling rancor? I once asked myself if finding love and being happy myself was a truly worthy goal? Is it not better to bring happiness to someone else's life? Now I believe that the realization of the one does not necessarily make the other impossible."

"No?" he asked.

"No. I could not make Mr. Worthington truly happy if I was not happy myself. I could not love him because I am in love with someone else. I am saying that I love you, Richard Edmond. Not as a father or a brother or a friend. Not as a guardian or a mentor or the man who has saved me again and again from tragic errors. I love you, Richard, as a lover, with all of my heart and for all of my life. If you cannot return that love, at least the words have finally been spoken.''

Now she turned to face him and waited for his reply, his acceptance or refusal of her sentiments. But when he spoke she did not understand what he was telling her. At first.

''My father did not like to travel. He crossed the Channel to meet you, but he commissioned me to cross it a second time and bring you back to England myself. I do not know that you recollect the day, but I shall never forget it. It was the early fall. The chestnut trees that lined the streets were just beginning to turn gold. I remember thinking the air had never smelled fresher, the sky had never been bluer, the songbirds never more noisy and cheery. I think I had a sense of some great impending event, but I may only have invented that in the years since.'' He smiled at her apologetically and still she waited for his response to her declaration. ''When I knocked at the door of 417, rue Saint Jacques, it was opened by a heathen. A savage. A bedraggled, ragged slip of a girl who might have inspired charity and compassion if it had not been for the fire and fury in her eyes. A little Gypsy with a dirty face and tangled black hair and a torn skirt. She glared at me fiercely and assured me she could take care of herself.''

Richard paused, reliving the scene in his memory, picturing the wild, lonely girl as she stood there, daring him to pity her. Then he turned to look at the woman she had become, his eyes bright, a catch in his throat. ''Can I return your love? Julia Masonet, I have been in love with you since the moment you opened that door. But you were thirteen and I was twenty. You were a child, my ward, and I was your older, wiser guardian.'' He stopped again and smiled at her ruefully. ''Older and wiser,'' he repeated, shaking his head. ''As much as I loved you, longed for you, cared for you and feared for you, all I could do was try to protect you and guide you to *une bonne vie*. I did not believe the years would ever bring us together.''

They sat facing each other, their knees nearly touching in the close confines of the railroad car. With her finely boned

hand she took his and pulled herself across the slight gap
that separated them to sit next to him, near to him, closing
forever the space of time and distance between them.

"They have at last," she said. "Despite my blindness and
the foolish mistakes I seemed determined to make, and despite your relentless insistence on 'my own good.' It has been
a difficult trek for both of us, Richard Edmond. Traveling
alone as we were. Let us hope that, together, we can help one
another over the remaining obstacles in our life's journey."

She laughed, a happy, lighthearted, forgiving, free-
spirited laugh, a laugh he knew he would hear often in his
life. He took her in his arms and kissed her smiling lips.

Journey's End

"I suppose we ought to change trains before we reach the
Scottish border. My mother will be expecting word from
me."

"Your mother expects me to be married in Gretna Green.
Let us not disappoint her."

* * * * *

Harlequin Historical

HISTORY IN THE MAKING!

Join Harlequin Historicals as we celebrate our 5th anniversary of exciting historical romance stories! Watch for our 5th anniversary promotion in July. And in addition, to mark this special occasion, we have another year full of great reading.

- A 1993 March Madness promotion with titles by promising newcomers Laurel Ames, Mary McBride, Susan Amarillas and Claire Delacroix.

- The July release of UNTAMED!—a Western Historical short story collection by award-winning authors Heather Graham Pozzessere, Joan Johnston and Patricia Potter.

- In-book series by Maura Seger, Julie Tetel, Margaret Moore and Suzanne Barclay.

- And in November, keep an eye out for next year's *Harlequin Historical Christmas Stories* collection, featuring Marianne Willman, Curtiss Ann Matlock and Victoria Pade.

Watch for details on our Anniversary events wherever Harlequin Historicals are sold.

HARLEQUIN HISTORICALS . . .
A touch of magic!

Jared: He'd had the courage to fight in Vietnam. But did he have the courage to fight for the woman he loved?

THE SOLDIER OF FORTUNE
By Kelly Street
Temptation #421, December

All men are not created equal. Some are rough around the edges. Tough-minded but tenderhearted. Incredibly sexy. The tempting fulfillment of every woman's fantasy.

When it's time to fight for what they believe in, to win that special woman, our Rebels and Rogues are heroes at heart. Twelve Rebels and Rogues, one each month in 1992, only from Harlequin Temptation.

HARLEQUIN® Temptation®

the Fortune Boys

A funny, sexy miniseries from bestselling
author Elise Title!

LOSING THEIR HEARTS MEANT
LOSING THEIR FORTUNES....

If any of the four Fortune brothers were unfortunate enough to
wed, they'd be permanently divorced from the Fortune
millions—thanks to their father's last will and testament.

BUT CUPID HAD OTHER PLANS!
Meet Adam in #412 **ADAM & EVE** (Sept. 1992)
Meet Peter #416 **FOR THE LOVE OF PETE**
(Oct. 1992)
Meet Truman in #420 **TRUE LOVE** (Nov. 1992)
Meet Taylor in #424 **TAYLOR MADE** (Dec. 1992)

WATCH THESE FOUR MEN TRY TO WIN
AT LOVE AND NOT FORFEIT $$$